"Taitz's fresh, funny, and whip-smart new novel deliciously probes both legal and human partnerships, the mysteries of love and justice, and what it really means to be a mother, even as it follows a wonderfully flawed group of characters struggling to give birth to their truest selves. Enchanting, honest, delightfully sly, and not to be missed."

—CAROLINE LEAVITT, *New York Times* bestselling author of *Cruel Beautiful World* and *Is This Tomorrow*

"Prepare to be charmed. Wooed by one man while pregnant with the child of another, Abigail Thomas is one of the pluckiest, cleverest, and most delightful protagonists to come down the pike in a long time. Sonia Taitz explores the plight of the unwed mother and the maneuverings of a corporate law firm with equal grace and dexterity and a light yet brilliant touch. A delectable novel to savor . . . and remember."

—YONA ZELDIS McDONOUGH, author of *The House on Primrose Pond*

"This modern-day Jane Austen winningly and wittily takes on love, sex, pregnancy, and working motherhood."

—MARIAN THURM, author of the *New York Times*-praised *The Good Life* and *Today Is Not Your Day*

PRAISE FOR *DOWN UNDER*

"A sly, subversive take on the familiar boy-meets-girl, boy-loses-girl, boy-becomes-a-world-famous-movie-star-and-tries-to-win-girl-back story, *Down Under* is a sheer delight. Sonia Taitz has written a fast-paced, quick-witted novel filled with trenchant observations about celebrity, aging, culture wars, and the search for true love. I raced through this witty and insightful book, anxious to reach the end. It came not with a whimper but a bang."

—JILLIAN MEDOFF, bestselling author of *I Couldn't Love You More* and *Hunger Point*

"*Down Under* is a beautifully constructed farce that reaches out in many directions—some amusing, some disturbing. The novel portrays a young boy's thrillingly brave and heroic struggle with his domineering father. We are hooked on the character of Collum Whitsun, and on his girlfriend Jude's obsession with this young, courageous boy. The writing is at all times so subtle and so right. When the middle-aged Collum sees himself become his father, the author brings a tragic dimension to her tale, even as the hero begins to go kablooey. It is all very enticing to follow her intelligent lead.

"While very much of the moment, and no less than a witty take on the zeitgeist, this novel is at the same time imbued with deep, dark truths and a sense of warped wisdom. Sonia Taitz is able to segue from an arch scene or grotesque moment to a heartfelt observation or smart insight with ease, finesse, and an unerring sense of literary mischief. A bravado performance, full of truth."

—WESLEY STRICK, screenwriter and director of *True Believer*, *Cape Fear*, and *Final Analysis*

"*Down Under* is a sharp, sad, and funny trip to the emotional antipodes. Weaving a story that's based, in part, on the broken soul of one of the world's erstwhile heroes, the author takes us from the northern exurbs of New York to Australia and back. Love, madness, and the meaning of loyalty form the backbone of this fabulous (in every sense) yarn. Sonia Taitz combines depth, pathos, and hilarity, creating a love story that is part legend, part cautionary tale, and entirely delicious."

—SUZANNE FINNAMORE, bestselling author of
Otherwise Engaged and *Split*

Named a Best Memoir of the Year by Foreword Reviews

*Nominated for the Sophie Brody Medal by the
American Library Association*

"Not your typical coming-of-age story . . . American Sonia Taitz, born to survivors of the Holocaust, lives under its long shadow in *The Watchmaker's Daughter*."　　　　　　*—Vanity Fair*

"Taitz writes beautifully about religious roots, generational culture clashes, and a family's abiding love."

—DAWN RAFFEL, *Reader's Digest*

"An invigorating memoir . . . especially noteworthy for its essential optimism and accomplished turns of phrase." *—Kirkus Reviews*

"Funny and heartwrenching."　　　　　　　　　　*—People*

"One of the year's best reads. This poignant memoir is a beautiful and heartfelt tribute to the author's parents. Funny, yet moving . . . It is the story of an ambitious and gifted daughter whose aspirations and goals collide with those of her parents."

—The Jewish Journal

"Heartwrenching, moving, and yes, hilarious . . . Fiercely tender and gorgeously written."
—CAROLINE LEAVITT, *New York Times* bestselling author of *Is This Tomorrow* and *Sad Beautiful World*

"A haunting meditation on time itself." —MARK WHITAKER, former editor-in-chief of *Newsweek*and managing editor at CNN

"*A heartbreaking memoir of healing power and redeeming devotion, Sonia Taitz's* The Watchmaker's Daughter *has the dovish beauty and levitating spirit of a psalm. . . .* A past is here reborn and tenderly restored with the love and absorption of a daughter with a final duty to perform a last act of fidelity."
—JAMES WOLCOTT, critic at *Vanity Fair* and author of *Lucking Out* and *Critical Mass*

"Sonia Taitz has a good heart and an unmortgaged soul. Follow where she leads. You want to go there."
—JOHN PATRICK SHANLEY, winner of the Pulitzer Prize, a Tony Award, and an Academy Award

PRAISE FOR *IN THE KING'S ARMS*

"Beguiling . . . Taitz zigzags among her culturally disparate characters, zooming in on their foibles with elegance and astringency."
—JAN STUART, *The New York Times Book Review*

"Evelyn Waugh, move over. . . . Even the heavy moments have verve and wit." —JESSE KORNBLUTH, curator of *HeadButler*, cultural essayist for *New York* and *The New Yorker*, and author of *Married Sex*

GREAT WITH CHILD

GREAT

WITH

CHILD

SONIA TAITZ

McWITTY PRESS

For information, address McWitty Press, 1835 NE Miami Gardens Drive,
Miami, FL, 33179.

www.mcwittypress.com

Library of Congress Control Number: 2017902202
ISBN: 9780985222796

Cover design by Jennifer Carrow
Interior design by Abby Kagan

The beginning of compunction is the beginning of a new life.
—GEORGE ELIOT

GREAT WITH CHILD

1 Falling into a rut in the road, pregnant, unmarried Abigail Thomas realized the literal gravity of her circumstances. Now in her sixth month, awkward and lumbering, she might have to rely on others to keep any sort of balance. She raised her eyes up and saw a handsome man, hauling her up on her swollen feet. It was warm for mid-October. Abigail was sweating in her "business" maternity wear—aubergine twill, black pearls on ears and neck, support stockings with a weirdly large belly balloon. The morning traffic whizzed by.

"Are you all right?" Abigail found herself leaning against the man's torso. She held on to his shoulders. Slowly, as she straightened, they parted.

"Thanks," she responded, her voice quavering. "I don't know what happened."

"You tripped into a pothole. You nearly got run over!"

"Oh . . ." Abigail felt so lightheaded now that she could hardly speak. This was unusual for her. The world seemed a blur that no words could begin to define.

"Well, I'm up now," she said dubiously. Was her leg actually bleeding?

"Must be hard for you," he said, checking her up and down.

"What's hard? This?" She pointed nonchalantly to the roundness at her waist. "Don't worry about it."

"You sure?" His voice was kind.

"I am just a little upset," she admitted, tonguing a tear off her lip. "My knee hurts—oh, god, ugh!" She was noticing the blood and the torn stocking.

"Here, you're OK," said the young man, leaning around to stroke briskly down her back. Abigail's jacket had picked up grayish street grit. He dusted off her shoulders, too, his head near her face as he leaned over to get all the spots.

Woozily, Abigail explored her Good Samaritan. He was of a pleasing height—not too tall, not too short. His thick hair was shiny and wheat-colored. She was close enough to smell him, and he smelled good, like fresh bread and cucumbers. In the base of her stomach Abigail realized she was starving. Could a nauseous woman feel hunger? During pregnancy, apparently, yes.

"Would you like me to call your husband or something?" he offered. Abigail, who suddenly couldn't walk a straight line, let him take her arm.

"I'm not—I'm not married," she said, aware of his firm touch through her suit sleeve. Then she toppled again, this time nearly taking the man down with her. He held her up and steadied her.

"Do you want to sit somewhere—maybe get something to eat?"

Had he read her mind?

"I'll be late for work," she murmured halfheartedly.

"You should take it a little easy; you've had a shock," he said, as she limped alongside him, gripping his arm.

"I'll be fine," she said, with what she hoped was conviction, stopping to feel if her leg was still bleeding. It was, but at least the flow was finally slowing down. "You fall, you get up."

He didn't quite seem to believe that. There she was, his expression implied, no wedding ring. A single woman—an unwanted pregnancy, perhaps.

"You're happy to take life as it comes, huh?"

Abigail raised her face and met his eyes.

"Happy?" she repeated in wonderment. It was such an old-fashioned word. People used it lightly nowadays, but for her, it had deeper meaning. She wanted happiness; she actually pursued it (as was recommended by the Constitution), but it always seemed to evade her.

Abigail looked closely at the stranger, noticing that he hadn't shaved. The tiny hairs growing from his skin were a mixture of brown, sand, and gold. She felt like touching them, fully appreciating the way they stood like little wheat stalks together. He had an approachable quality.

"Well, I'm happy right now, to be helping you," he said, smiling. His eyes were wide and willing. They were shining, almost glittering; if she looked really closely, Abigail could see herself in them.

Her father, a hardscrabble emigrant from South Wales, had no use for frivolity. He used to say, "Happiness is for half-wits." This was the word by which he labeled contented housewives, frolicking children, and what he called "ethnics." Was he himself one of the ethnics? In his native UK, yes. Like the Irish (and the Arabs, the Pakistanis, the West Indian blacks, the Jews), the Welsh were considered alien, a dark, elfin folk who liked to drink, sing, and weep. Even in America, where such things hardly signified (as long as you had money), Owen Thomas's ruddy face, lightbulb-shaped nose, and curly black hair seemed an embarrassment to him. Until it had thinned and unkinked through age, he had gelled his hair backward into a helmet of impenetrable dignity. A neat, thin mustache completed the look of natty self-regard. But none of this made him anything close to "happy."

"I really think you should eat something."

"You're really being gallant," said Abigail, coming back to the man in front of her. He seemed so gentle, so courtly. The men she tended to "go with" (though these occasions were infrequent) were more the Doberman type. Taut, alert, straining at the limits. Abigail never saw her suitors during work hours. When they met, it was in the dark: restaurants or fancy wine bars, once in a while ending up in her bedroom with its dimmable lighting. These men came predictably loose on aged single malts or flavored vodkas; they then made blunt erotic overtures. If she agreed, they fell tame and whimpering, grateful during the encounter. Afterward, they were silent again, lean and rangy, Dobermen breathing gruffly and slowly until the next chase and retrieval. They saw themselves as real men, career soldiers; like her, they did what they had to do.

What she now had to do was use the bathroom. Then she could eat. As though reading her mind, he steered her to a coffee shop on the corner.

"It's in the back," said the nice young man, discreetly letting her run pass him through the doorway so she wouldn't pee herself.

Sitting, sighing, Abigail reassured herself that she would not always be vulnerable like this. There was only a limited time for pregnancy; afterward, she would certainly be normal again. She would have the baby, drop the extra pounds, and reclaim her good old balance. She wouldn't be subject to these awful, unpredictable pratfalls.

Just the other day, she had nearly fallen down on the subway. No one had given her a seat, which she took as a politically correct statement that mothers-to-be are not invalids, just "differently able." Especially those in business clothing, primly enclosed in their corporate armor. She'd been trying to read her *Manhattan Law Journal* while soaring down the dark path to midtown. Abigail thought she felt fine; she thought she had the rocking and the pitching and the stopping in control. In the end, though, she had landed in the lap of a sour-faced woman in glasses. These were her humiliations for the time being.

To be waterlogged, gourd-like. Not exactly how she wished to be seen after three tough years at law school and nearly seven more at the firm. Sure, she'd passed the bar exam on the first try, and had survived a lengthy stint of hazing—which had not completely ended. (She wasn't partner yet.) But it was embarrassing to be a woman in the quintessentially delicate state. Pregnancy, Abigail thought, was a temporary disadvantage that did not fairly represent her. Before, if you'd woken her in the middle of the night, she could still parse sentences and chop up sentiments into their legal components and valences. But now, if you woke her in the middle of the night, she'd rush to the bathroom then fall back into bed like a big, heavy lump.

At this moment, though, unfair as it was, Abigail felt blurry. Were those actual tears in her eyes? There was a pain in her knee as she walked over to the sink to wash her hands, and probably some blood that she didn't want to look at just yet. Abigail tasted vomit in her throat, a familiar sensation these days. A tear slid down her face and she splashed some cold water on it. She felt ashamed of herself, as though she were not just falling, but failing.

Her dad used to say, "Good old Snowball, never melts." That was his way of praising Abigail when she was a little girl and didn't cry when she was hurt or sad. Griping, whining, complaining, weeping—these were signs of weakness, of softening with ambivalence toward the fact pattern. What worldly impact could ambivalence make?

Hardworking and gruff, Owen had built himself up from handyman to superintendent, from superintendent to building manager, and from manager to owner. As a landlord, he was sober and reserved. Whether checking out a basement boiler, meeting a banker, or initiating eviction procedures with his stalwart Armenian lawyer, he wore the same charcoal suit and pressed white short-sleeved shirt. His ties bore the only sign of his past—a tie tack dragon, rampant, clawing. This fierce Welsh icon pierced the middle of an otherwise blank chest.

Abigail's father was solid; he could make an impact. He had made a huge dent in his daughter, a negative space around which all her will had converged. Behind every successful woman, they say, is a dad who is proud of his girl. Abigail had had that. But she wondered if he'd feel proud of her now, collapsed and weepy, hair in her face.

For a moment, she almost surrendered to self-pity. It had been scary to be down, and now she felt sodden—and her hair did bad things when she perspired. It was curling up and wandering, a damp webwork. A twining, jungly cage of her own unwilling design. She could hardly stand to look at herself in the bathroom mirror.

Just this morning, she had carefully blow-dried it to a sleek, upmarket pageboy, but now, the mirror showed, it had gone wild. Abigail knew she must look slatternly, the sort of woman who wept in the gutters of the mainstream. The Greek chorus, at best. Abigail was genetically a sexpot, with lush, exotic features, but had spent the last few decades belying all signs of come-hither femininity. She had made her way solely "on the merits," as they say in the courthouse.

And now, she had the apartment: a one-bedroom with windowed kitchen on West End Avenue, doorman, pre-war. It had the color scheme: white, black, and ecru, punctuated by the neu-

tral geometric pattern of her pillows and the green of her potted jade plants, whose fat leaves needed only a torrent of water
from time to time to survive spells of neglect. Abigail wore the
outfits: expensive-looking suits and pumps (some bone, some
black), ersatz South Seas pearls, and knockoff scarves. Velveteen
jog-wear on weekends, boot-cut yoga pants for the gym. She had
the career: an associate on the final brink of partnership. This was
her seventh year at the firm, the critical year, in which the senior
members decided if she made the cut or not.

She had to make it. Before her fall, Abigail had been diligently
headed to the Library of the New York City Bar Association. Lying
on the gritty sidewalk, she longed for its cool marble corridors, the
tender-paged, leather-covered books, and the rich golden seal of
the bar, rising over all. Yes, one could research anywhere—laptops
had largely removed the age-old dignity of mahogany and vellum.
But the library gave her work the patina of professional status, the
classy sheen she craved. She, an honors graduate of Cardozo Law
(named after a Supreme Court Justice, no less), was steps away
from the Broadway express when she'd fallen down, smack on her
jumbo bottom. Despite the blood scabbing under her ripped support hose—she could now feel her knee stiffening—Abigail knew
she should still hasten down to midtown Manhattan.

She needed to find a precedent: Could a surviving spouse
collect from an airline if it were proved that her husband had
died of shock during the safety demonstration? But even without precedent, could it not be argued that such in-flight warn-
ings were unduly alarming, particularly for the many Americans
who suffered from heart trouble? Wasn't all the rest of the airport
rigmarole stressful enough? Now that you were vetted, x-rayed,
seated, and resigned, did they have to openly bring up disaster
and asphyxia?

The client's spouse had suffered from angina and premature

ventricular contractions. He had suffered a fatal heart attack while hearing the words "in the event of a loss of cabin pressure, oxygen masks will drop. . . ." The very mention of such a mask, popping like out like a goblin and seething with air, attached by a plastic umbilicus to a damaged mother plane, had scared him to death. The life support's fragility had been untenable to weak hearts: his soul had flown from the fickle craft. Someone had to pay for this. Or at least that was what the partners at Abigail's firm had said. More likely they were humoring the client, a wealthy woman with a large extended family, always good for estate probate every decade or so.

So there she was, having coffee with a stranger on a workday morning instead of doing her work. But it would be quick, and the man was exceptionally fetching and gracious, thought Abigail as she made her way to his booth.

The place was old-fashioned, the kind where you refueled quickly and continued on your way. It was the standard, reassuring retro: vinyl banquettes flanking Formica tables, sizzling grill, glass pots of coffee. Neon lights announced its hopeful name: The New Age Diner. Abigail's colleagues, who tended to drink skim lattes and foamy macchiatos, would never frequent such a "greasy spoon." In any case, they'd be at work by now, faces lit by glowing screens.

Abigail sat quietly, almost meekly, looking down at her paper place mat. It featured a map of the Aegean Sea. Despite her resolve to make this a quick pit stop, she was drifting into . . . something like the possibility of rest. It must have been the hormones—not just the pregnancy ones, but the endorphins that kick in when you've tumbled and bled. Even though she had looked at her watch (it was getting late), she had forgotten the significance of the big hand and the little. She looked, instead, at the tiny seconds, sweeping the face.

"What do you do?" she said, looking up at the man across the table. This was automatic to her, when meeting someone. What is your job, your career? And then she would proudly tell them hers.

"Yes, miss." A waiter spun over. He must have thought she had summoned him. "What you want eat." The young Samaritan asked for coffee. Abigail asked for decaf with skim, and seven-grain toast. The waiter spun away.

"Bring jam!" she heard herself blurting. A large nod, which did not slow his step, indicated that the waiter would comply.

"What do I do?" said her companion, picking up her question. "Oh, I do a few different things. A medley, you could say."

"Do you think that's good?"

"What?" His voice sounded a bit defensive.

"There. See it? Do you think it's good?"

Abigail pointed to a glass case of muffins and pastries. She was getting hungrier by the second. "Do you think it's fresh?"

"Oh, you were asking about the muffins," he said, regaining his composure.

"The corn muffin. Did you think I was disparaging you somehow?" She hadn't had a corn muffin in years. Now it seemed so humble and tasty.

"Yeah, my medley of work activities. Might have seemed a bit ad hoc to a smart professional like you."

"I didn't think that at all." Abigail flushed with pride. The man could tell she was someone.

"Well," he said, suave again, "as far as the food's concerned, everything's totally edible here."

When the waiter returned with the toast and coffee, the young man ordered two corn muffins.

"I only wanted one," said Abigail.

"The other one's for me."

"Oh. Sorry."

"Aren't you the hungry one," he said, a statement rather than a question, looking into her eyes and smiling. Abigail nodded, then focused on her food. She smeared her toast with grape jelly, then tucked into it, just as the waiter spun by, dropping off the muffins with improbable speed.

"What sorts of 'different things' do you do?" she said, trying not to talk with her mouth full but unable to keep it empty.

"Nope. I'm not answering until you tell me your name," he said, taking a sip of his coffee. He stared at her appraisingly.

"Guess," she said, surprised to be flirting.

"Marguerite? Esperanza?"

"What? No! Abigail. Abigail Thomas," she answered, chewing. She swallowed completely and added, "Esquire."

He seemed surprised by her name. Did he think she was a Latina? Or maybe he didn't know what "esquire" meant. It was a stately title, alluding to the days when knights rode on horses. Abigail loved saying it, and even more, she loved putting the "Esq." after her name. That *q* not only sounded fancy, it looked fancy.

"'Esquire' means lawyer," she said aloud, for his edification. She fished for a business card to brandish the proof.

"Yes, I know that," he said, now laughing, pushing the card back to her. "Well, Ms. Esquire, I'm plain old Timothy Vail," he said, extending his hand. Abigail wiped her own hand (shiny with corn muffin grease) and shook his.

"Vail? Like the skiing place in Colorado?" Abigail wondered why she'd had to say that. This smooth young man made her feel insecure. She had grown up on the wrong side of stylish and had never learned to ski, sail, or ride. Secretly, she was glad to have missed these experiences, which seemed like unnecessary brushes with death. Skiing was, in fact, falling; sailing, a chance to get hit by a beam and drown in the brine. As for riding, which appealed to her in the abstract—the idea of being carried along by an understanding force—didn't the horse often get spooked for no reason and throw you over? It could step on you, too, with its obstinate metallic hooves. Still, Abigail knew that any admission of these rational fears revealed her original low-classiness. Powerful people courted danger; they laughed at it and asked for more. They fearlessly introduced their children to it.

Something about Timothy Vail conveyed an intimacy with these cold-blooded pursuits. His golden hair and fine, straight nose; that strong, chiseled chin. He had an unhurried way of moving, and a calm, patrician tone of voice. But she was someone, too; she had done battle, too. If only he could see her in her element, strutting across the firm, documents in hand—or at her desk, signing triplicates. Then he would know her true, worldly status. And he would respect her hard-earned accomplishments and wins.

"You're a sultry little thing, aren't you?" Tim's voice was quiet, matter-of-fact.

Abigail's face reddened. Was that how she came across, even in her smart professional outfit? Still, a small smile crept, unbidden, across her mouth. "Sultry" was an even better word than "sexy"—and what woman (especially when pregnant) doesn't want to be thought at least slightly alluring? On the other hand, she had not dressed to entice (pregnant or not, she never dressed to entice at the workplace). She liked to be in charge of when and how she was sending those signals.

Apparently enjoying her befuddlement, Tim added, like a challenge: "Where'd you get that crazy hair? I love curls, by the way."

Abigail realized that her tedious blowout must have completely reverted, releasing her locks to their wildest state. The heat of the day, the fall in the street, and now the steamy coffee shop; she was done in. The Dobermen she dated seemed to prefer the straight bob, the smooth, unruffled surface. And here she was, all ringlets and flop sweat. All she was missing was big hoop earrings.

"Well," she said, trying to smile about what she felt was one of her biggest weaknesses. "It is naturally curly—both my parents had curls. Yours didn't, huh?"

"My family comes from Norfolk, originally. I don't think they allow curls there, over the age of three or so. You have to leave."

"Norfolk, Virginia?"

He cleared his throat with a touch of pride. "Norfolk, England."

"So they did leave."

"Pardon?"

"Because you're here. In New York, I mean. America."

"Yes. Here I am." He took a look around the coffee shop. Abigail's eyes followed his, suddenly noticing the blacks and Puerto Ricans, and the omnipresent Jews. The people like herself, the "ethnics."

"I think my folks just got bored," he was saying. "Here, they had an edge. In the land of the curly-wurlies, the straight-haired man is king."

He spoke without shame, like a real Anglo Saxon from the bygone ages, when the words and the concepts had bullyish heft.

"Not to mention the fair-haired boy," she said. "You're the heir apparent."

His pause and tiny nod implied agreement. "And you?" he said finally.

"What about me?"

"Your people?"

That was so un-American, she thought: "your people." She was herself, that was who she was, and she could define whatever that was. Wasn't that the meaning and the payoff of career? Still, to hedge the answer was to express a shame she wouldn't allow herself to acknowledge.

"You mean my family? Oh, we come from everywhere."

Abigail often thought of her family history. Her maternal grandparents, like her father, had been immigrants; they'd escaped Germany's midcentury madness and had clung tenaciously to their china service, silver candelabras, and Old World politesse. Not only German, they'd been Jewish, which added a level of high-minded history, a sense of thoughtful sorrow and lovingly kept traditions. Her mother, Clara (née Milch), had been simultaneously attracted and repelled by what she considered her Welsh husband's more barbaric influence. The Celts didn't worry about delicate matters, at least not the men, it seemed. The men were brought up to be tough.

Owen Thomas claimed to have liked hunting during his boyhood. You caught something, killed it, and then, as he put it, "you'd bagged it." (It was also the way some of his loutish peers referred to seducing a woman.) Clara, raised by cautious, bookish people, had considered this to be "goyishe naches"—gentile joy, by which she meant something callous, unworthy, and cheap. Bearbaiting, cockfighting. Decent folks devoted their lives to improving the world with love and caring. She had been a doting mother to her three daughters. Even here in America, she'd darned their white socks and made sure they had cod liver oil whenever constipated. Each of her girls was a pearl, a pretty seed pearl on a cashmere cardigan.

"Are you all right, Abby?" Tim reached out to stroke Abigail's cheek.

"Hey," she said, blushing. "I prefer Abigail." For a moment, she leaned her face against his hand.

"Excuse me," Tim said, sounding like a real gentleman. His hand went back to the other side of the table. Abigail tucked her hair back behind her ears again. She took a long drink of water and said, "Would you like to hear about how I usually spend my mornings?"

"Sure, anything you want to tell me," said Tim.

"Well, I actually work in a midsized midtown firm."

"Corporate area, I bet?"

"Not in the traditional sense. I mean, sure, we have a number of corporate clients. Small businesses, S Corporations. But I do estates. And aviation disasters."

"What? Both? At the same time?"

"No, not at the same time. Not usually. I mean, it could happen, I guess. I'm not at a famous firm," she continued, "but it's a quality firm, to those in the know. I could have worked at Cummer, Sachs & Veitch, or even Grimsby, Levin & Twain downtown, but I'd be a faceless drone. Then, at partnership time, they could easily pass me over. At Fletcher, I'm on the track. Unless I'm a screwup, I'll make partner this year," she concluded, her phrase coming out with another quaver. This pregnancy was definitely beginning to lead to "screwups." Like sitting here and telling her life's agenda to a stranger. On a work day.

"Partner, huh? One of the lucky few."

This gave her pause; it was like his "happy" comment.

"Oh, I'm not lucky," she said, thinking of her mother's brutal, prolonged cancer death and her own lonely personal life. "I've planned almost everything that's ever happened to me.

"For instance, I worked hard for my grades," she continued, with a bit of an edge. "No luck there, and no one handed them to me. And I work extra hard at my job. Meanwhile, I'm still paying back my law school loans." Leaning forward, Abigail confided, "You look more like the lucky one to me."

"What makes you think I'm lucky?" said Tim, a tiny tinge of sadness in his voice.

"Oh, you. You have that lucky look. I bet everything falls into your lap." She blushed again at the implication. She had virtually fallen into the lap of this charming, handsome man.

"Nothing falls into my lap," he said quietly. "I've got my eyes open. I saw you falling and I reached out and grabbed you, Abby. And here you are, about to run off to work and never see me again."

"Abigail," she corrected. "And here you are, relaxing in the morning, and look—you've got this great watch."

She took his wrist in her hand and examined the blue-faced Rolex. Then she looked under the table. "Just as I thought. Those comfy walking shoes that look like Hush Puppies but cost three times as much. Just to amble around Broadway. What are they called, Mephistos?"

"Why not call them Mephistopheles, since only a lucky devil like me can afford them, if that's what you're implying." Tim's voice seemed unduly harsh, she thought. And suddenly so different.

"But I need these very expensive shoes," he continued, the edge still hardening and the pace quickening. "I need my Doctor Faustuses, see, because there's all the extra walking I have to do, back and forth from the bank, checking up on my trust fund, and then to the accountant to find all those tax loopholes.

"You know, too much talk about money is kind of crass, Abigail."

Crass was what spoiled people called those who had to make it on their own.

"Maybe it's crass, but on my planet, Richie Rich, we do talk about money," she replied. "We talk about it a lot. All the time, and with gusto. And you know why? Because I've always had to fend for myself."

"I know your planet. The planet of money and 'Where do you work?'" Tim raised his pitch to sound like a demanding, peevish female, which affronted Abigail.

"On my planet," she began, "work is a—"

"OK, here it is," he burst out. "My father's a banker. Investment, not commercial. And my brother, the clone, the chip, he

of course works for McKinsey. Have you heard of it? It's the top
of the top. Management consulting. Whoop-dee-do. Maybe the
thrill on this end isn't as great as it should be. I mean, I have no
special fetish about wearing a tie around my neck."

"I can see that."

"You can."

An awkward silence followed.

"So what do you actually do all day?" said Abigail. At ten
fifteen, he was dressed in a soft flannel shirt, his long legs out-
stretched in faded black jeans.

"Are you checking me out 'for partner'?"

"No, no, I'm totally out of that market," she said, self-
consciously covering her ringless left hand. "I was just curious."

"Curious, that's all it was?" His eyes narrowed, and he looked
kind of sexy.

"Yes, just pregnant and dizzy and curious."

"OK," he said, wiping his mouth with a paper napkin. He was
fully pleasant now. "I'm going to do my little career speech." He
paused. "I'm in IT. Information technology. I work at home as a
consultant for small companies. You know, ad hoc. Projects. On
my weekends, I teach an entry-level computer course to kids.
They make their own books; I sort of publish them."

"Doesn't the IT consultancy pay your bills?" said Abigail sym-
pathetically. She often worked weekends, and knew how exhaust-
ing seven-day workweeks could be.

"The kids' course isn't just for the money, Abby. I do it because
I like teaching, and . . . ." he trailed off. "I don't do it for free,
you may be relieved to know," he continued. "They pay a hundred
bucks per two-hour lesson. Each. That way, they tend to take the
work seriously. The parents, I mean.

"By the way, speaking of money, I'm good for both of our
breakfasts. Even if you do eat like a—what shall I say?"

She found herself laughing. "A pregnant fallen woman?" Tim laughed mildly along. He had beautiful teeth, of course. "I've actually got to get home now," he said, tossing some bills out on the table.

"Wanna come with me?" he added casually, as he stood up from the table.

"What? No!"

"It's not a proposition. I live right around the corner. If you still feel dizzy, you can come back and lie down on my very comfortable sofa. I'll watch over you until you feel better, then walk you back to the One train."

"You're taking a lot for granted," said Abigail. "I might be dating someone else."

"In your condition?" he teased. "Who'd be interested in a pregnant lady?"

"I don't know," she replied humbly. "I guess someone sort of—unusual."

"At your service," he answered. "I'm not remotely usual." Tim watched Abigail as she rose to her feet. She was normally voluptuous, and pregnancy, she sensed, cheeks reddening under his gaze, only italicized these attributes.

"I don't need sofas," Abigail said, as he held the door open for her. She felt a lot better after having had some food. "I need to get going."

"To work?"

"Where else?" she said.

Tim could probably think of many other options, but Abigail was a fast one, tearing away to the subway as though nothing could stop her anymore.

2 ❀ The bar association library was like a second home to Abigail. The dusty smell, the dark wood, the sibilance of rustling pages—all these spoke of order. Things were set down, black on white, printed and beautifully bound. Even cases about disasters and their consequences were concluded with jurisprudential calm, the language itself majestically padded. The pages of the old Federal Supplements flipped quietly, with whispered good breeding, dispensing answers and dispelling chaos. Computers had their obvious place—speed, efficiency—but in this traditional milieu, many lawyers still preferred the dignified heft of these grand volumes. Abigail used both, but she felt most like a member of the bar when she flipped through the tomes. In her unusual field, it was good to be eclectic and thorough.

And it was wonderful to be in a profession with such a deep sense of its rich tradition. The library, her office, both so luxuriant and spotless, so hushed with elite purpose. Her own upbringing had been much rawer. Abigail's parents had always lived modestly. They were fearful of poverty, which (they often repeated) they'd both known firsthand. No one but her mother had ever cleaned their home. Like a servant she had toiled, scrubbing the toilet, slapping a long-haired gray mop to and fro around the floors. Owen thought maids were nothing but migraines—money down the drain and pilfering to the bargain. He didn't trust outsiders.

"I know how the poor look at the rich," he'd say, twisting his face into a sneer that looked almost stagy. "And you don't want people looking at you like that in your own home." Abigail's mother hadn't minded the housework. She'd been brought up to cook and wash, iron a blouse, darn a sock. Her own immigrant parents had been nothing if not practical. On her mother's watch, their home was spotless, down to the last piece of cutlery.

Abigail knew her parents' story so well it was like a fairy tale to her—with the attendant obstacles to be overcome by the heroes' noble efforts. Like her husband, Clara Milch was born an outsider to the easy American scene. Her parents, she often told her daughters, had lived in a displaced people's camp in Germany after the war, a temporary world of homeless Holocaust survivors. A distant cousin had sponsored her family, eventually setting them up in a refugees' enclave on the Lower East Side. That was where Clara had been born into the world. This displacement and the sudden rescue were both ideas Abigail was never allowed to forget, and the lesson had sunk deeply into her. You had to be safe, she understood. It was a frightening world. You had to be vigilant.

The story of her parents' romance was another major part of the family lore. At twenty, a secretary living with her parents, Clara Milch had met Owen Thomas. He was her building's new superintendent. Mr. Thomas was younger than she, Abigail, was now—only twenty-five. From photos, she knew he'd been red-faced, big-handed, curly headed. Clara had been leaning out of her second-floor window. Abigail imagined her mother looking at the immigrant kids bouncing balls against the walls of the narrow brick courtyard. She imagined her father looking up (like a ruddy Romeo) and calling to the pretty girl above him. But she didn't need to imagine his first words. Abigail knew them and never forgot them, not even now, in her safe, American life.

"Watch yourself," her father had said. "You might fall all the way down."

Then he had disappeared. A moment later, Clara had heard a knock on the door. The knock was so loud, it had initially frightened her. Police? Eviction? When she told the story to her children, there was always a tremor in her voice at this part of the story. But it was nothing bad at all. The young curly haired man was there, hat in hand, and he said, "Let me fix that safety grille so's it can hold."

His first words, face-to-face, were to offer a service. A good deed just like Tim's, Abigail realized with a thrill. Just like Tim lifting her up from the hard ground and holding her up.

"Oh, yes, please, sir, you're very kind," Clara had answered. (Abigail could hear her mother's over-correct diction; she could always imagine her deferential stance, which she never quite lost.)

"My name is Owen," he had said. "Please feel free to call me that."

The fairy tale had gone well after this initial meeting. It had apparently taken Owen no time at all to fall in love with the dark-eyed girl, an outsider like himself. ("None of this constant dating and getting nowhere, like today," Abigail's mother would often remind her.) In time, the good young man had won the lady's trust. Owen Thomas had impressed Clara Milch with his practical skills, his helpful deeds, and his simple, solid values. He knew what her folks had been up against, he'd said; he knew what the Old World was about, firsthand. Battles and boundaries, and all that petty hatred. He, too, had lost a language and a culture.

Their black curls mingling, Clara and Owen had fallen in love. It was a kind of mutual relief, a double rescue, Abigail thought. He would keep her safe, and she would make him strong with her trust in him. Despite the wishes of Abigail's maternal grandparents—they had hoped to perpetuate their ravaged Jewish customs—Clara and Owen had married, at City Hall. They wanted a fresh start in the New World, together.

Clara had borne three children in quick succession: Elizabeth, Abigail herself, and Anita. Anita, the youngest, had become a suburban housewife, house-proud in Woodmere, Long Island. "Annie gives me the honor of teaching her," Clara would say, proud to pass on her knowledge of how to bake a *babka*, how to fold a sheet, still warm from the iron, in just the right way. Elizabeth and Abigail, however, turned out to be "career girls."

"You're so busy, you have no time for this kind of work." Abigail often heard her mother's words in her ears. By "this kind of work" she had meant handiwork, sweat work. She had meant work that left a tactile impact, however brief and forgettable, on the cozy life of a family.

"Let your mama do it."

She had let her mama do it, glad to have someone like that behind her as she raced ahead. It was harder and harder to appreciate motherhood in these modern times, when her very humility seemed like a lack of ambition. But Clara's illness, cancer, had made Abigail more aware. Her mother had gradually become too tired to do all the things she had always done. And Abigail's homey world, the world she had always taken for granted, unraveled.

After suffering for years, Clara Milch Thomas had eventually died in a hospice. Tended by women, loving strangers who knew their work as well as she'd known hers, she had vanished back into the earth. Not long after, Owen Thomas had retired from his real estate business, packed up, and moved to the Sunbelt.

Now he lived in North Miami Beach, at the Versailles Hotel and Condominiums, with a woman called Darlene Shanks. Clara, Abigail thought, would have considered this woman cheap. All the more reason, then, to treasure her own promising career, which lifted her out of the realms of the sad or sordid.

Her big sister used to question her about her choice of practice. "How could you deal with those morbid issues?" Elizabeth had wondered. "Plane crashes? Widows and orphans?" Abigail was nonplussed. There was nothing disturbing in these matters, from her point of view. By the time she got to them, the whirlwinds had settled. Broken bodies were gently buried, plane parts retrieved, photographed, and cataloged. If time healed all wounds, law translated them into claims for hard cash, money damages for inchoate pain and suffering.

If only, thought Abigail, the real world were more like that: "actionable." When her mother had died, suffering, there was no possible "action," no "upside" to the matter, no "making the client whole." Abigail would take mechanical malfunction over biological disaster, any time. At least it had an ostensible cause, a starting point for debate from side to side. At least there were attempts at restitution.

Liz was a private banker. In her world, as in Abigail's, tough men and tougher women marched and barked all day and long into the night (with time out for power yoga and polytheistic Brahmin chants), then did it again the next day. The pay was magnificent, more than most people make in years toiling as nurses, teachers, or home care attendants. (Mama's attendant had been up all night with her toward the end, wiping, turning, and lending an ear to her fretful imaginings.) Liz wore Armani, La Perla, Louboutin, Peretti. She kept a pair of Siamese seal points called Rupert and Framboise in her half–town house condo on the Upper East Side, and a dappled mare called Dare Me in North Salem.

At forty-three, she had pretty much decided never to bear children. Still, the possibility of adoption, when her career flamed out at fifty or sixty, remained. Liz's husband, Art Gruen, a well-known essayist, had persuaded her that a needy child might be a rewarding addition to their future lives. For now, however, with years of bond work ahead, Liz didn't think she could give the child enough of herself.

Shunting children off on babysitters, she told Abigail, seemed annoying, if not pointless. "I'm not great at delegating," she'd say. "I'd go mad thinking, 'Is she doing it right? Is she giving her all?' and knowing that she probably isn't. I mean, who are these people? From what I've seen, they're not like us. They seem to be either snotty or slow, sometimes both." From what she'd casually observed, Liz was equally put off by the British nanny type (with her crisp vowels and compulsive rule-making) and the warm Jamaican childcare worker (whose grammar left much to be desired).

Notwithstanding these arguments, Abigail did plan to shunt her future child off on a caretaker, knowing that with enough time and patience, she could find a perfectly good one. People had relied on "help" for centuries. And what did babies need anyway? How much did it take to keep them out of traffic, feed them, play peekaboo? Abigail, who had never so much as touched a baby (she'd been appalled when her little sister Anita was born), knew she wouldn't mind delegating those dreary tasks.

What mattered was the firm to which, after tough years in law school, she had given seven even tougher years of dogged labor. Abigail would demonstrate how motherhood need not ruin productivity. It was infuriating when men—even in these modern days—would still whisper, "She's never coming back full-time" when a female associate got pregnant. It was even more annoying when they were right, depending on what you meant by "coming back." Even if the women returned to the office (and many did not, guiltlessly absconding with the training they'd been given), they were often distracted, ambivalent. Partly there, partly elsewhere, either literally or figuratively. And "elsewhere" was with that child, a being who seemed to transform women into brand-new creatures with pasts erased and all their goals reshuffled.

Abigail Thomas was not one of those women. Focus was her forte, and she would show them all. She was ready for the fight. Never again would men dare think women were not up to the job once their mammaries flowed. Never again would male partners assume that "career" was a relative term, dependent on emotional weather. She was a proud soldier, and she would not desert at any point.

During her fifth month, Abigail had been called in to speak to Bertram Fudim, the senior partner in her area. They openly discussed his worries—that after she'd given birth, she would "change," reverting to stereotypical female type (warm, worried, self-sacrificial) despite the years that her firm had invested in her. As Abigail protested that her work was "everything" to her, Fudim held up his large, hairy hand.

"You and I know this a taboo subject. The personal arena."

"No, it's fine. I'd actually love to address this."

"I've said too much. Some ladies would sue. Can of worms here."

"Feel free to open the can. I'm not one of those people. Those 'ladies,'" Abigail said, wincing slightly as she repeated his dinosaur term. "I get what you're saying. I'd be saying it, too. And I'm here right now to show you—"

"You can show me when it happens. Wait 'til then."

"No, you wait," she said defiantly. Such chutzpah would be crazy in most other contexts, but Abigail knew that men like Fudim appreciated gutsy women. That was the point of this awful conversation, wasn't it? To prove that she could take a rude, crude battering?

Bert Fudim had enormous dark brows, and they flew up expressively. Had she gone too far? Was her tone too gutsy? Would he slam her down? In the dramatic pause that followed, Abigail's eyes traveled the room, following the angles of beige carpeting and mahogany wainscoting, desk and armchair. Dust motes bounced in the air near the window, buoyed by the air-conditioning. Their dance, Abigail thought, was both endless and slightly sad.

"Turn around, Ms. Thomas," barked Fudim suddenly.

Swiveling her upper torso around the gravid roundness of her middle, Abigail saw a large samurai sword, hanging from the wall behind her.

"Gift from a client in Kyoto. Hara-kiri come to mind?"

"Context?"

"Giving birth."

"I'll let you cut the cord with it," she joked.

"It won't do the trick, dear," said Fudim kindly. "Those cords go very deep. And that's my point. Speaking off the record, 'cause I like you, OK? Pregnancy, childbirth, the whole nine months? No matter what you hear, let me give it to you straight—it's the true hara-kiri. Blood and guts. The killer."

"Oh, no, Mr. Fudim, certainly not," said Abigail, laughing nervously. Was he referring to her inability to handle labor? She'd be aces at that. True, with a Caesarian, you could pick the date of birth to coincide with a weekend, or better yet, a holiday, but she'd handle baby's exit either way.

"I've got the best prenatal care," she rattled, almost happy to share these strategies with another practical soul, "and I'll be going to Lamaze class, so I'll be in control of my labor—and— what's wrong?"

Fudim was glaring.

"You don't know what I'm talking about!"

Abigail blurted, "Oh, hara-kiri—did you mean symbolic—uh, suicide? Career down the drain and all that? No, please, with all due respect, I refute that stereotype about women getting hormonal, not wanting to leave home and put in the hours. We're not animals, ruled by some primitive nurturing 'instinct.' We're enlightened professionals, with seven years of higher education behind us, not to mention the invaluable work experience and training. Why would I ever throw it all away?"

Fudim got up from behind his ridiculously large desk and walked over to the door. He shut it. Then he came back and hovered over Abigail's shoulder. She was seated in a deep leather armchair, her arms wrapped around her middle.

"Let me tell you something," he said, stepping away to draw a cigar out of a humidor. He held it up in midair. "Oh—I'm sorry—should I not do this?"

"What, smoke a big cigar?" said Abigail. "No, no, of course it's fine." That was surely a test, to see if she was tough enough. Well, she was, although she couldn't speak for the baby. Maybe she'd just breathe shallowly.

Fudim took his cigar over to a small guillotine, chopped off the end, lit it, and sucked slowly, finally releasing a plume of strong smoke. "Let's talk about career suicide. Off-record, still."

"Of course! I appreciate your frankness," said Abigail, who knew that most partners wouldn't touch these subjects—gender, sex, pregnancy—with their risk of nuisance lawsuits. Wouldn't engage, wouldn't discuss, wouldn't admit. She loved how frank Fudim was being in her presence. She felt like his secret protégée.

"I know this is all about personal choice and privacy and all that nice, impractical ACLU, Legal Momentum crap—"

"It's actually a penumbra, they call it," said Abigail, ever the apt student. "An emanation from the First Amendment, the one that guarantees life, liberty, and the pursuit of happiness." There was that peculiar word again, "happiness." "Coupled with the Fourth Amendment regarding illegal search and seizure," she continued, "taking what belongs to someone, their secrets, for instance—"

"Took constitutional law in law school, did you?"

"Yes, Mr. F., I did."

"Well, you're not in law school anymore!" he bellowed.

Abigail's body jolted in the armchair, and her fetus kicked.

"You're in the school of real life," continued Fudim, lowering his voice. "And this is where A leads to B even if Oliver Wendell Holmes and his Harvard ass don't like it. You've got some memory for legal principles, kiddo. Me, I only remember that if a client dies, will or no will, the relatives are gonna get ugly. Money talks and greed screams. Did you know that?"

Abigail nodded uncertainly. Some law partners, in anger, had aspects of the thug.

"You remember that girl, Dana Kidder, the one in tax?"

"Sure," she said, wincing again at the word "girl." Dana Kidder was no mere "girl." Abigail had always been impressed with Dana's educational pedigree. Chicago Law was hard-core, conservative, with the worst grading curve. If anyone had virtual testicles, Dana did.

"Do you know what Kidder's doing now?"

"I hear she's living on the West Coast, right?"

"Living? Is that what you call it? I call it quitting, dying, losing, the sideline, the tar pits. Here's the scenario. First comes birth. Baby's gorgeous, what a miracle! Everybody's so happy they send fruits in those nice baskets. The ones that look like flower arrangements, you know? Those.

"Time passes. Things seem to be getting back to normal. Is she coming back to work? Is she gonna make me sorry I ever hired her and broke her in, hoping she'd finally earn her keep? She asked for three weeks, but now she wants more. Baby's not nursing, or maybe he is but now he won't take the bottle, or maybe he'll only take it from mommy. And oh, he's still not sleeping through the night.

"Now it's seven weeks; two months. Baby's got hair on his chest, he's ready for the soccer team and the Suzuki mini-orchestra, he's ready for the black belt Tai Kwon Do. But mommy's still not ready.

"Then, one day—she's back! She *is* ready! You buy another basket, flowers for the desk this time, and let's go make some money. But she's not really back. There's a picture on her desk of baby, with that sweet bottom tooth. Awwww. . . . What if he gets another one of those little teeth when she's not there? Who would want anyone to miss that? The bad old law firm, that only cares about money?

"Now mommy's torn. She's worried. She's on the phone all day. Yakking to nanny. Talking to doctor. Cooing to baby: 'Did you make a little doo-doo? Mommy will be home soon to wipe it and put on the special tushy cream.' 'Soon?' I want her to stay until eight, ten, like she used to! But no, at six thirty, she's out the door, and the client can call, but who cares? Not mommy! She's rocking baby. She's feeding him that milk she pumped out on office time, with that machine that makes everyone sick in the john and fills up the fridge like you wouldn't believe. Weekends? No way. Forget travel. Who could be so cruel to baby?"

"Couldn't she just do—something like flextime?"

"Yeah, sure, let's tell the client that she's only here between the baby's upchuck and his diarrhea-caca! Or maybe the day of deposition, kid's playing a pumpkin—and you can't miss the school play, right? Can you miss the Thanksgiving play when your kid's the actual pumpkin? Huh?"

Abigail didn't know the right answer. On the one hand, of

course, it was "yes," you can miss the play. But the way he was screaming addled her.

Fudim saved her by carrying on:

"Sometimes 'here' is never 'here,' OK?"

"Yes, exactly," said Abigail, on safer ground now.

"But of course, we can't spell this out. That's 'actionable.' So sure, we'll treat her just as good as the people who work their tails off, who actually get the job done! By the way, what are you talking about, Abigail—compromise? I thought you wanted to make it to the top here! 'Flextime?' Is that what you want?"

"No! Mr. Fudim, I know about the mommy track, and don't want any part of it. I will lean all the way in and push forward as hard and as long as anyone. Pregnant, not pregnant, play, not play, poop, not poop. I mean, even on the day I'm giving birth, seriously, I'll have my phone on me. And not just on vibrate."

"And you'll travel?"

"Of course!"

"Uncomplainingly? Without boring us with your miserable personal life?"

"Yes, anywhere!" Abigail pleaded. "Just send me."

Fudim made his mouth into a large O. At first, Abigail thought that she had shocked him with the idea of her traveling in her condition. But after a moment, a ring of hot smoke emerged from Fudim's mouth; it widened, then disappeared. He spoke again of his wayward associate.

"The funny thing is that 'mommy,' I'm sorry, Dana, does decide to work part-time. Oh, yes, she's a flexer, that one. An on-and-off ramper. Despite all the years we pumped into her. We find a way to satisfy her, give her dull cases with sleepy clients, trivial knots no good associate would touch, and she works less and less. She haggles over hours. 'Nine to five isn't really part-time,' she whines, or 'My baby is running a fever, I have to leave early'—she means even earlier, because she's already leaving early, right? Fill in the blanks; she's not happy, she's not, what's the word they all use, 'fulfilled.' Like I'm running a spa here, a Canyon Ranch with stretching by the, by the infinity pool. And by the way, I'm not thrilled, either."

Fudim carefully rested his cigar in a heavy crystal ashtray. He reached for an antacid and bounced it around in his mouth. It made his saliva thick, white, and slushy, then disappeared, leaving a pasty blob on each corner of his lips. Abigail couldn't help staring at these bright white spots as he resumed his lecture. Something about Mr. Fudim said "sad clown," she thought, but she fought that notion away.

"And then she goes and what does she do? She gets pregnant again. By this time, she's acting like she's doing the firm a big, humanitarian favor just by showing up. After all, she's been part of the great miracle of life, and we're just money-grubbers, right? Use you up for cannon fodder?"

"I never think like that," said Abigail, daringly meeting his eyes. Even at college, she'd been one of those who talked unabashedly about "big bucks," starting from orientation. Some freshmen in her sorority had even subscribed to *The Wall Street Journal.* Abigail's mother, visiting in the first term of law school, had gazed at the *Fortune* magazine in her daughter's room, along with some fancy books on "business units." She had said, with a soft, mourning tone, "I suppose you wouldn't want this, hmm?"

She had brought Abigail a woman's magazine. Despite the fact that the layout had made the words "Lady" and "Home" virtually unnoticeable, with the professional-sounding "Journal" large and proud, and despite the fact that the subheading read, intriguingly, "Never Underestimate the Power of a Woman," Abigail had said, "No thanks, Mom, I really have no time. I mean, the workload here is crazy."

And she was proud of that crazy workload. It meant she was somebody. A trooper, a Green Beret. An elite force.

"But I will eat that lunch," she'd added, generously. Her mother had brought her a breaded chicken sandwich, like a schnitzel, homemade, of course, and some fresh lemonade to go with it. Abigail felt pinned by her mother's hungry gaze as she watched her eat and drink.

"Mom, what? You're kind of staring at me," Abigail remembered how she'd complained, even as she enjoyed her meal. She also recalled her mother's reply:

"It feels good to feed a child, even a grown one. It feels good to take care of somebody else."

"Maybe you're different," Fudim was saying. "And maybe not. But let me finish up the Dana Kidder saga. So, the second baby comes, right? Thank goodness, it's not the same sex as the first, otherwise she might have to have three. Anyway. Probably right here, the nanny leaves. You thought they were part of the family? Not so. They always leave; there's turnover. The job is brutal, let's face it.

"So what's the story? Family problems in the West Indies. A landslide in the Philippines. Whatever. She's got a real family, this nanny—and it's not yours. Surprise!

"Now, mommy has to find new help, but now she's not just anxious, she's kind of, well, let's be technical here. Let's be clinical. She's depressed. She's having what you'd call an 'existential crisis'—see, I paid attention in psych class, or was it philosophy? Anyway, an existential crisis. 'What's it all about?' And now it's not college, you know, it's real! Life, work—the disappointments, right? Could you write the closing argument? Could you schmaltz up the summation, and make it come out tragic, Ms. Thomas? We want the jury crying, sobbing!

"Because mommy—I mean my part-time attorney—really did

think the nanny was 'part of the family.' Now baby misses her, and finding another good one—not that the first was all that good, in hindsight she was a lazy bitch and baby can't read or play piano yet—that isn't easy. Mommy's beginning to think about how hard she works here, at the firm, what we pay, and what she's got to pay the new girl to keep her. Now the new girl has to watch two kids; that's harder, that's more challenging, more ways to screw up. And it's more expensive, too. You get what you pay for. So mommy decides to take time off, to 're-prioritize.' Big word. How many syllables? Five. And what does it mean? Give up.

"Start a heading here, Abigail. Open a file. Call it 'End of Career.' The husband—he's got a job that runs smooth as Grey Goose—he tells her she's making the right choice. He has to. Otherwise she'll keep him up yakking about it nightly for the next four or five years. Already she's been moaning every day about how hard she has to work, two jobs, the office and at home, and baby's getting too close to nanny II, and prefers daddy to everyone, and what does he do, anyway, change a diaper? Wiping some crap off makes him a hero? JD, MBA, what difference does it make? She's knee deep in crap every day!

"So daddy tells her, 'Do what your heart tells you.' He means bury yourself in Diaper Avalanche for all I care, if you'll just shut up. 'Would you even think of giving up your career?' she says. And he'll say, 'Anyone would love to stop slaving all day and just play with his kids.' That's verbatim what he'll say, almost believing it. 'To watch them grow? To love and be loved in return by an innocent child? I'd give anything to trade places.' But of course, he can't, he won't, he wouldn't.

"But she does. She takes her 'leave of absence.' In the beginning, she'll do a little legal work at home. Send a couple of e-mails, do some research online. Billables come in, it's true, and no overhead. But time passes. She begins to forget. It seems normal for her to be a Mrs., a housewife, someone's mommy. And such rewards! Those wet kisses, applauding that pumpkin at the end of the play, the artwork on the fridge, all dedicated to her. And it looks, it really looks, like it'll last forever. Like time doesn't pass. Like she's the only mommy and those are the only kids, like the story's new and fresh.

"She's new and fresh and us lawyers, we're old and cynical. We don't get it, right? She snuggles the babies and pities us. Right? She gets to feel especially snotty about those mean bitches in suits and high heels. They have all the bad nannies now! They have the psychopaths, and her child's got her, the Woman Who Gave It All Up."

"Sounds like you've had a lot of experience with this," Abigail ventured, only slightly shaken. She had always beaten the odds, and she would now.

"I've seen it from all sides, dear. I'm a father—here, look." He motioned over to a side table near a side window. Within a gilt frame was his most recent family, several small kids in ski gear, his wife's lineless face haloed in lavender fox.

"She had a degree in interior design from Parsons," he said ruefully. He took his cigar up from the crystal ashtray and put it to his lips again. "But you know how it goes," he said, dragging. "Now she decorates our houses. The Sun Valley lodge is actually a knockout."

"Beautiful," said Abigail politely, referring to the wife, the snow, the house, Sun Valley. All of it. What else could she say? In some way, she saw that Fudim felt proud of his silver-framed story. But she, Abigail, would not be silver-framed.

"And then one day the husband decides to move to San Diego, and she goes," Fudim continued, releasing a billow of smoke. "True story. Dana Kidder, tax attorney, JD Chicago, law review, federal clerkships?—an appendage, mere chattel. Her husband parks her in the Spanish-style mansion that it takes a team to clean, waves goodbye, and hits the road running. In fifteen years, her kids'll do the same. Run off to the East Coast, you know, Williams, Wharton. Maybe they'll come back, and maybe not. But meanwhile, Dana'll get real good at tennis. Renovate the kitchen. Again. Take a puff pastry course. Have a midlife crisis when the kids get mouthy and her husband gets quiet. Get a liquid facelift, lift her boobs, Brazilian ass job. . . ." His voice trailed off.

"Sounds like you know a lot about this," said Abigail diplomatically.

"Autologous fat transfers," said Fudim, as though he were speaking a different language. He knew so much from keeping that third wife of his in shape.

"Ridiculous," she replied. How awful he made women sound, and how wonderful that she, Abigail, would pioneer a new era of values. It was an effort, though, to continue to keep her nerves steady. Despite her resolve, a little of Fudim's sexism was a lot, and Abigail was starting to feel queasy. Not just the cigar smoke and the thought of a South American "ass job" (whatever that was), but this talk of renovating kitchens? How dare he! She was satisfied with takeout; no, she preferred it. What difference did it make if you cooked the food or someone else did? What was wrong with salads, wraps, and yogurts? And—come to think of it—who were these people who matched fabric to wallpaper? It seemed bizarre to have such fixations. Whenever her mother had asked her to choose a color for the towels or a pattern for the tablecloth, Abigail had been proud to feel bored and above it all.

"Everything you said, it's not going to happen to me, Mr. Fudim. I'm not that kind of superficial person. I want to go all the way here. I don't even know what a 'Bugaboo' really is—my younger sister, Annie, she's got four kids, believe it or not—says I won't be able to live without it. It's a fancy stroller, I think, with great accessories. I'm still pretty sure I can live without it. But what I know I can't live without is work. It's my life. Without it—and I do mean full-time, in-house, on-call—I feel completely . . . not me."

Abigail was starting to feel unlike herself even now, talking to a senior partner about caca and Bugaboos. "As far as I know, Mr. Fudim, I don't even like babies until they start behaving like people, you know, walking properly and talking clearly and not spilling and touching everything." She was thinking of Annie's four little challenges. "I'm relieved that there are such things as professional caregivers. I'm not in the least maternal, and if some-one else wants to do it, I'm thrilled to pay for it. Fair exchange of goods for services. As for stay-at-home moms, I had one, and that thrill, on either end, isn't apparent to me. If you must know, sometimes I've felt like yelling 'Get a life!' at my fertile sister."

"Just wait, you're going to be one of these people."

"I've already got a great life. Here at the firm."

"Sure, let's hope for the best," said Fudim, generously. "I have kids, and it hasn't changed me one iota."

That seemed true.

"Ask any of my wives," he continued. "Took the little one, Jor-dan, into the office last year on his birthday, remember?"

"Yes!" Abigail vaguely recalled a stout ten year old who kept diving under the secretaries' desks to touch their legs. "He was so interested in everything," she attempted, politely.

"He's a pistol, that kid, and I love him to bits. But some people think you have to give, give, give like Mother Teresa in her hey-day. 'Taint so, dear."

"Me, I give at the office," said Abigail. "And that's a fair exchange, too."

"Good," said Fudim, distracted now by a pinging text.

Abigail stood up and left without further disturbing his routine.

3 ✗ The obvious questions—why, how, and with whom she'd gone and gotten pregnant—hadn't come up in Abigail's meeting with the senior partner. There were rumors, of course. Perhaps Bertram Fudim—who'd been so rashly frank in general—had thought these areas too personal to explore, verging on the actionable borderline of harassment as well as of employment discrimination. That was lucky, because if he had "gone there," Abigail couldn't have given satisfactory answers.

What were the real answers? Hard to put into rational words. For a brief time, Abigail Thomas, organized and focused, had been possessed by blind emotional need.

It had been a while since she had gone to that dark place. During her late teens, between childhood and *Business Week*, Abigail had been magnetized by anything bad, sad, or dangerous. Her parents' respective immigrants' blues may have had something to do with this, but it was also the spirit of the times, echoing the hormones that carried her on a rough, shocking journey from stick figure to full-blown vamp. Dark and dingy was a common place for young people's imaginations to dwell.

Abigail had had more company during this stage than she had ever had before or would after. Together, they sat in East Village dives, listening to singers croak about hard-knotted love, or lounged in hookah bars, feeling numb. Nietzsche (like other harsh existentialists) was big, as were fingerless gloves, Little Debby snack cakes, Cheetos, and clove cigarettes from Nat Sherman, held like sticks of incense as the ashes dropped. Soul mates were chosen from some endless weirdness cornucopia: Korean cellists with callused fingers that scratched, Irish Kabbalists, black hip-hoppers from Bronx Science. In those days, Abigail fell in love over and over. It hurt.

In college, the same. A graduate student from Norway played with her heart during sophomore year. It had taken her almost a year to soften him, and then he was all passion, all in. And then, one day, he seemed angry at her, as though caring for her had diminished him. Now he would make love to her, eyes aflame, weeping. Now he would storm out of her dorm and give her three days of silent treatment.

"I love you too much," he explained. "And you don't care, do you!"

"Of course I care!" she'd howl.

Both of them played this scene over and over, as though they enjoyed it. And then, one day, he told her they were through.

Because of him, Abigail had come close to committing suicide. "Where I come from, that is not so unusual," said Anders, refusing even then to melt, even a little. Abigail had suffered even more, unable to stop loving this ineffable man who finally went back to Bergen and, she heard, committed suicide himself. Over a different woman, nothing like herself. Some Norwegian singer he'd heard at a café.

She seemed to like unstable people. Abigail's best friend that same year was a gorgeous, tortured bulimic, Sydney, who, despite her habit of vomiting into the plastic bags she carried everywhere, grew so fat that her parents had her institutionalized in Bedford Hills. By the time Sydney was released—slim, serious, and ready to study the history of art—Abigail had decided to do pre-law. That "big bucks" motif had spoken to both her despair and her wish to escape it. This way, I don't feel. This way, I don't need anyone.

Since then, she had marched along the straight and the narrow, with the occasional boyfriend who never entrapped her. Abigail's real goal, like that of her infrequent dates, was long-term and practical. It was ordinal, sequential, like a well-wrought video game. You got one diploma, then another, and then you got a job. You got raises, you got promoted. It was all as rectilinear as the corners of her office, as her hard, wooden desk. It was doable if you worked hard and didn't fall down.

Her mother's sickness, however, her mother's slow death, had put some crazy, free-form lines into the picture, some retrograde motion and infinite loops. No one should have to shovel clods of earth onto their mother's coffin. Thud. Like the most horrible winter—a winter of hailstorm and mud. But that was her mother's tradition, and Abigail and her sisters followed it. Just after she had seen her mother obliterated by dirt, in a grave, finished, Abigail had experienced some of the old, strange hunger. And she'd felt herself drop into longing, a hole so deep it had no earth below to end it.

This past March, not long after the burial, Abigail Thomas had fallen hard for an older man. The death of her mother had opened up a bottomless need, and this man had seemed to satisfy it. He was a lawyer—a senior partner at Murdock & Hill. One of the best firms in the world.

Richard Trubridge was tall, subtly handsome (in a way that had crept up on her), and just beginning to gray. He appeared to be in his early forties. His glasses were thick black Peter Sellers/Dr. Strangelove frames that suited him. Abigail had encountered Richard on a golfing weekend. Senior associates and partners of several equally prestigious firms were sent on a junket with the purpose of honing their handicaps on a Palm Springs course. Abigail had stood alone with a borrowed set of clubs, astounded by the vista. A calm, planned greenness went on for rolling miles, just to entertain them. Outside of her mother's graveyard, she had not seen such a vast expanse of weedless lawn. The breezes ruffled her white shirt, cooling her back, down the spine.

Richard Trubridge had noticed her solitude and momentary stillness. In a quiet tone, he had offered to coach her game. His actual words were:

"Do you need some help there?"

"Yes," Abigail had admitted, finding that phrase very tempting. She did need help.

The scene was, as lawyers say, paradigmatic: the mentor's arm around her shoulder, helping a girl through the moves. Richard wore a pleasant outfit: peach Lacoste shirt, crisp white pants, brown-and-white golfing shoes. She smelled his nice bay rum as he lingered behind her. His breath tickled her ear. She heard his deep voice, kindly: "Hey, that's not too bad." The voice was familiar from somewhere.

"Really?" She turned around and looked at him searchingly. Richard's salt-and-pepper hair was long, curling at his neck. There was a touch of pomade, an old-fashioned gloss. She recognized him with a jolt. He had briefly worked at her firm.

"Now, just a little bit more like this." He swung her arm again, at the sky, and over her shoulder, and over his, behind her. They walked on to the next hole. Their steps seemed to fall into rhythm together, the length of the strides, the tempo. There was a harmony of bodies as he taught and she learned.

Hours passed, and the skies began darkening. Abigail could feel Richard looking at her lips. She hoped she looked pretty in the twilight on the fairway. He suddenly kissed her, and she let him, and she sensed that he sensed he could go on. His lips felt full as they sank deeply into hers. The kiss became possessive, questing. Richard held Abigail, his hands on her cheeks. He asserted his right to this kiss, to that touch, and she gave it, over and over.

As the orange sun slipped downward, Richard and Abigail walked to the short green grass by a water trap. Just beside a fecund pond, covered in algae, surrounded by swaying cattails. Abigail knew that he wanted her to lie down. She did, and she held her arms up to him. He looked down at her and sighed, and sank.

Yes, Richard sank, as though prayerful with gratitude, to his knees. She saw him sway above her. Then he stretched his length across and blanketed Abigail, pressing his weight into her, and into the earth. And then he came in, deep and slow, as though driving a shot. Richard Trubridge took his time, whether drafting a brief, talking matters over with an associate, or making love. As the world disappeared into a dizzy darkness, Abigail felt proud of herself somehow. Nothing sentimental, no fear, no prudery. A mutual agreement. She tried not to think too tenderly about the person, Richard Trubridge, who smelled of the sun and bay rum. This was just sex with a man, rough and ready. And yet he was so tender, even awkward at times.

◆ ◆ ◆

Afterward, back in her own room, Abigail reflected. She had not been with a man since she'd broken up with an old law school classmate, Jed Tayler, a long and disappointing on-and-off relationship. When her mother had begun to radically decline, Jed had pulled back, refusing to come to the hospice with Abigail. True, she hadn't spared him any details. As though threatening him to look away, she had forewarned him, told him that the cancer had now gone to her mother's bones, lit them up with poison, and that there were tumors in her brain as well, making her alternately stuporous or frighteningly blunt.

he had warned Jed that her mother might scream. One time, she had told him, her mother had said to her, to the daughter she'd served for over three decades: "I hate you, really! You snob, du falsche katz! What good you are to me? Du kenst mir nicht! You *don't know me*, all right? Now go away from me, go far, you tricky puss!"

Abigail could not go far, but Jed could. He had looked away, begged off, changed the subject. Finally, with a forced calm (as though it were Abigail who was ill), he had said he couldn't "take women when they were emotionally upset." From that time, she had soldiered on alone.

If Abigail could handle this, helping her mother suck from an orange as her lips trembled and the juice spilled over them both, if she could take the sight of her sunken eyes, lifeless as a snapper on ice, or ablaze with ferocious lunacy, if she could take in the sound of her mother's mouth bursting into fierce, disappointed German, then why couldn't macho Jed? Jed, who had always called her "darling," and "sweetheart"; Jed, who was currently facing down adversaries in the Federal District Court like a warrior, two briefcases and a mean mouth—what good was he to her? When Jed had no words to describe or rebut, no words to fight with and win, he got out of the ring.

The skill came gradually, but in the end Abigail grew inured to horror. She was able to stroke her mother's oval head and her knobby, aching feet. She could lay her ear next to her mother's sunken heart (loyal, Abigail felt, despite the cruel words) and listen to the weak but steady beat. Abigail had finally felt she didn't need anyone. She was working then, of course; she was always working. She could check her watch, leave the terminal ward, put in the hours at her job, then go right back to her mother's failing life.

◆ ◆ ◆

As she got dressed up in her evening attire, Abigail reflected on how privileged her life was now. Yes, she'd come from an immigrant family. Yes, her mother had died a lingering death that nothing anyone did could avert. But she, Abigail, had worked hard all along, and that work had paid off. And here she was, on a flashy junket in Palm Springs. All expenses paid. Abigail felt ravenous as she anticipated the evening's elegant four-course meal, the cocktails, the cassis sorbet, the cognac after dinner. This was the expense-account life, and she was determined to sup with passion, like those to the manor and country club born.

At the same time, she had misgivings. How unreal it all seemed—and how easily it might still be taken away from her. Earlier that day, as Richard Trubridge's body lay upon hers, shudders waning, Abigail had felt how tenuous her grip on fortune was. As they'd parted, each walking off in a different direction, she had actually thought of grabbing some of the hotel stationery, the pens, perhaps a small white towel to lay, cool and wet, upon her face when she returned to her little apartment. She suspected that what she and Richard had experienced, however beautiful (the sunset and his touch), had most likely meant nothing to him. After all, unlike her, Richard Trubridge was certainly used to trips like this.

And she was right to be cynical. Her tender new lover had not even shown up later, skipping the lavish supper she'd so looked forward to. Not that Abigail would have dared sit with him at his partner's table—she was too smart for that kind of exposure (already a few observant associates were making smarmy cracks). But she would have enjoyed merely sharing a secret across the room, and the promise of more to come. (Yes, more "nothing," but still better than actual, literal nothing.) The conference wasn't over. They'd have to weather not only this night but other days; wasn't there some sort of tacit agreement about how these things went?

There was far more to it than manners. Abigail remembered how they'd met years earlier, and how different Richard Trubridge had seemed, even then, from other men. So different that she'd never forgotten him. So different that he'd really hurt her now.

Tender, old feelings began to return. Abigail had felt oddly attached to Richard, connected in some way, from the time she'd first laid eyes on him. He seemed like a decent person, someone who had a soft, pliant heart—and these were few in the corporate-law business. In those early years at the firm, still dating callow boys like Jed, Abigail had wondered about men like Richard Trubridge. Thrillingly, he caught and held your glance when you spoke to him. There was an electric connection there, along with the sense of a personal gift. She'd asked him something in the reference library once, and he'd actually put his book down and considered how best to help her. That quick availability, that submission, the sudden access—it had been somewhat erotic. And not in any of the ways she'd felt before. It was as though he'd gently cast a spell.

There was also a sensuous, almost languorous quality to Richard's movement. While other lawyers raced purposefully through the hallways, as though translating the importance of their work into velocity and pushiness, Richard walked slowly, almost humbly. His tread was graceful. He let people pass him. He stopped here and there to look in on another lawyer, to chat. Even with associates. He was especially considerate to the support staff, and would often be seen simply listening to them talk about their children, their hobbies, their weekends. He always seemed to have more time than other people. To make time extend a little. He'd made time extend for Abigail, and it had stretched generously before her when she'd first met his eyes.

Yes, she remembered that sense of how good he was, how he'd linger in attention in a rare and moving way. But he seemed to act that way with everyone. Had he ever really noticed her? Yes, he'd helped her in the library, of course he must have "noticed" her. But associates like her, even attractive female ones, were many—and Richard was one of the partners. There was an aura around him, even if he seemingly did nothing to maintain it. It drew her in, from the bottom of her feet to her scalp. But had she done the same to him? It was foolish to think so.

Abigail remembered their first conversation. She'd asked him about finding a precedent to extend the scope of "undue influence"—the phenomenon in which a signatory to a contract, usually elderly, is thought to be coerced by a biased party. Richard had carefully asked her about the facts of her case, then mulled them. It was as though he wanted to see if there actually had been undue influence. This was strange and new, because in law firms you typically just took the side you were given. Abigail had not been asked to decide if there had been any undue influence; she was supposed to show that there was. She was supposed to find a precedent that would push the fact pattern her way, to that predetermined conclusion.

Richard had wanted to hear the story—her story—fresh. He'd wanted to hear it without the "undue influence" of his professional position, the "side" the firm wanted to take, or anything else that was extraneous or contaminated by bias. Richard actually seemed interested in the truth of the matter. When his eyes had met Abigail's, when she realized this man wanted to simply know what had happened, something else happened. It happened inside Abigail, deep inside her. A tiny revolution. A lurch out of the ordinary orbit.

She'd almost started crying. It had been a fleeting moment, but Abigail had been moved to tears by an honorable man who seemed strangely irresistible to her. Not only did he arouse sensual fantasies (imagine his attentions on the horizontal plane), but these were coupled with a sort of hero worship that felt as delicious as blind trust. She felt—she knew—that Richard Trubridge was one of the few who cared about the right things. And he would take his sweet time to set them right, to make them go in the right direction, however slowly, however long it took. In the end, this was a kind of power, Abigail thought, longing to know this power.

When her mother was diagnosed with cancer, Abigail had thought of telling Richard about everything that was going on in her personal world. She wanted to know how a kind person should act and would act. She wanted to pour her heart out to him, and to have his own good heart receive—and heal—the painful aspects of her life.

But she and Richard Trubridge were not friends, or even professional peers. They had simply had a moment together—one that was now sparking deep feelings in Abigail—but perhaps only she had experienced it as special.

◆ ◆ ◆

Having just made love to that very Richard Trubridge, Abigail's dormant attachment came back, full blast. The man's absence from dinner invited even more emotion. She had taken so much care to wear a gorgeous dress and the very uncomfortable shoes that made her legs look longer; she had taken great pains with her hair and her makeup, shy to be seeing the man after sweating with him on the greens. But he wasn't there. Was he actually avoiding her, or was he sick of rich, long meals?

This confusion created energy: as quickly as she could escape the banquet, Abigail began searching for Richard. But to her consternation, he wasn't at any of the bars, either. Keeping her voice businesslike, Abigail asked the front desk for his room number. When she rang Richard Trubridge, his line was busy. She took it as a direct rebuff; it inflamed her with need.

She wasn't sure how to act now. She felt lost. She wasn't used to doing nothing. Letting go. Instead, she turned fierce, as though that meant she was strong.

There she was, then, knocking on his door, the sound reverberating.

"Is someone there?" Abigail heard Richard's voice call out. Despite herself, it thrilled her. She hesitated, wanting to run away and desperately wanting to stay.

"It's me," she said, finally, her voice rising up like a wail.

"Who is it?" She realized he might not even know or remember her name.

"We played golf together earlier. Remember, we stopped—for a while—near the water trap?"

After a moment, Richard Trubridge opened the door.

"Abigail," he said, and the sound of her name in his mouth, and the way his warm baritone voice said it, reassured her even as it made her hungrier. Richard was wearing a white hotel bathrobe, his dark hair glinting as though he had just showered. A room-service tray sat off on the side table, the dome of the main dish glowing by lamplight. Richard's face was tired. It was now ten fifteen. Abigail took a step toward him.

"Uh, listen, I was just about to turn in," he said, too polite to take a step backward. He loomed over her, so close she could smell the elegant hotel soap, and murmured, "Long day, don't you think?"

"It's not my bedtime, kiddo," she heard herself retorting, as though she were in a bad forties movie.

"You should get some rest." He spoke quietly, and not unkindly.

"Can't I just come in and stay for a minute?"

She hated the way this was going. Now she sounded like some kid whose parents are heading out on a Saturday night, leaving her behind with a game of Life and a dish of Mott's applesauce.

After a minute, Richard nodded. Abigail brushed into his suite, past the small living area, and into the bedroom. A great big bedroom, much nicer than hers. A huge bed, bigger than king-size, a four-poster. She propped up a pillow and impetuously flopped down on it, kicking off her heels. They tumbled on the floor with a clatter. After a momentary standstill, Richard followed her inside.

"What's going on?" he smiled, just a bit. Abigail's feet were tiny, the arches high and vulnerable. Richard wasn't standing at the doorway, but he wasn't moving all the way to the bedside, either. He stood apart and somewhat frozen.

"I seem to need more of you," she said quietly. "Just for tonight. I can't seem to let you go for now." She spoke to her own small feet.

Richard took off his black glasses and rubbed his eyes. Now, looking up at them, Abigail could see their color for the first time: a surprising ocean blue, with lots of teal.

"I feel like we have kind of a history together," she said. She felt an unusual ache, the pain of missing something precious, something lost.

"You mean now that we—? Of course—"

"No, before that. Nothing big, but—"

"Yes, I remember you. We've met before," said Richard. "We used to be in the same firm," he went on, finally sitting down beside her, on the edge of the big bed.

"I remember you, too," she said. "You used to wear wire rims, and your hair was a lot shorter."

"That's right," he said kindly, and smiled.

Abigail looked into Richard's eyes. Their soft, honest gaze seemed to take her back to a better time. She remembered his slow lope down the carpeted hallways, his calm greetings. He had seemed different from the other partners, even then. That aura of goodness, packaged in the alluring form of a mature, responsible man.

Looking at Richard now, Abigail saw that the goodness in his eyes had only deepened since that time. The deep yearning opened up inside her again.

It wasn't just that they'd now slept together. It was that in the years they'd been apart, she'd only grown more and more sure of her utter aloneness in the world. The few inadequate relationships she'd had had only confirmed that.

"What do you remember about me?" she ventured. She knew he might hurt her by saying, "Not much." But she needed to know if he'd felt anything that day. Did he know, for example, that he'd started the process that made her leave Jed? By the time she finally did, Richard was long gone, under a cloud of secrecy. Dark things were said about him for years. She remembered having a drink with Jed and some of the associates one night, a few days before their final breakup. Jed had called Richard Trubridge a "loser." But then, to men like Jed, most people were losers. Her mother was probably a "loser" for getting sick and dying.

"What do I remember about you? Back then?"

"Yes—if anything."

"Well, of course I remember you, but let me think." Richard

closed his eyes and a smile came over his face. "You were ambitious, eager. Always rushing, working—a real go-getter."

Abigail did not return his smile. The look on her face was that of a lost soul. Was she that much of a boring, sexless cliché? Just another worker bee?

"And of course, you were very pretty," he added. "You still are. More than ever, actually. You're lovely."

Abigail still didn't smile.

"Do you really remember me?" she said softly. Because she remembered that electrical charge between them, not only this day but five long years ago. She remembered more and more. It almost hurt.

"You're a funny creature, aren't you?" For a minute, Richard Trubridge looked turbulent, conflicted. But then he turned fully toward her. He ran his hand up and down her leg, inhaled, and pulled her across him.

"Wow, you surprised me," he said, completely gone.

"I surprised you?" He had sort of grabbed her, which she loved.

"You totally caught me off guard, coming back to me tonight."

"Oh, yeah," she said, leaning up on her arms, looking down on him. "I'm just fearless." She looked down at the myopic turquoise eyes, vulnerable beneath her. Then Richard reached up and kissed her, pulling her down with strong arms. She peeled off her top, aware of the power of her breasts. His eyes caught the view, brightened, widened all the way to the pupils—so enormous—then closed again.

They moved together in surprising synchrony. It was great, more than great. It was a homecoming.

She heard him mumble a question, "Do—you?"

"What?" she said. "Do I—what?" But she wanted to answer, "Yes, yes I absolutely and wholeheartedly do."

"I don't remember saying anything," he laughed, hugging her warmly. "I like being with you," he added, kissing her all over her face.

He had smiled, and she had smiled back, and they had continued moving together, pleasing each other, seeking, playing. It was as though they had always been lovers. There was as much comfort as pleasure, and there was a generous sense of sharing in joy.

◆ ◆ ◆

Richard gave a lecture the next day, but Abigail had to attend a different meeting—"A Colloquium on the Nature of Honesty." So they didn't get together until lunch. When the meetings cleared out, they looked for each other. Abigail hung back, making herself visible, until Richard spotted her standing outside the large dining room. She was looking at the menu, or at least pretending to. Mesclun, kale, salmon, sole. She wasn't hungry.

"I'm not leaving," he said, as though reading her mind.

"You're not what?" she replied, looking up and trying to act surprised to see him. Of course, he was all she could think about all morning.

"I'm not going to leave your side today. You made quite an impression on me, and besides all that, I want you to hide me from these people."

"You mean all the big shots?"

"Big shots, little shots, I gave my talk and now I want to kick back a little."

"Wish I could have seen you. I had to do the thing where you let someone lead you blindfolded hither and yon, and you pretend not to be frightened by it."

"Did you get a good partner?"

"I'll tell you later. He might be right behind us. The whole thing was very creepy, very stealthy. Who thinks of these things? Who thinks trust can be established through fear?"

"I think you're right," said Richard. "Let's take a stroll, we can grab a snack at the coffee place later. They even have wraps—OK?"

"I'd love that," she said. And they opened up a huge double door made of glass and went out into the fresh air.

There were flowerbeds and fountains on the grounds. Farther off, down a pebbled path, stood a gazebo covered in wisteria. It looked as though grapes hung in heavy, fragrant clusters around it. A bountiful harvest, something sweet and generous. An enveloping light violet color, punctuated by dark green foliage. And all of it wrapped around a wooden bower.

"Let's go there," said Abigail, pointing.

As they approached, they could both see that no one was around. What a treasure. How odd that they had so easily slipped away from the world. On one side was the clattering cafeteria, buffet-style lunch with every kind of meat to be carved, fish to be sliced, and leaf to be heaped in a salad bowl, and all of it crowded and depressing. And on the other, this gazebo, this nest of stillness.

It smelled like heaven in there. The bench they sat on was hewn from wood, as though an integral part of the gazebo. It wasn't comfortable, but it was perfect. The leaves and flowers shaded them, and the fragrance wafted to and fro with the breeze.

For a long time, they didn't speak. And it was fine like that.

And then they spoke, and everything that passed between them was easy, and agreeable, and comfortable. Richard seemed like an angel to Abigail. An old-fashioned gentleman, almost too good to be true.

He said, "How's your mother doing?"

Abigail was stunned that he remembered.

"She's—she recently passed away."

"Sorry to hear that. I know you—"

"It was a long battle; we tried everything."

"I got exactly that sense. That you would try everything."

"Weren't you too busy being a big partner to notice that?"

"No, I wasn't, actually. It made a strong impression on me."

"We really tried. We both did. What can you do?"

Richard gave a big sigh and looked downward. He seemed to be attempting to collect himself. Abigail wondered if he had also faced illness or death in his family recently, but was wary of asking.

"There's only one thing we can do in the presence of this—" he suddenly stopped and looked at her.

"In the presence of sickness, you mean?"

"Yes, sickness, breakdowns, all of these horrors—chaos happens to everyone, and sometimes when you least expect it."

"I'm in estates and aviation disasters, so I know."

"You do, Abigail. Of course, you do."

"I wonder if anything can hurt more than losing your mother."

"Were you close with her?"

"Not so much. I mean, I loved her very much, but we were so different. And that sometimes makes the parting worse."

"Yes, I think I understand."

"It's an ambiguous thing, when you're not close but you keep wishing you were so close, you know?"

"You felt up in the air with her."

"Yes," said Abigail sadly. "And then she floated away from us all. So, anyway, what's the one thing?"

"The one thing you can do?"

"Yes, you said there was 'one thing.'"

"Sorry, do I sound like I'm lecturing you? I don't mean to."

"No, not at all. I'd appreciate having your insight here."

"Well, I've had my own ups and downs. And—well, the one

thing we can control is that we behave decently to each other. Help each other. You were kind to your mother, Abigail."

"Not all the time. I used to—I'm ashamed to say that I sometimes kind of looked down on her, and I think she sometimes knew it."

"You were good to her when she most needed you. And that's the real and only test."

Abigail pondered his words as he leaned over to kiss her. Richard was good to her when she needed him, Abigail thought. When she'd gone to his room, and openly asked him for "more," he'd given her all she wanted, all he could give. These memories warmed her. She felt both friendship and lust grow and intermingle inside her, a wonderful and unfamiliar combination.

When they walked back to the main building, it seemed as though hours had passed. They were still able to pick up the coffee and wraps, and they took them to Richard's room.

They kept talking.

"Shall I order champagne?"

Did that mean he was having as wonderful a time as she was?

Did he do this all the time?

Did he do this with everyone?

"Go on, ask me anything," he said. Abigail knew her face showed everything. No amount of professional training had changed this. She felt herself flushing, and tilted her face downward.

"No, I don't think I need to," she said shyly. The very fact that he wanted her to open up, that his life seemed accessible to her, was all the answer she needed.

"I love champagne," she added. Abigail didn't know it sounded naïve, as though she rarely had it.

"Me, too." Richard, too, was no big drinker. "I love it, too."

They made a night of it.

4 ⚖ On the last day of the conference, Richard had designed and would judge a moot court exercise. Abigail had volunteered to write one of the arguments. The topic was whether depriving a father of the right to see his child could be actionable against the state—under a plea of "cruel and unusual punishment"—harming both father and child. After all, it was by now a well-known truism that men loved their children as much as women did, and that it was in the best interest of any child to know and love his father as much as his mother. Pregnancy and lactation did not determine quantities of adoration, and men, though by definition not fecund, incapable of bringing fully fledged, viable fruit into the world, were no less biologically and spiritually bound to their little ones. They bonded, like women; they loved, like women. In that case, why was it not cruel and inhuman to separate a man from his kids, and these kids from their father? And if a state court did so—as it still frequently did—well, then, did it not thereby violate the Eighth Amendment?

There were, of course, no precedents for a ruling like this. And law, especially appellate law, was nothing if not rooted in the past. But times moved on, and new laws were made. Richard, Abigail saw, was a maverick, trying to create new legal perspectives, penumbras and emanations that the court hadn't seen for decades. On the other hand, this was just moot court, and moot court on a junket, at that. Golf was more the order of the day than jurisprudence, and this exercise seemed aimed simply at earning the tax deductions, to make the whole thing seem more work-oriented. Bonding experiences—rope climbing and the like—had been done to death, and this old-school exercise was, in its way, fresh.

Abigail, a daddy's girl, found the topic compelling. This was why she decided to volunteer for the more innovative (more difficult to argue) position that yes, depriving a father (or mother, for that matter) of the biological imperative to see his or her child was so harsh as to touch the conscience—that it was a punishment, more than a mere decree, and that family courts which so ruled without sufficient grounds were violating not merely statutory regulations but the United States Constitution itself.

"Can I ask you one little question?" she ventured to Richard after breakfast.

"You can, but you know I probably can't answer it. I mean, on ethical grounds. We're—we're—I'm partial to you, you know. And—and—I'm the judge of this, you see?"

"I'm not asking you to help me win. I just had a question."

"All right. Then ask away."

"You designed this case, right?"

"Yes, right."

"Well, I can tell what side you're on."

"Really, how?"

"I just can."

"Continue."

"You're on the side of the dad who can't see his kid. And I know that you're a good man. And why else would you have written things this way? And if that's the case, how appropriate is it for you—clearly biased you—to judge who wins?"

"Without addressing your comments in full, I'm—I'm not the only judge. But I can recuse myself if you want to raise the issue. . . ." His tone was mild.

Abigail couldn't answer for a few moments.

She could feel Richard staring at her, and she reddened. This was the man who had known everything about her, just last night. How she smelled, tasted, looked, and acted while lost in sensual ecstasy. And she knew the same about him.

"You're blushing," he said.

"Yeah, so are you," she replied.

"I think if I recused myself, however, people would know more about us than they need to."

"I like that word."

"'Need'?" he smiled.

"Yes," she said, smiling, too. "Need. And also, and especially, 'us.'"

And though it was the morning, and though she really should have been preparing for the moot court scheduled for four o'clock that day, Abigail had the distinct sensation that she harbored fairly rapacious thoughts about Richard. What a complex man he was—with his keen, original legal ideas and his almost mystical bedroom manner.

"Yeah, we should probably take this inside," he said, smiling.

Abigail also loved feeling how tall he was, especially compared to her. Richard was smiling down on her like a benevolent elm. Looking up into his face as though into a warming lamp, Abigail let Richard take her hand and lead her back to the room where they'd begun to know each other. And now it was even more familiar, kinder, slower. More beautiful somehow, and far more sweet.

Later, Richard did recuse himself. And Abigail did lose the hearing. Some icy woman with a pale yellow bun had declared, in startling reactionary opposition, that fathers, bodies intact, knew nothing and could never know anything of "cruel and unusual punishment." It was the mothers who knew it, daily, monthly, yearly, always, the endless cycle of menses, reproduction, nursing, and, later, the menopause. What did men know of all this, and how could anyone dare deem a legal decision to be equal in cruelty to that of nature?

Abigail was surprised to hear a woman use biological imperatives to win a case—but that was often the way, still, in parenting trials, and she took her loss graciously. After all, she knew that she had absolutely won the heart, the mind, the body, and perhaps even the good soul of Richard Trubridge.

◆ ◆ ◆

Still later, that night, in the darkness, Abigail awoke, thirsty. She got herself a glass of water from the bathroom and slipped quietly back into bed. She and Richard were both naked, and she was tired and happy. She had never felt so protected from the chaos of the world. Even the luxurious small bottles of cream and bubbles in the bathroom had cast a charm upon her. She felt safe and nurtured.

But then her mood changed, and fear stepped in as she thought about tomorrow. They would be leaving this place in the next few hours. Back to the normal, lonely grind. Abigail leaned over Richard, as though to ask him to change all that.

He slept exhaustedly, snoring lightly, turning when she hovered too near, seeming to need space and freedom. Sleep made this man feel unreachable again, as though he'd never known her, not before, not at the firm, not yesterday, not mere hours ago. There were moments, Abigail thought, trying to detach, that he looked like a corpse, mouth open, eyes slightly parted. Hospice patients looked like that. They passed away, and you couldn't tell when the transition happened. But Richard was actively alive. He snorted periodically; a worried moan would emerge, rising up and down the scale like a plea.

Toward dawn, as she sensed the time running out, Abigail reached for Richard and wrapped herself around his undefended frame. To her great relief, he snuggled closer to her. He rose up, kissed her face, from chin to forehead, then sighed and closed his eyes again. Another hour must have passed.

At the moment the phone rang, Abigail was feeling as though the room, and everything in it, was hers. The bottles of champagne, his clothing, him. She had it all. She was lucky. She was wrapped in rare comfort and happiness. She got up to pee.

"Let me get that," said Richard, at the third jarring ring. He grabbed the phone so quickly Abigail could hear the base fall off the table and clatter to the ground. Then, his tone intimate, she overheard him say:

". . . You are? Oh, good! Yes, of course I do. Say hi to the kids for me and give them each a kiss. You're a trouper, holding the fort like that, you really are, hon. Love ya."

A very quick and tender conversation.

Abigail heard Richard Trubridge put the phone down. She remained frozen in the bathroom, stunned. Wasn't he ever going to tell her he had at some point gotten married? Was he telling her now, in some blasé, sadistic fashion, or did he think she was deaf? Kids, too.

Maybe that's what he had meant, earlier, by his comment, "Do you do this often?" Not sex, but adultery. Jaded junketeering. Of course, he hadn't worn a ring; that would have been disrespectful to "hon," not to mention the fort she was so laudably holding down. Abigail knew that people were often cynical, that they used others, but this level of cool deception disgusted her. And she'd fallen for all of it. Golf tips, gazebo, champagne. Some manipulative flattery, a few sensual spots woken up by a pro. So obvious, really. What a fool she was. Men like Richard knew exactly which buttons to push. That looking into your eyes thing. Classic.

Abigail left the bathroom, picked her clothes up from the bedroom floor, and put them back on. She dressed with a philosophical slowness. Then she spoke, her voice just a whisper:

"OK, I guess I'm leaving now. It was—it was fun."

Richard was asleep again, his body radiating its tempting, treacherous warmth. She watched him breathe, enthralled still. She would have loved to lie back down, snuggle this man, forgive him, beg him for more. But Abigail fought her weakness back: If the longing hurt now, how much worse would it be in the end?

How could she be so wrong? *How* on earth? And was this why he was so pro-father? He had his own brood stashed somewhere? She even felt sorry for his wife—to be married to so sociopathic a liar. How smooth he'd been. She'd been completely taken in!

She wanted him to know she was leaving. She wanted to rouse him, jar him awake. So Abigail raised her voice to the level of a closing argument:

"Richard," she pronounced, "I have to go now."

She was glad to be in his room, a room she could leave. She could not have borne his leaving her alone in her own little rectangle of space. She'd walk out, take a shower, start packing. Her head would be high. She was not the happily married one. She was not the cheater.

"What, sweetie?" he said, stirring. Richard's voice was scarcely audible. "Sweetie": Was he burbling to her or to the other one?

You know, the wife he'd conveniently forgotten (and forgotten to mention)?

"Open your eyes and look at me," said Abigail, looking down. She felt cold and cruel and sad.

"What—what is it? Oh, I must have fallen back asleep. You're getting up?" Richard rubbed his eyes and looked at Abigail. "Come here, hey now, where're you going?" His voice was thick with sleep, vulnerable.

"I've gotten in over my head," said Abigail, not moving, though.

"Please don't leave; what time is it?" He reached for his glasses as his weak eyes searched pleadingly for meaning. They were near the phone. By the time he had put them on, she was stepping out of the suite.

"I want more," said his voice, calling out from the bedroom. Abigail froze at the doorway. Those were her very words, that first night. It had cost her some pride to say them, and it shamed her to think he remembered them enough to repeat them. His audacity in the face of the sordid facts said something about Richard Trubridge's character, but it was something Abigail, surprised to be openly crying, was in no position to explore.

5 As she walked away, Abigail coldly recalled that she had not taken her pill that night. She'd have to take it as soon as she got back to her room, at the less chic end of the grounds. Apart from the fact that she'd just met this man—this unavailable man—the last thing she wanted was a baby to need her.

Since her younger sister had become a mother, Abigail had avoided visiting her. Annie's brood, Abigail's niece and nephews, were as wired as terriers. The seven-year-old boys, Jared and Jesse, tore around the house touching everything; the five-year-old, Jaycee, whined chronically; and the baby, Todd, was a projectile vomiter. Annie, of course, acted as though they were precious gifts from heaven above, but was it not more likely that these blobs of flesh were punishments, put on earth to prevent women from remembering what they were put on earth to achieve? Like Bottom's ass, they bewitched you into cooing love notes. Then they grew up, becoming hairy and rough and smart-mouthed, and then they left you. They stole your mind, as Fudim had said.

They stole your life, thought Abigail. Annie had no life now. She'd been thoroughly annexed.

Though she held an M.A. in developmental psychology, Annie never even thought of applying her skills outside the house. (She might have had an office! There might have been clean walls, with no fingerprints, grape-juice splatters, or ketchup smudges on them!) Instead, Annie was usually to be found stuffing the fridge with free-range poultry, fish (which the children threw at one another), organic fruits, and cruciferous vegetables, or checking the catalogs for next season's cotton children's clothing from Sweden.

How could Annie stand it? Was she some kind of saint, or a brainwashed fool? And what had brainwashed her? Motherhood itself—with its infamous hormones of gestation and lactation? Was it the trend now, to have kids and drop out? Hadn't Annie learned a thing from the past?

Abigail thought about her own mother. If only Clara Milch Thomas had gotten out of the house and made a contribution in all those years. She was responsible, good with children; she could have taught somewhere. She might have lived longer, left more of a mark. As it was, her life was a moaning wind, a twist in the bedclothes, a raking of nails at the air. She had needed her children too fiercely; she had needed to be a mother even when her children had grown and gone.

Abigail was never going to let that happen to her.

When she entered her room, however, she had a shock. Searching first her cosmetics bag and then every corner of her purse and suitcase, she didn't find what she was looking for. Her little beige pill case was there, yes, but the card was empty, with punched-out holes where the pills had been. She had accidentally packed last month's used package. Abigail had followed her usual travel checklist, but perhaps she'd been duped by the tranquilizers she'd taken on the morning of the journey. She'd enjoyed the rare tranquility they brought as she packed her pills (as she'd thought), electric toothbrush, high-SPF sunblock. Since working at the firm and hearing about all the different ways that aircraft fail, Abigail had developed a secret terror of flying. Two Ativans in her system, and she could get to Palm Springs in unashamed calm. But apparently not with a full pack of contraceptive pills.

After returning to New York, she told herself, she'd get right back on schedule. Besides, Abigail was sure she was the type, common in these hectic times, who did not impregnate easily. (Half her sisters' friends complained about this.) No matter what she had done (or forgotten to do), there had never been even a single missed period in Abigail's life. She would be all right this time, too. Just to make sure, she did fifty jumping jacks before showering in a haze of boiling water and antibacterial soap. Science had never been her subject, but Abigail had often heard that tense people did not easily conceive—in which case she'd be fine. Being with Richard was the first time in her life she hadn't been tense.

But now she was rigid with fear whenever she thought of the man, married liar and powerful lawyer, husband and father of kids. No condom for this guy. And he would probably tell the next girl nothing about her and their baby scare. Not that there would be any baby scare. Tense people did not conceive, right? And even if they did, there was always the smart girl's early out, still legal. She could probably get some quick little sucking procedure done, a touch of blood, and be none the worse for wear.

◆ ◆ ◆

When, despite resuming the intake of birth control, an incredulous Abigail missed a period, then another, she had had to concede that there were some inexorable forces she had not tangled with before. Whatever she did next, she acknowledged her surprise—that a living being was taking form inside of her, even as she and Richard did not speak (or need to speak) another word to each other, much less touch.

With her mother gone, death had become something Abigail took less abstractly. This new lesson—in the form of a spinning mass of life that took off inside her, without her permission— seemed even more invincible. It was stronger than her will, stronger than her plans, stronger than her wish that she be left alone, free and untouched. Death would leave you alone and at rest. Not so new life.

Abigail went back to the obvious option of "losing" the baby— the fetus—but something (new hormones, perhaps?) made her feel, instead, as though her shrinking sense of self was all that mattered in this world. What was this weird, surrendering awe? Was this what pregnancy did? It felt almost painful, fate taking over all the plotting and planning, ego stepping aside and letting a mystery grow. Yes, it was a growing pain she felt, an instructive pain, and these were rare.

There were even times that Abigail sensed her own mother alive still, within her, a quickening love she could carry to term. Could she really bring a wandering soul into the world? Would her mother have wanted her to?

Abigail thought guiltily about her mother's death. There had been such fury in it, not only at cancer, but at her, Abigail. There had been a bitter scorn. She had had her eyes opened by illness, and had seen Abigail for what she was—a cold person, absent of vegetative growth, a withholder of life and of love. And now, Abigail could feel it, see it —the daughter who had rejected her own mother. There must be a place in hell, she saw, for those who spurn the teat. And she had spurned it, preferring the steely gray embrace of male ambition to anything else in the world, however sweet.

There were glimmers of painful new knowledge inside her now. Her mother had been good! Her mother had helped others! Her mother had done all she did to make the world more comfortable and safe! Abigail felt humble. If goodness were the ultimate lasting status, she would have to explore it. Was motherhood goodness? The hormones were making her say "yes," not only to that question, but to all unanswered questions, and to life. Maybe Richard was rotten after all—her heart ached at this reversal—but she could become a better person.

And then, too, maybe it was better this way. The timing was somewhat advantageous, Abigail thought, her mind struggling to be practical. She was no longer young enough to presume fertility for very much longer. If she was ever going to be a mother, she'd better act before it was too late, before the well was dry. As for her single state—how contemporary, how brave it was! It would actually be like some challenging extra-credit problem: Could she reach for partnership, be a mother, succeed at both— without a husband? The answer, she knew, was "of course." Best foot forward, and always marching away from the Dana Kidder paradigm.

She'd actually be a pioneer. Someone to watch, like Susan B. Anthony, if perhaps more vulnerable, and already prone to acid reflux.

6 A week later, at five o'clock in the afternoon, Abigail's cellphone vibrated. It pierced the late afternoon library silence even with that smallest of sounds. Abigail felt vital when summoned that way, as though she were an emergency room doctor. Swiping it up before the second shudder, she expected to hear Mr. Fudim's secretary, Leona. Instead, she was greeted by a flirtatious male voice:

"Found you, didn't I!"

"Who's this?" she whispered, keeping her head down.

"Tim!"

A pause.

"'Coffee Shop' Tim!"

"How'd you get my cell phone number? Hang on."

She walked out into the echoey marble hallway.

"I called your office," he said. "Took me a long time to remember the name. Then it came to me. Fletcher—the bow and arrow, shades of Cupid. I called them, and told them it was urgent, so they told me where you were."

"Who'd you say you were?" It was a pretty small firm, and reception knew the clients, by and large.

"I told them it was Tim Vail from the offices of Vail, Sun Valley, and Gstaad, and your gal put me right through. Even asked me to spell 'Gstaad.' It is hard to spell."

"A silent *g*, I know." She'd seen the place in magazines, gossip columns. He, of course, had probably been there, schussing from peak to peak.

"And don't forget the double *a*."

"No, rest assured that I won't." Abigail paused. "Let me call you back. I'm in the middle of something," she said, almost hanging up before Tim could give her his number.

◆ ◆ ◆

Pacing the library, Abigail felt herself getting annoyed, not only by the topic of conversation (if that's what it was) but by the fact that she was having one at all. During work hours. In the sanctum of the Bar Association library. Where were her doorkeepers? No pro like Fudim's Leona, Abigail's assistant, Tina, was a chatterbox who mixed up messages and asked impudent questions about her gestation. For example, Tina was very interested in who the father was, and frequently let Abigail know about the office "pools" in which the support staff voted. Was the "baby daddy" (she'd had the nerve to say) someone Abigail knew, or just some sperm from a refrigerated bank? Why did she need to go to a bank, the gossiping staffers had argued, when most of the guys she knew were probably tall and brainy anyway? Pick any of the associates, you'd make a winner—and these guys were going to be good providers, too.

"So you know who I guessed it was?" Tina had confided not long ago at the office. "Someone you knew, definitely. That psycho guy who used to work here, Richard something?"

"Trubridge?"

"No, that doesn't sound right. I'm sure it was Richard, though. Wait—you're right! It was Trubridge. Funny name, Trubridge. Hmm."

"Did you say you knew him?"

"Don't you remember why he left? Fired. Some big crooked deal he was in. Got caught with his hands in the cookie jar. That happens more than you or I would like to think, you know?"

"I do know." Abigail was a lawyer, after all. Crookedness, both in the field and out (where lawyers policed it) was not altogether new to her. And in the case of Richard, it was, sadly, no surprise.

"But you mean he—" she began.

"Maybe he hid something—anything to win, huh?"

"Well, there are rules of discovery for that—"

"Hey, rules are made to be broken. We're all human. But who's surprised, not me. Come on, the rich get richer, right?"

"That's what I hear," said Abigail, more confused than before the conversation started. But Tina was just warming to her subject.

"So you're human, huh?" She chuckled in a weird, warm way, like "Welcome to the club, girl. We're none of us perfect." Tina had continued reassuringly, "He was over in Palm Springs, right? Heard you two spent some time together." Tina was silent for a moment, as though trying to imagine what a junket like that would be like, to "spend time together" in a nice place, far away from the office.

"You—you say he used to work here?" Abigail stammered. "I—I don't fully recollect, there were a lot of . . ."

"Yeah. He was cute in a way," said Tina. "I could see the attraction. And he smelled nice, like a kind of woody thing. But didn't you know about the scandal?"

Abigail tried to remember. A few years back, there had been some buzzing in the higher echelons about hidden evidence, and then a few lawyers had seemed to leave rather abruptly. At the time, she hadn't thought much about it. Richard had been in the family law division; not her area.

"Of course I heard something about it," said Abigail. "So—so that was Richard?

"Yeah, but he looked different then, I don't know, I haven't seen him lately. But they say he's got a different look. Supposed to be a lot hotter—"

"Tina," said Abigail, cutting her off. "I'm serious. He's not the guy, I'm not interested in his 'hotness'—and I'd appreciate it if you didn't sit around spreading these rumors at the firm."

"I'm not the one making the noise here," said Tina with sudden exasperation. "He is, believe it or not. This Two-Bridges guy, or whatever his name is. He had the nerve to call you the other day and was so pushy—I transferred him to personnel to get rid of him! I mean, he acts like he's still a big shot here, which I can tell you he's not."

"Well, what did he call for?"

"Look at you. You're all red."

"I'm pregnant, Tina. I'm overheated." Did men have these intrusive conversations with their assistants? At the same time, part of Abigail liked having another woman she could talk to— one who was down to earth and all too honest.

"You just said you don't care."

"Yes, I did. But—but maybe there was some legal issue I need to know about. Or assist with." She cleared her throat in a professional's way. "Like getting down to brass tacks, come what may. Important matters to be discussed."

"Nope—wait, you OK? First you get red, now you're choking—anyway, no, we don't do any business with him anymore.

And Abigail, he sounded kind of, like, quiet, like a stalker. You know, creepy. So that's why I thought, I'll get rid of him. I like to think I keep the weirdos away, right?"

"Oh. Oh, good work, then."

"Thanks. So tell me, if it's not the stalker, is it the freezer sperm, or what?"

What could have prompted this call, thought Abigail, wondering if Richard Trubridge knew just how much of a fix he'd gotten her into (not that she couldn't deal with it masterfully on her own). Did he want her to "take care of it"? Promise not to shame him? Pay her off? No, she argued with herself. Despite Tina's confidential prattling, no one knew what had actually happened between her and Richard. Certainly no one would have taken the leap and told him. Either way, she didn't need this man, with all his complications, professional as well as personal. Not with her career, her resourceful mind, her savings.

". . . so it's been almost a week since he called. I think I really got rid of him for you," Tina was saying.

Abigail hesitated, then spoke with her customary authority. "Excellent, Tina. Thanks. You absolutely did the right thing."

Now that she thought of it, Richard's nondisclosure of evidence, if that's what it was that led to his leaving the firm, made sense. It was consistent with what she now knew about the man. Had he told her he was married? No. Some more "nondisclosure." And here he was, unashamedly trying to get through to her again. If she'd picked up the phone herself, she wouldn't have been able to resist him, even now. That low, slow voice, and the hands that went with it. Despite everything, he tugged at her heart, and had made her feel that she'd tugged at his. That's what makes him such a dangerous con man, Abigail reasoned. She should be glad Tina had cut him off and "got rid of him."

◆ ◆ ◆

But now, with her working at the library, of all the people for Tina to patch through: Tim Vail. A stranger who'd picked her up off the street, literally. Yes, he had seemed nice—more than nice. But for all she knew, he could be as big a cad as Richard. In a world of romantic schemers and her own responsive weakness, she was glad to have real, important work to do.

Still, the idea of Tim—the way he'd rescued her that day, his wheat-stalk hair—refused to let her concentrate on legal matters. And her awful conversation with Tina about Richard's dubious past made this other man look especially good.

Abigail stepped outside, took a deep breath, and called him back.

"Are you that busy?" Tim said cheerfully, picking up on the first ring. "I've been sitting by the phone like a lovelorn teenager. But you're worth waiting for."

"I'm always busy when I'm working." She noted that most men would have been annoyed to wait for her for several minutes like that. Some would even have hung up when she did call, refusing to be inconvenienced by another person's delays, however exigent. But Tim seemed easygoing. He seemed, moreover, to really like her. It was sort of nice to be pursued, especially when she wasn't making the slightest effort.

"Well, Abigail, I was working, too. In fact, I just finished a difficult spreadsheet and felt like taking a break and answering more of your questions. I find I like being cross-examined by you."

Abigail took a moment to feel out all the vibes. On the rebound from Richard, steeped in hormones, and against her better judgment, she decided to play on.

"So you like being cross-examined, do you?"

"Any kind of examined, I like, and the more thoroughly, the better," said Tim.

"Oh, you should try being exhaustively deposed by me," she said.

"You're on."

"We could meet later. I'll leave here around six thirty, six forty-five."

"That late?"

"I'd usually work 'til eight, nine, sometimes ten. But this pregnancy really makes me weak and wimpy."

"Oh, you slacker! I'll take advantage of that."

There was a pause on Abigail's side.

"Why would you want to take advantage of someone's weakness?"

"You mean, that's not a nice thing to do?"

"No. It's a very not nice thing to do. So why are you stalking me in this condition?"

He paused only slightly. "I told you, Abigail. Your condition interests me. You're a hot little gypsy with a big round crystal ball in front of you."

"'A big round crystal ball'—that's actually a baby, Tim. The product of coition with a man, other than yourself."

"You mean there are other men besides me?"

"In the big world, apparently, yes. In my little world—not currently, as I think you've worked out. But I don't think you should feel this way about a mother."

"Only if you're my mother, I think. You could look it up in the law library, though. To make sure."

"My field is death and taxes," she said soberly.

"Don't worry, I'll widen your horizons."

"Double entendre? If so, rejected. Seriously, what do you have in mind?"

"I want to cook you a nice meal to bring back your strength."

"So you're going to mother me?"

"Just to prove it's not such a dirty concept."

"You're the dirty concept around here," she said, cheering up at the idea of someone—particularly someone as cute as Tim—cooking for her. Now that her real mother was gone, she missed that.

◆ ◆ ◆

Later that evening, Abigail sat on Tim's corduroy futon, sipping a grape juice–Saratoga spritzer. Tim, drinking a hearty merlot to go with the roast, bustled around his galley kitchen, separated from her by a counter. He lived on the ground floor of a brownstone, a space filled with faded denim cushions that blended with his baby blue walls. Tim, wearing well-worn jeans and a faded madras shirt rolled up at the elbows, seemed to blend in, too.

As he chopped onions, whistling, Abigail peered around. There was a large white mica desk, with a computer on it. Just beyond it was a windowed door, leading to the backyard. What a luxury in the city. Your own fresh air. She walked over and saw several tricycles, scooters, and a small round trampoline outside. For his little computer club, she supposed.

"Hot onions smell homey, don't they?" said Tim. "They're going on top of the rice. With some cremini mushrooms. Just another minute and I'll come sit with you. But you're not sitting. You're standing and looking at my yard."

"So I am."

"Want to go outside?"

"No, I'm good. Can't I help you with anything?" said Abigail.

"No, just sit back down and relax. Say, how's your knee?"

"Still smarts a little. I got some Betadine and this big gauze bandage, so I could graphically demonstrate my devotion at work. The picture says: I was on my last legs, but I still punched in."

"Did you get your just rewards?"

"I spent the day in the library, so no one noticed."

"Show it to me then," he said, wiping his hands on a tea towel and stepping over to her.

Abigail sat on the couch, and Tim kneeled at her feet.

She raised her hemline, revealing the bandage, surrounded by an aureole of orange-red liniment.

"Tell me how brave I am."

"You are very brave," he said, getting up from his knees and perching beside her. "What if a bus had run you over while you lay there? You could have been totally killed!"

"Tim," said Abigail, adopting the tone of legal counselor, "you have a point." Tim had sat so close she could feel his body heat, and out of the corner of her eyes, she saw that bristly chin of his. She spoke quickly: "Speaking as a lawyer, we always advise young people to draw up some documentation about their disposition of property. Just in case a bus runs over them. On the other hand, you seem to have very little by way of personal property, and as for me—"

Tim grabbed her. "Shut up, motormouth."

Abigail stiffened, expecting him to kiss her. She couldn't wait. She was planning to try to resist, but only briefly. Tim let her go and walked away.

"Too soon, right?" he said.

"I think so, yes." She was pregnant, she thought—what were the rules anyway? He was not only too soon; he was too late.

Standing by the garden door, as Abigail herself had stood moments earlier, Tim nodded, as though readying himself for a challenge.

"What is it, Tim?" She felt an intimacy in the air, as though he had, in fact, kissed her. Not kissing her was even more intimate, in a way. Getting so close and then swerving away.

"What if I revealed that I was married, briefly, two years and three months, to an irresistible woman who looked a whole lot like you?"

"Is that what you see in me? Someone else?"

"She had the same Crazy Curl hair and neat little chin, but a completely different expression in her eyes. She had no 'career,' Abigail. She married to start a family—another major difference from you. And then, and this was the funny part, it turned out we couldn't have children."

"Oh," said Abigail, seeing Tim's face darken, "that's sad."

"Is that the word?" Tim looked down and pinched the tip of his nose. He seemed ashamed to be seen this way.

"Yes. It's really sad. But if you loved each other," Abigail ventured, "why didn't you compromise? You could have taken care of each other, comforted each other, cruised through the Panama Canal."

"Whom are you trying to convince?" said Tim, looking up through clouded eyes. "I wasn't the one who dumped the marriage."

"She left you?"

"She was fine! Just perfect! I was the one who couldn't—"

"Who couldn't—oh, I understand," said Abigail.

"Dud sperm. Unlike the one that got to you. It turns out I shoot blanks."

Life was so strange, thought Abigail. Those that wanted didn't get, and those that didn't want—got. She walked over to Tim and looked into his eyes. With the tears in them, they looked green and clear.

"You really wanted a kid, huh?"

"I love kids."

"And she didn't want to adopt?"

"I would have! Whether they're my 'biological' children or not, what's the difference?"

"I know it makes a difference to some people."

"Those people are narcissists, Abigail. It has to be their flesh and blood? Otherwise, no love capacities? God! Well, you've just described my darling ex-wife. She said she 'wanted to feel life inside her,' or she'd 'never be a real woman.' Her mother once told her that."

"That's so cruel. Lots of women can't—"

"Can't, or don't want to. Exactly. But she had to be a brood-mare. Filled up with sperm and a cloning bunch of cells. That's the real deal to lots of people. Blood ties. The gene pool.

"She'd have envied you right now. Look at you, so self-contained. It's all between you and your own little tummy."

"Little?" Abigail patted the high, round sphere. The way Tim had described his ex-wife's views, she almost felt privileged. The envy of some women, and even of some men.

"You know what I mean. The way you pat it. And you don't even mention the other party. Doesn't he count at all?"

A silence hung in the air. Abigail wanted to tell Tim about fertile, married Richard, who didn't even know about her condition. But to embark on that topic would open her up to questions for which she wasn't ready.

"All right," said Tim, sitting back on the couch and putting his arm around her. "Forget the details for now. I sense you've been abandoned, one way or the other. Right? You poor baby," he murmured. "I honestly know what that feels like. No one's ever loved me in my life, my adult life, that is. No one's ever given me their total heart."

"Aw, that's sad," said Abigail.

"No—I've learned a lot about being there for someone. You

can't just leave people in the lurch. So, you know what, I'm here," said Tim, stepping back into the cooking area, "if you need me."

"Don't worry," said Abigail. "I won't burden you. I—I really don't need people very much."

The words hung in the air as Tim bustled in the kitchen.

"Just a little, though?" Tim returned, putting a plate of warm and savory beef, accompanied by caramelized onions and sautéed mushrooms, in front of her.

Abigail nodded, and started to eat. She ate everything, heartily. The warm food thawed her. And later, when she and Tim drank coffee on the couch, she let him take her mug away, and at last press his lips to hers.

Wow, thought Abigail, he's pretty good at this.

7 Not long after, Abigail signed up for a "course" in childbirth. It was a truism among the experts that no one could do it properly without a period of study and practice. Once they learned how to do it properly, they could go ahead and give birth with the full confidence that they had been professionally trained and would do it with skill and finesse, as they did everything else in their lives. They would be prepared like professionals to meet all the mysteries of life. Not for these women the screeching and the twisting in pain. They would know the secrets of birthing power.

A partner, or "coach," was also required. This coach would bring ice chips, a stopwatch, a tennis ball, and other esoterica. Also, of course, they would coach the woman properly, and with skill, until the healthy baby would emerge, awake and alert (and, ideally, ready to learn the alphabet). After that, they would all bond in some way.

Abigail, initially partnerless, had put off thinking about these classes, but now she had Tim and could proceed. He had readily consented to accompany her. "I've always been curious about these things," he'd said wistfully, which puzzled Abigail, who had never been.

Now that she had a coach, Abigail had begun to research these birthing classes. She had learned that they taught people to control pain by varying their breathing rhythms. Concentration on something so simple as the air, flowing in and out, could lessen the deepest pains of life. She tried this theory out, breathing deeply as she considered the fact that she could never be with Richard Trubridge again. Somewhere inside her still hurt, no matter how many times she inhaled and exhaled. Abigail hoped that the actual classes gave you better information about pain management.

As though to ward off an inner gnawing (estrogen, Abigail suspected—that hormone always gnawed), Abigail had also begun eating supper at Tim's regularly. She grew fatter and happier, scarfing down his potpies, his casseroles, his seven-layer fondant-topped cakes. It pleased Tim to watch her need and, especially, her greed. He'd suspected her of having a deep yearning for love, and this seemed to be proof of it. She was passionate—now about food, but later, perhaps, about him. As the spindly trees in his garden shed their leaves and the air grew colder, Tim built a fire in the hearth. It gave surprising heat to his little blue cave of an apartment.

They sat before the fire, holding hands. Tim brought Abigail's fingers to his face so that she could feel the stubble. For some reason, she let out a tiny, encouraging (if involuntary) moan. Her condition, with its hormonal surges, multiplicity of neurons, and networking vessels, seemed to activate the sensual centers most especially.

Cupping her face in his hands, Tim began kissing Abigail with force and need. Yes, he was amazing; he was gifted, even. Abigail enjoyed him, but a curious sense of detachment persisted. She liked the way she could passively lean her head back against the sofa and let Tim press his weight against her. His gorgeous wavy locks brushed across her face as he ravaged her mouth, searching for something. She felt limp, as though she had no needs of her own. True, she felt like yearning up toward him in truer abandon; she felt like grabbing that hair in a hunk. Somewhere inside her, a current was rising. How could it not be?

But the baby inside was more compelling; it kicked; it was kicking her all the time now. Abigail put her hand on her stomach and pulled away from the embrace.

"He's probably jealous," she said, to Tim's confusion. He looked at her, pupils wide, bewildered.

"Who?" She noticed that he was panting. "Who's jealous? The real father?"

The "real" father? Abigail wondered if Tim thought that he was now, de facto, some kind of father, albeit less real. He was not going to slide into being her partner this way. She would get good, professional help after this coaching business was over.

"The baby is jealous, Tim. The baby doesn't like us to do this."

"That's not true," Tim said, his voice weak and his gaze besotted. He began nibbling at Abigail's neck, his warm tongue an interesting contrast to the cool pearls it lifted and dropped.

"You're just going too far here," said Abigail, still feeling the baby kick.

Tim mumbled into her neck, "But I'm your birthing partner."

Annoying. Sometimes Abigail wished she had asked one of her sisters to partner her. Tim had become possessive so quickly. But Liz never had time for anything but work, and even if she had "re-prioritized" temporarily—which she wouldn't—she'd have overused the data, marking the length and strength of the contractions, as though this were some kind of uterine Dow Jones.

And Annie had her hands full with her own little ones. Some days, she said, it was a victory for her just to get her hair brushed and her lipstick on. And some days, she had once told Abigail, she just sat on the Cheerio-embedded carpet, surrounded by noise and toys, and cried.

"So we're taking this on together," Tim was saying. "Now listen, breathing partner: I'm noticing that you breathe differently when I do this," said Tim, moving his face down the front of her sweater. "Let's explore what happens when I touch you here."

He reached down into her V-neck and touched her breast. A light touch, but he lingered. His ear was at her mouth.

"That's a different sound," he said. "Did you notice?"

Below her chin was his mop of golden hair, shining in the firelight. She didn't answer but gave a short nod, which he felt.

"And if I do this," he said, slipping his finger under her bra, "you might respond first by—"

"Tim, that's it for me," she said, grabbing his hand in a fist.

"What's the matter," he whispered into her ear, easily putting his hand back where it was. "What do you want to stop? This?"

"I want to stop everything," she said. She had never felt her body so alien before, such a clarion female advertisement. She felt fallen, and loosened, and weak—not so much by the pregnancy itself as by the knowing power it seemed to give Tim. If love was a wrestle, he could pin her now.

Tim slid his body downward, bringing his mouth to her partly exposed breast. "It's tidal, and you have to go along with it," he said, pulling her sweater farther down, stretching the V below the point he needed to get to. He pushed her bra cup aside and licked her nipple. Like her breasts, it was different, swollen and more sensitive.

"The baby!"

"Mmmm?"

"It's kicking."

"Where?"

"Inside me." She sensed he'd wanted her to say that. "I told you, he's jealous," she pleaded.

"I'm jealous of him, inside you," said Tim, moving to the other breast.

"Stop it!" said Abigail, blushing. His mouth was crazily good.

Tim's eyes took in the thin layer of perspiration that moistened her face. He blew on it until the little hairs that surrounded it flew.

"Do you really want me to stop now?"

"Yes," said Abigail, her voice soft and uncertain.

"OK fine." He let her go abruptly. She felt dropped from a great height.

Abigail fixed her sweater, touched at her pearls, smoothed her hair. She knew he was annoyed. When he didn't get what he wanted, Tim could be as peevish as a child.

"I do want to get closer to you," she said, later that night, more open on the telephone. "But come on, it's so strange. I'm pregnant."

"It's OK," Tim responded. "We're traveling into unknown territory. I have time. I'm not going anywhere. Not yet, anyway," he added, teasingly.

◆ ◆ ◆

Late that night, she got a call from the office. It was a young partner, Dave Biddle-Kammerman, his voice manic with significance.

"Get dressed and go to Newark," he said. "You're being sent to depose some witnesses in Grenada."

She reared up a little in her bed. "I'm heading for Spain?"

"Not Gre-*nah*-da. Gre-*nay*-da. West Indies. You know the

place where they had the invasion in the eighties? No? Well, anyway, your plane leaves in about two hours and forty minutes."

"What happened?"

"Prop plane fell on some old lady's house—not a native, of
course, a greedy, litigious Brit. She's suing for the loss of her
house, well, the back part of it, her 'conservatory' she calls it, plus
a couple of dogs—big dogs, show dogs, can't remember the breed.
And last but not least, she lost a leg. Not all of it, just from the
mid-thigh or something."

"Uh-huh. Whose plane was it?"

"It belonged to a son—I think Preston, or Parson, some *P*
name with two syllables—of our own lucrative Mr. Cranebill, but
it was a friend who was flying it. A new girlfriend. Kiki. The Six-
Foot Hun, they call her. She's been on the cover of *Face* magazine.
How could Cranebill the Younger say no to her need for adventure?"

"Is she dead?"

"Yep. Kiki's had the ultimate adventure."

Mr. Cranebill was a fast-food entrepreneur. He was a wonderful client, doing not only all his trust and estate work with the
firm (and with Abigail) but numerous pre-nups and post-nups
for himself and his various grown children. Though never one to
wince at the firm's staggering fees, he was a stickler who would
refuse to pay a penny that he viewed to be unfairly extracted from
his fortune. Being sued by the Grenadian dowager after what was,
most likely, an act of god—single-engine planes being, of course,
notorious—was bound to engage Cranebill's sense of challenged
honor.

"We have to litigate this with vigor," said Abigail excitedly.
How wonderful to have a big case come up, just as she was moving up to partnership. She could also prove that the pregnancy
was not slowing her down.

"With vigor is right," said Dave. "The plaintiff is some kind of madwoman."

"Are you coming, too?"

"No, can't. My wife's having twins this week." After a telling silence, he said, "Look, I've paid my dues. Remember where Fudim sent me last year?"

It was somewhere in West Africa, and Dave had nearly been in a crash himself. And now he was the firm's newest partner.

"You'll be fine alone, Abigail. You've got the hunger."

"I do?" She wasn't sure all the time anymore. Sometimes, lately, she had noticed lapses. She had even begun to take senile little naps in her office, with the door closed.

"Sure you do. You're a howling coyote."

"Guess it is my chance to impress the old Fud," she agreed.

"You want to make partner, don't you?"

"I've got no time for rhetorical questions, Dave. I've got to pack for my trip to Granada."

"Granada. By the way, you're flying WIS out."

"What's that?"

"West Indian Skies."

"Never heard of them."

"That's good. That means they never crashed, 'cause then you'd have heard of them. It's a local airline. Very reliable, safety-wise, if a bit on the late side. Don't worry; you'll get there in one piece, two pieces counting your kid."

"I appreciate your wit. How long do you figure I'm staying down there?"

"Figure a week. Things move slowly down in the tropics. When are you due?"

"Mid-December. I really shouldn't be flying much later than my eighth month."

"Well," said Dave, "as far as the case, I can't tell you how it's going to go. It might be quick and easy; I'm not sure. But if you're not up to it—"

"No, I—"

"I can call Fudim and—"

"No, don't. Dave, I'm really, truly up to it."

"You sure?"

"Hey. I said I'm on my way."

Abigail hung up, momentarily wondering whether it was a great idea for a woman in her seventh month to fly to the deep Caribbean. Googling it, she could see that Grenada lay almost as far south as Venezuela. This would be a trip of at least five hours' duration, maybe six. Without tranquilizers this time; they weren't safe for the baby. With this airline, the trip could take half a day, door-to-door, with her heart in her mouth.

Abigail had not been feeling at her best during the night. Cramps strong enough to wake her had gone on for about an hour, then subsided. She had been scared to go into labor, then been struck by the realization that in a short time she would do so whether she was scared or not. Maybe the trip would be just the thing to take her mind off these worries. And, as Dave had said: the more pressing and impossible her circumstances, the more she showed her partnership potential by doing the impossible. Or at least the horribly inconvenient and possibly life-threatening.

8 ⚖️ The turbulence started somewhere over the middle of the Caribbean Sea. Abigail was so scared she wanted to die simply to end the torture. The way the air currents took you, came upon you like a warlock and shook you, was a nightmare. It was a view of the dark face of life, horny crocodilian evil, ravenous and waiting to spring.

It was odd that Abigail's examination, routine and constant over the past years, of air disasters had never dulled her fear. In every deposition she took, in each act of discovery, she still sensed the proximity of death's trapdoor. There they were, people like herself, wearing penny loafers, picking at the chicken cutlet, eyeing the Scottish butter cookies, watching the movie. There they were, travelers, banally en route, and death was a bully, not letting them arrive. So, ya think you're goin' somewhere, do ya?

Of course, law was there to restore logic and order to, and provide compensation for, these nightmares. It graphed the horror, tucking it into folders much as the grave tucked in the bodies. But if it should happen to her, if the winds cracked her out of the sky—that was different, and no law would restore, specifically, her. Was there no one to appeal to about this? Well, God, of course.

Abigail prayed, as she had sometimes heard her father pray, "Our father, who art in heaven . . . thy kingdom come, thy will be done, on earth as it is in heaven." What did heaven have to do with her life? She had work to do, right now! But she was going to deliver a baby in two months, like it or not. God's will was scary.

Abigail tried her mother's prayer, "Sh'ma Yisroel, Adonai Eloheinu, Adonai Echad." The initial "*sh*" sound of the Hebrew was comforting, a sound her mother used to make when soothing her at bedtime. Shhh—it's fine, just listen to the night, silent and velvety. Shhh. . . . And those words: "Listen, people: The Lord God? He is One." What did that mean? That he, unlike all others, had no conflicts? That (unlike the overscheduled human) he could be and was everywhere, in the office, in the nursery, and even in the bone yard? One thing was sure: he had found a space to be between herself and a stranger, lost in the night. He'd sparked in the midst of that dark tryst with Richard. And he'd made them one, together, blended in this living child she carried.

Abigail turned the word "one" around and around in her mind as the plane pitched and vibrated. Breathing in and out, she thought of God spiraling around her, a bunting-cloth deity spun of cloud cotton. "One, one, one . . . ." As her breathing slowed, she felt her mother and her child embrace her and embrace each other. They circled around her and within. The rolling plane became a cradle adrift in a gentle, rocking universe. She slept. How odd, she thought, as she slipped into unconsciousness, how soft and strange the comfort, incapable of the burden of proof. Not needing logic.

Abigail arrived safely, processing once again the notion that the sure feeling of imminent disaster—at least in her case—meant nothing. She could return to the banal thoughts of the day. She quickly leapt up, grabbed a taxi, and sped to the hotel.

Her room was a sultry, exquisite surprise. At its center was a large four-poster made of glazed rattan, surrounded by potted areca palm trees. Above, a large mahogany fan rotated slowly, making the palm leaves vibrate. The floor was cool, polished terra-cotta. Stepping outside on the whitewashed balcony, Abigail inhaled the scent of bougainvillea, jasmine, and gardenia. A small green lizard skittered by, stopped, stared at Abigail, disappeared. She went back into her room to shower.

As she walked to the bathroom, she heard the rustling sound of an envelope being slid under her door. Opening it, she found a note from the local investigator retained by her firm.

Miss Abigail Thomas, Esq.:

Here's what I know: A single engine Cessna turboprop crash-landed on the property of Evelyn MacAdam. She is the widow of spice millionaire Jock MacAdam, they settled out here near Pointe Saline in the early 60s. Mrs. M. lost her right leg below the knee, and her dogs, a male and a female about to deliver, had multiple internal injuries and had to be put down. (This has caused the lady to have something of a breakdown, although word around here is that that's not unusual for her.) The garden full of rose and orchid specimens is ruined, not to mention the conservatory where she was trying to grow a hybrid of basil and rosemary (can you believe those were her dog's names, too? Basil the boy, and the bitch Rosemary).

First impression is, I see nothing wrong with the plane other than the impact damage. You might find that surprising, given that I found it in pieces over a kilometer, give or take. I'm guessing our pilot knew nothing about hydraulics, tried to land it too quickly, let the wheels drop out. Then she couldn't retract the wheels and couldn't land in the proper time, and with no space for it as well, right on top of Mrs. MacAdam's place. Yes, it was a girl, and the records I looked at show she had very little practice in flying even the single engine Cessna. Lucky the tank was nearly empty or there would have been no house left at all. Certainly no Mrs. M. to sue your client. But she survives, and she is suing. She has no living relatives.

Anyhow, I'll be over at the bar in St. George's all afternoon if you want to see me. I could take you to Mrs. M's, whatever you like. Let me know.

Jackson (call me Jay) Moss, P.I.

◆ ◆ ◆

Though it took a surprising hour and a half to get to the place, through winding roads crisscrossed by sleepy goats, Abigail's driver needed no help finding "the bar in St. George's." Arriving there, Abigail was surprised to find that all the people sitting at the bar were Grenadians drinking bottles of local beer. The bar she had imagined was high-ceilinged, with air-conditioning and rich mahogany decor. This one was a tin-roofed shack, open on one side, with a few rickety tables and a counter at which the West Indians drank and smoked.

As Abigail entered, pregnant and sweaty in a pink shift and white leather sandals, they stared. She hoisted herself up onto an available bar stool and found some kind of balance.

"You drinkin'?" said the barman.

"Yes, please. What do you have without alcohol?"

"Hmm. What I have like that." He seemed to be thinking.

"Give her a ting, man," said a patron in a neon orange shirt. "She gonna like it for sure."

Abigail didn't know what that was, to give her a thing.

"I'm not positive I would," she said.

"Don't worry, it good," said the barman.

A moment later, a fizzy grapefruit-flavored drink was placed before Abigail. This, she saw on the label, was Ting. It was good, and she did like it. The man with the orange shirt raised his beer bottle and smiled.

"Excuse me," she found herself saying to him. "Do you happen to know someone called Jay?"

"Jay? Jay who?"

"Jay—it's really Jackson—Moss."

"Hmm," said the man. "He from 'round here?"

"Yes, well, I'm not sure, really. He's working here. He's an investigator."

"Oh yeah? What he investigatin'?"

"Well, it's really privileged, uh . . . information," she began, then, noticing the young man begin to turn away, she added, "I mean, I can't tell you all the details, but I'm sure you heard about that plane crash over by the MacAdam estate?"

"Where you said that plane crash happen?"

"On top of Mrs. MacAdam and her dogs, basically."

"I mean whereabouts? Here, in Grenada?"

"Yes, here, but I'm not sure of the exact location."

"She white lady?"

"Yes, she's Caucasian, that's right."

"OK, then, she must have been from St. Edward side. I don't go there, but my sister work nearby, she might know something about it."

"Oh, really?"

"Yeah, she work over by the English people, the rich ones like you there by St. Edward's side."

Abigail chose not to explain that she herself wasn't a "rich" Englishwoman, but rather a hardworking first-generation American lawyer who had put herself through school. She worried that they wouldn't really see the distinction.

"What does she do?"

"My sister? What you think she do over there? She clean the house. Mind the children, all a that."

Just then, a tall man, wearing a pressed white shirt and brown trousers with a neat crease, walked into the bar. He walked straight up to Abigail and grabbed her in a bear hug that nearly threw her off her stool.

"Good to see you! You found the place."

"Mr. Moss?" said Abigail, wiping some sweat off her forehead.

"Call me Jay. Sorry to be late, friend of mine popped by a few minutes ago, and I was out on the street showing him my beautiful Harley motorbike. It's for sale," he said more loudly, "anyone here wants it?"

"Probably an old piece of junk if you sellin' it, eh Jay?" said the man in the orange shirt.

"Well, it's done good for me for the past ten years." Jay looked at Abigail. "My god, girl, you are presently making a baby. No one told me that."

"What's the difference?" she asked defensively, to the sound of hearty laughter. "What's so funny?"

"Nothing," said Jay.

"You put her that way, man?" said a man in a knitted hat in red, green, and black power colors. "You workin' overtime, eh?"

"We just met, you crazy?" said Jay. "Shut up now, Alfred!" Turning to Abigail, he said, more quietly, "Now, in your condition, I do wonder if you'll be OK on the back of the cycle, huh?"

"On the way to Mrs. MacAdam's, you mean?"

"Yeah."

"That's your means of transport?"

"Yeah, I'm worried about you now."

"Don't you have a car?"

"Take too long that way," said Jay. "With the Harley we can just zip by."

"Maybe she have the baby out there on the road," said a dour, grizzled man, causing a new wave of laughter to erupt.

"I will not have the baby on the way," said Abigail, feeling irritable. She was hot and tired, and the aforesaid baby was kicking her mercilessly. "Why didn't you tell me you knew Jay?" she charged the man in the orange shirt.

"This man? He Jay?"

"Actually, Ms. Thomas, they call me by a different name here."

"What's that?"

"They call me Big Whitey."

"What? You're African American."

"Huh?"

Abigail suddenly remembered he wasn't American at all.

"You're black."

Guffaws now. Jay waited until they subsided. Abigail flushed.

"Well, technically, I guess, yes, that's my color, you could say. Although my grandma was white, British, too, like our Mrs. MacAdam, actually. But that's not it, really. It's just that I work so much with the white people, investigating about these islands and being so helpful and all."

The man in the neon orange shirt snorted. Jay took it casually.

"Hey," he said coolly. "Don't be laughin' about it! Is my job, you know!" Jay's voice became lilting and "islandy" as he spoke.

"I see you've discovered the local drink," he said, now addressing Abigail. "Have you had enough Ting?"

"Yes, thanks."

"Let's leave then. Have a look at my bike, see if it suits you."

She let herself slide off the bar stool. One of her feet was not only swollen but asleep. She shook it back to life.

"Goodbye, pretty," said the barman.

"Not sure I like your choice of watering hole," Abigail muttered on her way out.

"Sorry about all that," said Jay. As they stepped outside, he added, "I pick up more talk at places like that than I do at swanky hotels. You get my meaning?"

"I guess so," she agreed. "It is very authentic. And someone mentioned a sister who worked near the accident."

"Yeah? Good info. Now let's see if you can climb aboard."

Jay stepped on his wide old Harley and pushed himself forward as far as he could. With some difficulty, Abigail swung a leg over the seat and sat behind him.

"Put your arms around my waist."

"All right. Do I get a helmet, too?" Jay wore a silver one.

"Sorry. Reach back and open the storage box."

Swiveling as best she could, Abigail found a smaller helmet, bright taxi yellow. She put it on, strapped it under her chin, and closed her eyes. She felt Jay kick down hard; she felt the engine roar, and then there was speed. Abigail bounced, the baby kicked, but despite the unusualness of the situation, she felt she was in safe hands as Jay drove her through the winding roads of south-western Grenada.

9 Evelyn MacAdam's home was large, breezy, and ramshackle. The ceiling fans, festooned with dust, were motionless; the abundant potted palms, brown; and the wicker furniture, cracked. The lady of the house seemed cracked as well. When Mr. Jackson Moss arrived with Ms. Abigail Thomas, Esquire (as they announced themselves, to Abigail's delight), the dowager boomed out:

"Cora-Lee! Twinings! Prince of Wales!"

The maid, a girl who appeared to be in her late teens, stared at the unlikely pair of guests. Her eyes traveled from white little Abigail, about to pop a baby, to tall brown Jay and back. Mrs. Evelyn MacAdam yelled out more loudly, "You're good for nothing, Cora!!"

"Yeh, I know," said the maid, nonplussed. She was concentrating on the measure of Abigail's stomach.

"You all want some water or somethin'?" she said finally.

"Yes, thanks, I'm parched," said Abigail.

"You parched, what you mean?"

"She's thirsty," said Jay. "And I am, too. Hungry, too."

"Didn't ask you, though," said Cora-Lee.

"Well, I asked you, then."

"Yeh, you did," said Cora-Lee, walking away.

Abigail looked around for a place to rest her legs. She decided on a worn settee, which seemed less likely to collapse than the two broken chaises that flanked it. It was made of dark, carved wood. A thin, hard layer of horsehair padded the seat, which was covered in faded, burgundy-colored velvet.

"Oof," said Abigail. "This is like a rock."

"Take what you get, eh?" said Jay, settling in beside her.

"Anyway, we're not here to have fun," she said, trying to agree.

"I wouldn't say that," Jay began, "I tend to like my fun and my work mixed up together, if you know what—"

Mrs. MacAdam whooshed in suddenly, her chariot an electric wheelchair. Jay's mouth paused midword, agape, and Abigail nearly laughed with surprise at the theatricality of the moment. Mrs. MacAdam had an antic, simian look in her eye. If she were not a bag of bones, and wired as a chimp, she could have been beautiful. Her clothing draped about her in Grecian style, the diaphanous fabric printed with paisley and tied here and there with a knot. Her high-cheekboned head was crowned by a loose ball of hair in which a four-tined, fan-shaped tortoiseshell comb stood up. The hair and the wheelchair were the same color, polished silver.

"Hello, Mrs. MacAdam," ventured Abigail.

"Lovely home," said Jay.

"Lovely? That's a damned, stenchful lie. It's ruined. Why are you lying to me? What are you here for? Chitchat?"

"Not exactly," Abigail allowed.

"Good!" said the woman. "My attorney's not here, as usual, probably drunk. Don't need him; he's a nuisance. Gets in the way.

"Want to see my leg?" She bent down quickly, reaching into her skirts and pawing around for the stump. Something in the way she moved the leg indicated that she still had her knee joint, but not much else below.

"No, thanks—we know the facts of the case, the leg and—"

"Not ready for it, are you?" said the woman.

"I—I'd rather not look at your leg, at the moment," Abigail said, clearing her throat. "It's relevant, of course, but I'm sure the doctor who examined you has excellent records, and we'll supply our own physician in due time. But to be honest, I've just had a long ride in the heat, and I'm not feeling—"

"Of course you're not feeling! You don't feel anything, do you, you lawyer?"

"Now, now—" said Jay.

"Look at you two, talking down to me just because you think I'm old and silly and harmless!"

"I wouldn't jump to conclusions, Mrs. MacAdam."

"I can't jump to anything, you hypocrites, and you know it!"

The woman hardly seemed harmless, thought Abigail. On the other hand, she reasoned, non compos mentis in a prime adversarial witness would be good for her client, Mr. Cranebill. How could anyone take this woman's testimony seriously? Abigail watched with detachment as the harridan continue to rebuke them.

". . . but still you manage to creep and crawl around the world, wanting to see the dirt of it," Mrs. MacAdam was saying. "Gives you a tingle and a jingle, right, my good friends? There but for the grace of god, and all that?"

She gave a merry, horrifying smile in Jay's direction. "So come on, you! You! Look at my leg; turn yourself on! I can even show you the part they tried to throw away—but I wouldn't let them. It's buried outside, wanna look?"

"You're not English," said Abigail, trying, with as much composure as she could manage, to change the subject from the woman's stump. "They gave me the impression you were."

"Shows what they know, huh? Just because I married a limey, does that make me love Marmite?"

"What's that?"

"Forget it, you ignoramus. It's a yeast spread. I'm from Bangor, Maine, and that's in the U.S.A. Heard of that?"

"Yes, I'm from New York, but I did think—"

"You think too much, and where does it get you? My husband was a goddamned Tory. He thought all the time, plotted, weighed the pros and the cons. 'What can I do for me, me, me?' What a philosopher. But now he's dead. See what I mean? And I'm alive and kicking." She kicked with her good leg. "Still can't jump, though. Can't jump to all those conclusions."

"What did he die of?"

"Shagging some whore on the rocky shore of Barbados. Where you from? Barbados?" This was addressed to Jay.

"Originally I'm from Bermuda, but mostly I work in the West Indies, ma'am."

"Bermuda. Very English. Very propah. What's your work?"

"I investigate matters."

"You look like you're having a good time doing less than nothing in the so-called sultry tropics."

"We're professionals in our respective fields, Mrs. MacAdam," said Abigail, "and although it is nice to be in Grenada, I'm here primarily to help straighten out the pertinent legal—"

"SHUT UP you big fat bull-crap slinger!" bellowed the old woman, as Cora-Lee came in with two tepid glasses of cloudy water.

"You're even worse," she said to her maid, taking one of the glasses. "Look, you can't even count to three, you ninny. And this isn't Prince of Wales. It's maid's water."

"I go get another one for the gentleman," said Cora, handing Abigail the second glass.

"Don't you have any Sprite or something?" said Abigail. Noticing the maid's uncomprehending stare, she added, "any Ting?"

"Why water is not anything?"

"I meant the drink, Ting, tell them, Jay!"

Jay was starting to laugh, but concealed it as a throat-clearing.

"Oh, just drink the water, girl," he said. "You lucky you got yours so fast."

Abigail put the glass to her lips. She took a big gulp of water and sighed with exhaustion.

"You're good and knocked up, aren't you, honey?" said Mrs. MacAdam, her tone still not quite human.

Cora-Lee, who had gone off to get Jay's glass of water, turned back to listen.

"Beg your pardon?"

"I'm not the one to pardon you, dear counsel, for your sins of indiscretion."

Abigail spoke as calmly as she could: "How is my 'indiscretion' relevant to you?"

"You like to eat dirt. All lawyers do. Well, so do I, so we're even!"

"All right, fine," said Abigail, giving up on all sense. "But why Mr. Moss and I are here," she said, reaching down into her briefcase and drawing out a yellow legal pad, her gold-plated Cross pen, and a mini tape recorder, "is to ascertain the facts of the case as they appear to you, the plaintiff."

"All righty. You're trying to get me some money. That's fine and dandy."

"Actually, your lawyer does that. I represent his adversary, that is, our client is on the opposing side."

"Do you think I'm stupid? I mean you'll help me get my

money because the truth of this case is going to hit all you phony liars right between the eyes!"

With that, she raised her skirt and displayed her stump. It wasn't so bad, actually. A blind end, healed over: clean, bald, and rounded.

"Now I do see," said Abigail, gulping. "That must be—awful for you. But it may not be my client's fault, legally speaking."

She waited for Mrs. MacAdam to interrupt her with another outrageous concept or display, but for the moment, there was silence.

"Now," Abigail continued, "My colleague, Mr. Moss, has explained to me that the unfortunate accident occurred roughly seven months ago—"

"Same as you, huh?"

"What? Oh, I see. My pregnancy. Well, I've come to see it as a blessing, actually." The baby moved just then. Abigail made a small, surprised sound, and placed her hand gently down on the settling mound.

"I sure wouldn't know," she heard Mrs. MacAdam saying. "Never liked kids myself. Neither did Jock."

"What I'd like to hear from you, to the best of your recollection," said Abigail, re-gathering her business wits, "is what happened as the plane fell—it was a Cessna 208 turboprop, wasn't it, that came crashing down onto your property, creating this cause of action?"

"How the dingleberries should I know what kind of plane it was? Jock used to have some kind of Piper, but that was a long time ago, and he'd use it to see the whores in Venezuela. He loved the way they'd yell out, 'Ay! Ay!' Such fakers. But anyway. This plane you're talking about was a killer. Knocked me down, took the breath away! I thought I'd died! Didn't feel any pain, though, 'til I saw my leg hanging off. And the bitch about to whelp."

"Uh-huh, you mean the dog?" said Abigail, who had forgotten to turn on her tape recorder.

"There were two dogs, my Basil and my Rosemary. They were prize Rotties, thick as planks and worthless at anything but winning ribbons. But each one, mind you, could have gone for well over a thousand, and the bitch was expecting a large litter, by the look of her. But afterward, my, oh my! They were horrifying lumps of fur, black and red. My husband, Jock, he used to take everything to get stuffed. Hawks, lemmings, alligators, didn't matter. But these dogs were roadkill. Nothing could be done. Had to bury them, along with my leg. Right next to Jock himself, they went."

"You must have loved him very much," said Abigail mechanically.

"Jock? Hated him! Never knew I was alive! Humping everything in sight—was he your father, too?"

This was directed to Jay.

"Thought you said he didn't want children," he answered.

"Not on purpose, he didn't," said the woman. "But as you know, sweetie"—she looked over at Abigail—"man proposes, but God disposes."

"Well, maybe," said Jay, "but I been told my father is Harling Moss. You can ask him; he lives up by the Beach Plum hotel out on St. Lucia. He bleaches the sheets there 'til they white enough for the guests."

"You mean that ironically, of course, and you hate us whites; well, we're not crazy about you either, hating us for being luckier than you."

"And not all whites are consistently lucky," Abigail reminded them sagely.

"Is that a fact?" said Jay, but pleasantly enough.

"I knew my share of poor white trash, young man," said Mrs. MacAdam, nodding. "In fact, we were poor white trash! Ate nothing but pork rinds and lard sandwiches until I met my Jock—and a good thing he had an eye for a shagging then, or I'd still be frying Spammy burgers for my supper!"

The maid came in with Jay's drink. It was a tall, cold glass of beer with a large head of foam. He took it with delight and, as he looked at her, drank deeply. He licked his lips, tasting the foam, as Cora-Lee winked quickly and disappeared.

"Oh, she wants you, baby," said Mrs. MacAdam to Jay.

"Don't they all," he answered breezily.

"And then I fainted," said Mrs. MacAdam, returning to her topic, the accident." I think I had a dream of death while I lost consciousness, and it felt swell, I can tell you."

"Then you came to, and what happened next?" Abigail prodded.

"Where was your girl?" added Jay, looking for an eyewitness.

"Cora-Lee? She was shouting and being ridiculous, and her friend next door, what's her name, Minnie or Mimi, I don't know, she was dabbing at my head with some eau de cologne, 4711 I think it was, nightmarish waking to it, and then the ambulance came, a broken down piece of crap, and some clumsy ox tried to lift me.

"Then we turned and saw this other person in bad shape, and he took her first, with another medic, and I saw a lot of blond hair fall out of a cap, and blood poured out of this person's mouth, and I fainted again. I suppose that was the damned pilot."

"Well, let's not jump to conclusions," said Abigail maturely. She had learned that this kind of moderation might well save a case. After all, perhaps the actual pilot had run away, and had nothing to do with her firm's client? Perhaps the plane had been hijacked at the airport and the poor dead woman—Kiki, was it?—had merely been a hostage. Maybe she wasn't even dead, but crawling right this minute through the bush. Litigators were good at creative supposition.

"You think someone else was flying the plane?" said Jay incredulously. "Didn't your client say that his son's girlfriend—?"

"Jay, please. It hasn't been stipulated, so it's not part of the record." Abigail was proud of her detached professionalism. Nothing was true unless proved in a court of law, and anything was "arguably" possible. She was proud of her creative imagination. Usually a vestigial trait in the legal business, at times like this—alibi-making time—inventiveness, even a sense of fancy, could be quite critical.

"And where do you suppose your imaginary pilot is now that I'm suing the pants off your very real client? Taking tea on Jay Z's yacht?"

"I don't know. Maybe he is, maybe he's not. It's not my business to prove my theory, but to disprove yours."

"Mine's not a theory. I got knocked by a plane that had a huge stupid blond in it! And you're going to pay, pay, pay!"

"No, I'm not. My client will—god forbid. And remember," she added a bit sharply, "I'm an attorney. Whatever happens, I get paid." Abigail was out of line, but she was tired of being harangued.

"Hoity-toity," said Mrs. MacAdam.

"What about your botanical specimens?" asked Jay.

"Thanks for reminding me. Yes—that ought to be worth something. I was working on those specimens for the last ten years. Had florists and botanists and horticulturists from Holland to Haifa calling on me, spying on me, wanting to know."

"Spying, you say?" said Abigail, thinking the diagnosis might now be paranoid schizophrenia. Witness impeachment would be a breeze.

"Yes. Spying. I'm not crazy, if that's what you're thinking. They'd always wonder, how does she grow roses hardy as carnations and fat as peonies? How can she cross-pollinate rosemary and basil? They didn't even know that I was planning to market that hybrid herb to every pizza house in the U.S. and the U.K. Ha! Ha! 'Basmary' would have filled every shaker from Hawaii to the Hebrides!"

"Maybe they did know," said Abigail, egging her on. Clearly, the woman had made this speech before, alliterations and all. It was useful to draw out all her delusions.

"How far did you get in your progress?" said Jay.

"Far enough. And if you ask me, someone wanted to have me stopped."

"So you are suggesting that this plane crash was some kind of plot to get you, or your ideas?" Jay asked.

"Yes, sexy. But I'm not done yet."

"You intend to start over?" said Abigail, with a trace of admiration.

"Not just yet. But once I collect from your deep-pocket client—didn't think I knew that expression, did you?—then I'm going back into business. Except this time I'd like to cross cucumbers with peppers, because making salad with all those different things you have to chop and dice gets tiring. 'Cupers' will be the wave of the future."

"Uh-huh," said Abigail, with a fond, fleeting thought of dinners with Tim. All those caringly cooked vegetables. Then, pulling herself back to the moment, she jotted on her pad that they must argue that Mrs. MacAdam was incompetent and thus should not testify. This was wonderful. Plaintiffs who were old and disabled could get an inordinate amount of sympathy up on the stand. Juries seemed to think they deserved special treatment; they thought with their hearts instead of their heads. Who wanted some sweet old lady in a wheelchair, sobbing in the box about her doggies? Keeping her out of the jury's way was critical. Even she, Abigail, representing the other side, would start to see things Mrs. MacAdam's way if she had to listen to her much longer.

"Do you have an official report on your pain and suffering?" she asked dispassionately. "The—the mental-emotional aspects of your ordeal?"

"I'LL GIVE YOU MY PAIN AND SUFFERING!" the woman lashed out. And then she was silent, with her mouth pursed up like an anus.

"Thank you," said Abigail in a small voice.

Mrs. MacAdam began again: "Oh, no, thank *you*! Do you think it's fun to be in this hot, hot hell in a wheelchair? And that's not all—I can't take a swim anymore, and I reek of perspiration! Smell me! You don't want to, huh? Sure, you don't! I *stink*!"

Abigail was too polite to agree. Flowers and 4711 could only do so much.

"And what about my romantic life? Who would want me now? Even he wouldn't, and I can tell he's like Jock, he'd want a knot in a tree!"

"Oh, please, ma'am," said Jay.

"Look how he 'ma'ams' me—that proves it! The pity! The distancing! What do you two really know about suffering?"

Abigail reflected on her mother's nightmarish cancer death, then realized, with shame, that her own suffering had only been vicarious.

"I'm an old cripple," whispered Mrs. MacAdam, "that's what I am . . . I haven't any money or family. . . ." Here she began to cry, so quietly and yet so deeply and wrenchingly that Abigail felt moved to console her.

"Your life's not over," she said. "Someone might be your family still. You never know who might need you, as a wife, or a sister, or a mother—"

Where did that come from? Abigail was embarrassed.

"As a mother?" said Mrs. MacAdam, sniffling like a child and looking up. "Do you really think so?"

"It's—it's—anything is possible," said Abigail, attempting to resume her legal distance.

"Oh," said Mrs. MacAdam, her voice disappointed. "Another one of your possibilities." She paused, then added shrewdly, "and I suppose you're not lonely at times, now, in your condition, far from home."

There was a laden silence then.

"Excuse me, I have to use the facilities," said Jay.

"You mean you have to pee? Cora-Lee!" she shouted. "Get over here and show our man-caller where the toilet is."

Much more quickly than anyone expected, the maid appeared and whisked Jay off. Mrs. MacAdam addressed herself to Abigail in a surprisingly soft and human tone.

"You're not such a tough nut as all that, are you, lovey?"

"Who, me? Yes, I am," she answered, mechanically. "Tough, very tough."

Mrs. MacAdam whirred her chair closer to the horsehair settee.

"And you haven't got anyone in the world, either, have you."

"Well, I'll have a child soon—and . . ." She cleared her throat and began again: "This is not really what I'm here to deal with."

"And you can't trust anyone."

"If you say so."

"So you come on hard, as a defense, to keep 'em away."

"Professional training, my war mask," said Abigail, surprising herself by starting to prickle behind the eyes. "Where's the bathroom?" she said abruptly. "I assume you have another one."

"Cora'll show you when she gets back from dealing with Jay. Just a second. I want to show you this picture of my daddy—" she wheeled herself over to a decorative mantel. "Wasn't he handsome? Distinguished?" she asked, wheeling back, clutching the photo.

Abigail nodded miserably. She needed to pee.

"You're a daddy's girl, aren't you? I always know, all that drive, need a tough husband who knows what he wants."

"Where's Cora—I can't wait—"

"Oh, listen—" said Mrs. MacAdam, head aloft, eyebrows raised, as though she were about to reveal the secret of life.

"What is it?"

"Listen!"

"I can't hear anything. Please, where's the bathroom?"

"You don't hear anything?"

After a moment, Abigail thought she could hear the sound of weeping far away.

"What is that?"

"You don't know the sound? Think harder."

"It does sound familiar, but it's so faint."

Abigail listened. At first, there was silence, then the stray call of birds. But finally, within it, she discerned familiar sounds—cries, really—crescendoing and fading into silence.

"Stray felines in their heat. The dumb strength of nature, huh?"

"Yes," said Abigail, morosely. This was a new low in her life as attorney. She was being forced to listen to a yowling feline reproduction—and she had peed in her pants.

"Don't worry about it, honey," said Mrs. MacAdam, her eyes fixed on the rivulet traveling down Abigail's legs, puddling on the floor. "I do that all the time."

10 Abigail and Jay went over to visit Mrs. Mac-Adam's neighbor. The maid who had seen the accident turned out to be called neither Minnie nor Mimi, but Miranda. She was a servant who "came with the house" as it was rented to various Americans each winter. Miranda was used to being alone, she explained, observing the goings on around her. She had no close relationships, save with her neighbor Cora-Lee.

"That lady want to get killed, believe it," she was saying.

"Who? The pilot?" said Abigail, who kept wondering why someone with so little flight experience would take out a single engine all alone. Had she run out of gas en route to the airport at Point Salines?

"No, I'm not talkin' about the pilot. I'm talkin' about the old lady, Mrs. MacAdam. Cora-Lee's mistress. She moody."

"What do you mean?" MacAdam could hardly sue Abigail's client if she wanted "to get killed." This could be great news, better than contributory negligence, real proof of the plaintiff's instability.

"I saw it with my own two eyes like I'm seeing you now. I saw her driving a car along, under the plane. A real nice car, you know. The Jaguar she have all those years. Could run it fast, fast, fast."

"Trying to get away, probably," said Jay. "Wouldn't you run if you saw a plane coming down on your head?"

"No, no. You're not understandin' me. The plane goin' down, I think the pilot tryin' to land beyond, over there by the fields, where there no folks livin.'"

"And Mrs. M—what?" said Jay. "You're telling us she wouldn't let it land?"

"That's what it look like. And I see the pilot go up again, and the wheels don' go up for her, and she try to go up and not hit down on Miss MacAdam, but Miss MacAdam, she drive right under, even when the plane start to go in all directions, and with the wheels stuck halfway between up and down."

"Hydraulics can be murder," said Jay.

"Could you be clearer about the causality here? I mean, maybe her driving right under the plane confused the pilot into crashing, but how could you tell what Mrs. MacAdam's actual intent was? Maybe she was confused," said Abigail. "The plane being so close to her land, and all. The dogs must have been barking, and she must have felt terrified, helpless."

"Why you care how she felt?" said Miranda abruptly. "You're working for someone else, anyway. Your boss in New York, right?"

"I didn't say I cared 'how she felt.' I'm simply appraising the legal situation. Her state of mind is certainly relevant to that."

A thought occurred to Abigail. Could her client, Hutton Cranebill, countersue—hauling Mrs. MacAdam and her wheelchair into court and blaming her for causing the loss of his plane? If the crash was her fault, then so was the death of the young female pilot. Kiki's parents would also, doubtless, get on the bandwagon. They might even claim that she was a new model with a promising career, worth millions in lost potential income. With the information Abigail was hearing, Mrs. MacAdam could be shaken down like an old sack of coins. Countersuits could be fun for defendants, a little table turn and Whoopee! We're in the money! This scenario might really make her a star at the firm. And just in time.

Miranda's employers were out shopping in town. She led Abigail and Jay out to the back, and laid out a towel on the beach. The waves lapped at the shore, rhythmic and soothing. Abigail picked up handfuls of warm yellow sand, feeling it pour through her fingers.

"Miss MacAdam kept under it, you understand. Under that little plane. She was followin' that thing. And Cora-Lee, when it come to understanding the old lady, she no dummy, and she tell the truth, all of the truth, and she tell it to me alone. And you know what she tell me?"

"This is hearsay, anyway," said Abigail, now questioning the countersuit. What reason could MacAdam possibly have to want to kill some new girlfriend of a man she'd never met—and lose her leg in the process?

"I don't know what 'here-say' is, but here what Cora-Lee say. Cora-Lee tell me that the day before, Miss MacAdam cry she don't want to live no more, that she want to die and be done with the pain of all of it." Miranda sighed and stared out at the waves. "The work of it, you know."

"So your story is that MacAdam was basically trying to commit suicide?" Abigail interrupted.

"Is not my 'story'—is the truth, and Cora-Lee the one that should know it, because she know the lady for a long, long time."

"Hang on, though," said Abigail. "Maybe MacAdam should have known that running under a plane would make the pilot crash, although now that I put it into words, it seems ridiculous. But even so, she might not have intended to kill Kiki, or cause damage to the plane. She wasn't capable of any such intent, because, according to you, she was suffering from clinical depression. And when that happens to you, the world outside your misery just stops existing. It's there, but you can't feel it."

How did she know all this? She had never been depressed in her life. Maybe she got a sense of it from watching her mother making all those sandwiches and smoothing all those blankets, and for what? To be remembered by someone, she supposed. To give some person a memory of love's sweetness.

"Girl, you hit the nail right on its poor head."

There was a long pause. Up until now, Jay had been listening coolly, nodding his head from time to time. He had appeared to take the possibility of Mrs. MacAdam's fatal—to others, that is—instability with a certain man-of-the-world quality. But now he seemed preoccupied. He scribbled into his notebook for a moment, then looked up at the darkening sky. Abigail noticed that the sun was beginning to set, the tide to rise. The waves were getting choppier and whiter. She was thinking, too: If Mrs. Mac-Adam wanted to kill herself, it still lent support to Abigail's theory of incompetence. Could such a "looney tune," as lawyers liked to term unstable people, be taken seriously in court? The desire to kill oneself was prima facie evidence of mental illness. That would benefit Cranebill and son, and that was all she would need. Pilot error was exacerbated by a suicidal on the ground. Leaving Cranebill with his deep pocket untouched would make her enough of a hero to the firm. The idea of countersuit might well be overdoing it.

"When I came to her, after the accident?" Miranda was saying. "I wipe her head with cologne from the people living here now, and she beg me, 'Take me away from this, Mimi. Take me home.' 'Where,' I say. 'Where your home at? You live here now twenty years.' 'No, Mimi, no,' and she stroking my face so tender. 'Let me go where I belong. Let me go there.'"

"She's from Maine, originally," said Abigail, knowing as soon as she said it how flat-footed that sounded. Home could be figurative—her library, for instance.

"She didn't mean that, honey. She meant, 'Let me go home where I'll see my Jock, and he'll see me,' she say. 'Let him know that even without a leg, or a heart, or a head, I'll still know him. And he'll know me better than he ever did.' 'You'll get better, Miss MacAdam,' I said, kind as I could. 'No!' she said, kinda loud. 'I promised Jock I was coming for him, and now I'm just stuck, just stuck here. I want to go home, I want to go home,' and on and on, and she cry like a baby."

"But I wonder," said Jay, "if she was so depressed before, why was she growing all those roses and herbs? Depressed people aren't usually so productive."

"Things ain't so much black-and-white like you think, honey," said Miranda, getting up slowly. Looking down at Abigail, she said, "You're fighting her in a law court, I know that. You think one side is right, and the other is wrong. And he helpin' you," she said, looking at Jay. "They call you Big Whitey, right?"

"Yes," said Jay. "But you see my skin is as black as yours."

"Yeah, well. Ain't anything so much black-and-white like you think. OK? And she a nice lady, remember." She brushed the sand off her wrap skirt and walked, barefoot and dignified, back to the beautiful white oceanfront home of her employer. "I got work to do before they get back. Laundry and all."

Abigail and Jay watched her go.

"Thank you!" Abigail called out. There was no answer.

"Well, that was interesting," she said to Jay, when Miranda had gone in. "You looked preoccupied at one point. Were you thinking of a countersuit, too?"

"I don't care who's suing who," said Jay. "I'm just looking for the detail of it. But I remembered something about the old lady. They say around here that she had a good business sense when her husband was alive—that she's the one who got them both rich as they were."

"You mean she wasn't crazy?"

"Oh, no, no, no. Just, you know, different."

"Uh-huh."

"Dance to her own drummer."

"OK."

"But people are always jealous—just like she said. Lazy people without drive and ideas. You know, they wondered how she could think of a scheme and it would work out for her all the time. But it was brains and a lot of hard work, I think."

"Oh, come on. That old loon?"

"They say she was getting somewhere. I wonder why that plane was there in the first place. No planes go flying that way, over the houses on the coastline. Spying, maybe, like she said? Fly real low and take some pictures?"

"You're wondering about that? Why would they send Kiki, of all people?"

"So no one would think they were spying. She could even land and ask for a cup of tea, a nice blond model girl like that."

"You're speculating."

"Not really. I found a camera nearby," said Jay, looking straight at Abigail.

"A camera?"

"From the plane, battered up. A really good one, an old-fashioned Leica with telephoto."

"Maybe Kiki was island-hopping."

"Maybe. Taking pictures of Carriacou. Nice dolphins there. Or maybe she was hopping over by Mrs. MacAdam's to see something growing on there."

"You mean, steal her ideas—such as they were? Who'd sink that low?"

"Your client's rich and greedy, right?"

"How'd you know that?"

"They all rich and greedy!"

Jay laughed out loud. Abigail smiled weakly, nodding. Knowing about the camera would mean her own client was not right, and her client not being right (or provably right) could mean she'd lose the case, and losing the case would mean she would be passed over for partnership, and being passed over for partnership would mean she was not a success (or provably successful), and being a failure (as corollary) would mean she would forever be a disappointment to herself, her father, her mother, and all the striving people who had suffered, striven, and disappeared before her.

"We ought to take a look at the pictures, you know," Jay continued.

"Maybe we should," she answered vaguely. She did want to know what was in them. What the truth was. Ignorance was never the right way, was it?

An orange sun was setting over the ocean, and the sand began to chill between Abigail's fingers. She was sifting it again, picking up piles, letting them pour out in streams.

"Look Jay," she said, "it's actually plausible, what Mrs. Mac-Adam says. My client, Mr. Cranebill, does in fact have something of an interest in agriculture, among other ventures. He runs a chain of pizzerias, and they use a lot of oregano. And Mrs. Mac-Adam did say she was going to invent some kind of herbal combination. . . ." She broke off into silence, realizing the implications.

"So what you gonna do about it? Want me to check into it?"

"No. That would hurt Cranebill. I'd get called on the carpet in about two minutes. This is not a good time for me to get a negative profile."

"With a child coming, you mean?"

"Yes. I'm kind of in a fix. I'm all alone to support this baby. Plus I'm up for partnership, which is all I've worked for—I guess all my life. So my job is to go 'Rah-rah!'"

"'Rah-rah'?"

"Yes. 'Rah-rah.'"

"You don't feel stupid saying that?"

"I don't actually say it, Jay. I mean, unironically."

"Are you being ironic?"

"No. And yes, it does feel stupid, now that you mention it. I bet you'd say it, too, though, if they paid you as well as they're paying me."

"Wouldn't. Would not ever."

Jay turned and started walking. Abigail followed, and he turned his head.

"I'll run you back to your hotel now. It's getting dark."

"So don't talk to me about cameras," she pleaded, "not now and not even later."

"OK, Abigail, I hear you. Just thought you'd want to know."

"Oh, it is useful to know, yes. In real life, it's often critical."

She stumbled on the sand, and Jackson Moss extended his hand to her.

Abigail accepted his large, warm hand and the ride back to the safety of her hotel room.

11 ✗ The next morning brought a disturbing e-mail:

Ab—

Cranebill is going to play hardball, and so are we.

He says "not one red nickel," so you know that makes your job just that wee bit harder. Basically, we've got to cream old Mrs. M. Tell me that you've found something that clears Kiki the Hun. Have you checked the record of that Cessna? It wasn't bought new, coulda been some metal fatigue, or a loose circuit, etc. Are they suing the manufacturer? So could we, now that I think of it. Hey, maybe Cranebill can make money on this! Another idea: You could say Kiki had an epileptic fit—hadn't told anyone about it, maybe it was her first grand mal. These things happen.

Actually, I'm just making that up, but you can use it if you want. I'd believe it!

Dave Biddle-Kammerman, Esq.

Instead of immediately responding, Abigail found herself calling Tim. Back in New York, she had thought the relationship was moving too quickly. Here, in Grenada, she'd tried to focus only on her work. But Mrs. MacAdam, so weak and yet so fierce, had tapped some longings in Abigail. What was that about? Maybe it was the dowager's talk about her faithless husband, or the way Cora-Lee was now there to cater to her every need. Tim was a good man, Abigail realized. He'd been single-mindedly loyal to her. He seemed to really care about her. In her motherless world, she was his baby. He had asked for nothing in return. Tim was a gift, plain and simple.

It was early, about seven in the morning. The sun was bright and warm, another gift. Like the food Tim prepared for her, undeserved and deeply needed.

The answering machine came on. When the beep sounded, Abigail said: "Tim, I don't even know why I'm calling. I'm supposed to be working on a pressing bit of litigation, right? But I'm tired and I'd rather be with you than with anyone or anything else, because you care about me. I mean, I'm beginning to feel that you do."

Tim picked up his end.

"You know I do."

"Do you miss me?"

"I've taken my first Lamaze class without you, and believe me, a man alone at Lamaze is a lonely, lonely man."

"Oh, Tim, that was brave."

"It was actually kind of fun. There are some characters there. And the teacher's a real pistol."

"Uh-huh."

Abigail had gotten back into her king-size bed. She wore a long white T-shirt that said "Sun-Waves-Fun" in citrus colors, the word "waves" billowing out over her ripe stomach.

"Abigail, you really should take this stuff more seriously, this birthing stuff. You really shouldn't miss classes."

"OK, I know, but I had to go down, and right now, I—I want you to come down here and be with me. I need you." She was surprised at herself. She'd admitted something. Even Tim seemed to freeze for a bit, before he hurtled on forward:

"All right, let me think, today is Wednesday, and I can get away until—well, Saturday's my mini-publishing session for the kids, and the next class is on Monday—"

"Which class?"

"Birthing class, and you're going with me this time!"

"I'll do whatever you want if you just come now."

"Let me hang up and I'll check Travelocity."

"No, wait a minute—Tim?"

"What?"

"Nothing." Abigail was trying to say she cared about him, too; she was reaching for some loving words.

"What?"

"See you soon."

◆ ◆ ◆

That was all she could say. Despite everything, Richard Trubridge stuck in her mind, a phantom husband. It had been years since she'd first laid eyes on him, but certain moments had a way of sticking—and somehow, maddeningly, didn't get displaced by what happened later.

So Abigail kept seeing an incomparable man walking through the halls of the firm, tall and serious, earnest as Abraham Lincoln. She kept hearing his voice, low and rich, as he stood in the library asking for a Supreme Court amicus brief, just before he had come to her aid.

At the time, she remembered, he had practiced a subset of family law involving custody disputes. Caught up in her own field, crushed by her workload, she had tried not to think too much about him, at least not in a "crush" way. Anyway, office romances were frowned upon, particularly those between associates and partners. But her excitement had always dwelled as much on his presence as on his potential as a mate for her. Richard Trubridge just seemed to have gravitas—a moral seriousness, the weight of conviction. There seemed to be a meaning and purpose to his life.

Abigail and her mother had loved watching Jimmy Stewart movies together, films in which he stood up for what was right. Richard had something of that persona to him, the modest everyman who is anything but ordinary.

What Tina had mentioned about Richard's professional disgrace was a painful contrast to these musings. Yes, he had left the firm under a dark cloud. There were whispers about some controversy—a client dropped in the middle of litigation, evidence hidden—and then Richard's name was blackened. He had seemed to disappear for a while. But somehow, these people never fully did. They remorphed, and the more sociopathic they were, the better they were at reemerging, in new form, demonstrably strong as ever.

When the new, improved Richard Trubridge had shown up at the resort in Palm Springs, he didn't have the air of a black sheep. No, he was a conquering hero, greeted by the senior Fletcher colleagues with a deferential friendliness. If they and he had history, there was no overt sign of it now. Now he was a partner at Murdock & Hill, a larger firm than the one he'd left, and he seemed to have no worries about what anyone at Abigail's firm thought of him. Certainly not about what she thought. Why would he? Why would she matter? Abigail had been, in his world, just a kid, a novice. And compared to Richard Trubridge at the top of his career, she still was.

Abigail had not placed him immediately. First, there had been only the sense that she knew him from somewhere in her past. Those new (to her) Peter Sellers frames had thrown her off—and the fact that his hair, so short before, now sexily tickled the collar of his polo shirt. Furthermore, she had never seen Richard without his three-piece suit, a navy blue pin-striped costume of authority. But that slow, loping walk, as he took her around the links, seemed familiar. His scent tugged at her heart—bay rum and cloves. And his thrilling, low, sensuous voice was the same.

But it was his touch that defined him. It was when he had lain there, vulnerable, in his hotel bed, no glasses, myopic, that she had begun to retrieve the feelings she had once had for Richard Trubridge—and then some. Though she did not remember ever seeing his hands at the firm, Abigail had always known that his fingers would be finely carved. They were, and they had moved gently over her that night in Palm Springs. He had caressed her in a way that no other man had ever done. Tenderly, with curiosity.

Abigail had, perhaps, wanted to fall fully in love with him now that she was older. The age gap was much less important—less than ten years, and what did that mean in the larger scheme of her now longer life? And he worked at a different firm. No obstacles, then. Abigail had stepped to the ledge of her feelings. She had almost begun to fall, and it would have been a huge drop, because she felt like she was falling from a height.

But to Trubridge, of course, she would always be just a "funny creature," to use his own words. Had he meant them disparagingly? Was he saying that he could never take her seriously? And how could he, when it turned out he was married? That call on the phone. That really hurt. No, she wasn't in "big" love, not yet, but she was connected, too far gone not to care. It was too late to hear him say "honey" to someone else without feeling left out and ashamed. Abigail was pretty sure he'd been single while at

Fletcher, but she should have realized that a man like that—with prestige; a good, solid income; and that deep, quiet attractiveness—would eventually marry and have a family. She should have realized that he'd send them kisses over the phone when he traveled away to Palm Springs. Even if he was with her, for a time. She didn't really count at all.

And of course Abigail would now feel, when she thought of Richard, wounded and abandoned. He didn't know he had left her this way, pregnant and longing, and he didn't need to know, either. Let him remember her as the hard, plucky lawyer, out for a bit of sport. His ignorance of her true state gave her the only victory she could savor—a form of one-upmanship. With that slight advantage, Abigail determined not to think of Trubridge too much. She would put their tawdry little escapade behind her.

How lucky she was to have Tim now, someone who cared, who would come when she called him, no matter how impulsively.

◆ ◆ ◆

When, after his long journey, Tim arrived from New York, Abigail was determined to unwind. After all, there she was, in the sultry Caribbean. She had flown down on short notice and worked hard.

She was still working until the minute Tim knocked on her door. Papers all around her in her room. He took them from her and said, almost severely:

"It is now officially time to spoil yourself."

"What's that in your hand?"

"Planter's punch. They gave it to me in the lobby."

"Mmm—looks good. I never got one."

"You probably ran in reading a memo and missed the tray.

Anyway, you can't have it. I'll get you a lemonade, though. And then we're going down to the beach. No, you know what? You can order one down there—let's go."

"Can I at least put on my flip-flops?"

The ocean waves, like sighs of relief, had helped Abigail surrender. As Tim sat drinking on a chaise, she had tossed off her flip-flops, walking barefoot into the water and letting it carry and cool her. The next day, she bought a cheap snorkel set from the hotel gift shop. Now she floated, breathing through the little J-shaped tube. She could hear herself breathe, in and out, a living creature like the ones around her.

Under the water, slowly, life emerged. First a few small fish, dotted like leopards, and then a school of angelfish, turquoise and brilliant yellow. They glanced at her, then flicked away, some circling back to look again. As Abigail parted the water with her arms, more fish appeared, darting amidst the coral. Her heaviness lifting, a screen parted, revealing hidden treasures that gracefully changed. Abigail was hypnotized, succumbing to the embryonic beauty below the surface.

12 ⚖ While Abigail snorkeled, Tim had a few more planter's punches. He was getting to like them, but the climate really jacked up the potency, he thought. Was that a good thing? Sure. He considered going to bed for a brief siesta. The Caribbean sun was blistering. Better to go inside than bake on the chaise. Abigail would be OK in the water—he'd never seen her so relaxed. If only she could sustain that feeling. . . .

He was a little disappointed that he and Abigail had separate rooms at the hotel. She had thought it best to appear professional—what if Jackson, the investigator, were to visit and see a strange young man in her bed? She was on a business trip. Anyway, Abigail wasn't sleeping with Tim, so why give the wrong impression? If they shared a room, even the maids would think he was her husband. And on some level, despite his willingness to coach the birth, maybe Abigail didn't think Tim should be taken for the baby's real father.

Tim pondered his months-long history with Abigail. Where was it all going? And why on earth did he stand for it? She was typical of her type—the up-and-comers. They always, always cared about their image. Maybe his career wasn't showy enough for her. How ridiculous. How sad. These things put space between people.

He didn't need to be a corporate type—leave that to his father and his brother. Rich, entitled, self-important, hard. They felt themselves to be real men, while people like him were—well, weak. They had never—no one had ever—seen the real him, and business clothes would only have obscured him more. He'd have fit in, vanishing into his class. He'd have fit the bill, as the awful saying goes.

I don't have to wear that yuppie drag, that ruling-class mufti, he thought, bristling. Clothes didn't make the truly elite, the seasoned Anglo American man. Who should be free to wear comfort and ease if not him, born to privilege? When someone like Abigail dressed casually, she'd probably be taken for the au pair or the maid. It wasn't just the curves or the curls—she was on the smallish side, too. No more than five-foot-four, barefoot.

Yes, this one was vulnerable. Her cross-examination style—the sort of thing she'd subjected him to on the day they'd met, was a put-on, he sensed. The clothing, too. Her typical corporate disguise. She wanted to look like a Meredith from Greenwich, a Kristin from Darien, but there had been "tells" everywhere his eyes had lingered. The way her breasts swelled—they must have been big even before the pregnancy. And the dusky sheen to her skin, that touch of olive below. That's why he'd guessed she was Latin—and hoped she'd have a lilting name like Esperanza, Dulce, Sofia. Hispanic or not, Abigail had such large brown eyes, the kind that stopped his breath. The tears he'd sometimes caught in them—the subtle shades of weakness—had moved him even more than her frailty, so bravely disguised. Yes, underneath it all, this was a fragile woman, an aeolian harp through which the winds made lovely, captivating music.

Tim wondered if Abigail's vulnerability included this pregnancy. Was it actually planned, the way everything else in her life seemed to be? She had said so little about it, keeping her own counsel in that prim manner she often attempted. Given her personality, maybe Abigail was actually one of those women who, reaching a certain age, firmly decided to have a baby, no matter what. But why hadn't she just waited a little longer, until the partnership was in the bag? And why had she obeyed the simple biological clock? These days, there were smarter choices. Couldn't she have frozen her eggs, or just gone to Somalia and picked up a sibling group?

That solo, oddly timed pregnancy, if nothing else, spoke of a deliciously daring nature. And if—as it seemed—it was an accident, it spoke of impulsivity at best, sloppiness at worst. Tim found all this alluring, Abigail's not being all in control, no matter how hard she tried. That's what made her worth the wait.

And suddenly Tim, too, felt out of control. Trying to stand up, he found that he wasn't all that stable on his feet. It's definitely time for a lie-down, he thought, stumbling as he rose from the chaise and knocking a glass off his cocktail table. Ice and a small umbrella fell to the ground, and Tim stepped around them as carefully as he could.

As he attempted to walk, a beautiful young woman, a servant, rushed over and asked him if he needed anything. In his current inebriated state, that seemed such a lovely, sweet invitation. Tim smiled affectionately at her. He could see her trying not to smile back. To her, he knew, he was a handsome, rich American. A golden boy, kissed by the sun. But to him, she was nothing less than an angel. The idea of their service, these girls, these women, so selfless . . .

"What did you say, mi amor?" he found himself saying, in the old language of his favorite nanny.

The waitress stood before him.

"I ask you if you need something, anything? Maybe another drink?"

So wonderful, he thought. Serving the food, bringing in the clean towels. Some woman smoothed his bed in the morning, some girl opened it at night, leaving foil-covered chocolates on the pillow. They were wishing him sweet dreams—that's what the notes they left said. What was he dreaming of now? The cool motherly hand, like tonic, on his brow. Checking for fever. Soothing the pain. Taking away all the wrath of the sun.

"Actually," said Tim, swiping off his sunglasses and peering off in the general direction of the hotel. "Could you possibly help me get up to my room? I seem to have drunk a little bit more than I meant to."

"Let me get these orders to those people over there," said the waitress, cocking her head toward the full tray of colorful drinks on her shoulder. "I'll come back."

Tim waited for her, watching the dark-skinned employees race about, making white folks happy.

"OK, now," said the woman, returning, breathless, looking at her watch. "I'm off for ten minutes. Where your room's at?"

"It's no more than a few yards away, there, by the main house. Ground floor, kind of by the hammock thing? Near the big coconut tree, you know?"

"I think so. You can walk a little?"

"I'll try. . . ."

As she gave him her elbow, Tim thought, again, of Abigail, and the day she had fallen. He had picked her up and restored her, and here she was, letting go and finally having some fun. He had not wanted to call out to her, seeing how happy she was snorkeling in the ocean. It was so rare to see Abigail surrender, to just let go. She deserved this time in the sunshine. As for him, he wanted nothing but shade and darkness. Like this lady on his arm, this sweetly subservient woman. The reassuring dun shade of this woman's soft skin.

"This way, right?" said the waitress.

"Yes, that's it. We're almost there. Hang on. OK, there it is, there's the door, the, wait . . . the next one. Could you—could you do the key? I'm just a little wobbly here."

Taking the key card from Tim's hand, the woman opened the door into his large, airy room. A ceiling fan turned slowly over a huge bed draped in swirls of aqua and coral. Tim kicked off his flip-flops, raced to the bed and tumbled onto it, face forward.

"Ahhh . . . Thanks so, so much," he murmured into the cool, smooth bedspread.

The woman stood near him as though expecting something.

"So kind of you," said Tim, turning over on his back and propping himself up on an elbow to look at her. He knew she probably wanted a tip, but he could do better than that.

"Did you say you were having a break?" he said. "Do you want something? I can order in."

"Room service take longer than my break to come here," she replied.

"OK, well, at least have a cold beer from my bar, how's that? Always getting drinks for everyone. You must get thirsty yourself."

"No, I'm all right," she insisted, but Tim sensed some hesitation in her voice.

"Take something. Key's over there, next to the coffee maker. That's right," he said, as the woman knelt down at the mini fridge. She took out a Heineken.

"Expensive," she said.

"Yes, it's imported from Holland."

"Never had one. Never really drink much, anyway. Not in the day."

"Well, enjoy it!"

"It's good cold," she said, snapping open the top and taking a long draught of the beer. "Like how I serve you guests here."

"Well, be my guest," said Tim, patting the bed near him. "Come on, it's OK. Sit down and relax." He heard himself sound like he did with Abigail. Why was everyone else so stressed? Why was he always the one who showed them how to let go?

"Not supposed to be here anyway," she said, as she sat down next to him.

"I won't tell anyone," he whispered into her ear. She kept drinking the beer. He impulsively took her earlobe in his mouth and gave it a little nip.

"No one going to fire you," she said, not smiling and not moving. "'Cept your wife."

"Oh, no, I'm not married," he said hastily. "I'm divorced, in fact. A failure. Essentially unlovable, you could say."

"Who's that woman I seen you with, then?" she said.

"Oh, you saw her?"

"I watch all the people."

"Oh, I do that a lot, too," said Tim. "Well, my situation with this woman, it's hard to explain," he sighed, falling down flat on the bed. "Even to myself. She booked me a separate room, so you figure it out."

"Well, that cost more money, anyway," said his companion, draining her Heineken. She stood up to go. "Two rooms and all."

"I wanted to make her happy, but if she needs her, what's it called, space . . . Oh—speaking of money—here."

Tim scrabbled into his pockets, then handed a bunch of bills out at the drinks girl. She tucked the money away in her pocket, and left.

◆ ◆ ◆

And now, alone again, Tim found that he couldn't sleep. Abigail would be back soon to look for him, he realized. Had he gone too far with that drinks girl? Maybe so. Probably. But it was really Abigail's time to show him how she felt, because he'd waited long enough. No other man would tolerate her maddening coyness. He'd had it with being humiliated.

Lying back as the world spun, Tim now graphically imagined Abigail on top of him, clinging to him with all fours. Soon—he knew it would happen soon, if not before the baby, then after. He'd make up for lost time, spin her around, pin her, ravage her. He couldn't wait for that moment to finally arrive. It would be worth it, a payback for all that ambiguity and so often feeling shunted, to finally feel that luscious body wrapping around his. Even after the birth and her inevitable, futile diets, Tim sensed that Abigail would always be shaped like an odalisque, a harem girl in a frankincense lair, lying on satin pillows. That low center of gravity, shortish legs and broadish hips—that draw to the hot horizontal—had always beguiled him.

He relaxed into a comfortable sense of desire. Abigail always tried too hard, something a Meredith or Kristin simply wouldn't do. Dogged self-improvement was not on their privileged roster. But this one, this poor girl, was clearly trying to better herself (she felt she needed bettering). But didn't she know her tactics were obvious? Didn't she know that the WASPs she emulated didn't try that hard or worry that much? That to be like them, she'd have to be the opposite of her noble, striving, meaning-seeking self? He could tell, looking at her almost-Hermes-but-not briefcase, that she had all the rote bourgeois aspirations: money, power, status. She wanted to "arrive" somewhere, to prove some impossible theorem—and only then would she feel legitimate.

Tim was different from most men in his circle. His friends, schoolmates mostly, confined themselves to magazine, television, and computer images. In their world, women were tall, feature-less, hairless, muscular, and reed thin. They tended to favor the leggy blonds and sporty redheads found conveniently around them in Connecticut, thighs taut with tennis muscles, calves triangular. The boobs they dreamed of were either sporty little A-Bs or the occasional pointed, rock-hard silicone missiles.

Tim, on the other hand, had spent his early years in the Caribbean, where nature was allowed to flourish and tendrils to wrap luxuriously around trees. His personality-free father had worked for Barclays in Barbados, and his frigid mother had found it necessary to find amusement in cocktails and elaborate dinner parties. (He remembered her mostly receiving guests, hair long and scarf streaming, torches standing by the entryway, tabletop tapers flickering in the wind.)

He had been brought up first on that English island, and later in the Dominican Republic, by beautiful servants, and always felt a sensual resonance with women who had that softness. Mixed with their gentle subservience was passion—the way they kissed him, chastised him, fretted over him (what he ate, how he slept, whether or not he played outdoors) in ways his parents never had. Tim grew up favoring the tawny, the ripe, the languid, the outraged, the wild. In his teen years, he had spent hours gazing at loose Polynesian breasts in his father's collection of *National Geographics*. Some of the boys at boarding school had better pictures—smoother women with heartless smiles. But these nature-touched women were his favorites.

They always had seemed free of hypocrisy, honestly exposed, real in an almost animal way. Pregnancy seemed that way, too.

What testimony it was to the sex act: the mark left on the woman to carry around for nine months, for a lifetime. While males walked away, unscathed.

Abigail would never walk away unscathed. She was aspirationally corporate, yes, and maybe one day she'd have enough money to buy the look of lazy privilege. But right now, to Tim's eyes, she looked frankly post-coital. Not just her tummy—which was more than a giveaway—but the flush and the sweat. Her hair sticking to her sweet little neck. And how her legs had buckled when she fell.

He was so glad he had caught her that day. Whatever had happened to her before, she'd been safe in his arms. Strong as she thought she was, he'd protected her. Just the way that he'd felt protected as a child, for that brief island of security.

And now he was surprised to find himself weeping. . . .

I'm thinking of Milagros, Tim realized. That cocktail waitress had brought her vividly back to mind. Milly, he had called his favorite nanny. "Mi amor," she had called him, and the words had seemed so true. A tear trickled out of his left eye. He let it skate to his mouth, where he licked it, sniffling once, with a quick shudder. He was a grown man, after all. He had no need of the woman who had raised him, during his years in Santo Domingo. It was so long ago that it no longer seemed real anyway. His father was running the branch of his bank, and his mother had always been busy, dashing off in her white sandals, her blond hair glinting in the heat. It was Milagros who had busied herself with him, worn herself out on him. Then she disappeared, as all maids eventually do.

Tim hummed a little song, "Y por eso los grandes amores, de muchos colores, me gustan a mi. . . ."

Milly had come into his life when he was a toddler. She was probably in her late sixties now, unrecognizable to him. He thought of her chasing him around the tall, dry grasses, catching him, holding him high in the air, nibbling his feet. He would kiss her feet, now, if he could, for her loyal service. Knowing his parents and knowing the world, he knew they had probably paid her pennies for her loving service, better and more intimate than his own mum could ever, ever give.

And that was the problem, in a nutshell, with the world of cold commerce.

13

Abigail returned to her room after her nice long swim. As she showered and changed for lunch, she pondered a work-related conundrum.

Dave Biddle-Kammerman's e-mail had clearly instructed her to find some unforeseeable flaw in the Cessna, but Jay's research had turned up none beyond a loose rivet in the wing. The fact that these small planes often crashed made the whole thing cut both ways.

On the one hand, pilots ought to know better than to fly them too near residences; on the other, didn't the frequency of accident (and ground accident) prove, paradoxically, that the craft itself was unpredictable? And if the craft were inherently to blame, why not assign culpability to the relevant corporation—and not her client? (Of course, they could argue that, as with cars, the cost of making small craft accident-proof would be prohibitive, outweighing the benefit—however large—of getting everywhere in a hurry.)

Abigail tried to factor in Mrs. MacAdam's contribution to the accident. The plane, she knew, might have been perfectly good, but MacAdam's alleged mad circuit in her Jaguar certainly could have contributed to the tragedy. In fact, not only was Fletcher on solid ground vis-à-vis MacAdam, but they really ought to advise their client to countersue for reckless disregard for human life. With nothing wrong with the craft, and Kiki properly licensed (if inexperienced), they could hold MacAdam up by her one good leg, turn her upside down, and shake her out.

There was just one problem. The camera. Still, no one knew about it but her and Jackson Moss. Should she ask him to just "lose" it? Wasn't that the opposite of what good investigators do? Still, her firm had retained him. Maybe he would do it for her if she asked him to. But she just couldn't ask him.

Abigail's conscience was getting in the way, a vestigial organ when it came to litigation. Where had it come from, and why was it blocking her path? Hadn't she spent three years at law school, and seven at the firm, learning to temper her own personal qualms? Right and wrong were amateurish terms, she now knew, not practical, legal ones. After all, she was a professional.

So she tried to shove her conscience back. Logic was a good tool for that. Thinking clearly, methodically, dispassionately. First of all, MacAdam seemed bent on self-destruction, so what would be the harm in suing her? Secondly, suggesting counter-suit to Fudim (and tidying up the bit with the camera) might just push her over the line and into partnership. A trip well spent, he'd think. Perhaps he'd even use his legendary word of praise: "Kudos." "Kudos, Abigail," he'd say, raising her up to the inner sanctum. "You think like a lawyer at last." Her father used to say, "You think like a man," and she'd be flattered.

This was much the same thing, she thought, drying herself and putting on her espadrilles. These were the type with ribbons wrapping around the lower leg—and in her case, this part of her anatomy, especially the ankles, was swollen. Men didn't have these hormonal problems and sudden body bloats, but she could think as lucidly as they did, even with such disadvantages. Making her even stronger than a man, she concluded with a bit of satisfaction, tying double knots to secure her bows.

Speaking of men, where was Tim? Here she had gone to the trouble of putting on a nice outfit for lunch together. As the time neared one thirty, Abigail called his room. The phone rang nearly a dozen times, and she was on the verge of hanging up when Tim answered drowsily.

"Hu—hullo?"

"The sun made you tired, huh?" she said, her heart suddenly fond. He was tired because he'd flown all the way down to see her. Here was a man she didn't have to chase.

"Abigail?" His voice was friendly. "I thought you forgot all about me."

"No, I thought you were going to get me."

"Little mother?" said a gravelly voice in the corridor.

"Hang on a sec, Tim, someone might be talking to me from outside my room."

"Weird. Maybe a maid?"

"Maybe—I asked for more towels. But it doesn't sound like one. Hang on."

Abigail went to her door and opened it. In sailed Mrs. Evelyn MacAdam herself on her motorized wheelchair.

"Who're you on the phone with, little mother?" she said. "Tried to call you, used the house phone, line was tied up. Speaking of which, you should loosen those laces."

"No, it's fine, I'm just a little waterlogged."

"Well, don't get gangrene, all right?"

"I won't. Listen, I'm on the phone."

"YES I KNOW! I told you I tried to call you. Who're you talking to?"

"Oh, it's just my—my new boyfriend, he's just across the hall-way," said Abigail. She said "new" because she really couldn't stand the thought of Tim being taken for the baby's father.

"Your new boyfriend, the one who's shagging the tawny maids? Saw her leave the floor a few minutes ago, thought I detected a trace of a post-coital limp along with a knowing smile. They're all like Jock, I tell you. Jock the roving cock o' the walk. She was counting the money with a gleam in her eye. Jock was a good tipper, too."

Abigail, dismissing the information, cupped the phone and spoke to Tim: "Could you meet me in the dining room in about fifteen minutes?"

"Sure, I'll just lie back down for another minute here."

Tim hung up and promptly fell asleep. In his dream, the drinks girl—he'd noticed her name tag; her name was Harriet—was pregnant. She was carrying his child. Unlike Abigail, Harriet was nimble and lithe in her pregnancy; she had been born for it. And she was weightless; Tim could raise her in the air like a tray full of drinks. Despite the fact that she was pregnant, she liked to have sex with him all the time. She thought he was the best lover in the world, and she adored him. He felt the same way about her.

To show his devotion, he had got her a servant. Her maid looked like Tim's mother, Mary-Ellen, ash blond with pink lip-stick, white sandals, and a martini in her hand. Mary-Ellen was sort of lazy and sour, but they kept her anyway. Harriet was too great with child to sink to the level of floor-scrubbing, and Mary-Ellen needed the money to support her own family. In time, Mary-Ellen would learn to scrub the floor, and like it.

When the dream child was born, Mary-Ellen not only scrubbed all the grime away, she grew to love the child and raised it as if it were her own (far more lovingly than Tim's real mother had raised him; this was the most beautiful part).

As Tim dozed, Abigail continued to converse with Mrs. Mac-Adam.

"Abigail Thomas, Esquire," Evelyn MacAdam was saying evenly. "I am going to level with you. For some reason, I like you. I don't like many people. Let me just make that clear."

"I can see that."

"Yes. You can. And I think you like me. I can see that. Am I right? Don't answer. I'm always right; that's why everyone hates me."

"I don't hate you," Abigail admitted.

They looked at each other.

"No, I know that," said Evelyn MacAdam. "I can detect the strength of your emotions, and the fact that they're completely uncorruptible. That's another reason why I like you so much."

"You like me so much?" Despite her legal training, and the utter incongruity of emotions in this context, that felt good, and fun, to say.

"If I had a daughter, I'd hope she was like you. Not necessarily the pregnant situation you currently find yourself in. Something about you yourself, not the bovine hanging-titty aspects. I mean any bitch can whelp; who knows that better than I? No, it's not that, Abigail. It's you yourself, my dear girl, without embellishment."

Abigail, despite herself, wanted nothing more than to listen to this all day. But instead, she cleared her throat and looked at her watch.

Mrs. MacAdam took the hint. "Always in a hurry. Stab, grab, and go. That's what they're training you to do. To become. Well, you'll grow out of it. I can see that, even if you can't. Of course you can't. You're too busy being young and idiotic. Anyway—I'm not going to ask you to blow your side of the case. After all, you're a legal beagle or whatever the current word is. And I know you need the money, even if those creeps you work for and represent don't. Right? Still paying off the tuition?"

"Yes, and it'll take forever, especially now that I'm—"

"Yes, babies cost a lot. Far too much, if you ask me."

"I didn't ask you."

Evelyn laughed appreciatively. "Sassy-pants."

Abigail couldn't help cracking a little responsive smile. It was such a funny thing to be called. Sassy-pants.

"See, I know a little bit about who you are," Evelyn continued. "And I know a lot about who they are. And for them, it's all about power and pride and winning, Abigail, things you and I don't begin to care about."

Don't I? thought Abigail. I think I have begun to care about those things a lot. More than ever, even. It was hard not to care when you'd worked seven years and were finally up for reward.

"It's not too late to save yourself from being a soulless shark in a suit. You might want to take a different role model. Me, for example. I'm thinking about doing you a good turn and giving you some of the money I get—how does that sound, dear? Keep you out of the gutters of the law, you know."

Abigail cleared her throat again and said, "It sounds like a bribe to make me throw the case your way. And that's exactly how it'll look to everyone in charge of me."

"It does. It will. OK. Don't worry. Do your worst. Hit me in the stump. Call me crazy. Countersue, sure, I know all the tricks, baby. Tit for tat. I know that one. Hurt me back so I never hurt you again. Go on, doesn't that feel good?"

Abigail felt sick, listening.

"No, really, take my farming ideas, take my last nickel. But no matter what, remember: No one is in charge of you, and don't let anybody tell you different."

"I wouldn't, I wouldn't knowingly hurt anyone," stumbled

Abigail, knowing that, as a lawyer, that was what she would do, if asked, and wondering how Evelyn MacAdam could already know about her idea of countersuit. She supposed that was an obvious tactic, the best defense being to behave as offensively as possible.

"Little mother, just remember one thing, though. It may give you some comfort on the days that your conscience works: Even if you do everything you, or is it they, can think of, I'm going to win anyway."

"No one ever knows about the disposition of a case," said Abigail, trying to displace Mrs. MacAdam's sureness with legal rationality.

"No, I will win, because I'll be right, and fair. I'll be good to the people who did good for me. That's how I'll win, regardless of material outcome," said Mrs. MacAdam. "I'll win in the only way that matters."

Abigail fell silent.

"You like that one? 'I'll win in the only way that matters?' Yes, I can turn a phrase when I want to. Now, should I go to law school and exploit this talent of mine? I'm kidding—this mouth should not be monetized, isn't that the word, 'monetized'?"

"I've heard it," said Abigail, although it was used more by the MBAs than the JDs.

"I wouldn't be caught dead in the rat race. Too many rotters gnawing the bone. I'd constantly be vomiting."

"What are you saying? What do you mean by 'the only way that matters'?"

"Guess!"

"You mean—are you referring to the truth or something?"

Abigail struggled to remember the guest lecture on moral philosophy she had attended one afternoon at law school. By the time the speaker had finished, she had had no idea what the truth was, or if it even existed. That was what law school did to you. It cleared your truth meter. Tabula rasa was what was needed: A blank page to fill as suited the needs of the current case at hand. A page on which "right" and good" were sentimental words, used sincerely by only lesser, mushier minds.

"Never mind, you'll get it sooner or later. It'll come to you," said Mrs. MacAdam.

"Come on, Cora-Lee! Teatime!" she shouted to her paid companion, who was standing quietly outside all the while. With that, Cora-Lee came in, nodded quickly to Abigail, and escorted her boss back to her new red Jaguar. Abigail followed, turning back before she could see Mrs. MacAdam being lifted from the wheelchair into the car. She preferred not to see her look so vulnerable. Evelyn MacAdam was right. Abigail didn't hate her at all.

◆ ◆ ◆

Shortly afterward, Tim and Abigail enjoyed lunch on a terrace that grandly overlooked the sea. As they ate, thieving blackbirds darted over the empty plates on neighboring tables. Sitting on the rims, they would snatch at crumbs of rich cake, morsels of potatoes au gratin, then fly up to the eaves. Their cries, short and jealous, mingled with the whoosh of the soft turquoise waves. Tim sat cool and crisp in a white linen shirt, his hair ruffled and lifted by the breeze.

"Either you really are one gorgeous guy, or you're finally starting to grow on me," said Abigail.

"Is it me you want or just my food?"

It was true: Abigail had finished her main course, sea bass with mango and ginger, and was looking with interest at Tim's pasta with julienned squash. He pushed it closer to her and picked up a goblet of ice water.

"Enjoy," he said. "And by the way," he added, "you look pretty good yourself." Abigail had browned beautifully in Grenada. Tim wanted to kiss her plump mulberry lips.

"I feel good, too," she said, pausing. "I think we can go home soon." Noticing his disappointment, she added, "I know it's hard, Tim. You just got here, and we're both unwinding. But I can't justify my expenses much longer. My research here is as complete as it needs to be," she said, looking for the waiter to bring the desserts. "And don't forget, you need to be back for that computer thing on Saturday."

"I could miss one session. The kids love to get a break from me."

The idea of missing a session at work would have shocked Abigail before she had gone down to Grenada. But she was beginning to change. She could relax, if Tim wanted. She owed him that much. What father figure would the baby have had, if he hadn't come along?

"We don't have to go right away," she conceded. "But do you mind if I check with the airlines and see if they can get us a couple of tickets for tomorrow night?"

"No, I guess I don't mind."

A steel band began to play on the beach beyond them. The notes reverberated, blurred, jangled, as the melodies moved forward.

A waitress finally brought a selection of sorbets to the table.

"You know, I wonder if you'll ever really slow down," said Tim, with a bit of an edge. "I mean, I get that you want to cut your work short, but under the circumstances—I mean you dragging me down a long way for such a short crisis—how considerate is that? And how much time have you spent with me, anyway?"

Abigail heard the resentment in Tim's voice. She guessed it was related to not only the length of their stay but the quality of it. She had insisted on separate rooms, and they had not become lovers, even in this sensuous paradise. She knew that women in her condition did not always refuse male advances, and Abigail's doctor had never cautioned her otherwise. But Abigail felt that she couldn't yet, and that Tim was beginning to resent it.

"Well, let's enjoy the time we have, OK?"

"OK," he said grumpily. "But I'd really enjoy grabbing you and smashing my lips on yours."

"Mmm," she smiled. "Try this." Abigail sampled the mango sorbet, a tiny dab on her spoon, slipping into and out of her mouth. She was thinking about having something more filling with the ices—maybe a slab of that coconut cake over there? She was feeling excessive, and liking it.

"Why don't you feed me some of those ices," said Tim. Abigail complied as he bent his head forward. Then, leaning over, his lips cold, he kissed her. A waitress, passing by with some coconut cookies, laughed appreciatively. Abigail's mouth was streaked with gloss and sorbet, and she wiped it. He pulled her back and messed up her mouth again. He was the best kisser in the world, and they both knew it.

Their eyes met.

"Hey—what do you say you come up to my room?" she said, as though it were an original idea.

"Why do you think I flew down here?" said Tim, his voice cracking. "All I wanted was to be closer to you."

Tim came into her room, and they were closer than ever—as close as two people can physically be—several times that night, and once the next morning. And though she was carrying a child, another man's child, Abigail's body responded as though she and Tim were made for each other. In Grenada, an island in the middle of a sighing sea, she went just a bit out of her mind.

14

The flight back was delayed for hours, giving Abigail a chance to brood about her fear of airplanes. (Was there an unclaimed bag? A loose rivet? A leak in the hydraulics?) Tim tried to distract her, telling Abigail about all the times he'd flown back and forth between the United States and the Dominican Republic when he was a boy.

Abigail's contracted mood seemed to shrug off the help he was offering. Tim's arm went around her shoulder, and her muscles tightened, resisting. Just yesterday, she had let him make love to her over and over; her body had been loose, fluid, fluent. She'd melted in his arms like hot wax. What's wrong with me? she thought, as he slowly took his arm away. If I were Tim, I'd be losing patience. But it was hard to relax on a plane. She'd never been able to.

What she needed, Abigail thought, was a good, strong tranquilizer. Without it, fears rattled every nerve. But pills could harm the baby. Abigail wondered: Did nerves like buzz saws also harm the baby? The books didn't address that question. They assumed that mothers, and mothers-to-be, had the appropriate bovine temperament to handle life's greatest surprises.

The airplane took off just as the island sun began to set. Midway into the journey, as Abigail was beginning to relax into the darkness, the sky was pierced with arrows of gleaming greenish light. A thunderstorm.

"I knew it," thought Abigail, at her worst and taking it personally. She felt adulterous for having slept with Tim (though Richard couldn't know, nor would he care). The physical union was different from what it had been with Richard, who had been so tender with her. With Tim, Abigail had felt as though she had been expertly blasted to outer space, upside-down and weightless, screaming. Tim was sui generis; he was a sex genius, a carnival ride. The kind you'd get addicted to, your body in one place, your true self in another.

So now God was trying to take her plane down and really separate her body and her soul, she thought ruefully. And the puzzling thing was: despite her current funk, Abigail was desperate to live. Suddenly, she wanted the baby born and seeing her, holding her, damp from heaven and testifying to permanent trust. She wanted to feel God's good side. Too often, she had felt the other, the side that broke hearts and killed off hope. This storm was an example of how little He might care.

But divine grudge was unlikely, Abigail reasoned, trying to be mature and professional. In her work, she dealt with aviation disasters every day. Most of them, terrorism aside, occurred in small planes, charters, and fly-by-night (literally) companies. She was in a 747, and Tim had insisted on their switching from the local airline to a more established one. But even on the lesser airlines, hydraulics and engine problems rarely doomed a monster carrier. And bumpy flights, particularly on this route, were par for the course. Abigail forced her mind to explain the true (scientific) sources of choppy air, parsing subjective horror into facts and statistics.

Turbulence is a reflection of the air's movement. It is analogous to the rocking of the ocean's waves, to the bumps in a road, she told herself. It's actually like a cradle rocking in the sky. So God had a rough hand sometimes; so what? Did that mean the cradle would fall?

But what about the thunderstorm? Had she ever worked on a case where the plane had been hit by lightning? No. But she remembered something she read in a fear-of-flying book she'd once hurriedly read through in the bookstore (she couldn't be seen to own such a book): "The plane's engines are powerful, and even if all four were hit by lightning—a near impossibility—the plane could, theoretically, coast to a landing."

Theoretically wasn't good enough right now. Abigail had never heard of a 747 coasting to a landing after losing total engine power. Could a plane "coast" down from thirty thousand feet? Abigail's mouth became dry. She realized how little she knew about planes, how much less she knew about the essence of catastrophe. But she did know that if God felt like letting millions die in a war, thousands in a flood, landslide, or bad mosquito-bite epidemic, so it was. When it came to "acts of God"—the term lawyers gave to disasters—there were no clever alibis, nor even the meekest apology. Lawyers took off their glasses, rubbed their weak eyes, and looked blindly out into the void. And for once they kept their Maalox mouths shut.

But God, Abigail thought, nearly crying about it, why do you bother making people in the first place? She rubbed her stomach. Remember him? Look, he feels my adrenaline. He's bouncing around like a cat in a bag. Are you planning some mean trick on this wee little kitten? As her baby kicked and writhed in the turbulence, Abigail pitied his mortal state for the first time as she perceived the true fragility of her own, and everyone's.

"Did you say something, sweetie?" said Tim, who was all this time sitting by her side, headphones on. He was calmly reading a programming manual and jotting a note here and there.

"Aren't you scared?" said Abigail, taking his hand and squeezing it.

Tim looked outside as though he hadn't noticed the storm before.

"Oh," he said, sliding his headphones off. "Well, that's not so great, but I'm sure the pilot knows what to do. Go higher, go lower, go faster, go through it."

"You're so trusting," said Abigail. "Hasn't anything scary ever happened to you?"

Before Tim could respond, the plane hit a large air pocket and plunged, shutting off her mind. A few people screamed as the plane lost altitude. It fell for only a few seconds, maybe five or six. When it regained its equilibrium, the captain got on the PA system and chuckled, then cleared his throat to say:

"Well, ah hah, that was a pretty bad little bump back there, and I hope you're all OK. Ah, I think I'm gonna keep the seatbelt sign on from here on, because as you probably detected, there's a little bit of storm activity on the right there. I'll get back to you in a little bit, when it's clearer, and then I hope it'll be a bit smoother all the way to New York."

Abigail found it hard to listen to him. She was engaged in staring at the lightning still streaking around outside. Its antic motion disputed the calm in the captain's manly voice.

Tim said, "Do you want to ask me if I was scared just then?"

"No, Tim, I—I have to be quiet for a little while now, or I might vomit."

"Just close your eyes and relax," said Tim. Abigail closed her eyes and leaned back. She tried to breathe deeply as flashes passed light through her lids. Pink, white, yellow, and then blackness. And more blackness. Yes, staying dark, wonderfully.

The storm was slowly, slowly ending. Abigail began to feel safer. Seatbelts unlatched, trays came down, and long lines formed for the bathrooms. Abigail, who badly needed to pee, began to navigate her way down the aisle to the nearest toilet. Though the lightning had stopped, there was still some turbulence, and the plane was shaking. First, Abigail dropped into the lap of a man to her left, and then, when she had finally gotten off it, a violent lurch threw her at an opened tray on the opposite side of the plane. The tray caught her on her right flank as she fell. A can of cola spilled onto a woman's pale linen suit. The woman screamed.

Abigail felt a sharp pain, as though she'd been stabbed from within. As she got up, she was surprised to see the line parting to let her through. Locking the door inside the cubicle, Abigail saw the blood drenching her skirt, dripping down her legs. For a moment she stared. Then she sat back down and noticed a button with a flight attendant shape on it. She pushed it. There was little pain now. They were about thirty minutes from the airport.

Abigail heard a knock at the door.

"Did you call for help?"

Abigail rose up a little from the toilet and let a woman in uniform come in.

"What's wrong?" the flight attendant said perfunctorily.

Then she looked down and saw all the blood.

"What's going on, hon?" she said, taking in the fact that Abigail was pregnant.

"I fell a minute ago and I think I hurt myself."

"Let me make a quick call and I'll be right back," said the woman.

Returning to the bathroom, she gave Abigail two thick sanitary pads.

"What month are you in?"

"Late seventh, early eighth."

The flight attendant was in her forties. "I've got a bunch of kids myself," said the woman. "By the time you've had your third, it'll be like getting your hair trimmed."

"Really?"

"And some women make a big deal about that, too, don't they?" The attendant's own hair was short, thick, and straight. She opened the bathroom door and helped Abigail, whose bottom was now securely bundled, over to a row of unoccupied seats in the rear of the plane. She lifted up the armrests, and Abigail lay down, curling up into fetal position.

"Could you cover me, please?" she said, beginning to feel better.

"Sure." The woman went to the back and pulled out a blanket and pillow. Then she lifted Abigail's head and tucked the pillow under it. As Abigail lay back again, the flight attendant smoothed the blanket over her.

"OK now?" she said.

"Could you stay with me until we land?"

"I'm not going anywhere." She sat down next to Abigail. "See, now," she said, "it's a good thing they've got some of us old hands on the plane. Some of the young ones, twenty-three, twenty-four, they'd be in as much as a panic as you were. Age before beauty, right?"

"Oh, yes," said Abigail peacefully. She closed her eyes. When you needed a kind heart, or some wisdom around you, beauty was very overrated.

◆ ◆ ◆

When Tim came back to see what had happened to her, he found Abigail asleep.

"What's going on?" he worriedly asked the flight attendant.

"She had a slight tear back here, probably some kind of placenta problem, some bleeding. My sister's a labor nurse. Usually heals up just fine. Eighth month, huh? Wow—you're nearly there. We're gonna land at LaGuardia in about ten minutes, and I've called ahead to the hospital to admit her. Long Island Jewish. They've got a good obstetrics and neonatal. Don't want to take any chances, right?"

Birthing classes notwithstanding, Tim had a hard time associating himself with the actual, imminent appearance of a newborn baby. And though he loved children, this talk of blood and placentas was alienating, like having to kill, gut, and de-feather your own chicken before you could eat it. He tried some Lamaze breathing.

"Hon, you all right?" said the flight attendant, looking at the man hyperventilating. "You'd better sit down, huh? Yeah, that's right, go over and sit on the other side of your wife, there. You'll feel better in a minute."

Tim made his way over to the other end of the row and sat down. His eyes were closed, and he was taking long breaths through his nose.

"Want some ice water? Some Coke?"

He shook his head.

"Hey, hon, OK, alrighty, now, just put your head between your legs. You're looking green around the gills. Not Irish, are you?"

He shook his head violently.

"Just a little joke. Green and all. We'll be landing in a little while."

Tim complied. With his head between his legs, his mind calmed down. The woman passed him a bag and Tim breathed slowly into it. Whenever his thoughts returned to scenes of bloody birth, he brought them back to the paper bag on his mouth. He puffed in and out, the way he had learned in the birthing class.

They landed safely. When the flight attendant roused her, Abigail was surprised to find herself peacefully snug on an airplane, of all places. And there was Tim at her side, looking at her with such worry in his eyes. The woman helped Abigail sit up and said, "You and your husband are getting out first. They're all gonna stay seated until you come out. There's gonna be a stretcher to keep you nice and comfy. Don't want you to be hurt again, right? How you feeling, hon?"

"Pretty good," said Abigail, trying to sit up more fully and get the big picture. She wasn't used to being treated this way, "playing the invalid," as her father would call it. But there was a crampy feeling in the bottom of her groin, and a continuous sense of dripping. Abigail did not resist as the attendant gently but firmly pushed her back against the seat cushions.

"Do I have to wait a long time?"

"There's gonna be some emergency people getting on in a couple of minutes. We're still gonna taxi a little to meet up with them, OK, hon? So just relax and you'll be off the plane in no time."

"I really feel a lot better," said Abigail. "Do you think I can go to my own doctor—he's on Park and Ninety-Third?"

"Course he is, hon, but we're closest to this hospital and that's where you'd best go. Don't want to drive all over the place if baby's not getting oxygen or whatever."

"What do you mean—do you think he's suffocating?" Abigail said in a panic. Having a child was a big enough sacrifice—she still had no idea, despite the bluster, how people managed—but having one whose brain was oxygen-poor was more than she could take.

"I really don't know, but that's what the ambulance is gonna give you, sweetie. Lots and lots of good air, and your baby'll get more than he needs. Why, I'll bet with you and your husband so good-looking and smart, this boy will turn out to be a world-class athlete, and a doctor to boot. How's that?"

"Well, I didn't want them to tell me what it was. But boy or girl, athlete or doctor or none of the above, all I want is a healthy baby," said Abigail seriously.

"That's the way, mom, and I'll pray for you."

Tim had resumed breathing into his bag at the mention of brain problems. Abigail, looking over, turned to the woman and leaned over to whisper in her ear.

"Can I tell you a secret?"

"Sure, sweetie," said the flight attendant, pushing Abigail's dark, damp tendrils out of her eyes.

"That guy over there, the one I'm with? He's not the father of this child. The actual father is married, with kids of his own. But the guy I'm with is—well, he's unbelievable in so many ways, he cooks well, he kisses great—I mean I'm lucky he loves me in this state. . . ."

"Aw, that's a bittersweet story, sweetie. Don't dwell on it just now when you need your strength."

"No, it's not bitter . . . even without either one of those men, I'm fine. I pay my own bills, and—and my law firm needs me, so that's why I went to Grenada, and—I'm up for partnership this year. . . ." said Abigail, straining to pull herself up again. The woman again firmly prevented her from rising.

"There, relax now. You're saying you're 'up for,' for"—the woman was looking a bit anxiously toward the front of the plane.

"Partnership. Real security. Forever."

"Real security, isn't that something!" said the flight attendant, nodding to the EMS personnel who'd boarded.

15 One of the surprises of being hospitalized, Abigail found, was the havoc. She had remembered her mother's hospice as a quiet place where even the sunlight was gentle and tempered. But that had been her last destination. All you could do in a place like that was wait for the inevitable, which rendered a certain sabbatical peace.

Here among the salvageable, the hospital bustled with raucous, rolling gurneys and shouting orderlies, nurses sprinting down the linoleum. There was also the endless beep of the monitor attached to Abigail's abdomen, recording a heartbeat quick as a rabbit's. Her baby was alive within her. I'm coming, I'm coming, I'm coming, it seemed to be chanting, its voice low, relentless. Abigail's heart answered with the plea, Not yet, not yet, not yet.

If she was very careful, the pregnancy would go on to full term. Premature birth terrified Abigail even more than the usual sort; placental detachment had never been part of her plan. Abigail calmed herself, remembering that her condition had stabilized. Though she had not even had a chance to return home since leaving for Grenada, the baby paraphernalia would be arriving at her house any day.

Some months ago, per her sister Annie's advice, Abigail had ordered a wicker bassinet and changing table, a nursing pillow, a rocker, and an assortment of soft toys. These would go into her dining area (which angled off her living room). That space was never used, since Abigail tended to dine on takeout food, eaten on a tray in front of the TV. Annie said that some people felt that not waiting until the baby arrived brought bad luck, but that they were wrong. Abigail had of course preferred to be prepared.

Now, in the hospital, Tim had brought Abigail a pile of classic books about child-rearing, and she had begun to leaf through them. She had culled the gist of the matter. There were five basic points to parenting:

1: Never leave the baby on the changing table.
2: Support the head.
3: You can do no wrong as long as you love your baby.
4: Love, or bonding, can take some time.
5: Parenthood changes your life. There is no going back from it. Ever.

That last one gave her pause. Abigail did not want her life changed too much; she had worked too hard to make it what it now was. She had put together a list of potential caretakers from a reputable agency. Just before her trip, she had begun calling some candidates, all claiming to be "experienced, mature," and to "love children."

Some voices seemed disappointing. One of the answering machines featured a woman saying, "I'm not here, I'm out," in an apathetic, unsure way. A pause, then, where Abigail could hear children screeching in the background, and then a slow, clattery hang-up. Another was answered by the rumbly voice of a male, saying, "Who the hell is it?"

To the best of these candidates, Abigail gave information about her need for "an absolutely take-charge person." The sound of her own voice, crisp and confident, reassured her. She could settle this matter satisfactorily. Every pot had its cover, as her mother used to say. And every child, doubtless, had a nanny out there, ready to help a frightened mother through the shoals of baby love.

Despite these preparations and consolations, Abigail was aching to get back on her own two feet. At first, the firm had not forgotten her any more than she had forgotten them. They had called her at the hospital with a few questions about her Grenadian case. But how could she think with all the noise and bustle around her? Her work product was beginning to suffer.

It tortured Abigail to imagine the office wisecracking about her being like all the rest of the women, whose brains said one thing and their bodies another. She would become a long, windy anecdote like Dana Kidder. It rankled that she couldn't, at that moment, disprove them by jumping to her feet and running to the library. There was a baby in her uterus, a thick napkin between her legs, and a large waterproof pad—the kind used for puppy-training—under her behind.

Already, she was being replaced. Dave Biddle-Kammerman would pick up the threads she'd left and begin weaving them into a coherent strategy for their client. He had sent Abigail an expensive bunch of flowers, with an attached note that said, "Everyone is pulling for you." What did that mean, exactly? Was her life in danger? But no one actually came to the hospital see her. It was as though she had leprosy.

Abigail didn't have many personal friends, either. There was a woman she had known in law school, but they had fallen out of touch when Gwen had decided to drop out and become a playwright. Abigail had once seen one of poor Gwen's "showcases," which took place in a dank room somewhere near the West Side highway and featured two markedly hideous actors, one more miserable than the other, talking about "anomie." (She remembered an exchange. One actor: "Oh, anomie." The other: "I know you know yourself, but brother, do you know *me*?") Gwen would probably not be good company in a health-care crisis.

There were also some old college girlfriends who had called from time to time over the years, but they now lived out in the suburbs, Scarsdale and Summit, and none of them "needed to work" anymore. Some kept on expanding and wallpapering their houses, laying down tiles within and paving stones without, and planting perennials up and down their gardens. One said she might go back to school when the kids were grown, to be a therapist, and the other had joined the Junior Leagues. The momentum of success seemed to have stopped for these women; something in their lives had slowed them down to the pace of human growth. In many ways, Abigail felt, they were the lucky ones to whom real life—the invisible, non-corporate one—belonged.

Abigail felt she now wanted to talk to these old friends, to plumb their world and understand it. But she dreaded the weight of their contempt. From their perspective, she would be the freak now: an unwed, pregnant, workaholic woman with a detachable placenta. Men might be more understanding of her anxiety to get back to the mill—provided she kept mum on the gory details—but all the men she'd known, boyfriends and platonic male friends, had married.

Of course, there was Tim, who visited faithfully, bringing good, hot, homemade food. But somehow in his presence Abigail felt bereaved. She was missing her real mother, she realized. That quiet, strong, forever love that nothing else had ever equaled. Now that she was going to be a mother herself, Abigail began to see how rare and irreplaceable it was.

16 ⚖️ There were a few career women at Fletcher with whom Abigail had shared moments by the office microwave, but only one, Rona DeWitt Miller, cared enough to visit her now. It was odd; they had not had much in common before, and had rarely spoken more than a perfunctory word or two. Now their shared condition—motherhood—seemed to open the floodgates, at least on Rona's side.

An associate in divorce law, Rona had recently had her own baby and was on maternity leave. Abigail had not even realized that her colleague was pregnant, she had "carried so small." Now, Rona arranged herself on the corner of Abigail's hospital bed and burst out:

"Oh, Abigail, just look at us now!"

"What do you mean, Rona?"

"Forgive me," said Rona, weeping, "I didn't mean you, Abigail, you're just stuck in bed with that big, you know, baby in there, looking pale, guess you lost lots of blood, huh? I meant me. This week I'm dealing with a green poop situation. Giving birth was a nightmare, but then you have to do all these things, and see all these things, and the weirdness of it all does not *end!*"

"Boy or girl?" said Abigail, willing herself to be calm.

"Oh, the baby? Girl. Dylan Molly Miller." Reciting the incantatory name seemed to fix things for a moment, and Rona's face lit up. Then her face fell again and she resumed: "The green poop's better than the awful Grey Poupon stuff that came before, or no, maybe the worst was the black tar—"

"The black tar?" said Abigail, despite herself.

"Comes out in a glob like toothpaste from the devil. Those first few poops? You will freak, Abigail. But does it end there? Apparently not. Sometimes I can't *wait* to leave that nursery, and get back to my nice clean desk!"

Abigail understood that. "So you're back at work?"

"No, not yet. It's only been four months."

"Four months! But I thought we only get six weeks."

"That's paid leave. I'm actually taking a longer break—unpaid."

"But why? They'll forget you—you'll never make partner, and Rona, I saw you, you worked so hard!"

"Oh, Abigail," said her colleague, her voice warm with pity. "'Partner.' It all seems so far away. So pointless." She paused and looked at Abigail. "You really don't know what I'm talking about, do you?"

Abigail did not immediately respond. "I guess not," she said finally.

"You're due any minute, huh?"

"Early December."

Rona was silent for a moment. "Abigail, your situation, as I see it, is fraught with obstacles. And as I understand it, you're entering this foreign territory alone, without a—without a partner. In the family, not law firm sense, I mean."

"I do have someone."

"You 'have' someone? We're not teenagers now! Substantially, do you have someone? People are talking, they know you have someone, a cute guy, I've heard. But you don't even live with him, right? Kind of 'now you see him, now you don't'?"

"I live alone and like it that way," said Abigail mechanically. Having Rona sit on the edge of her hospital bed and judge her love life as she lay there with a torn placenta (and pre-term fetus) under her blanket was just about intolerable.

"Well," said Rona, "I have my own theory. You're a bright woman. An independent woman. A practical woman. And in your mid-thirties, my age, right? Your fertility was about to start falling off the charts."

"Well, I don't know about you, but I'm only thirty-two."

"Great, but what if you wanted more than one, adequately spaced? Right? So I figure you went out and found some genius sperm."

"Hey," said Abigail, "have you been talking to Tina?"

"Who's Tina?"

"My administrative assistant. That's one of the pet theories she mentioned, that I haunted some Mensa meetings, then used a turkey baster. Well, she didn't actually mention Mensa. But you get the point. Tots in the test tube."

"Well, OK, let's not judge. I may end up doing that to get a normal second one. I'm just kidding—Dylan's my heart and soul."

So weird, thought Abigail. No matter how much mothers complained, how many awful truths they divulged, their children were always the "meaning" of their lives, their "heart and soul." Where was that meaning and soul before? And would Dylan's life be just the same—no meaning until she had a baby herself? It was all so absurd.

"Now let me tell you my theory," said Rona.

"About what? Child-rearing? Normalcy?"

"Stay on point, counselor. I'm talking about your conception."

"OK."

"It was love-based."

"And then what happened?" Because clearly, these days, love was nothing you could lean on.

"Right. Something must have happened. Maybe you did have a real guy, you might have even loved this guy—but something prevented you from being with him."

"No comment."

"You're taking the Fifth?"

"I'm calling on the entire Bill of Rights, and the fact that it's nobody's business."

"And if that's the case, and I hope it wasn't, that's sort of sad," continued Rona. "Because then it could have been that Richard Trubridge."

"You have been talking to Tina!"

"No, but thanks for the confirmation. I had my own hunches. I knew Richard way back when, and I think he always had his eye on you. He used to be in my department, you know. And—well, Abigail, you were seen with him down there in Palm Springs."

"I was?"

"Of course. People have eyes. And ears. And mouths to talk with."

"And what do they say?"

"Here's what I say: What a mean way to treat a smart, accomplished girl like you. I know you're not a 'girl'—you're a professional, accomplished woman—but deep down, you're a 'girl' at heart, and easily swayed. So he did what he did, and he swayed you."

"Huh?"

"He knew you had a great career ahead. But did he care? He wanted what he wanted, as ever. Bad enough he hurt his own career with the stuff he got up to at the firm before they kicked him out. But to take it out on a promising associate on the verge of partnership, to grab someone and knock her up for a cheap thrill. Or wait—do you think he was getting back at the firm? Like a 'fuck you right back' sort of thing?"

"Rona, please, that's not what happened. But I really don't want to talk about this."

"Right. Sorry, sweetie. I mean it's probably not him anyway, huh?" Rona paused, but Abigail said nothing. After a moment, she spoke again.

"Hey! Do you want to talk about what it's like to give birth?"

"OK." Abigail was glad to change the subject, although the sudden gleam in her friend's eyes warned her that Rona's memories of birthing would not be reassuring. In a sense, this comforted Abigail: if Rona always saw the worst of everything, maybe Richard was not as professionally venal as she had just suggested.

Rona took a deep inhalation and then sighed it out.

"I was in labor for twenty-four hours," said Rona. This was her war story, Abigail sensed; she had told it before, and she would tell it again. As a prospective mother (and stuck in bed), Abigail knew she was the perfect audience.

"I absolutely thought I was not going to make it. Either the baby would die, or I would die. You really begin to understand how it's possible to die. In fact, you want to die, Abigail. You want them to cut your throat so it can be over. And yet it's just beginning."

Abigail wondered about this. Had her mother really given birth three times? Had her sister? She'd seen mothers all her life. She just hadn't realized that they were all veterans of a battlefield. And yet here she was, in a hospital. And Rona had a post-traumatic glaze in her eyes.

Her voice went monotone: "By the end you're no lady. You're

ready to shred your twat in Macy's Christmas window *just to get it out!* But you know what happened to me?"

"What happened?" said Abigail, dragged along. Like the baby itself, she was caught in the long tunnel of Rona's maternal darkness.

"After all this, they tell me I have to have a C-section, which of course I had vowed never to have. That's the credo, isn't it? Breathe, and pop, simple. Who wants to admit that they've failed at the first challenge? The Demerol was really nice, like being drunk in the sun. I wanted to keep pushing. But the baby's heartbeat was slowing. They started rushing me into the operating room. Of course, then I begged for the famous epidural."

"Good for you," said Abigail, who had also hung on to the concept of getting out of this without pain. She was relieved to be learning about the drugs that brought relief. First the Demerol, then the epidural. A C-section didn't sound too bad, either—someone helped you get the baby born, quickly and efficiently.

"Do you have any idea what an epidural really is? *It's a huge needle jammed into the middle of your spine.* And what's more, you hurt so badly that you *want* this needle in the middle of your spine!"

"Oh," said Abigail, her voice conciliatory. Rona was having a flashback, and she tried to be kind. "That does sound terrible."

Rona, silent, had apparently worn herself out. She'd blown some kind of anecdotal fuse. She sat down, pulled up her shirt, and put a small apparatus on her breast. It looked like a big plastic test tube with a rubber funnel on the top and a large bulb on the side. Rona pumped the bulb and grimaced. Finally, she resumed speaking:

"It's dripping, two ounces if I'm lucky, and then I've got to rush home to my little darling and let her drink it. That ought to hold her for the next, oh, ten minutes," she added miserably.

"Why not just give her a bottle?"

"And let her have diseases, and deafness, and bad teeth?" Rona looked at Abigail as though she were a pedophile—but since that technically meant "lover of children," perhaps the opposite.

"Is that what happens?" Abigail felt shaky. She had browsed the classics of child-rearing but had not yet absorbed all the horrors." You mean I can't just get someone—someone else—to give him a bottle here and there?"

"Not if you want all the benefits, Abigail," said Rona. "I'm sorry. I have to be blunt. You seem to know very little."

"For how long?"

"Oh, at least half a year. Minimum, three months, for the benefits."

Abigail felt like asking what the benefits were. But she wouldn't have been able to face them, or the fact that her own child, yet unborn, would receive them incompletely.

"I have to get back to work!" she protested. Rona should understand that more than anyone.

"You want a sick, dumb, overweight child? That'll be even more work in the end!" Rona had moved on to the other breast. "Think long-term!"

"I didn't know I had anything to do with all of this," said Abigail. She had been expecting a brilliant prodigy, and good-looking, too. After all, Richard Trubridge was tall, athletic, smart. And she was no slouch, either. She had thought this paragon would emerge and do its thing, more or less.

"But with all this nursing, how will you ever get back to work, Rona?"

"Oh, I might not," said Rona, sealing up her test tube of breast milk and putting it into a padded bag. She put her breasts back into her bra and closed her shirt buttons and patted them down. Abigail watched it all with a growing sense of dread. What an enormous rigmarole it seemed to be.

"What are you talking about?"

"I'm getting close to the little imp. She grabs my boob, she looks at me, she falls asleep in my arms. I don't know, my hormones sometimes make me cry." Rona abruptly started crying. "I'm sorry."

"No, it's fine," said Abigail, surprisingly beginning to wail along. Rona put her arms around Abigail, and Abigail gripped her tightly. They hugged each other for dear life and rocked.

"What's the difference what happens, Abigail?" said Rona, sniffing. "We'll be replaced by the next generation anyway, like our mothers before us."

"And they by the next, and the next," said Abigail shakily. It was all tragically true and utterly illogical.

"Listen," said Rona, detaching herself with a yank. "I have to go. Dylan has to go to Tumblin' Toddlers. Otherwise her brain won't grow."

"Who says?"

"The folks at Tumblin' Toddlers. They've done their research. And experts back them. Babies need their bilateral symmetry and multi-zonal auricular maturation. They need music, too, both Western tonal and—eventually—Schoenbergian twelve-tone, which—oh, never mind. It's hard to explain, and won't be relevant 'til Dylan's mastered the flugelhorn. For now, I've been singing 'The Grand Old Duke of York,' and of course doing some East African clapping games."

"Uh-huh," said Abigail, rendered momentarily mute. She wasn't sure she knew "The Duke of York." Was that some British song she'd missed? She felt left out and stupid. How could she teach it, or even sing along? And how was she at clapping games? It was like that bad dream where you haven't prepared for the finals. Or was it the one where you went outside naked? Both at the same time, maybe. The naked finals, unprepared, boobs dripping and uterus sectioned.

Rona looked into her date book. "Oh crap. I forgot to do the big math dots today."

"The math dots?"

"You know, the stickers on the oak tag boards?"

"Oh yeah, those." She made another mental note.

"Look, Abigail," said Rona, kindly, "you have time. They recommend waiting as much as a week after the birth, so their eyes are clear and focused. But you should be starting the language lessons now. Have you downloaded?"

"Have I—?"

"You know what, get the tapes and put them in your Pregaphone."

"What's a—"

"I'll lend you mine. You're clearly not ready. Thank goodness, you can accelerate. I'll give you the fast-track version, and don't forget to play it as much as possible."

"I'm lost here."

"Well, you can choose—I have the French, the Japanese. Latin. Kind of aim the speaker at your tummy, so the baby learns the phonemes. I can come by tomorrow and set you up."

"Do you have to?" Abigail whined. "I feel tired."

"It's up to you," said Rona pertly.

"But you did it?"

"Oh, yes. What does tired mean to the modern woman?"

"I don't know, what?" said Abigail miserably.

Rona sniffed. Her face brightened. "Come to think of it, I brought you something."

"What?"

She reached into her diaper bag, the multi-compartmental pouch into which she had tucked her breast milk.

"It's a book I really liked. I started it at the hospital, and it helped me get out of the postpartum thing. It's called *I'm a*

Horrible Mother, But You're a MUCH MORE Horrible Mother."

"I'm a horrible mother? Already?"

"Well, I know I'm not horrible," said Rona. "Anyway, it's supposed to be funny, you know, satirical, so you, with your sense of humor, will eventually love it I'm sure. It's all about the perfection thing."

"Oh, the perfection," said Abigail tonelessly, taking the book. The flyleaf promised that the book would describe "the two or three things that are *not* fatal to your baby," then listed all the ways that baby could die: buttons, radiators, cats, sandboxes, cling wrap, too much dust, too little . . . Abigail, trying to live up to her reputation for wit, attempted a smile.

"It *is* funny," she said.

"That part? It's not meant to be. But dip in. You'll love it."

Rona stood up and hoisted her diaper bag. It was stuffed to bursting and seemed momentarily to affect her balance.

"Got to run, Abigail. I've been away from the little darling for an hour, and one of my books says that it'll lead to 'endless and bottomless angst, need and resentment.'"

"I'm really touched you came," said Abigail, recalling, again, that no one else had visited her. It had probably been too awkward, not knowing how it would all turn out. And sickness, like parenthood, was not too much acknowledged at the firm.

"Oh," said Rona, "I had to see you. I was going nuts; I'm probably hiding it well. And misery loves company, right?"

17 Soon after, abruptly, Abigail was notified to pack up and get out. Although the sonogram showed that her baby was a bit small, not only vis-à-vis full-term babies but also normal babies of its age, the hospital had decided the numbers were adequate and sent Abigail back into the world. Her placenta, at least, seemed secure enough, and the worst of the bleeding had stopped. Before her discharge, Abigail was advised to rest as much as possible and avoid stress. They didn't seem to realize that she was a lawyer on the verge of partnership. Any mistake she made in any direction seemed consequential.

A few hours later, on Tim's arm, Abigail entered her little apartment. It was now strangely altered. Yes, there was her good old closet, full of business jackets, skirts, and dresses, handsome work clothes in an array of sizes. There was her blond-wood desk, with the computer and modem, for working at home, and there, on the wall above, were her diplomas and bar association certificate. But now, in her dining nook, she saw the new bassinette and changing table, delivered and signed for in her absence. So much white, and the bassinette was lace-fringed. Peeping inside, she saw its little mattress—a pattern of ducks and many downy ducklings. And some of them wore clothes.

The phone machine was lit up with messages. Abigail popped the button and listened warily. She'd asked Tim to keep calling around for babysitters and housekeepers. One paper in particular carried ads from these workers, immigrants from Ireland and the islands, mostly. Here and there an elderly widow, a young student, or someone whose English was poor.

"I try to call you but no answer. You call me about the job. You not here. No problem, anyway. I here at home. Tanya."

"Hiya!! This is Stacy? I'm here for the next year or so? I'm from Jacksonville? Florida? I am thrilled about your baby? You won't be sorry? It'll be so much fun?"

"*Yes. Yes.* It is Angelica Corones speaking. I am waiting for you call me sooner. You call me about job babysitter?"

"Hello, good afternoon. Mary-Ann from Dublin. Could take care of the young one fer ye. I may charge a bit more but I'm wert it, got my papers in order, too. But I won't scrub yer floor, I'm not a maid. Right, tanks fer listnin.'"

The next message was her sister Annie.

"Welcome home, Abigail! Your cellphone was off, and anyway, I don't want you getting all that radiation in your present condition. Daddy just called me. He's flying up here with Darlene for Thanksgiving. I'll do the honors again. Do you want to come a day or two early and stay with us?"

"Thanksgiving?" Abigail shouted at the machine. It was bad enough that the pregnancy was moving along so inexorably, but the calendar, too? It was now wheeling her into a family gathering she could hardly bear to face.

"I'll put the kids all in one room," Annie was saying. "The little ones just crawl into my bed anyway. Daddy and Darlene have to have their own bedroom. Liz and Art, too. You can have the third room. But listen to this: Liz said she couldn't be in until late Thursday—Thanksgiving itself—because of a breakfast in Chicago. Can you believe it? Working on Thanksgiving? You probably can, you're two peas in a pod, drive yourself nuts for no reason.

"Anyway, get a good rest and I'll come and get you on, like, on the Tuesday? Would that be OK? You can settle Daddy and the girlfriend. You're good with him."

Abigail fell back into bed and stretched her arms out to Tim.

"Welcome home," he said, hugging her.

"Could you please come to Annie's with me?" she pleaded, hugging him back gratefully. One challenge after another, and he was always there for her.

Abigail found it hard to envision seeing her father in her current state. They had never really discussed the details of her pregnancy, only that it would not interfere with her work. And now, with the order to take it easy, even that was not so certain.

Tim stared into her eyes. "You want me there on Thanksgiving?"

"I want you there very much."

"Am I part of the family now?"

"I hope so," she answered. She wasn't at all sure. Displacing his anger from his unwed, pregnant daughter, Dad might lay into Tim. There might be a blowup. And of course, he'd give her a hard time as well. With all his ambitions for her, how could she have let herself end up like this? Abigail needed someone there to hold on to, someone with whom she could leave Annie's house if she had to.

"Well, you know I'm a total sucker for you. But I have a family, too—and Mom gets upset if we don't go home on these holidays. Of course, she loves my taller, more successful, and more corporate brother more, even though I'm the one who was always more tenderhearted. But that's not the issue, and—you're really not listening, are you?"

"Yes, I am listening," she said quickly. "Your brother sounds like a Doberman. I used to like the cool and callous Dobermen, but now they fill me with dread."

Tim knew the reference all too well. Abigail often praised him for being more of a spaniel. "I don't think I fill you with enough dread, which may be the trouble. But anyhow, I'll see what I can do. My folks like to eat early," said Tim. "Because that's when the real drinking begins. Then my busy big brother leaves—something work-related, or that's his story—and mom cries all over me. She cries when she's drunk. I think she enjoys it. But I don't. So maybe I'll come over later in the evening and skip the maternal pity party."

Abigail grabbed Tim's head and kissed him on the mouth. She lay back again. "You're the best, and just to show my appreciation, I'm going to study all those birthing handouts you brought home from class," she said.

"Oh, my god!" said Tim. "I just remembered. We have class in half an hour! With all the excitement of bringing you home, I nearly forgot!"

"Don't shout, you scared me," said Abigail. "So what?"

"*So what?* What do you think, Abigail, that I'm the one who has to do this and you get to stay home? I'm your coach, remember? They all probably think I'm some freak with an imaginary friend."

"You mean you're not?" said Abigail.

"Nothing about this situation is imaginary, Abigail," said Tim, sternly. And then he helped her to her feet, the way he had done on the day they met.

18

"This is terrific! Everybody give Abigail Thomas a big, beautiful *Hello*!"

Casey, the birthing instructor, circled the room, her powerful legs striding around the expectant couples, who sat on cushions on the floor. She wove her hands in circles in the air, like pinwheels.

"Hello, Abigail!" everybody said, as she beamed at them.

"Now, since this young lady hasn't been here all this time," said Casey, kneeling down deftly behind Abigail and putting her hands on her shoulders, "I think she should let us all know why she's taking this class and what she wants to get out of it."

Casey bobbed on her ankles, waiting for Abigail to speak. For the moment, words failed the usually articulate attorney.

"Come on, Abby, everyone has shared their reason for being here. We've got our older couple, right, Maggie and Joe? It's never too late to learn how to give birth the right way. Why, just the other day I heard about a fifty-eight-year old woman, first baby, and completely natural!"

The class, including Casey herself, applauded.

"And we've got Toni, who used to be scared to death, remember, honey?"

Toni, a pixie with scalp patterns shaved into her straw-colored hair, nodded vigorously. Her enormous husband, the sure cause of Toni's outsize protrusion, smiled proudly beside her.

"Ah, go on, Casey," said Sheryl, sucking on a mint and staring at Toni's future ten pounder, still stuck under the tiny woman's pink muumuu. "You know that half of us are gonna have Caesareans!"

"Did I hear someone say the *C* word?" said the instructor, lowering the heat on Abigail. She stepped over to Sheryl, her expression mock-horror, and a few students chuckled knowingly.

"Well, you did show us the movie," Sheryl protested.

"We have to cover all our bases, Sheryl," said Casey, shaking her orange curls. "As a matter of fact, the surest way to get a C-section is to feel the way you do, that it's unavoidable for—what did you say—half of you? Because class, as we know, it's the last thing nature wants for you!"

"Except for when it's breech, right? With the big head at the end instead of the front?" said Toni.

"You weren't listening either, Toni. That can be an obstacle, but with a few headstands and a skilled practitioner, you can turn a child around in utero. No, there are few exceptions to the rule of heavy breathing and vaginal expulsion. Now, Abigail," she said, turning back and smiling, "I haven't forgotten you. Where've you been all this time?"

"Working, mostly," said Abigail. "I guess I feel I have to give it my all."

Mara, who wore what seemed a custom maternity suit in fawn faux-buckskin, complete with fringes, shook her dark straight hair, all three feet of it, in indignation. "Yes, that's what we're about," said Mara. "But *we* give it to the next generation."

Many of the class participants looked at Abigail as though she might be a narcissist. Abigail, returning their gaze, enjoyed her own inner conversation. They were making precisely the fallacy her own mother had made, she thought. Nurture the next generation, and leave yourself out. And then they nurture the next, and leave themselves out. Who actually got to nurture their own lives and promise? Men?

"Well, anyway," Abigail found herself saying, with a voice she hoped sounded maternal, "I'm here now, and from here on, all I've got to think about is having this baby." A smattering of applause registered her classmate's growing, if wary, acceptance.

But Mara persisted. "What kind of work was it?" she said suspiciously. "Corporate?"

"That's a judgment," said Tim, shutting her up. But only for a moment.

"No. No. My lover, Gorse, is not here, as I said at the beginning of these sessions, because she is in the theater. She is an artist. But what were you doing? Some commercial exploitation of people? Some rape of the environment our babies will breathe? *When will you finally be satisfied?*" she shouted.

Good question, thought Abigail.

"Is this your first child?" she asked.

"Fourth," said Mara.

"When will *you* be satisfied?" she parried. And before Mara could answer, she drove onward. "I'm a lawyer," Abigail said. "True, I don't work for the poor, the hungry, or the oppressed," she added, suddenly hearing how bad that might sound. "Not right now, at any rate. But I don't breed like a bunny and judge people I don't know. And I do my utmost for any client that pays me. Right or wrong, I am an attorney." That didn't come out quite right, but there it was. It was what she had learned at law school and at work. She was a professional, after all.

"OK, class, that was interesting, and now we can get back to—"

"No, Casey—I won't take that comment. I'm a rabbit? I'm a—"

"I was asking Abby where she was. We got off topic. Let's finish, OK?"

"I'm trying to," said Abigail. "Yes, I missed a class or two. I was in Grenada, finding grounds to defend someone against a frivolous lawsuit."

"*You went on an airplane in your late seventh month?*" Casey shouted. There was a hushed, shocked silence until Casey leapt to her feet, exulting, "that is *so great*! You gave your baby a vision of true dynamism, and I'm all for it. Class? Let's hear it for Abby!"

They applauded, louder than before. All but Mara and now Toni, who folded her arms.

"What is it, Toni?" asked the teacher.

"She endangered her child," said Toni. "We all know what happened. Timmy told me all the details."

Timmy? "Abby" was bad enough, but "Timmy"? Abigail turned around. Her partner was flushed with nerves, and whispered, "I did call her; she was worried."

"We were all worried," said Toni, easily overhearing.

"Yeah, she set up a phone chain," said Mara. "Because we actually care about one another. That's what we do. We don't simply—"

"And since when did I become everybody's business?" Abigail interrupted. "I don't even know any of you."

"And whose fault is that?" said Mara.

"And we're trying to know you," said Toni, appeasing.

"We're bonded in care for each other and for our babies, all our babies," Casey patiently explained. "That's the contract of this class. And I want you all to know, class, that what happened to Abigail can be a tremendous learning experience, not just for her but for all of us. Life is full of accidents and surprises. The Olympic runner trips on a pebble. Your water breaks on the bus. Who are we to judge what this mother-to-be was traveling for? What she meant to prove to her child? Maybe her karma is to fly, to be free, to express herself in the broadest strokes!"

Abigail nodded awkwardly. She had never heard herself described in such creative terms. How wonderful to be off the hook, and in the good graces of this birthing guru! But Casey wasn't quite finished.

"Would you say, Abby, that you came here for that reason? To fly, to be free, to express some undiscovered side of yourself, and to share it with others?"

"Well, yes, maybe, but also it's sort of what everyone does, and—"

"Yes? Can you go a little deeper?"

Abigail tried. "And I guess I wanted to, to kind of get used to the idea of being a mother, going in there one way and coming out another. . . ."

"Good rhyme," said Casey thoughtfully. "Mother, another."

"Purely accidental," Abigail mumbled. But she was flattered, nonetheless. "I mean, I'm no poet or anything."

"See, class, these categories, 'corporate,' 'artist,' 'us' and 'them'— they do more harm than good. Abby doesn't even know that she's creative. We all are, we all have our inner poetry, class, and I want you to listen for it as you—

"IFFFFFFFFFFFFFFFF!"

Here, suddenly, Casey took in her trademark bellyful of air, and let it out with rapid, forceful puffs:

"HUH HUH HUH HUH HUH HUH HUH!"

After her initial surprise at observing an entire class of adults huff away like engines, Abigail tried to go along. Just as abruptly as she had started, however, Casey stopped. She put her finger to her lips.

"Shhhhhh. Shhhhh."

Abigail did the same, lifting her finger and going "Shhh . . ." Then, appalled, she realized that Casey wasn't doing another exercise. She was just asking the class to be quiet. Casey's voice fell to just above a whisper.

"Today, class, in our continuing journey, we are going to do something exciting. Something we've never done before. Now, some of you may find the following exercise unfeminine and even ugly, but let me assure you, when it comes to having a natural baby, there is nothing so beautifully female and gorgeously strong as . . ."

She paused dramatically.

"*Pushing*! Uh! Uh! Uhhhh!" Casey made a few guttural sounds, as though she were having a torturous bowel movement. She squeezed her eyes tightly, pushing even harder. Her face grew round and red, as though she'd pop.

"Uh uh uh uh uh! OK. Try it." Casey relaxed. Abigail waited until everyone else started. She didn't want to be the only one again. Then she tried it.

"UH UH UH!" This was embarrassing. Tim looked at Abigail approvingly, but she knew she was actually holding back. It was worse to do this one if you didn't really do it. Sillier, more pointless. Mara, meanwhile, was giving it all she had:

"UUUUHH! UHHHH! UHHHH!"

She looked up for a moment.

"Casey?" she panted.

"Yes, Mara?"

"I think I pushed something out of my butt. Is that good?"

"*Excellent*, Mara! Class, I should tell you that when you do this one, especially in the birthing room, there is a good chance that you will expel some amount of fecal matter."

"What? You mean I'll shit myself?" said Sheryl.

"Yes, and it will be *great*, because it will mean you're really, really pushing. So let's all give it another try."

"UH! UHHH! UHHHH! Come on! Squeeze, tighten up, push from the belly, PUSHHHH!"

Toni shouted: "I think I peed!"

"Terrific!" said Casey, loping past Toni and over to Abigail.

"Hey, Abby—OK, you're being too hung up here. Come on. Tim, move over a little. Let me in there; I'll coach her. Now give me a big one, Abby.

"I'll count to three, and then you hold your breath, and *push, push, push* for a full count of ten. Got it?"

"Umm, I think so," said Abigail, mortified to see that the class had completely stopped to observe her. Bad enough that she'd been called a corporate monster and destroyer of the environment. Bad enough that she'd called some pregnant woman a rabbit. She did pee in her pants nowadays (very notably in Grenada, in Mrs. M's drawing room), and had no desire to be doubly incontinent. Nevertheless, in her state, Abigail was in no position to argue with a professional birthing instructor. And part of her wanted to impress Casey with her strength. Tim patted her encouragingly on the shoulders. She'd do it for him, too.

So Abigail gave it everything she had, which was always a lot. Abigail pushed so hard that a little head began to emerge.

"I think it's the baby!" she shouted in disbelief.

Casey, confirming, was too stunned to cheer.

19

Earlier than she had planned, Abigail had indeed given birth. It was a good thing that the birthing class took place at the hospital; they'd rushed her straight off to the delivery floor. She had to smile about it. Nothing, so far, had gone as intended. In a sense, she'd gotten off easily. She had come to expect childbirth to be a long, slow, arduous ordeal. But instead, she lay flat on her back on a gurney, filled with disbelief that it was all happening so fast.

Where did *you* come from? she found herself wondering as her clothes were removed and her legs were raised. (Vaguely, she sensed Tim being pushed around, given a yellow paper gown to wear, and disappearing behind her head as the doctor knelt before her.) Yes, she knew the technical sources of human reproduction. But how, really how, did a living, breathing, radiant being come into your life? (Exit your body and enter the birthing room—really, where had it come from?) It was as though an angel, a fairy-tale sprite, had perched on her windowsill, or a fluttering, upside-down hummingbird. Wings beating so fast they seemed invisible.

So all of a sudden, she saw her baby, topsy-turvy, held in the air by a man's huge hand. It was a girl, and her mouth was toothless, open, silent, shocked, then crying. A layer of wet, powdery wax covered her wrinkled skin. She was flailing, her toes splayed. Her cry was strong and rhythmic: "Aa, Aa, Aaaaa!"

Abigail's body began shaking. She was not sure if she herself was crying, too, an echo of her child's immense arrival. She didn't know if their voices blended, where she began and ended. A moment ago, they'd been together, fused, as one—and now they were strangers in a room who needed to reach for each other. The baby's cry was meant for Abigail. She wanted her mother. Abigail heard herself ask for the child.

A moment later, the little girl was laid on Abigail's stomach. She was weightless but wriggling, so new she seemed flawless. Abigail put her hand on the perfect little head, touching a black web of hair, soft as feathers, as silk. Putting the child to her breast, Abigail was amazed to see her root around, searching blindly, with clenched eyes, for her nipple.

"Here, here," she whispered, guiding it into baby's open mouth. The newborn latched on to her mother and sucked violently. She'd never tasted milk before, and this first milk, Abigail knew, was creamy. "Colostrum": she had just learned the name of it in one of her books. But nothing prepared her for her daughter's avidity. Tiny as she was, her bony gums were vises. She would thrive if given half the chance.

"Ouch!" Abigail yipped involuntarily. But she admired her daughter's strength.

"You'll get used it," a nurse said. "You'll toughen up in no time." Inserting a finger, she eased the baby's mouth off Abigail's nipple. It seemed throbbing, outraged; nothing any lover had done with his mouth compared to this ardor. Abigail found herself stunned by a kind of joy. She was thrown by these powers outside her. She wanted to speak, but the words didn't come to her. Her mouth hung open, as though she'd had some tasty colostrum as well. So this was manna, heaven-sent. Like the baby, this lovely gift from nowhere. This creamy, first mother's milk.

"Let's clean her up and take some measurements," said the nurse after a moment, picking the baby up in one hand, like it was nothing, just a little handful, and taking it away. The baby began crying again, more loudly than ever before.

"Oh, she wants to come back," said Abigail, her heart dilating with odd, responsive yearning. "She didn't finish," she pleaded.

"She'll be all right. At first, they're not so hungry." Another nurse wiped Abigail's face with a damp cloth, briskly. The mother was a patient, too. Tended by kind hands and hearts.

"Should I count her toes and fingers?" she said, a helpless worry quavering her voice.

"She's perfect, don't worry," said the nurse who was rubbing her face clean. After that, she placed a new pair of socks on Abigail's cold feet. Warm, woolly, thick socks.

"How much does she weigh?" asked Tim, suddenly stepping over to a cold metallic table where babies were dealt with, wiped, shod, hatted, and tagged.

There was a brief silence. The newborn was wheeled away, out of the room.

"Say—where are you going?" said Tim. His voice sounded worried, and Abigail picked her head up to see.

"How much did they say?" asked Abigail, hoarsely. What was happening?

"Well, that's the thing," said a nurse, bustling now to remove bloody pads from below Abigail. "She's just a bit scrawny, five pounds ten, but that shouldn't be too much trouble. I've seen much smaller. We're just having Doctor Appleman take a look."

"How was her score, you know that test they give them?" Abigail remembered something about that from another of her baby-care guides.

"The Apgar?" said the other nurse, who was scrubbing her hands somewhere behind Abigail's head.

Apgar. Colostrum. Latching on. All these once theoretical words were real to her now.

"I think it was six."

"Not too bad," said the nurse closer by, who snapped a clean white sheet over Abigail's legs, tucking it around her cozily. What with the warm socks and the crisp sheet, she felt almost ecstatically spoiled and beloved.

"But it goes up to ten, doesn't it?" Was this like a bad grade? Did it "count"? She knew the nurses would know how to comfort her.

"Don't worry, Abigail, she's great," said Tim. "I got a good look at her as they were wheeling her out. She was in this little plastic basket on wheels, and I think she saw me. They popped this pink beanie on her head."

"They are pretty sweet, aren't they," agreed one of the nurses. "The boys get baby blue ones."

"But I hardly got to hold her," Abigail whimpered. "She's probably missing me by now." She had also read about how critical it was that the child bond with its mother during the first few hours. Didn't the hospital know about these studies?

"You'll get plenty of chances later, dear," said the nurse who'd tucked her in.

"I'm just going to let you lie here for a while until things settle down." She massaged Abigail's deflated abdomen. "I know that hurts a bit. But it helps it go back to normal. Now go on. Shut your eyes and rest."

Abigail dutifully shut her eyes. But even with her eyes shut, all she could see was her tiny little girl. Her heart nearly broke, thinking of that red, needy mouth with no words yet to ask for what she wanted. Despite herself, Abigail lost interest in these thoughts and yawned exhaustedly. A part of her was relieved to be given some respite.

Another nurse began wheeling a pile of messy laundry out of the room. "We'll check on you in a little while."

Abigail and Tim were finally alone.

"Hey, you total woman," said Tim, stroking her face gently. "Are you all right?"

"I'm just really thirsty," she said, with a cracked voice.

"I can run out and get you a milkshake."

"No, just some water. With ice, if you can."

"Anything."

After he left, Abigail thought she could hear babies crying insistently. Imaginary, surely. She was on "birthing floor"—the maternity ward, they'd told her, was upstairs. Still, Abigail was sure she heard those cries. Soon, they dwindled and she could hear only one particular cry: it was the aching call of her own daughter, no less disturbing for being imagined. It seemed to come from some bottomless misery, some insatiable need. An agony of longing. Abigail's breasts prickled. Her eyes filled, and her heart almost stopped with fear. What a responsibility. How could she, weaker and more confused than ever before, take care of someone else?

20 ⚖ Tim was sorry to hear that the doctors thought it best to keep Abigail's baby in the hospital for a few more weeks. Still, she was a little small, and they were just being extra careful; they wanted to observe her. During her stay she'd receive formula mixed with her mother's milk. Though Abigail tried pumping her breasts, even buying the same apparatus that Rona DeWitt Miller used, she couldn't squeeze out more than a few drops. One nurse would take her offering (the half ounce of grayish, watery liquid only a "top-off" to a hearty can of processed milk). Another nurse would feed the newborn baby. Different people came and went. As for herself, Abigail was free to go the next day.

With Tim by her side, Abigail stared into the transparent box in which her baby lay.

"She seems so alone, so fragile," she said.

"No, she's strong. She's got your go-getter quality," Tim said. "Poor us," he had thought to add, but Abigail seemed too listless and wan for jokes.

She seemed almost as lost, at times, as she had down in Grenada, after hours of great sex. She had lain there, beneath him, limp and abandoned. Afterward, Tim thought he had even seen tears in her eyes. Abigail was sometimes so puzzling. So complicated. The very things that pleased almost everyone else (like his stellar lovemaking, like bearing an exquisite child) only made her travel off into solitary brooding. Was this a form of ingratitude? He thought it might well be.

However much he cared about her, and he cared so much it sometimes hurt, Abigail often seemed to take him for granted. Had she ever really thanked him for all he did for her? Maybe with words, now and then with her body, but Tim sensed she didn't mean any of it that much. He'd hoped they'd be closer after the baby came home, when some of that tension drained away. But for now, he needed reassurance.

"Say, do you still feel up to us having Thanksgiving with your folks?" he asked her.

"It's what we do every year—I mean, it's expected."

"Well first of all, this year, I'd be coming—you told them, right? And that's a pretty big thing. And secondly, you look so weak right now. Will you be OK to travel, Abby? Can you sit through a long, rich meal with lots of noisy kids?" Tim needed to confirm his own plans. Did it even occur to Abigail that offering to be with her showed caring and commitment on his part?

"I—I think so. It'd be nice to be with family. Anyway, what are my choices? I can't sit home alone on Thanksgiving with all the baby things around me and no baby."

"You wouldn't be alone. I would stay with you."

"No, that's really sweet of you, but you have you own mother and brother to see—"

"Only for about an hour; that's my time limit—"

"And anyway Annie wants me to come. I mean, us."

"There's the magic word—'us,'" said Tim, and grabbed her in a hug.

◆ ◆ ◆

Thank god for Annie's always open arms, Abigail thought. She was surprised to be so drawn to a sister she had never understood before. Without her, the family would have no center, no hearth fire. Abigail and her sister had talked on the phone for an hour the previous evening; Annie had asked all the right questions. She was hungry for details, and lavish with comfort and praise.

"I think this baby looks just like our mama," Abigail had told her. No one else but Annie would have cared so much about bringing Clara back—in the form of a grandchild. Even her father, who'd loved their mother so much, seemed loathe to speak about his losses.

He had flown up from Florida with his girlfriend, Darlene Shanks. The girls knew that Owen had planned to spend two weeks at Annie's house—the week before Thanksgiving and the week of. But Abigail had suddenly given birth, and her father had come on the first flight the next morning.

"Hey, kid," Owen Thomas said when he raced into her room at the hospital. He sat down on the edge of the bed and talked softly into his daughter's ear. "Ya did it, and no question."

"Daddy," she turned, warm and cozy. "When did you land?"

"Just now. I'm comin' straight from the airport."

"You look tired. Go to Annie's and get some rest."

"I'm right as rain. How're you feelin', peppercorn?" This was one of his pet names for her. Abigail hadn't heard it in years. She couldn't remember her father being so—well, motherly. Perhaps when she'd been very, very little. In her cradle, perhaps, before much had been expected of her. Before he'd taken over the mas-

SONIA TAITZ

culine order of things, the passing on of toughness and of mastery. But now that her mother was gone, Abigail needed this side of her dad.

"I'm doing OK."

"Bit knackered of course?"

"Not so tired I can't greet you like a human being." She tried to rise up to a sitting position, straight back and all.

"Hey, settle down. I know you're not fakin'."

"I am knackered, actually," she laughed. Was this the man who used to pour drops of cold water on her forehead on school mornings, even when she'd felt sick?

"And how's the little one?"

"She's little, all right. But she's a strong, determined one. Anytime she gets the bottle she guzzles away. Try to get it from her!"

"She has your drive, bless her," he said, and Abigail's eyes had filled. She was a softie when it came to her dad. And when he was proud of her, she melted. Not that she could cry outright in his presence. He wouldn't like that. She held that back.

"I hope so," she said, finally.

"She'll do us all proud," he said, smiling. "And you'd better come to Annie's next week and tuck into some turkey, or there'll be me to answer to."

"I'll be there for all of that," she said.

"Good then."

"Wouldn't miss it for the world. And I'll get strong again soon, and I promise—I'll be back at work in a flash."

"Good girlie," he said, standing up. He paused at the doorway and looked at her once more. "But you rest now. You've done a job."

"Have I?" she mumbled, falling back asleep. She had not slept so well in months and months.

21

After lengthy consideration, Abigail decided to call her daughter Chloe: a combination, she fancied, of her parents' names, Clara and Owen. Now, at the Thanksgiving table, surrounded by her father, her sister, her brother-in-law, two nephews, two nieces, and Darlene, she asked her family what they thought of the name.

"Haven't heard it too much," said Owen, chewing. "'Glowy,' did you say?" He had a way of making things sound Welsh.

"Shine little glowworm, glimmer, glimmer," sang Jared, and Jesse laughed uproariously. Annie smiled at her boys.

"They each have a toy glowworm that lights up when you squeeze it."

"Chloe," said Abigail. "Not glowy. No *G*."

"With a *K*, then?" asked Annie's husband, the dentist. Wayne was large and manly; Annie had made steak for him as a special order. He hated turkey.

"No, not a *K*, a *C*. It's properly spelled *C-h-l-o-e*." She wished her big sister, Elizabeth, would get here already. Sophisticated

Liz knew how to spell chic names, whether from the classical period, the Continent, or the English peerage. Not only had all Liz's friends already had babies, but she liked to look in the baby names book and choose one for the future, when she would settle down and adopt. (Annika was in the running for a girl, Asher for a boy. That last one was Hebraic—also currently acceptable.)

Owen persisted as though the name were as rare as Rumpelstiltskin, "How d'ya say you spell it? *C-l-o-e*?"

"You forgot the *h*, Dad. It starts with *C-h*."

"*Ch-loe*?" he said tentatively, pronouncing the *ch* like a Scotsman saying "loch," or a Yiddish yenta saying "yech."

"No, dear, it's French," said Darlene, delicately picking some corn from a back molar. "*Clo-ay*? Right? Je parlay Cloay? All French names have just that particular sound, don't they?"

"That they do, Darlene," said Owen agreeably.

"Tim says it's actually Greek," said Abigail. "Some people put two dots over the *e* to pronounce it separately."

"Ah, Tim—that's your special friend, I suppose," said Owen, suddenly seeming dark-spirited. "Annie's told me he'll be here later. Tim wants it to be Greek, with two dots, does he?" He looked over at Darlene and she gave him a compassionate shrug.

"He doesn't 'want' it to be Greek; that's just the name's origin," said Abigail. "You can ask him when he gets here."

"Greek's a dead language," offered Wayne, scornfully.

"Tim likes it, though?" said Annie. "The name, I mean?"

"Uh-huh. He loves it. But I picked it myself." Abigail had wanted to tell what the name meant to her. How it combined Clara and Owen. But she no longer felt the impulse.

Later, she watched, overwhelmed, as Jaycee was playing the drumsticks on her mother's head (she was the musical one, Annie explained). Jared and Jesse's faces were covered with cranberry sauce (they were artistic), and little Todd was projectile vomiting.

"How do you cope?" she wondered aloud.

"You mean with Todd?"

Abigail had meant all of it.

"He is kind of hard to feed," said Annie, wiping the table and floor. "It's not gluten or anything. We're still trying to figure it out. Poor li'l nugget. He can't help being the way he is."

"That's what I love, a blanket vindication," said Tim, waltzing in. Abigail felt a thrill as everyone stared at this handsome young man. His face was flushed from the cold autumn air, and a slight air of drunkenness made him dapper.

"Come on in," said Annie, after a moment. "I didn't even hear the door. Jared, did you let this nice man in? Next time tell Mommy."

She cleared a clean space for the new guest. "There's certainly lots of food."

Tim sat himself down next to Abigail with a lot of commotion. Moving the chair outward and back was a prolonged scene in itself. Then he grabbed the nearest wine carafe to fill his glass, unbidden, to the top. While it was understandable, his slight tipsiness annoyed Abigail. "Stayed for a couple of drinks with your mom, huh?" she said, sotto voce.

"You could say that again, and louder," Tim affirmed, reaching over to the marshmallow yams and tucking the spoon in deep. "Because if a man can't spend Thanksgiving with his mom, who can he spend it with?"

Annie stared as Tim flung a large yam pile on his plate. He was clearly buzzed; his cheeks glowed and his eyes glittered.

"Would you like some turkey with stuffing?" offered Annie. "That's the main course, after all."

"Did you have any turkey at your mom's?" said Abigail.

"No—we had what you'd call the liquid dinner. So I'm famished."

"Let me serve you a plate, then," said the hostess.

"Yes, please, lots of everything," said Tim, smiling at her like a hungry little boy.

"Anyone else want something?" Annie looked around the table.

"I'll have a nip of something wet, I reckon," said Owen. He stared fixedly at Tim, his face twisted into a scowl. Late to the table and eating like a pig, he seemed to be thinking. Darlene pushed her plate away and reached into her handbag. She took out a lipstick and applied it, then pursed her lips.

"Shall I open another bottle of red then, Daddy?" said Annie.

"Just a beer would do nicely," said her father. "Lager, whatever you've got, I'm not bothered."

"We do have beer, right, Wayne?"

"Yeah," said her husband, chewing on his beefsteak. "In the garage fridge. I've got those great big bullet ones. Get me one, too, would you, honey?"

"What about you?" he added to Tim, in a gesture of welcome.

"Can't say no," Tim answered cheerfully, polishing off what was left of his wine.

The phone rang, and Annie ran to get it.

"Well, that was our Lizzie," she sighed, returning "She says she's not going to be able to make it at all. Some part of the deal is delayed, I don't know, anyway, they'll be at it all night. She didn't even sound upset," said Annie, bewildered.

"She has her duties," said Owen.

"But on Thanksgiving, and the whole family here," continued Annie, half to herself. "And she doesn't even seem to mind it. Said they'd order in and keep going."

"Good on her," said Owen.

"I wish you'd told me she was on the phone, Annie," said Abigail. "I would have told her about the baby's name. . . ."

"She was in such a rush, Abigail. And you forget that she's been an aunt four times before. It's old hat to Liz. I'm not sure she cares all that much. About names, I mean," she added.

"I guess," said Abigail. It didn't seem as real when Annie had had the babies. But for Liz, apparently, it was all the same. Abigail and Annie were now on the same discountable mommy dinghy, bobbing out to sea. And one of their discoveries would be that no one really cared that much about all their domestic details.

"Don't forget the suds," said Wayne.

"Oh, honey, I almost did!" Annie now trekked out to the garage fridge. She came out with several large silver cans of beer.

"Everyone all right now?" Annie sat down and cuddled her youngest. Todd drifted off to sleep, his lashes casting shadows on his fat cheeks in the candlelight.

"I'm more than all right. I'm fine and I'm dandy," said Owen, drinking determinedly. When he'd finished his can, he crushed it, squeezing it with his hand and laying it out on his plate like a corpse.

He stood up and spoke. "I'd like to formally introduce myself to you, young man."

Tim rose quickly and extended his hand.

"I am, of course, this young lady's father. Owen Thomas."

"I am, of course, this young lady's—uh, I'm Timothy Vail. Glad to meet you. Happy Thanksgiving."

Owen grabbed Tim's hand and held it in a vise-like grip, which Tim, wincing, attempted to return.

"What are you thanking me for, now, exactly?"

"Ouch! Excuse me?" Owen squeezed harder as Tim squealed out, "Do you mind—?"

"Pardon me. These are working man's hands," said Owen.

"You must have worked really, really hard."

"Oh, Tim, yes. I did. I worked very hard. Everything I have, you see, is paid for. Legitimately mine. I've got no bills to settle on my own account."

"That must be reassuring."

"Don't you talk down to me, lad. One thing's not settled, understand? It's not settled, not for me and not for my dear daughter. And I'm getting on in years."

"But I'm actually not—"

"Don't interrupt your elders. I've got a daughter alone in life with a newborn baby. And I've got, sittin' just beside her, at my family table, a young man who frolics and drinks."

"What—you mean this beer I was just offered?"

"And the wine, which you filled to the brim, and whatever came before them in your nightly crawl. Now hear me well, son. I'm no prude. I grew up in South Wales, and I know the interior of a pub, I can tell you that. But holiday or not, don't be arriving to my family dinner swaying like a young birch tree and smelling like a brewery."

"Daddy, Tim isn't really—"

"Drrrrunk?" said Owen.

"No, Abby," said Tim. "Your father is correct. I am a little buzzed, I'll be the first to admit it."

"You're not the first. And are you so buzzed you can't remember she hates that very nickname?"

"Dad! I don't really mind it anymore!"

"So drinks," said Tim, seemingly oblivious to this sidebar on nicknames. "Mother did put out the martini pitcher at a quarter to five, and you should have seen her when I left! But what does that have to do with—you don't actually think I'm the father of Abigail's baby, do you?"

"I don't. Annie's told me outright that you're not."

"I hope I didn't overstep," said Annie. "Daddy did ask, and I thought it was OK to share as much as I knew."

"Sure," said Abigail. As long as no one knew about Richard

Trubridge, she thought. Because that story would really make her father mad. And just as her mind formed that thought, Owen confirmed it:

"And it's a good thing that you're not the man, for it's a bigger cad that got her with child." He took another can of beer, popped it, swilled it, and crushed it flat.

Abigail cleared her throat. Whatever Richard's moral flaws, she hoped he'd never have to come face-to-face with her father. Short as he was, Owen Thomas was formidable.

"But you see, my soused table guest, whoever you are. Check your motives, and do so now. I hope you're not toying, for don't you know she needs a husband and a father for that poor baby lying there in hospital?"

"Oh, god," said Abigail. "What makes you think he's toying with me? We have very special feelings for each other."

"Oh, I can well imagine those special feelings," said Owen.

Tim was too handsome for anyone to think anything but the worst of him, Abigail realized. Being that kind of good-looking was something of a handicap in decent circles. Daddy wasn't exactly sober now himself; if he got into his primitive man-woman-child thing, the night would be long, if not murderous. Abigail looked over to Annie for help.

"Dad," said Annie, picking up the cue. "You're getting yourself worked up. And my kids are listening to this blather. Come on. Let's save it for another time."

"Are you saying it's time I married her?" said Tim, leaning forward menacingly.

"You should, and soon, if you're serious-minded."

Abigail looked at the two of them, shocked. Was she to be part of this discussion or not?

"Well, what about you and your lady over there?" Tim was saying.

"I do plan to marry Darlene, thanks for asking. Not at the moment, but presently. She's not carrying a bastard child, by the way. You're an impudent newt. And since it's clear as day you're naught but a playboy—or you'd have at least proposed to my child before now—promise me you won't touch her anymore. Because as her dad, I don't want to see Abigail pregnant with another fatherless babe. Two babies with two different cads don't add up to an honest life. Modern or ancient, I didn't raise my girl that way, nor did her poor dead mum."

"For god's sake, Daddy!"

"Sir, Mr. Thomas—Owen, if I may—I take your daughter very seriously. She's one of the most interesting and intense girls I've ever known," said Tim. "And she's extraordinarily modest in her way," he added. "She didn't even want me in the birthing room. I mean, it went quickly, and I couldn't help seeing a few personal things here and there, but my point is—she was prudish. And believe me, it took ages before we—"

"Tim! Enough! I don't need you to defend me."

"An odd prudery, Abigail, given the circumstances. Knocked up by god-knows-who, and now this man comes to table. . . ."

"Please, Daddy," said Abigail, "I was out of town, nervous—"

"Oh, you're always nervy, since the day I met ya, scared of yer own shadow. Were you hungry then? Was it war time?"

"I was out of town in a strange place, and it all seemed so competitive and cutthroat, in a subtle country-club way. You know, Daddy? I wasn't used to this level of sophistication. I was intimidated. And he—this man—was patient and kind to me—"

"Yes, I'm sure, very kind to take advantage of your fears," said Owen, irritably. "Well, why doesn't this wonderful man marry ya, then?"

"Yeah," said Tim loudly. "Why doesn't he marry ya, then?"

"This man. OK. He has a name. His name is Richard Trubridge. He's a law partner. And he—Dad, I'm sorry to say that he's already married." Abigail just couldn't keep the secret anymore.

"Jesus Mary Joseph what a thing!" said Owen. "Married?"

Now it was Tim who turned to Abigail with a shocked expression. There was a heavy silence, and Abigail hastened to fill it:

"No, I didn't know that about Richard at the time—didn't know he was married. He didn't seem like that kind of man. He protected me. Taught me a good swing, as a matter of fact. He didn't seem one bit the playboy, Dad."

"I don't recall the golf game requiring a lie-down," said Owen.

"No, it doesn't, not typically," Abigail admitted quietly.

"And what are you teaching her?" said Owen, turning to Tim. "What is your particular ball game?"

"You know, Daddy, Tim is the most caring, giving person I know. He went to birthing class for me, he came down to Grenada when I had to work there, and—and here he is with us at this table, fielding all these questions."

"Well," said Owen to Tim. "A knight in shining armor then, is it?"

"I guess I am, a little. Attempting, at least." He suddenly felt sober.

"Gainfully employed—or leeching off my girl?"

"I pay my way, Mr. Thomas," said Tim, his voice quivering slightly. Abigail felt for him. People often thought he was a gigolo, simply because he was good-looking and never seemed to go to work.

"He's an expert computer man, Daddy," she said. "In the business of information consultations." Her voice carried a touch of her father's Welsh lilt now. "To the corporations and all that."

"Aw, then you do need your fingers, then, for the keyboard," said Owen, his manner finally relenting. "Sorry I squashed them together so hard. You know, with the handshake."

SONIA TAITZ

"I'm beginning to regain some feeling in them, sir," Tim replied, staring at Owen's flattened beer cans.

"Well, that's great!" said Annie brightly. "Now, who wants some pumpkin pie and who wants some hot deep-dish apple, and who wants both?"

"A sliver of each," said Tim, "if you made them." For all the insults, Abigail sensed that he was glad to be there, among these earthy, direct folk. In Greenwich, his mother was probably about to serve the candied, gingered orange peel that everyone admired, then chewed and discreetly spat into their linen napkins. Better to be confronted. Better to have it all in the open.

After dessert and an assortment of liqueurs, Annie sat on the sofa. She seemed too exhausted to lift another plate or rinse a bowl. Her four little ones tumbled, curled, and molded around her, stroking her face and kissing her knee and tickling her chin. Abigail sat, watching her sister and her family. A circle of wordless, unprovable truths.

"You look so tired," said Annie. "I've fixed up your bed. Got a bed for you, too, Tim. Sorry about Dad. His bark is worse than his bite. You might want to take Liz and Art's room though. It is empty, after all."

"I've heard worse," said Tim. Abigail came over to him and sat on his lap. Tim kissed the top of her head.

"Thanks for everything, Annie," he said.

"Mm hmm," she peaceably replied. "I think I'd better get these little peaches settled upstairs soon."

"Can we help out with the dishes?" said Abigail.

"I've put most of them into the washer already. Darlene's helping out in the kitchen. You go to bed."

Abigail looked over to Tim. He looked like he could use a good sleep under one of Annie's huge duvets.

"Shall I show you your bedroom, li'l Timmy?" she said. Tim

nodded like a small child. Drinks, the dinner, and Dad had chastened him.

"I would marry you, you know," he said. "If you wanted. You know that, right?"

"Shhh. I know that, sweet boy," she replied, as they trudged upstairs. "You're a fine person, Timmy. Now go to sleep."

The house felt secure to Abigail that night, full of the warm breath of children, of close-knit family. Overriding the worries, the drudgery and conflicts, was a precious sense of trust. That was Annie's doing, Abigail realized. In her own way, she was a great provider. Not the way Fudim was, not the rich kind, but, as Evelyn MacAdam had so perfectly put it, "in the only way that matters." The kind that brought safety and joy.

22 ❁ Late Sunday afternoon, Abigail returned to her apartment. Already, there was an e-mail from Dave Biddle-Kammerman. Didn't he have family? Didn't he celebrate Thanksgiving? It was a letter of thanks, in a way.

Indeed, Dave thanked her "on behalf of the firm" for all that she'd contributed to the MacAdam case. The tone seemed valedictory, as though Abigail had to leave—and take her gold watch with her. How does Dave even know what I've been doing and thinking? Abigail felt preempted by a pro. And one who worked through national holidays, weekends, and the fortunate (for him) pregnancy and childbirth of his rival.

No slouch herself, Abigail promptly sent a returning volley—a forceful document for Bertram Fudim, Senior Partner. In it, she outlined the extensive research she had done in Grenada, the many strategies she was exploring, and her considered legal recommendations—not to mention the billable hours, which were massive. Boldly, Abigail also laid out the possibility of a countersuit asking for punitive damages in the multimillions. This ground-scorching approach would finally ensure that she not be forgotten when she took maternity leave.

That leave would naturally be brief—just a week, after the baby came home. Abigail knew that she had already spent too much time outside the office. Yes, she'd had reasons—crises, lives almost lost. And yes, the accident that had caused all this mayhem happened on company time, on a client's behalf, on a work flight. But all they'd remember at the firm was that she hadn't been there. The reasons never mattered.

◆ ◆ ◆

Damage control accomplished, Abigail rushed to the hospital to see her little girl.

Poor tiny Chloe. Less than a week old, her challenges were primal, and far more consequential than anything that happened at the firm. By the time life entered the corporate legal arena, it had been packaged and parsed into causes of action, dollars and cents, plaintiff and defendant; these diminished it irrevocably. And by the time the lawyers were done with it, life was unrecognizable as a formerly organic thing.

But Chloe—she was life in its purest form.

Simply eating and breathing were all she could cope with, and she did, with all the strength she had. At times, her eyes, which were frequently open, searched left, then right, then crossed, retreating back into an inward arena.

"We've still got to fatten her up," said the nurse, as the baby approached her seventh day. She popped the bottle into the little girl's mouth. Chloe's skin was still wrinkled, her limbs like bent sticks. What hair she had been born with was silently and mysteriously disappearing, day by day, and she looked like a wizened old soul. Sometimes, when the bottle left her lips, she'd drop her head to the side and sigh. Her hands, still often clenched, seemed to hint of an ancient, unforgettable vendetta.

Life was tough. It was full of mean people, accidents, betrayals, and misunderstandings. And on top of it, you had this body to take care of, with all its needs. Abigail felt so sorry for what she'd gotten Chloe into—this world.

"Will I ever be able to comfort my baby?"

"Comfort? What do you mean?"

"Breastfeed, I guess. I'm not even sure that's what I mean," Abigail said, ashamed of her utter ignorance, her lack of even the words to express her ignorance.

"Did you express any milk for us today?"

"Not yet, I'm sorry, I guess I should have," said Abigail. "I've just got back from my sister's house, and I didn't feel up to it."

"It just takes practice. Don't beat yourself up. Want to burp her now?"

"I'll watch you. I have a confession. I'm still sort of scared of her."

"Everyone says that. She's new to this, and so are you. Just try to breastfeed as soon as she comes home," said the nurse, putting the baby over her shoulder and patting her back gently. Chloe obliged her with a huge froggy belch.

"A lot of mothers get the real 'let down' once they're settled."

"The 'let down'?"

"The 'let down' reflex. It's involuntary. The milk starts to prickle in your breasts and then it comes."

To Abigail it sounded like crying. That prickling in the chest, and then the flow. She felt she understood this.

But nursing Chloe when, eventually, she did take her home, seemed impossible. Why should any child pull pointlessly on her empty (though swollen) breasts, when with far less effort and a fraction of the time, she could empty a two-ounce bottle of formula and sleep contentedly? (Or, as Abigail's father used to say, why buy the cow when you can get the milk for nothing?)

The new mother kept offering herself and being rejected, offering and being rejected. Her baby screeched rejection. But the nurse had said try, so Abigail did try. Chloe needed to be fed every half hour, and the feedings took a half hour, so slow was the flow of nourishment. She would wriggle, clenched to the source and twisting, desperate. Abigail, too, began howling in pain. Her nipples cracked and bled; all that seemed to flow was red and angry, wrong and unmaternal.

"I can't do this!" she wept, trying another position, switching to the other breast. Somewhere she'd read that Guinness helped. She bought a bottle and drank it. That helped her relax a bit, and she did "let down" more than before. But it was never enough. She still had to "top off" with formula. At least it dulled her nipple pain. Both internally and as a topical salve.

Abigail, exasperated, decided on a plan. She would get someone in. Now. It was stupid that she hadn't made arrangements yet. True, the baby had come early, but she had known that that could happen. How had an efficient woman like herself managed to dawdle like that? She should have found someone right after the accident. But the voices on the machine had seemed so awful! At the time, it was laughable, but now she wondered how she could return any one of those calls, much less hire the women who had made them.

She could call an agency and take the high road. People like herself—professional—always delegated. It was simply a personnel issue. Agencies, she began telling herself, could do all the sifting, selecting the cream of the crop. Why else would they be in business? Obviously they had years of experience in sizing people up, getting and checking references, and—most critically—making love matches between employees and families.

But what type of person would she want to have working for her? Abigail still had no idea. Of course, the agency would know. They knew how new mothers were. They, too, were a sort of mother, sister, and friend. If their staff could save Abigail time and worry, they would be worth all the fees in the world. She worked hard; she deserved a little peace of mind. Agencies saw to that. All the ads said, "Leave it to us," or, "Mother, your worries are over."

True, it seemed a bit callous to let her worries be "over" so soon. The baby was still a newborn, after all. And no nanny could breastfeed her. But if she was going to quit trying, then anyone could care for her child as well as she. Or better.

Having resolved to call the agency, Abigail filled a bottle with formula, heated it up, crooked Chloe in one hand, and fed her. The baby drank gratefully. Then a great calm came over the two of them. They slept.

23 Domestic Delites had the biggest listing online, and although the name did suggest the sale of sexual favors, Abigail had to admit that they seemed experienced with the needs of new mothers.

"You sound tired," said the sympathetic man who took her call. (Abigail was surprised that he would understand so well, and so quickly.) "Call me Gary, and tell me what you're looking for. A little help, huh?" He seemed to know everything.

"Yeah. I'm really exhausted, and she never sleeps."

"So you've got a little girl, huh? And she doesn't sleep through the night? And you've got to get some sleep yourself, huh?"

"Right—you're exactly right—and also I feel like a klutz because I don't know anything. I paid attention at the hospital and did read a lot of books, but—"

"Nothing like havin' some experience, right? What's your name and address?"

Abigail told him.

"So you're lost and upset, and you need someone in there yesterday. Am I basically right, Abigail?"

"Yes. Can you help me?" For the first time in a long time, Abigail felt like the people who chose to sit in the back of the classroom and not raise their hands. The people who needed to look over other people's shoulders, or they couldn't make a move. They must have felt like idiots, too. And now she would feel that way, at least in the motherhood department, for the next eighteen years or so.

"Hey, Abigail."

"What?"

"You're in luck. Hang on."

"Sure." What else could she do? She heard Gary clicking on his computer. Then he seemed to smother the phone with a cupped hand and do some yelling. After this, he said, suavely, "I think I've got someone great for you, and she's available right now. What kind of hours do you need, Abigail?"

"Well, I guess, all hours, live-in maybe?"

"What kind of work are you in?"

"I'm an attorney in a small firm, involved in a huge case—"

"Good. Listen. You have a job. But your nanny has also got a job. Working for you. And you gotta respect those limits. I mean, let me ask you this, Abigail. Would your boss ask you to work day and night with no sleep?"

"He has asked me, and I've been glad to," said Abigail, quickly, with pride.

"Oh. Well, Abigail, listen, you gotta be flexible in the beginning."

"No, you don't understand, I've got to get back to work soon—I'm about to be made a partner at Fletcher, Caplan—"

"I understand," he cut her off. "Say no more. So you're going back right away. That's good, that's better. Let me tell you something in complete confidence, Abigail. As one professional person to another. You know law, the contracts, the torts. I know the domestic employee.

"They don't like it when the mom's around, Abigail. It kind of cuts into their act, their routine, as it were. They can't let their hair down with you there. And that's a good thing, contrary to what some people think. Your kid doesn't need more tension, let me tell you."

"Do you mean my kid specifically? Do I sound tense?"

"No more than the other moms I deal with. OK, I can tell you want someone easygoing, with a light touch, right?"

"Well, I also want someone very experienced, you know, with CPR and all the other emergencies."

"Very sensible. Accidents do happen."

"They do?" she found herself saying. She of all people, with her legal background in aviation disasters, should know that accidents happen.

"For the most part, yes. But not with Domestic Delites, though. My girls are super careful. And you need someone calm. Everyone wants competent and calm."

"Right."

"Do I know my business, Abigail? Abigail, you're a normal mom, what can I say. And we're the professionals. Anything else on the wish list?"

Abigail thought.

"Can I add 'loving'?"

"Abigail, I hear you. We do loving like nobody else. And who wouldn't love your cute little baby?"

"I know," said Abigail. "But maybe if she cried too much, or you were a nervous type, no, you said calm, right, but what if you weren't so maternal, I mean, all the time?"

"Come on, Abigail," he continued, "I've screened these ladies. We're talking about nice folks here at Domestic Delites. They all love babies, or they wouldn't be here. I got pictures all over my wall, you should see. The babies, the nannies—it's one big happy family. Some of these nannies, you wanna hear something touching? They get invited to the wedding twenty years later."

"You've been in business twenty years?"

"Long enough to know about happy families," he demurred.

"One more thing. I want my baby to know I'm her real mother," she blurted. She knew it was a non sequitur, but it was still important.

"Scientific certainty, Abigail: every creature, every single animal, knows its real, actual mother. They get that smell, that feel right away. It's nature, it's biology. It's not an adopted baby, right?"

"No."

"Good. Sometimes I put my foot in my mouth with that one. Adopted, biological, step, whatever, love is love. Believe me, you're the one they come to when you come home, tired, from work, with all the complaints. You couldn't get kids off you with a crowbar. I'm just kidding.

"So let me read this list for you: Competent, calm, experienced, loving. Hours? Probably eight a.m. to six p.m.; how's that for a start?"

"Could we do eight to six thirty?"

"We'll negotiate that. That's a long day. But you work outside the home? That's a premium, trust me."

"I will be working full-time, any day. Just for the moment, I'm still home. But I promise I'll try to stay out of the way."

"Now you're talking. Too many cooks spoil the baby."

◆ ◆ ◆

The agency sent Arlie. She was a thirty-six-year-old woman from Guyana, of East Indian ancestry, divorced and childless.

"My husband was faithless," she'd said in slow and intermittently queenly English," so although I was pregnant, I did have my abortion."

Because of this confession, and because of her tinkling ankle bracelet, which Abigail found disturbing (alluding, as it did, to both sexuality and slavery), Arlie nearly didn't get the job. Her references, however, had been amazing. One letter said:

Never in my life have I met anyone like Arlie Rajani. Without a question, she is the most gifted person with children. My twins, who were born a bit early, needed constant care and supervision. With the patience of a saint, Arlie fed and diapered them, bathed them and took them to the park, twice daily. We trusted her implicitly, and she was worthy of our trust. We recommend Arlie without any reservation.

The other said:

Arlie came into our lives as a godsend. Though we had a lot of trouble with Cassidy, Arlie knew just how to handle him. When we got home from work, he'd be bathed, dressed in pajamas, and watching his ABC tape or his 123 tape. Even in the beginning of his infancy, Arlie showed him the dots. Later, she played clapping games with him and did difficult puzzles. Now he is a good student in the Huxley Academy. Anyone who has this woman for a nanny is lucky. We will miss her.

Good with twins, premature at that, and good at being a "take charge" sitter when parents worked full-time? Arlie seemed just the ticket. Besides, Liz, who had always been shocked at the "dreck" her friends had hired, was right. There weren't many quality people out there. Most of the other candidates had seemed dull, surly, or both. They had not been able to handle Abigail's prepared list of questions.

"What would you do if the child was rude to you?"

One said, with a thrill, "Oh, Lord, I'd teach him how to behave."

"How?"

"Oh, you just leave that to me," she'd said, narrowing her eyes and grinning boastfully.

"What would you do if I couldn't get home on time?"

This question stunned another candidate.

"I got my own child, you know, in day care, and I must be home at least by seven, miss. It's a two-way street." Then she reached into her handbag, took out her notepad and pen, and jotted something down on it. Abigail noticed her underlining her own note two or three times before replacing it, and the pen, in her bag.

Abigail needed someone flexible. And the fact that this candidate, like many others, had a child of her own that she didn't see all day was guilt-inducing for Abigail. How did nannies feel, taking care of a child in its own home, when her own child was taken care of somewhere else?

So Arlie, poised and unencumbered, seemed to have many advantages. It was true that she dressed up too fancily for her interview, lots of jingling jewelry and a silk suit that bore a lingering, sultry (though not unpleasant) aroma. The abortion saga was more than she needed to know. But Gary had explained:

"When you're dealing with this caliber of employee, Abigail, you're getting someone who dresses well. She's basically solid middle-class, like you and I, you know, not some lady from some slum. And as for that comment—you understand, the termination situation—I think, quite frankly, that she considers you a fellow woman, a woman of the world in fact, right? And she wants to be totally frank with you. You like honest, right? All the cards on the table? You get that, and more, with Arlie."

"I do?"

"And more."

24 ⚖ As soon as Arlie began working in her home, Abigail could see how indispensable she was. Arlie had patiently explained that, so far, Abigail had done nothing right.

"It's not your fault, you know. They don't teach you anything in the schools, so what on earth should you know about?"

It was true. Abigail had had no idea, despite her years of schooling, despite her Phi Beta Kappa and French award and National Merit Scholarship and Honors JD, that babies' bottoms needed to be creamed with the thick white cream and not the yellowy jellowy stuff. She did not know, despite graduating summa cum laude with a cumulative grade point average of 3.96, that talcum powder was dangerous and caused "lung clouds," and she did not know, despite a clerkship with a federal judge, that they needed to sleep only on their sides or they could swallow "the milking vomit." Arlie had explained all this, but if Arlie had not been there, who knows what might have happened?

"And see here, see she cries all the time with you."

It was true. Many hours had been spent walking with Chloe, holding and rocking her, settling her down with infinite cooing and pats on the shoulder. At times, she still seemed all but inconsolable, and needed to be put in her special little swing to calm down. This was even after feeding, burping, bathing, diaper changing.

"But look here—see here, look at me. See how calm, how nice she lie down and go to sleep for me?"

Abigail looked, and she saw that it was so. She looked and saw a perfect stranger curled up in blissful peace with her own Chloe. A baby who, minutes earlier, had been howling with rage, now spooned with a paid employee. And seemed to like it. To prefer it, if the truth be told.

"How—how do you get her to do that?"

"If I could tell you snip-snap, you wouldn't be paying me all the money, eh?"

She got up, laid the baby down in her bassinette, and went to the kitchen to prepare the next bottles.

Bottles were fine, Arlie said—how apt that she'd prefer them to Abigail's breasts, which were technically irreplaceable. And formula was fine (she preferred the rarer brand that cost double.) But never powdered formula, even with the best water. Only the canned liquid would do, because powder was "too thin." And when Abigail had gone along to the park with Arlie and Chloe, she'd learned that Chloe must sit in the sun for so many minutes (wearing a bonnet of course, but shoes optional), and in the shade for so many minutes. Abigail had not known that either. It was not in any of her books.

The things Arlie knew went far, far beyond book learning. This made her especially inimitable. One had to learn the lore at her very feet.

Arlie had been kind enough to let Abigail push the stroller

when park time was finished. But she had been shocked to see how she did it. Abigail had stepped off a street corner with the front stroller wheels first.

"Always you must lead with the back wheels, please, miss, always the back! You want to tip the baby out?!"

Contempt, on one end, and abashed silence on the other. Thus the two of them stood at the corner, the stroller hauled up again on the safe curb. Arlie had yanked it back with a harsh, punishing force.

"Hmm, you want that? Baby falling quite dramatically on the street?"

"No," said Abigail, dying to mutter, "obviously."

"Well then, why you lead with the front wheels then, see her flying forward?"

"But she's totally strapped in," Abigail had protested. The stroller was top of the line. Its strap was beyond effective, too—it tucked between the little legs and over the little shoulders and around the little waist. It was no seat belt but a truss. A harness. A test pilot could not have had a better strap than young Chloe Thomas.

"You relying on a *strap*?" Arlie snorted with an expression that held deep disappointment, almost contempt. As though saying, I know you all, you rich idiot matrons. You want to kill your babies. How low can you sink?

"Yes, the—safety strap," Abigail stuttered. "Isn't that—?" She looked at the traffic light. It had changed to "WALK" many times now. And yet Arlie would not allow them to proceed. This was like a game Abigail used to play with her sisters: Mother, May I? Except that now, she was the mother, and her paid helper said only "You may not."

Arlie was shaking her head and looking alternately up at the sky and at the passersby, as though to beseech heaven and earth with the words, See what I have to deal with?

What she actually said, to Abigail, was, "So someday you forget to close the *strap*, and the baby falls in the street, eh? I seen this more times than you can imagine, so don't tell me about it."

With that last testimony, Arlie took control of the carriage with a curt, "Take a rest now." As Abigail walked alongside her nanny, she felt like a great burden had been briefly lifted. No more mistakes could be made for the time being. But she had made so many in her short term as mother. Deep down, all the time now, she felt empty and foolish in Arlie's presence. How had this essentially illiterate lady gained such confidence? And why did she always look so cool and clean in her silky blouse and tight skirt? Stumbling alongside her, Abigail knew that her utilitarian sweat suit was covered in baby slime and smelled of spit up. My other outfit is a success suit, she wanted to scream. But no one would take notice of a woman who reeked of the stomach contents of newborns.

Later that evening, when the baby slept, Abigail stared into the bassinet and whispered, "Don't you know me? Don't you know your own mother?"

The softly sleeping baby gave no answer, but Abigail continued, "I carried you. I gave birth to you. Why don't you give me a little sign that you care! Just a little one!"

As Abigail's voice rose with the burden of her argument, Chloe awakened and shrieked.

"Aaaaaaaaaah! Aaaaaaaah! AAAAaaaaahhhhh!"

Abigail picked up the baby. She smelled of Arlie's moody perfume. Rocking the wriggling, disconsolate child, Abigail wished Arlie were there. She felt ignorant, harmful, bad. The perfume gave off a midnighty, hopeless atmosphere.

"Aaaaaaaaaaah! AAAAAAAHHHHHAAAAAAAA!"

"Please, Chloe, don't scream at me like that. I want to help you. I want us to be close."

The baby kept on screaming.

"Are you hungry? I've got some formula."

"AAAAAAAHHHHHHHH!"

"Like Arlie says, you know? Liquid?" The baby stopped crying and stared hopefully at the word "Arlie," or so it seemed to Abigail. She was silent as Abigail put her back in the bassinet to run and fill a bottle with formula. But when Abigail picked her up again, the baby screamed and slapped at the bottle as though trying to push it away.

"Arlie isn't here to give it to you. May I?"

The baby clawed at the air with curled, insistent fingers.

"Tear my bottle out of my hands if you could," said Abigail, sadly. "Tear me to pieces, too."

Chloe seemed to listen with interest to this synopsis. But then, retreating into some internal hell, her eyes darkened and she bawled like a succubus. Abigail exercised the next option.

"Maybe you're wet. I haven't changed you for a while."

She put the baby down to check. Chloe was dry, still covered with a thick layer of Arlie's good, white, smeary cream. Abigail tried to reclose the tape tabs of the diaper, but could never get it as neat and snug as Arlie had. When she was done, in a fashion, she shifted Chloe in her arms. The baby seemed to root for her breast.

"Is it me? Do you want to have some of my milk?"

Abigail sat down with the baby on her lap, and quickly yanked off her nightdress. She offered her breast to Chloe. For a moment, the baby sucked and pulled at the nipple. Then, red, furious, disgusted, she tore her head away and bellowed, hiccupped, and blasted:

"AH-AH-AH-AH-AH-AH-AH- AH- HA-HA-HA-HA-AHA -AAAAAAAAAAAAAAAAAAAAAAAAAAAAAAHHHHHH-HHH!"

Abigail nearly threw her child back into the basket. Chloe

was screaming harder than ever, legs and arms out straight, digits splayed wide in agony. Her crossed eyes fixed on her own red nose.

What do you want from me? Abigail thought fiercely. She struggled to choke back her own scream of pain.

Hours later, the baby slept, sniffling reproachfully, but Abigail still didn't know what she had wanted.

When Arlie returned the next morning, Abigail told her about the horrible tantrum, as she called it.

"What kind of tantrum?" said Arlie, taking the baby up swiftly and cradling her in one arm as she walked to the kitchen to boil bottles.

"You know, where they scream and kick their legs?"

"Oh, the gas colic," said Arlie, stretching Chloe out face down on her forearm and rocking her gently. "You just go like this, and poof!"

Indeed, the baby, who had been gurgling happily at the sight of Arlie, passed a blip of gas and fell promptly asleep. There was a smile on her lips that Abigail would have died for. Chloe had never smiled before.

"Oh, a smile, eh?" Arlie, though pleased, was calm, as though to say, Oh, a smile, I've seen those before. Nice, aren't they.

"Was it really a smile?" said Abigail, biting her lip to keep from crying. She was wearing a stained nightdress, and her hair was tangled and matted. Arlie discreetly averted her eyes and sang softly into Chloe's tiny ear:

"A little smile for Arlie, Arlie, Arlie . . ."

Chloe cooed. A real "mm-gooo" of pleasure. Arlie responded, nuzzling the baby's neck.

"She's gonna laugh soon, too."

"Uh-huh," said the mother, listlessly.

Abigail, listening and watching like a spurned lover, wanted to let go of herself and do something. Grab the baby and run out of the house (her house)? Wail out in pain (like a big fat Chloe) and see what happened? Instead of taking these options, she used her brain to rationalize the situation.

Abigail knew that Arlie was just doing her job. She was being paid (by Abigail herself, in fact) to make that baby love and trust her, pass gas in her face, smile, and go "mm-gooo." She also knew that if she, Abigail, the wrong person, showed her tears, Arlie would not soothe them, because that wasn't part of her duties. And she knew that wanting Arlie to console her was neurotic and needy and in any case impossible. You could buy a fake mother for your child, but not for yourself.

Turning her back on the nanny-and-baby scene, Abigail retreated to the haven of her room. If everything were taken care of—if it were all hunky-dory, as it seemed to be when she wasn't around—she might as well go back to work in earnest. Mr. Fudim would cite Abigail Thomas as a favorable precedent for the modern age: the first mother who had taken virtually no time off from the job! What a trouper! She would be setting a precedent for the books.

Abigail would be like O-Lan in the *The Good Earth*, who gave birth in the rice paddy and never stopped toiling. But she would be better than O-Lan, because she was a lawyer, not a coolie. Future generations of female associates would thank her for setting a positive example of what women, albeit mothers, could do with force and will. When she got her big corner office, she'd be able to shut the door and cry. But not just now.

As Abigail stood in her slip, deciding between the black suit with the black shoes or the gray suit with the gray shoes, she heard the doorbell chime. A double ring, Hello, hello: Tim. He visited so frequently that the doorman no longer announced him.

25 "Hi, Abigail, hi Arlie," said Tim, breezing in.

"Good morning, Mr. Vail," said Arlie, with respect for the man of the house (there was no other candidate, she'd noticed).

Abigail called out from her bedroom:

"Tim, is that you? I'll be out in a sec. I'm getting dressed."

Arlie stepped out of the kitchen, unpeeling her apron and fluffing her hair. It was shoulder-length, pitch-black, and blow-dried into a chic pageboy. Leaning on a hip, she took a good look at Tim, which he returned.

"I like that skirt," said Tim. It was long, and white and billowy, a strange contrast with Arlie's body-flattering turquoise sweater.

"I try my best, sir," she said, lowering her eyes.

"How's Chloe?" he said, after a moment.

"Sleeping like a lamb," she said, now looking up at him. "I gave her the bottle just now, and she went off after the two ounces. Just what she needed."

"Was it? We so rarely get 'just what we need.'"

Arlie hesitated before replying. "Want to see her now?" she finally inquired.

Tim thought she was referring to Abigail. "Of course I do. What's taking her so long to come out?

"Hey Abby!" he shouted, taking off a tweed jacket with well-worn leather elbow patches and tossing it down on the beige bench in the foyer. "What are you up to in there?"

"I'm getting ready to go back to the office, Tim," Abigail shouted, her tone deliberately carefree.

"What for? Did they call you or something?"

Abigail thought for a moment. She hated the feeling that any response she gave would be heard by Arlie as well. To Tim alone, she could have confided that no one in the office seemed to have any interest at all in her. Since her return from Grenada, they had seemed to wrest information from her, then leave her for dead. To Tim, she would have admitted that she was frightened not to be at the office, afraid of professional obliteration.

Her wonderful idea of a countersuit against Mrs. Mac-Adam seemed to have been swallowed with a gulp—perhaps absorbed by and currently nourishing the career of Dave Biddle-Kammerman, partner and father of twins. Dave hadn't taken, and wasn't about to take, any maternity leave, paternity leave, leave to love and languish. Dave was acting normal, that is to say, unstoppable. She could act that way, too. Apparently, she had to.

If Arlie were not there, Abigail would also have confided to Tim that she felt de trop in her own home. She knew Arlie looked down on new mothers, both working and not: the working ones, said Arlie, were "hard-hearts," and the nonworking ones, as far as she was concerned, "dumb-headed and jumpy." What did that make Abigail?

No wonder she felt unloved and unwanted. Chloe didn't need her. She looked up with delight when Arlie arrived each morning, and with disappointment, it seemed, when she left. After all, who had the experience, and who had none? Who had the energy, and who was exhausted? Who did the job with professional aplomb, and who did it as an ambivalent amateur?

Despite everything, I'm the one who really loves you, Chloe, thought Abigail. This isn't fair. This isn't real, or true. If I didn't pay Arlie, do you think she'd be here tomorrow? She'd be on to the next lovely baby, the next first smile, and the next. What was hardest for Abigail was knowing that she'd never be able to share these facts with Chloe. That would be cruel, a last laugh at her innocent child's expense.

If Abigail thought about these domestic matters any more, she knew she would start crying and ruin her office mask. Good old snowball, never melts, her father had said. It wasn't ever really more than a pose, her self-containment. It was a stunt, performed to impress. But if she melted now, who would support Chloe? Who would make sure Arlie kept coming back to love that child, on cue? Abigail couldn't let herself get lost in emotional webs. She had to get up and get out and get going.

Tim's question about the firm calling rang in Abigail's ears as she stepped out of her room, dressed in the armor of the legal world. The firm hadn't called, perhaps, but she had called herself up to the task. She had on a good wool suit in a rich shade of bronze, creamy opaque hose, a silk blouse, and—of course—her heels, brown faux-crocs with a high vamp. She had also sprayed herself with a classic, Chanel No. 5, to challenge Arlie's lighter drugstore scent.

"Hey, you're wearing your best suit," said Tim.

"And you've got some cologne on," said Arlie. "I can smell it from here. Baby don't need such strong smell around her little nose; she'll start sneezing. You see, already she starting to get those allergy pimples, look."

Abigail couldn't believe what she was hearing. She felt like saying, pettily, "well, you wear perfume, Arlie, and it has penetrated my home like a flea bomb," but she wasn't going to sink to that level. Besides, what Arlie wore wasn't real perfume but merely toilet water. Or was that Arlie's point? Abigail felt stupid again.

"I can't smell anything on either of you," said Tim, helpfully.

"She's wearing something heavy," said Arlie. "Maybe White Shoulders."

"Is there really a perfume called 'White Shoulders'? That's pretty poor marketing, geopolitically, I'd say," said Tim, looking at Arlie's tawny face. A small smile played on his lips. "I mean, what if they called some men's cologne Arabian Thighs? That'd be pretty offensive," he continued, beginning to openly chuckle. "Or maybe erotic, depending on your taste."

"I'm saving up for Bal a Versailles," continued Arlie. She sniffed the air with a thoughtful expression. "That one is elegant."

Abigail sensed that Arlie delved into her medicine cabinet while cleaning the bathroom. She owned many good perfumes, as well as a dizzying assortment of lotions, creams, and potions, some of which came with their own spatula for application. Every few days it seemed as though the quantities diminished. Abigail of course noticed all of this—tiny dabs added up to almost empty jars—but could say nothing.

"Bal a Versailles? That's pretty old-fashioned. Don't you mean Brown Sugar?" said Tim.

"Never heard of that one," said Arlie, puzzled.

"I'm wearing Chanel," said Abigail, who wondered why Tim was making up names for perfumes, and whether (and why) he was flirting.

"I wonder why you need to criticize me, Arlie. Just because

you know more than I do about babies doesn't mean you—please don't demean me."

"I did not be mean to you," said Arlie, with dignity. "But if you really think that I—"

The fact that Arlie clearly didn't know the word "demean" (and that she, Abigail, naturally did) gave her no satisfaction. Being smart and verbal had nothing to do with the contest for love in her home.

"I don't think it, I feel it!" she said, almost shouting. "I feel put down all the time now! You don't know what it's like to be a new mother!"

"Well," said Arlie, quietly and calmly, "you know I had that abortion, and so I was not lucky enough to have the experience directly."

Both Abigail and Tim looked stunned by the frank, bold intimacy.

With a small, bitter smile, Arlie continued, "And I honestly never knew I needed to give birth so I would finally please you—"

"You please me. You're more than competent. I would like you to support me."

"How I support you, you with all the fancy house and the money, excuse me? You understand?"

"You could try to notice that I'm a person, a woman, like yourself. I'm a human being, too, Arlie."

"But Abigail," said Tim. "She can't do that when you're from a different class and power structure. Don't you see that it's unfair to make that demand? That's why you two are getting so emotional."

"Yeah," said Arlie. "Don't yell at me for nothing I can't do."

"No, Tim," Abigail persisted. "Arlie has status here. Don't you see? I'm in Mothering 101, and she's like—postgraduate. I don't even know the alphabet, and she's writing the thesis and grading the papers, and giving me Ds—"

"You're jealous of her?" It was as though Arlie were no longer there.

"She knows so much more than I do. I never knew how much I never knew."

"So go to the library."

"Books! First of all, who writes them? Experts, mostly men. And the books are so confusing, they all say different things. It's more a hands-on thing, it's an art, and a feeling, you know?"

"You'll get there."

"Will I, Tim? Have you seen the way the baby looks at her?"

"You want the baby to look at you the way she looks at Arlie?"

"Yes, I really do," said Abigail, her voice betraying a trifle more sadness than she intended.

Arlie seemed to feel that this sidebar had gone on long enough. She took a breath and resumed her own argument:

"Well, if you think I'm not doing my job properly, Ms. Thomas, then call up the agency, you know, and get a refund and send me promptly on my way. Because no one is ever unhappy with Arlie Rajani."

Suddenly, Arlie's face contorted downward. In a gesture Abigail understood, she held herself back. Standing very still, she covered her eyes with her hands. Tim put his arm around her shoulder and held her. Turning her head toward his tweed jacket, Arlie took a deep breath, inhaling all the wonderful Tim smells. Abigail knew exactly what she was inhaling.

Now, she cleared her throat loudly. Tim's body made a slight shift, drawing her closer. Arlie exhaled, trembling, and pulled away from him. Standing alone, she faced her employer with an expression of strength regardless of outcome.

"I am ready now, Ms. Thomas. Call the agency. There are more babies and more jobs for me."

"Listen," Abigail said, trying not to dwell on the fickleness of nannies, or how plausible they looked in the arms of one's lover, as though it were possible for them to fill your shoes—and your nightie. "You know I have confidence in you."

"Yeah, the baby's doing great," added Tim. "Abigail told me she's getting to almost twelve pounds."

"Yes, that is true," said Arlie, in proud, dignified tones. "Eleven pound, thirteen ounces. I weigh her just this morning before her first bottle that I give her."

"Well, wow, that's great then, isn't it?" said Tim. "She was just a little peanut when she was born, and now she's a—a—"

"A Brazil nut!" said Abigail, encouragingly. She looked at him and he looked at her. "A cola nut," she tried again, thinking of an old commercial featuring these huge dark seeds.

"At least a filbert," he said, exploding in laughter as Abigail did, too.

"What do you think, Arlie?" Abigail said, trying to include her. "A chickpea? Garbanzo." The woman stayed somber.

"All kidding aside," said Abigail, abashedly, "I really appreciate you. You're indispensable to me and to Chloe. Please believe me."

"I must quit if I make you unhappy," repeated Arlie evenly. "Domestic Deliters send you someone who make you happy. Make you laugh like that."

It was funny, Abigail thought. Arlie wants love just like I do.

"Arlie Rajani treat every baby like it was her very own," continued the nanny, taking a step closer to Abigail. Abigail could feel the warmth of her body. She sensed a spice to it, beyond the manufactured heat of her eau de toilette. She wondered if Arlie had a boyfriend who could siphon off some of this heat.

"And that is why I make that comment about the perfume," continued Arlie. "I need my child to be comfortable. That is my job, and I must do it."

"I don't want to start up again, but since we're talking openly, why do you say 'my child' when she's, you know, mine?"

"Chloe's yours until the day you die. But she's mine when I'm on the job. That's how it works. You understand?"

"Yes." She didn't completely. Who could?

"My last boss, she make a big dinner party and tell me to serve it. I never say 'boo.' I serve, I clean up, and then I quit. They want me back now, they say Arlie, they cry Arlie, but I refuse them. I am a nanny, you understand? Not a maid and not a slave. And I know my work. My children always gain the weight, and they grow up tall and strong. And then I go on."

It seemed noble, thought Abigail. Unrequited love in its purest form, perhaps. Planting trees for someone else's shade. For hers.

"Now you go and do your job," said Arlie. "And leave her to me. I will keep her clean and wipe her bottom. I will give her the milk and I'll burp her. But all the time, you are the mama and she know it. She know it all the time. So don't wear that perfume. Go wash it off and let her smell her mother."

"All right, Arlie," said Abigail, dutifully going to the bathroom to wipe behind her ears. After that she checked the bassinet to see if Chloe had awakened. She wanted to see her own baby, be seen by her.

"This her big nap. Shhh. You go. Best not to wake her and she cry and you get so nervy again, eh?"

"I can stay, right Arlie?" said Tim. "I haven't seen the baby much lately."

Arlie hesitated. "She sleep for a long time sometimes."

"I can wait."

"Well, I've really got to go," said Abigail. No one said a word; no one stopped her.

For a moment, she hesitated. Was it proper to leave her nanny and her handsome man alone in the apartment? She had not slept with Tim since the baby's birth, and Arlie was beautiful. It was odd: she did not feel as threatened by the thought of Tim and Arlie as she did by that of her daughter with Arlie. Perhaps I'm not really in love with him, she thought. My body is, yes, she acknowledged, feeling a sudden regretful pang for him even as she walked away. But not me.

26 🌺 As soon as Abigail had gone, Tim rose up to lock the door behind her. Arlie walked silently toward the door, as though to check that he'd done the job correctly. The house was her domain, and she had to keep Chloe safe. Tim had locked only the bottom lock, so Arlie took care of the top one as well.

She bumped into Tim as he turned back to walk to the living room. For a moment he seemed to stand in her way. Then Tim walked over to the sofa, sat down, crossed his legs, and asked Arlie where she came from. She'd been on her way to check on the baby again.

"Huh?"

"I said, where are you from, originally? I used to live in the Islands, myself."

"Guyana." Arlie stood next to him now. Her expression read, Is that all?

The phone rang, and Tim swiped it up. He listened for a moment, then said, "Sorry, they're not here. No, I have absolutely no idea." He paused for a moment, then hung up and smoothly turned back to Arlie.

"That's where—off the coast of South America?"

"Yes. It's near Brazil."

"Some kind of colony—French?"

"No, English. Used to be. Not anymore, though."

Tim sprawled across the sofa and threw a leg up on the backrest.

"I grew up mostly in the Dominican Republic, believe it or not. At least my early years. So you're Indian?" said Tim, craning his neck up to get a good look at her. He looked down at Arlie's feet as well. That ankle bracelet was a nice touch, he thought. A thin little slave cuff. Some women wanted to feel that way—subservient.

"Long time ago my people came from there," Arlie was saying.

"Why?"

"Why they come there? Bauxite. They use it for industry. Workers, you know. My father had a general store, though. I was brought up real, solid middle-class."

"Oh, were you?"

"Yes. I had a good British education, you know, the uniforms and all, and here I trained with Domestic Delites to qualify for nanny."

"How long did you study?"

"Three and a half weeks. Then I did the CPR and got my certificate accredit."

"Come over here," said Tim, smiling. Mixed with mistakes of content and speech, her dignity and pride were irresistible. "I don't want to keep twisting around to see you."

"I was going to check on the baby when you stop me."

"She's sleeping, right? Otherwise, it's safe to say she'd be shouting and crying."

"Yes, so maybe I should boil some bottles in the kitchen," Arlie responded. "Baby will be thirsty after her nap."

"Wouldn't you rather sit by me?"

"I don't think Ms. Thomas hire me for that."

"Maybe she actually did. You do everything else for her. She doesn't feel like taking care of the baby, so you do it. You get to do all the dirty work, see?"

After a long pause, Arlie spoke: "You two are not happy together?"

"Oh, 'happy' is a complicated word, especially for a woman like our Abigail. She's a very complicated woman, and you can see all the joy that brings me. She doesn't actually know what happiness is. Even when it's staring her in the face."

"Yes, she has everything, luxury lotions, the best stroller, even a good job. . . ."

"Not to mention the gorgeous little baby girl you help her raise."

"But sometimes, you know," said Arlie, rising to a new topic within her expertise, "these new mothers, they get a little sad. The hormones, and that. Give her time to adjust. That can be the reason."

"Oh, sure. That must be it."

"Sometimes, men don't see it. But it's common, understand," she said. "It will pass, don't worry. Sometimes their bodies hurt for a long time from the soreness. The birth, it rip you."

"No, she's put back together, all right," said Tim. "She just doesn't—she just doesn't actually love me, Arlie," said Tim. "I can stand on my head for her and she won't really, I mean deeply, care." Tim looked into Arlie's face and felt he was about to cry. He hated himself for what he was doing. Who did he think this poor woman was, his nanny? Milagros? Did he think she'd hug him and make it all better?

Arlie looked away. "Excuse me," she said, "but it's not my job to talk about those things. It's not my professional training."

"Don't make your mind such a slave, Arlie. Don't be all 'professional.' I get enough of that from Abigail. Don't be rigid. I'm talking to you as a person. As a man with a broken heart—to a woman who might have a human heart inside of her."

Arlie hesitated.

"But Ms. Thomas, I see her smile with you, she laugh with you," she ventured. "And you talk like you like each other, you joke together, you hold hands and that."

"Sure. We like each other. We're friends, we're terrific companions." Tim sighed jaggedly. "And sometimes she holds my hand because her heels are so high she needs a strong arm on the side. To keep from falling."

"True! I try on some of those—" Arlie stopped midsentence, perhaps realizing she shouldn't have confessed that.

"No, who wouldn't? They make the legs look so, so hot, but can you walk in them? No."

"No," Arlie agreed.

"Couldn't you—couldn't you just sit with me, for one minute? The baby's sleeping." He patted the sofa and shifted over, giving Arlie room.

"Why you want to sit with me," she said quietly, even as she sat down. "Movie-star man like you. Well-dressed, talk smooth. Have anyone you want." Arlie's eyes were downcast as her fingernails circled, scritching and scratching at the thin, mesh fabric of her hose.

"I don't have what I want by a long shot, Arlie."

The phone rang again. Tim swiped it up, listened for a moment, then slammed it down.

"Who was that?" said Arlie.

"Someone who keeps calling the wrong number," he replied.

"Deep inside," he continued, looking intently into Arlie's confused eyes, "I'm actually as wretched a creature as you."

"What are you talking about, I'm not wretched!" said Arlie, bristling. "You be amazed how much I send home, how much dollars I put in the account. Thirty, fifty, hundred, sometimes more. I don't need anything. A dress, some shoes, a little rice, a honey cake."

"And that crazy cologne," he said, leaning over to breathe into her neck. Musk. He noticed the little bumps of skin, rising under his mouth. Goosebumps and a shiver.

"Arlie, I hope you won't mind if I ask a little question."

"What is it?" she said tentatively.

"You're a caregiver. But who takes care of you?"

"Don't trouble yourself about that," said Arlie, flushing.

"Don't you have any feelings?"

"Yes, of course I do. But I don't like to bring them here."

"But you do bring them here. You bring them everywhere, and that's what's so special about you. You're able to give love freely and receive it."

"To the baby, not freely, that's my job and I get wages for it."

"Get beyond that, Arlie. Come on; don't be like Abigail Thomas, Esquire! Think beyond the professional. Don't turn it on and off." Arlie stared at him as though she understood. "Be real, be a person," he persisted. "Have a heart, OK?"

"I do have a heart, what you think, I don't?" her voice rose up. "I was married and divorced, you know."

"Same as me. Married and divorced. We're both broken-hearted. Another Guyanese, was it?" said Tim, moving closer.

"Yes," she responded. "Marwan, that pig. Four years I give him my love and he—he—" Arlie began to cry.

"OK, OK," said Tim, soothingly. He put his arms around her. For a moment she stiffened, but then Arlie's muscles seemed to release as Tim hugged her. Slowly, slowly, he weighted her down until she lay prone on the sofa. She showed a certain blind obedience to gravity and nature. Then she stiffened again and spoke:

"Not here, I told you, not on the job. Maybe after work, all right? I mean it, after work," she repeated. His body pinned her, but gently. It floated above hers, touching lightly everywhere. Arlie was talking right into his ear, talking softly.

"Baby, what does it matter, I'm here now, let's not lose this moment," Tim responded just as softly, pressing her down again, feeling her blood pound beneath his body. He was madly challenged by their situation. Why did every single woman prefer work to love?

"Your heart is beating so quickly. Are you starting to like me a little?"

"Yes, a little, but the baby—" whispered Arlie.

"Remember, she's sleeping with a nice full tummy," he murmured, his face nuzzling hers. His stubbled cheeks scratched at her soft brown face. "I know how good you are at getting that baby into the deepest, most peaceful relaxation. Abigail told me that. You're a sorceress, you are. You have true female power."

Arlie was listening hard; Tim felt her buzzing concentration. With his own legs he pushed hers apart.

"Now close your eyes and just let me make love to you."

Tim's heart beat wildly as he felt Arlie surrender. Looking down at her face, he saw old hurts blurring into a dreamlike state of trust. And he hadn't even really touched her. How different from Abigail's wary sexuality. He felt as if he and this woman were both floating in a hot, dark space where all transgressions were permitted. No one had ever let him in so far, without fear.

Hands shaking, Tim lifted Arlie's billowing white skirt, a bridal veil that now hid her face from him. He put his hands on Arlie's surprisingly tight and resilient pantyhose and began to roll them down. The shoes were the last to go, delicate, strappy sandals that he gently unbuckled.

"There you are," he said, when he'd stripped her feet bare. The woman lay still below. Her breath came short and fast.

"Did your husband do this?" he asked, probing here and there with utter tenderness, alternating with rude demonstrations of will. "Or this?"

"No . . ." said Arlie. "No . . . Yes . . . I don't know. . . ."

Tim knew where she was, lost and floating in a sickly sweet haze. Her eyes rolled under their lids, the thick, dark lashes fluttering slightly. He was there, too. Only talking kept him from oblivion. A part of him was frightened by his own actions. What on earth was he doing here? Seducing someone just to get to Abigail somehow?

"Wait—" he gasped. "Let's stop. I don't want to take advantage of you. After all, you are her employee, and I don't know how Abigail would feel—"

"Oh, god, please don't stop now."

"But Abigail would definitely kill us both."

"No. Yes. Oh god, my job, my job."

"So should we stop?"

"No, please, let's go on, I wouldn't tell her. . . ."

"Don't you feel guilty? I do."

"No, please don't feel bad," said Arlie, weakly trying to rise and address him. "This was supposed to happen. I've been praying for love. Don't you know I was lonely like you?"

"I'd hoped so," Tim acknowledged, with a puzzling mixture of misery, panic, and elation. "Listen," he said, holding her face so he and Arlie could see eye to eye. Her hair was rumpled now, her expression fully honest. She was more beautiful than Abigail had ever been. "I know that in some way we need each other. But I need to tell you that I'm very confused."

"All right. Me, too."

Still pinning her eyes with his, Tim resumed his lovemaking.

"Ohh . . ." said Arlie, falling down again, down. Her head rolled left to right, right to left.

"You're not faking with me, the way you sometimes do with that baby. Look at you, squirming."

"I don't fake with the—" Arlie protested. The words caught in her throat. She could hardly speak.

"Oh, come on," said Tim, his movements stopped.

"If you got fired, you'd find another job. It's the love business, Arlie. I know. My own dear mother hired a nanny to love me, and she did, by god, she did her job and got paid for it."

"That's no shame, to need the money," Arlie spoke hoarsely.

"No, of course not. Tell me. How much does she pay you to love her little kid, Arlie? Minimum wage? More? My mother got me loved for pennies; wasn't that economical?"

His voice sounded harsh, but then it softened as he began frankly pounding her.

"What should I pay you for loving me tonight?" he murmured, his voice a mocking contrast to the brutal way he moved.

Arlie didn't or couldn't respond. Her eyes were now squeezed shut.

"Anything, yes, I don't care, just take me—"

"No, take me! Take my heart," said Tim, through his teeth, as though mad. "It's used, but it's free. Go on. Take it all!"

With these words, he pushed in hard, like a knife blade, stabbing. Arlie grabbed him with arms and legs, prehensile. Tim watched her, tears falling from both their eyes. He had not managed to get to anyone before. Not to Milagros, his nanny. Not to his cold ex-wife, and certainly not to Abigail. They had all remained at a safe distance. They had gotten away from him. But he felt he got through to this woman, pursued her to the end of where she lived and captured her entirely.

Arlie was lost in him, shuddering and dewy-lashed. They held each other like survivors of a shipwreck.

◆ ◆ ◆

The baby awoke. Tim sat up and quickly wiped his eyes as Arlie ran out to the child. As she changed Chloe, Tim adjusted his clothing. Then Arlie wordlessly passed the child to Tim, stepping into the kitchen to warm up a new bottle of formula. Her movements, he sensed, were efficient, practiced. She was back to her regular work; she was catching her breath and returning to the ordinary world.

Tim lingered in heaven. He was more tender than he'd ever been before, kissing the baby's head and sniffing her ten tiny toes. Chloe was getting to know him; she was quiet in his arms, docile and trusting. But Arlie's bustling pace was obviously forced. Tim sensed she wasn't his for the taking anymore. Fair enough.

As he was leaving, Tim spoke with an affected casualness:

"Look, what I said about the—your payment. It's not entirely facetious. I know you don't have much. You work hard. I make a lot more than you do. So here. Take it."

He took a rumpled bunch of tens from his pocket and held them out to Arlie.

"It's what I have on me, and I want you to have it. I feel bad."

Arlie looked into Tim's eyes with an expression he couldn't read. It seemed ardent, like fury, and yet there was dignity and distance in it.

"What are you doing to me now?" she spoke levelly. "Before, I don't know. But now, now, you're fucking me. Now. Piece of shit, you."

"Forgive me, I told you I felt confused," he responded. "I feel guilty toward Abigail, and I feel even worse about you. So please take it. Please. Money means very little to me, to be honest, but I'm aware of what it means for you."

Tim placed the bills in Arlie's hands, but she let them drop to the floor. He kissed her goodbye on her cheek. Her flesh felt cool as marble now. He imagined she would pick up the cash when he left. Somehow, that thought made him feel even worse.

27 ✕

Abigail walked into the offices of Fletcher, Caplan with a sense of nervous expectation. The receptionist, a statuesque redhead called Sherry, said, "You're back again," without expression. "For good this time?" she added, as Abigail walked down the hall, her heels sinking into the Oriental rugs. Associates and paralegals scurried as ever, too busy to do anything but nod as they raced here and there.

Abigail entered her own office, expecting to find piles of work on her desk, but it still seemed empty and hollowed out. There was nothing on her desk; the phone was not flashing; there was only one little note stuck to it. It was pink and it said "Trubridge."

"He called here again?" she asked her secretary, Tina.

"Yeah, a couple of days after you had the baby. Guess word gets around."

"Possibly. But no one here seemed to take notice except Rona—an associate in a different department. What did he want?"

"He was after your personal numbers, home and cell, but of course I knew not to give those out. Especially not to him. He tried real hard, and you know, he puts on a real good show, Richard, very tempting. I almost gave in. I mean, I thought he sounded desperate! But these acting jobs, and believe me, I've heard a few—they don't work on me. I'm a professional. And I work in a law office. Don't even try to manipulate me, you know?"

"Oh, that's good to know," said Abigail quietly.

"You know what I mean?" Tina repeated, continuing to be satisfied with herself.

"Yes, I do know. Thanks, Tina. Good work."

Abigail crumpled the little note in her hand, but held on to the ball of paper.

"Was that it? No one else called?"

"Nope. Most people didn't expect you back so soon."

After a moment, Abigail punched in Dave Biddle-Kammerman's direct-dial digits. He picked up with a curt "Biddle-K."

"Thomas, A.," Abigail replied. "Remember me?"

"Thomas, A.?"

"For heaven's sake, Dave, you officious jerk. It's Abigail Thomas."

"Oh, oh. Abigail! How—how's the baby?"

"Fine, Dave. She's fine, I'm fine. Everyone's fine."

"I really meant to come over and see you at the hospital, but—you'll get this—I'm all caught up in the twins."

"Uh-huh."

"You of all people know how complicated it is."

"Indeed I do."

"Jen's ecstatic," said Dave, referring to his wife. "She's nursing on both breasts at the same time. Can you believe it? Got a good sitter? That's key. Ours is a lifesaver. She comes from Central America and speaks to Lloyd and Drew only in Spanish. Problem is, I don't know what she's saying, and neither does Jen. Probably 'Keel the gringos,'" he laughed.

"You're so politically correct, Dave. We could really have used you in the Caribbean."

"So what's up?"

"Well, everyone says that when you have a baby, law firms act insensitive to the fact that your life has changed, and send you all this work you can never get to. However, that hasn't happened to me, which makes me feel left out. To be honest," she added, "I'm nervous."

"Hormones, Abigail, hor—"

"No, Dave," she interjected, raising her voice. "My hormones are in check. Here are some facts: a couple of weeks ago I gave Fudim a progress report about the case, but haven't heard from anyone—"

"Which case in particular, Abigail?"

"Which case 'in particular'? You know, the one you sent me down to 'Gre-*nay*-da, not Gre-*nah*-da,' for? The one with the plane accident and the leg and the non compos mentis plaintiff?"

"And you had your accident, too—the one where you nearly lost your baby. Aw, Abigail, I'm so sorry how things have worked out for you."

"How did they work out? They haven't finished working out yet, Dave. I'm still working them out. And I'm working them out pretty well."

"No, I mean, you had to go to the hospital and all that, and the baby came early, or so I heard. I mean, I wasn't counting the weeks to your due date or anything."

He probably was, thought Abigail.

"Everything's fine, I told you," she said. "Baby's great."

"Got a sitter?"

"What do you think? I'd leave her home alone with a note on the fridge?"

"Well, sometimes it's hard to find a good one. We had my wife's mother live in for a—was it the first month? Six weeks?" Actually, he hadn't given the matter much thought. He'd gone back to work the next day. "She was a real life-saver."

"But my mother's dead, remember?"

"Oh, sorry, last year, right?"

"Give or take." They used to be friends, and she was sure he'd seemed empathic over her loss.

"So sorry, really sad, I remember she was sick for a while." He paused. "So which agency are you using?"

"Domestic Delites."

"We used Premium Pamperers. Expensive, but they're worth the sacrifice, right?"

"The sitters?"

"No, the babies. Harvard class of 2038, Abby!

"Rah-rah."

"Start savin' up right now!"

"That is the plan," said Abigail drily.

"Right. So in terms of the near future, are you coming back soon, or have you totally fallen in love with the kid?"

"Not mutually exclusive. You love your kids, right?"

"You mean you're coming back soon?"

"I'm actually sitting here as we speak, Dave."

Dave Biddle-Kammerman was uncharacteristically silent for a moment.

"Where is 'here'?"

"The hallowed halls of Fletcher and Caplan. Check it out. Hang up your phone and come over to my office."

Dave came over to Abigail's office. When he entered, he found her sitting at her desk, her hands folded neatly atop it.

"Do you see my work space?" she said, indicating a vast expanse of bare, shiny wood. The desk was beautifully made, and its rivets and drawer pulls were polished brass.

"Oops. Do you want us to chip in and send you a floral

arrangement? They have those nice ones with the big bottle and the ribbon and the balloon."

"No bottle, no ribbon, no balloon, Dave. Yes, you have correctly observed that my desk is empty. True, there are no flowers, but more important, there are no files. So I would like—right now—to have access to all the work you're doing. Forward everything you have, and get some hard copies made. This way, I can help you on your cases, or you can help me on mine—however you'd like to put it."

"Oh, sure, sure. Well, we're fine-tuning that countersuit at the moment. It's a real good idea, Abigail."

"It really is. And does anyone remember whose idea it was?"

"No one's forgetting anyone, all right?" said Dave. "But if you don't mind being a real team player, which is, by the way, what the firm looks for in its partners, I'll take a little credit for myself and for Mr. Fudim. Remember that memo I relayed to you, about how the client wanted the earth scorched? I wrote it, which started the ball rolling. And that's what the countersuit will do—silence old granny but good."

"What do you mean?"

"MacAdam was suicidal, right? Well, if she wants suicide, we'll give her suicide. Legally, of course."

"Yeah, let's kill the poor old girl." Abigail had spoken without thinking. In fact, she had muttered. But Dave had heard her. He shoved his face into her space and spoke like a real litigator:

"Sarcasm, Ab? Whose side are you on with that 'poor old girl' crap? She's not your grandma, you know."

"It's an objective observation," said Abigail, "of the actual truth. Which is always a good place to start, don't you think?"

Dave did not seem to agree.

"Well, here are the facts, and I think I know more of them than you," she continued.

"Doubtless."

"Always room for doubt, as you yourself so often say, but thanks for agreeing. So. 'Poor, old, girl.' Let's parse that. Mac-Adam's been impoverished, and she's had misfortunes. Does that cover 'poor'? The reasonable man—or woman—would have to agree. She's lost her dogs and her garden and her leg, and part of her house is destroyed. That's unfortunate. And she is fairly old—even given our increased lifespans and broadening standards. So that adjective applies. As for 'girl,' while that can be a sexist term, she is sort of girlish, you know? Possessing the traits of a young girl. But you'd have to meet her to see that. And you'd have to be perceptive. It's kind of an intangible thing, Dave."

"But as for 'sides,' naturally I'm on the client's side. Cranebill's."

"Abigail. You sound funny. What happened when you went down there? You spent time alone with MacAdam. Just tell me. I'll understand. Trust me. I'm on your side."

"Good to know."

"Did she get your sympathy or something? Yeah, I bet she tried. She's very manipulative. We sent someone else down to depose her, some little associate, and that poor guy came out not only liking MacAdam, which is bad, but reluctant to work on the case against her, which is worse. Maybe she paid him something on the side. Same thing happen to you?"

"Oh, please. What happened to the guy?"

"Fudim told him to go work somewhere else. Let him work for the NRDC if he wants to hug a tree."

"Who was this pathetic softy?"

"A little second-year. Carl Granger."

"Carl Granger? I interviewed him for the job. He told me he just bought a nice condo and he's up to his ears in bills. I don't think he can afford to—"

"My point exactly," said Dave, giving her a hard look. "They pay, we play. We're lawyers here, and do our clients' bidding. Right? Now, I'm also going to do what you asked. I'm going to copy everything I have, and have my girl put it on your desk. But don't blame me if it's overwhelming. You'll be swimming in work, Abigail."

"Do you have that deposition?"

"The one the Granger kid took off MacAdam, that one, right? It's—it is somewhere, I know that. But I mean, we're simply not gonna use it. It's got some very damaging information in it. And of course, there was the other side, just lapping it up."

"What damaging information?"

"I'm certainly not going to tell you."

"Why not?"

"Because we would have a much, much weaker case if we 'knew' it. So we don't 'know' it. If I told you, it would mean that obviously I had knowledge of it, and then you obtained knowledge of it—and we can't have any of that. And you'd face a certain amount of exposure as an attorney."

By "it," Abigail suspected that Dave was talking about the camera that was found on the plane. Up until now, only she and Jackson Moss had discussed "it." Jackson had told her frankly about the camera, admitting the possibility that her client had actually been spying, just as Evelyn MacAdam thought. But how would she have gotten that information? Certainly not from Abigail. Jay must have leaked it to Miranda or Cora-Lee. Despite herself, Abigail was glad. The truth had a nice way of falling through the cracks and landing in your lap, whether you liked it or not.

So Jay was another one of those people, she thought. Rule breakers, like Evelyn herself. People who felt that principles trump procedure.

"Risky or not, I'd still prefer to see that depo," said Abigail.

"I'm a senior associate on the case. I'd like to see all pertinent materials. And I feel sure you can scrounge it up somehow."

"Why are you so interested in it?"

"Oh, don't look for trouble, Biddle. Partner though you are, it just doesn't feel right to have you know more about this than I do." Besides, she thought, if she left it to him, the shredder could be busy tonight.

"Talk to me later. I've got some paperwork to do now," he said, speeding out of Abigail's office.

After a few minutes, she leaned out and saw Dave Biddle-Kammerman lugging a heavy box of documents over to his secretary. Abigail waited for him to disappear, then checked his office thoroughly for the missing deposition. Not surprisingly, it was nowhere to be found.

28 ⚖️ When she returned to her desk, Abigail was delighted to find that Mr. Fudim, no less, had buzzed her. Perhaps, as she'd hoped, he appreciated her coming back after so short a time postpartum. As originally promised.

It seemed like ages since Abigail had last sat in this great leather chair, in this room with the samurai sword. Fudim had talked about hara-kiri then, she remembered; he had said that motherhood was "career suicide." And yet he didn't seem surprised to see her back so soon after the birth.

"I'm all geared up," said Abigail, trying to fan enthusiasm for her own grit. "I felt put out to pasture, but now I feel great. Ready to go."

"Did I ask you how you felt? I don't recall."

"No you didn't," she admitted, chastened.

"Thomas: Have you heard about that stupid associate?"

"Carl Granger? Dave Biddle-Kammerman told me something about him."

"Biddle had Granger's deposition. He tells me it was full of garbage."

"Do you happen to have a copy of it?"

Fudim took a moment to give Abigail a nasty stare.

"'Do I happen—'?" Had he used a falsetto to mimic her female voice? "*NO,*" he continued, thundering. "*NO.*"

"OK, you don't have a copy," she said flatly.

"The fewer copies floating around, the better. There's some very damaging information in it, facts alleged that we had no prior idea about. Unfortunately, our client has not been entirely forthcoming. More to the point, we can't use the information, and we're just going to have to pretend we never heard about it. Catch my drift?"

"Not entirely," Abigail confessed. "I've always been a real stickler for information. Facts have been my business for the last seven years, and now you want me to—"

"You know, Abigail," said Fudim, cutting her off with a slight edge of fury, "this really reminds me of another case we had here, it was a number of years ago. One of the lawyers, a partner, in fact, just could *not* keep his big mouth shut. It was the same kind of thing, the client kept a little secret, and we found out about it. It came to our knowledge."

Was he talking about Richard? Abigail's mind reeled, and she felt herself flushing deeply, as though she'd done this act with him.

"He disclosed?"

"He *betrayed.*"

"I see," she said quietly, trying to make sense of what her boss was saying. Richard had betrayed her, too, and she'd heard he was professionally rotten in some way—but what had he actually done? Something she now felt like doing? And would that be betrayal?

"Now, Abigail, what could we do, under these circumstances? We pretended not to know, and in legal fact, we didn't really, totally 'know'—and what is knowledge anyway, you get me? It comes, it goes, one remembers, one forgets to remember. And so, we won the case. Client was thrilled. We were thrilled.

"Until that big-mouthed attorney went over to opposing counsel, told them the info we'd omitted, and—well, it was devastating. We lost on appeal, and of course we lost our client."

Abigail's head was swimming, an almost pleasant sensation.

"Your own attorney came forward with facts favorable to opposing counsel?"

"Shocking, I know. To be fair, he didn't think of it as 'helping.' It was more a 'full disclosure' thing, he said."

"Is he still practicing?"

"Not by my definition, he isn't. Whatever he's doing, it's propelled by insanity. Who is he, Don Quixote? Anyway, who cares? You're not getting my gist!"

"What is the gist—the MacAdam case, right?"

"Yes, I'm worried sick about the widow MacAdam. See, even without that extra piece of ammo, I have this feeling MacAdam's gonna twist us around. She already got to Granger, who's fresh out of school and should have more spine. She's had a go at your sympathies, too, no doubt. And eventually, of course she's gonna twist the judge and the jury around. Why would anyone want to impoverish such a cute old gal?"

"I don't know. But I guess Cranebill wants to."

"Well, yes—of course he wants to, if it works to his advantage!" Fudim paused. "Are you admitting she's cute? I was playing devil's advocate," said Fudim.

"So was I," Abigail answered quickly.

"No, you weren't. Biddle-Kammerman told me that he thinks you're sympathetic. Cut that out. I'm serious. Are you nursing your kid or something?"

"Not really, not anymore."

"Those hormones'll kill you. Melt you into a puddle. I don't like to get personal, but there's a—a kind of motherly look in your face now."

"There is?"

"Yeah, there kind of is. Not that it isn't sweet. MacAdam probably has it, too, when she's not plotting to flatten us. And worse, she's gonna sit so sweetly in the courtroom, cute as a button, and show off her stump. Who's gonna argue with her? Some trampy Hun model nearly buzzed her off the face of the earth, killed her gorgeous doggies and hurt the sweet little herb garden that she lived for—and she's guilty and has to pay?"

"Well, I can see what you're saying. But our side might have probative weight. She did show reckless disregard and—contributory—"

"Weight, shmeight. Real people are trained to like all the ladies, the puppies, the babies, the plants. You understand me?"

"I do. 'People' can be so sentimental."

"Speaking of which. Go home. Come on, it's your first baby! I'm gonna get blamed for hauling you in here so soon. Dave Biddle-Kammerman's already accusing me of being a slave driver. Told me to go easy on your workload."

Abigail took this in. That snake Dave was definitely trying to shut her out.

"But if you're so worried, Mr. Fudim, I'd like to discuss strategies for keeping her off the stand—non compos mentis, for instance—"

"No, that might make it impossible to collect on countersuit. Don't worry. We'll figure it out. You've done your best, and for now it's not your problem. We'll factor it all in. You've got a baby that needs you."

"Needs me? That fact is not yet in evidence," she tried to joke.

Not laughing, Fudim went over to the door and held it for her, so out she went, heading homeward.

◆ ◆ ◆

When Abigail opened the door to her apartment, she walked in on a scene that once would have startled her. There was Arlie, patiently holding up a large piece of oak tag with two dots on it and saying, "Two, two, two."

"You're doing great, Arlie," said Abigail. "My friend Rona once explained about these dots to me." She remembered that she had not spoken to Rona for a while, and resolved to call her.

Chloe squealed with sudden joy at the sound of Abigail's voice, which made her so happy she found herself beaming.

"Had a good day, then?" said Arlie.

"I was able to go to work and not worry about anything," Abigail replied. "So thanks so much, Arlie. You make my life possible."

"Well," said Arlie. "I know you have to teach these babies, otherwise they don't get so intelligent. And even though you don't mention it to me, I do it. Because I want this child to be the greatest thing, you know. Maybe she'll be a president, an actress, a model. Anything."

"Terrific. Thanks again." Abigail was by now eager to get into her bedroom, shed the heels, and wriggle out of her tight, scratchy suit, but Arlie was speaking more and more urgently.

"And one day, she can be a lawyer, even, like her mama, and make so much money she can do anything she want!"

"Oh, Arlie," said Abigail, touched by the naïveté of the sentiment. She had once felt that law would let her do "anything." Maybe it could, but right now, she didn't see how. Still, it was nice to remember its potential.

"She lucky to have a mom like you, so professional, you know?"

"Thank you for that vote of confidence, Arlie. Not everyone thinks that mothers should work at a demanding career. I think you're pretty wonderful yourself," she added generously. "And what you do is very important, you know? It's vital."

Arlie didn't answer. She had moved on to the concept of "three":

"Three. See? One, two, three. Two on the top, one on the bottom. Only lonely dot on the bottom, see, baby? Oh, you looking to where your mother went? OK, she'll be back in a minute."

Abigail entered her bedroom to change out of her business clothes. When she came out, wearing yoga pants and an old T-shirt, Arlie was putting a light load of laundry into the washing machine. Chloe sat in her little chair, watching everything.

"She like the sound of the washing machine, look," said Arlie.

"She does? I didn't know that."

"Sure. It relax her. She look so happy."

"Shall I—may I sit with Chloe for a minute when you're finished loading up the wash? I just want to be with her."

"You don't have to ask me, Ms. Thomas. She is your own baby, you know."

"Thanks for saying that, Arlie."

Arlie left the room to straighten up the bassinet. Abigail sat with her child. Chloe gazed at her mother, smiling, openmouthed. Abigail looked into her eyes, transfixed by her joy. It spread over her like sunshine; it illuminated her. She didn't know that she herself was smiling, but she was.

Only after a few minutes did she notice that her baby was drooling. Abigail found a dishtowel and carefully began wiping the saliva off Chloe's face. The baby sat impassively as Abigail dabbed her chin dry. Then, all of a sudden, she began shrieking, as though stung.

Arlie came running.

"What happened, baby?"

Chloe sat there, her lower lip curled into a pout. Fat tears crawled down her round pink cheeks.

"I—I was wiping her chin," said Abigail. "She had some spit up, some drool."

"But what you wipe with? You use that?" said Arlie, indicating the dishtowel.

"It was all I could find."

"No, no, Ms. Thomas. It too rough for her skin. You need to use a cloth baby diaper, you know I keep a pile in the closet over there by the front door, and there is some by the bassinet. They are softer. She need that, especially with her face rashes that she get. Maybe you touch a pimple."

"Maybe," said Abigail humbly.

"Here, let me get one of those soft diapers to show you."

"No, I know which ones you mean. I'm just happy she's stopped crying now."

"I'm going to put some cream on that little face, all right baby?" said Arlie, taking Chloe out of her baby seat and lifting her onto her shoulder. They headed to the changing table, where Arlie kept the ointments.

"No—don't go yet," Abigail pleaded. "I need to tell you that—that I won't be going into work tomorrow."

"You'll be here?"

"Yes, I think I'll stay home for a while," said Abigail quietly. "I hope you won't mind. I know that Gary—from the agency—said the sitters like to have things the way they like them, but—"

"I understand. All the mothers, they say it's hard to leave the baby when they're so small and cutie-cutie, eh? Don't worry. I'll be going to the park if the weather's nice. You can come along with us. It's all right. Mr. Gary don't know Arlie. I'm not bothered."

"Thanks. I think I will go to the park with you and the baby."

Abigail was tempted to tell Arlie the truth: the firm, in a show of benevolence, preferred that she stay home for now. Privileged as she seemed to be, she too could not do everything she wanted.

29 🍼

There they sat, the three of them, on a park bench. Since Chloe was too small to do much, she lay in the carriage, at Arlie's feet. Abigail felt restless. She paced around, checking out the bucket swings, the mini climbing frame, the sandbox. Though it was a crisp day, the sun was warm and the air calm. Bundled children toddled around, watched at a distance by their caregivers.

Returning to the bench, Abigail found Arlie surrounded by a flock of nannies, each with a baby in a stroller. It was as though they had waited for her, the mother, to leave so that they could descend. Now Arlie was chatting and smiling with the other nannies, more comfortable than Abigail had ever seen her. The women seemed to know one another, including Arlie in their easy camaraderie. All the while, with calm professional instinct, Arlie pushed Chloe's stroller back and forth, soothing her. Chloe fell asleep under a canopy of branches above the benches.

Abigail remained standing, apart. She felt the way she'd felt when she'd walked into that remote bar in Grenada and didn't find Jackson Moss—alone, apart, and on display. She felt the nannies size her up, noticing her blue sweatpants and her big orange parka, her clunky running shoes and disheveled hair pinned down by a large barrette. She felt they had her pegged as they talked to Arlie in lowered tones, their eyes looking at her, then away. A nervous mother, a sloppy girl (and probably not that rich). No use to her child, a nuisance to her busy employee.

All at once, Abigail leaned over to her daughter's caregiver and said, "You know, Arlie? I just remembered. I have an important phone call to make. Work-related," she added. This conceit helped salve the hurt Abigail felt at being left out of this group. It made her seem sure and strong and necessary somewhere else.

"I'll just say goodbye to . . . to my baby," she said, stepping over to look into the carriage. Arlie held her back gently.

"She's sleeping now. See, Ms. Thomas? Best to let her rest."

Abigail felt the other nannies staring at her, as though to see what she would say to this challenge.

"Oh, you're right, she has gone to sleep," she said, gazing at her child with a sense of utter longing. How had all this distance come between them? Nannies, feedings, park trips, work—and sleep. This soul had once lived inside her; they could not have been closer.

"I'll just whisper, then."

Arlie gave no resistance, nor did she exchange glances with the other nannies, some of whom were bold enough to shake their heads.

"Goodbye, my darling baby," said Abigail, her voice cracking from the strain of not speaking more loudly. "I love you more than anything."

She had never said it before, and now she had said it in front of the world. Her heart felt like cracking in two. If it had, she would have taken one half away, wherever she was aimlessly headed, and left the other behind, with her little dreaming child.

◆ ◆ ◆

When Abigail returned home, she checked herself in the lobby mirror and found that her hair was matted with sweat. She had buttoned her parka the wrong way, and one of her sneakers had a loose and flopping lace. The doorman called out that he had a package for her. She took it upstairs, dropped it on her bed, and cried lustily.

She had been holding in this outburst since the baby had been born, and now, like the baby, it had to come out. Abigail sobbed out loud, walking through her home with a slow, nostalgic, ceremonial pace. She looked in the closet, at those soft baby-wiping cloths that Arlie had mentioned, and wept at the sight of them. She walked over to Chloe's bassinet, picked up her little sateen pillow with the lace trim, and held it to her face, soaking it with her tears. Maybe Arlie would think Chloe had done some more drooling.

Finally, spent, Abigail went back to her room and tore the package open. She could see the Grenada stamps—had it come from Jackson? Inside was a professional camera with a large tele-photo lens, the glass shattered. The camera was covered with dried soil, significantly battered, and loaded with film.

Yes, Jackson Moss had sent it to her, along with a note he'd handwritten. It bore a single, simple sentence:

You'll know what to do with this.

I will? thought Abigail. For a long, dazed moment, she wondered if the camera contained shots of a basil-rosemary planta-tion in the West Indies. She could even hear Evelyn MacAdam's voice, now proud about her plants, now enraged at the thought that she'd been spied on, strafed, sabotaged.

When she came back to herself, Abigail carefully slid the camera and note back into their padded envelope. The package sat there, wrapped up again but bulging, expectant with material.

"I don't know what to do with you," she muttered, as though apologizing to it.

And then, abruptly, surprising herself, Abigail realized that she had to call Richard Trubridge. At first, she couldn't remember the name of his firm. Finally, "Murdock" came into her mind. A sinister sound, but a start. She could find the rest from that little piece of the puzzle.

When Abigail finally got through to the office, however, the secretary said, "Mr. Trubridge is not working here at the moment."

"What do you mean?"

"Mr. Trubridge is not working here at the moment."

"Yes, I know what you said," said Abigail, who couldn't help sounding testy. "I asked what you meant. Is he working somewhere else?"

"No, miss. He's currently on a leave of absence."

"For how long?"

"I'm not aware of the details. All I know is that it's a leave of absence."

"What kind of leave?" Abigail asked. "Paternity leave?" she spat out, feeling reckless. She was finally getting sick of not knowing everything that mattered, at work and in her personal life. Sick of it.

"Oh, no, no," said the secretary, letting out a faint chuckle. "But I do believe it is some family concern."

"Oh," said Abigail, further deflated by the words "family" and "concern."

Hanging up, she found herself hugging the package Jay had sent her. She felt she had to hang on to something.

30 ❀ Richard Trubridge did have family concerns. Last spring, his older brother, Allen, had developed a heart condition, leaving him unable to work, and just as his family—Lauren and three children, Ellen, Hal, and little Martin—had adjusted to this, Allen had had a debilitating heart attack, and he needed lengthy rehabilitation.

Now Lauren Trubridge, Allen's young and high-strung wife, had developed what the doctors called nervous exhaustion, and she had to be hospitalized as well. This left Richard no choice: he had taken a leave of absence until his sister-in-law recovered and his brother came out of Rusk Rehabilitation.

It was a world that Richard, even with years of family law behind him, had never encountered. Married only briefly, in his thirties, he had experienced the vicissitudes of family as a paid professional, by proxy. Now it was real.

The two eldest (the girl was twelve; the boy, ten), were in school, with after-school activities taking them straight through to supper time. For high school, their parents planned to send them to an elite boarding school, and they both had the ability and discipline to thrive there.

But Martin, the three-year-old, had not even been admitted to the nearby Montessori, and his depressed mother had made no other arrangements. Thus Richard, unmarried, childless, and in his forties, had made his first acquaintance with the playground.

At first, Martin had refused to go anywhere at all with uncle Richard. Nor would he call him uncle Richard, as he'd been urged to by his mother on the phone. Even when Richard managed to strap Martin into his stroller (for which he was almost too big), wheeling him to a lovely playground on the Fifth Avenue side of the park, Martin had turned around and called his uncle "Big Stinky." He had said it with real malice, and then repeated it louder, with a variation: *"Big Stinky, I hate you so bad."*

After days of pushing this child in his stroller, Richard was exasperated. Martin wouldn't get out, wouldn't play in the sand, hang on the rope, climb on the rocks, or cross the little bridge. He wouldn't do anything.

"Why won't you play?" Richard kept asking. "Are you missing your mommy and daddy?" The answer: *"Big Stinky, I hate you."*

Then one day, for a lark, Richard pushed the stroller in the opposite direction, toward the East River. He was thinking that the child might like to look at the birds by the waterside. Besides, Richard was becoming embarrassed by all the sitters looking at him, unable to make a dent in Martin's obstinacy. Surprisingly, Martin did begin to look more game as they headed eastward, or at least more animated.

"Water park! Water park!" he screamed, kicking his large, heavy legs.

"Is there a—a water park there?" said Richard, leaning his long, Lincoln-esque face into the stroller. Martin stared into his uncle's friendly, aqua eyes with their rectangular black flames and finally nodded. It was like that first providential moment between Helen Keller and her teacher.

"Where is it?" asked Richard eagerly.

From the corner of his eye, he thought he saw another associate he'd vaguely known from his old firm. Rhoda something, he thought, or was it Rhonda? She was wheeling a baby in an elaborate stroller, heading for the same playground. For a moment Richard thought of avoiding her. Associations to Abigail could sometimes be painful. But Martin's wishes pulled him forward, and he went.

◆ ◆ ◆

I'm starting to get old, thought Richard, sitting down on a bench as Martin played. It was hard to chase a little kid around, especially one like Martin. Poor guy—he probably missed his parents, and that's what made him so hyper. Richard understood. Not that he'd stop taking him to the playground. It was the best thing for his body and his mind. Martin did seem to enjoy it more and more each day. On the other hand, he, Richard, was exhausted. His brother was sick. His sister-in-law a mess. Richard just wanted to rest. He could have used some love himself, someone to really talk to and be with.

Richard thought wistfully of Abigail Thomas. He missed the bold girl he had held in his arms not ten months ago. Why had she left him so abruptly? At first he had thought that he must have disappointed her in some way. But how? Had he said or done something? He remembered how unbelievably close they had felt together, as though they were destined to stay that way, to move through life in harmony. How could he be so wrong about someone? She hadn't seemed to be a cold person rather the opposite— everything he knew about her spoke to a great and yielding heart.

But if so, why hadn't she returned his calls? She had hurt him badly, and he simply did not know what to do.

He had even called her directly at home, hoping to get through without the screen of legal secretaries. A young man had picked up and curtly, proprietarily, gotten rid of him. That was clearly the problem. She had already moved on to someone else, and he, Richard, had been shoved out of the picture. How quickly people betray each other! Or worse—maybe he, Richard, had been a mere interlude in Abigail's longstanding relationship with this other man. She had been weak then, lonely, tipsy, perhaps. Afterward, after him, she wanted simply to forget. He'd been a mistake, then. Nothing more.

Now Richard watched his nephew play in the park. It was amazing to see how the little boy had changed over the course of a few days. In his beloved, familiar park, Martin had come alive. He ran across a suspended wooden bridge, played tic-tac-toe with a giant yellow game board, and jumped into the sandbox, burying himself and tossing sand behind him like a digging dog.

"Martin, my love, have fun, but watch you don't get sand in that little girl's eye."

"All right, uncle Richard. You are my goodie."

What an improvement! Richard sighed with deep satisfaction, then strolled over to the water fountain near the exit to take a long drink. As he lifted his head, he saw the associate again. Rona something. That was it. Miller? Not a bad attorney; she'd worked with him on a few cases at Fletcher, Caplan.

Should he be brave and ask her about Abigail? Rona and she were probably still colleagues, and he could pretend to a merely professional interest in the both of them. But just as Richard began moving toward Rona, she strapped her child into its stroller and began walking purposefully in the other direction. Of course, he could not follow her. Martin was fixated on the way he could spin a steel wheel around, as though he were driving a car.

"Uncle Richard, come watch me!"

"Yes, love, I'm coming."

He followed the little boy, watching him do all his favorite activities, and some new ones, until it was time to go home.

31   A few days later, Tim came back to see Arlie.

"Ms. Thomas is not home," Arlie said, her tone measured. She stood at the doorway, blocking his entry.

"I know she's not, Arlie. I called her earlier. She said she was heading over to the east side to visit a friend."

"Yes, a friend did call her," said Arlie. "She also have a baby, Ms. Thomas tell me. I think they going to the park over there for a play date."

"May I please come in for a minute?"

"I have work to do, you know."

"But the baby's not even here."

"I still have the washing and ironing."

"I—I've been thinking about you."

"That's good. Go home and think some more."

"Please. I won't stay long." Arlie looked at him doubtfully. Finally, she opened the door and let him in. Tim walked over to the living room and sat down on the sofa. Arlie remained standing.

"Don't you ever do any work?" she said, her voice low and unemotional.

"Sure I do, but I'm in computers and I'm a freelancer, a consultant. I can basically call the shots in terms of my hours."

"I did some computer myself back in Guyana. Word processing, we called it. Had a nice office job with an actuarial firm. Our biggest client was in that bauxite business, very important, you know bauxite? Industrial uses and all that."

"Was that before or after your marriage?"

"You don't know much about me at all," she said curtly.

"Well, I do know a thing or two," he said, trying to put his arm around her.

"Very little," she retorted, pulling away. "But you know, when I come here, I had no papers, so that's why I became a nanny, because you can get sponsored. And I sort of fall into it, deeper and deeper. It's hard, hard work, you know. Sometimes I wonder if I want my own child anymore."

"Oh, Arlie," said Tim, "you were made for it."

"For child-caring? Then why do you look down on me for my work, then?"

"What makes you think I look down on you?"

"Hm!" she snorted. "I'm good as you, even if you do have more dollars," she said, starting to speak with an edge in her voice. "Smart as you, yes, and maybe more hardworking. You think it's so easy? Look at how Abigail admire me, look to me for answers she don't know! But I think about what happened with us, and I think you don't know me at all."

"I'd like to know you better," said Tim.

Arlie did not look at him.

"Know this," she said at last. "I was married, divorced, and hurt."

"So was I," he answered simply.

"Don't ever compare yourself to me! I might lose my job for you and your games. Be fired by my boss."

"Don't think of Abigail that way. She's just a real person like you or me. She's a new mother; she's not going to fire you."

"Hm. You're probably right. I had my time to be a mother, too, you know. But the marriage wasn't good. Right from the beginning, Marwan had no respect. He was tight with his money, too, and he called it 'his' money—like I don't have any. And when I was pregnant, he made me feel so bad, so bad. Like now I was really a slave. So I got rid of the baby, and I left him."

"Arlie, I'm sorry," Tim ventured. He wanted to say more, to comfort her, but for once he could not find the words. His glibness was failing him, and he felt a melting sense of humility before her.

"You like kids? Ever have any?" Arlie now seemed in charge of the conversation.

"Yes. No, I've never had my own. I—I teach a class once a week, in my spare time. I teach kids to use the computer." He paused for a moment.

"My ex-wife was a beautiful, dark-haired woman," he continued. "Like Abigail, and even—even more like you, Arlie, when I think about it. Anyway, we kept imagining that we would have all these gorgeous kids. But after a while it appeared that I couldn't have any. It was a fantasy. Impossible. So she left me."

After a long silence, Arlie turned around to face him.

"Listen to me, Tim. I don't know what happened with you and that woman. Was she white?"

"Yes."

"Tim, I feel you are as potent as a rhino. Your body has great energy. When we were together before, I felt all your seeds racing, racing."

"Good god!" said Tim. "You felt my what! Aren't you on the pill or something?"

SONIA TAITZ

"Naturally, I have an intrauterine device, or I would have kicked you hard in your handsome face when you touched me the first time. But look how you jump when you think you could get me pregnant. Yes, Arlie is a fertile woman. Be sure of that! I can have a baby anytime.

"But it's all right," she continued, after a pause. "I don't want no baby right now. But for the rest, sure, I will give you what you need for now. I need things too, you know? But don't be disrespecting me anymore, eh?"

"All right," he said, his voice small.

"You're a little needy boy, but you don't know how to give, not really. But I'll teach you. For a start, leave my boss alone. Don't keep acting like her partner. She's not for you. I've been thinking hard about it."

"Leave Abigail alone? What do you mean?"

"You can be her jokey-jokey friend, but stop thinking you can ever be her man. You act just like a nanny to her. Feed her, hold her hand, keep her safe in the hospital. She lost her mother, she does need that."

"But we—I've just told her father we were practically engaged...."

"You lying all the time now anyway, so forget about that. She has a man already. The man who gave her a baby. And I think she love him—could be that's why she has no room for you. Yes. He gave her that baby and she growing to love that baby like a fool. I think from the beginning, she want that child. She didn't kill it when she was carrying, did she? Did she have her abortion like Arlie? And she such a worker all the time? No, she start to love the man who made her stop and grow. I can tell, all of it, how my boss always looking at her baby's eyes. She see more than a baby there. She searching for the love that she felt. She searching for it."

"He's searching for her, too," Tim conceded, after a long pause.

264

"You have a sense of it? As a man you feel it?" Arlie sounded impressed.

"No. He actually—he called here, but I have to admit I never got around to giving Abigail the message."

"When was that?"

"About a week ago. You know, when we were—you know— first together, and I got the phone a couple of times? That was him."

"I thought those were just wrong numbers. And anyway, I was not myself. But that was him, you think—and still you never tell her? You are selfish like Marwan. But you have your sweetness, too. Your eyes are good. Your touch is like magic, and right now you are going to love me more and more, do you know what I mean?"

"I think so."

"I'm not talking above your head, too smart for you?"

"No, I think I get it."

"Good. So now I'll teach you a lesson to bring you to my level. Take off your clothes and lie flat."

Tim complied at once. He lay there, nude and humble, looking up with innocent hope. Never, since he'd been a child, had he felt so vulnerable and at the same time so trusting. Yes, he was falling, and he was rising to her level.

"Close your eyes now," said Arlie.

Then she lifted her skirt, mounted him, and rode Tim until he felt he was almost dead. Throughout it all, he hadn't made a move. He couldn't have.

Afterward, Arlie dug out a crumpled roll of tens from a pocket in the skirt. She offered them to Tim, who was still trying to catch his breath below her.

"Money-back guarantee," she said, again expressionless.

"You're angry at me—still?" he gasped.

"We both want the same things, so don't play the big shot. And don't pay me money ever again. I'm not less than you."

"No, of course not," he said, still trying to breathe.

They were silent for a moment. Then Arlie dismounted.

"Something else," she said, in a new tone of voice, brisk and cheerful. "You say you teach computer information technology. Can you show me some lessons? I forget since the last eight years I'm in this country. But I learn very well, very fast. So teach it to me now. I'd like to have some kind of office, part-time work, like you, you know? Can you train me?"

"Sure," said Tim, his natural generosity returning as her lecture ended. "I'm supposed to be a pretty good teacher."

"My weekends are free," she said.

"You don't have to pay me, either," he added.

"I wasn't going to," said Arlie, allowing herself a big smile.

32 ⚖ Over at the firm of Fletcher, Caplan, Mr. Fudim was shaking his head. What a mess he had to clean up. Abigail Thomas had shown some promise at the beginning, but he'd been right to doubt her. He should have doubted her a lot more.

And now the kid's career was going to have to take a sudden, jolting nosedive. It was tragic, he thought, that she had hoped to become the first full-time mother partner. Deluded. For all her sassy bluster, she didn't have the goods for that kind of professional promotion. She'd been nothing but weak and emotional.

Instead of raising Abigail Thomas to their level, the partnership, instead, was preparing to force her resignation for "unprofessional behavior." Thanks to him. But he had to give some of the credit to Dave Biddle-Kammerman, too. That new partner had given his all to the firm (he hadn't missed a day since his twins were born). And he'd been at the forefront of Thomas's career U-turn. Earning his keep, Dave had been busy behind the scenes, catching on as the girl went rogue on the Cranebill case and fighting her bad instincts at every opportunity.

Damage control was the name of the game. Mr. Fudim was happy to have someone in the office who knew who was who and what was what. The picture Dave Biddle-Kammerman painted wasn't very pretty. But it could be altered—or it could be erased. In short, Abigail Thomas would have to go.

Over the past few weeks, it had become clear that *MacAdam v. Cranebill* was going to be settled in the plaintiff's favor—that is, against their client. This was a disastrous end to the matter, one that would mean the loss of Hutton Cranebill as a deep pocket for the firm. Every area of the practice would suffer thanks to this unruly senior associate.

The camera that had allegedly fallen from the plane was, of course, the source of the problem. When young Carl (another rotten apple) had deposed her, Mrs. MacAdam had boasted that she had friends everywhere who would vouch for her character, industry, and green thumb. More catastrophically, she had claimed the existence of a camera whose presence "proved" that Cranebill's fast-food subsidiary had been spying on her crossbred rosemary and basil plants. (The telephoto lens had also gotten a good shot of her cucumber-pepper seedlings, she'd added.) Whether Mrs. MacAdam really had those shots or not—and any one of her friends could have found it and kept safe it for her, as evidence—the threat alone had cowed Cranebill into buckling.

Firing Carl and discreetly shredding his deposition, while naturally satisfying, had done the firm no real good. The camera was out of the bag, as it were, and even though Dave Biddle-Kammerman had of course tried to deny the presence of the damning evidence (a common practice, and one that had led to a partner's quitting years before), such tricks were pointless now, in light of MacAdam's confirmed knowledge and probable possession.

Dave had made clear to Fudim that Abigail Thomas was "clearly the one responsible for this debacle." She'd been the one to go down there, find Jackson Moss, and relate the parameters of the investigation to this local investigator. Jackson, too, had patently mishandled sensitive evidence. He must have found that camera; he, like MacAdam, knew lots of people. In places so primitive, adversarial lines never remained as clear as they should.

Finding this "smoking gun"—with a tip, or slip, from either side—could have been a wonderful windfall. Had Dave been the one in contact with Jackson, Fudim mused, things would have gone very differently. Even before the find, Dave would have insisted that Jackson's job was to prove that there was no camera. Things disappeared all the time, particularly when they had probative weight, and it would have been ridiculously easy to lose this busted hunk of metal—or at least rip its memory out. But Dave "strongly suspected" that with Abigail at the helm, Jackson had received no such direction.

Thanks to Dave, Mr. Fudim now knew that the weakest link wasn't Jackson but rather the firm's own seventh-year associate. Jackson might have broken ranks and sent the camera to the old lady, but it was more likely that he'd simply sent it to Abigail, from whom he took direction. So it was Abigail herself who must have gotten word of this material evidence—or, worse, the evidence itself—to Evelyn MacAdam.

All along, Dave had stressed, Abigail had been sympathetic to their adversary. After all, both he and Fudim had heard her imply that she "felt" for her. This kind of sentiment, these "feelings," while acceptable in their place (at home), had no place in a law firm. It was inexcusable, even if, as they both knew, it was brought on by the destabilizing hormones of pregnancy and motherhood.

If Abigail Thomas could be blamed for losing the case, Fudim might now offer Cranebill some financial incentives to stay with the firm, some discounts on the billables. Naturally, he would assure his client that Ms. Thomas would no longer be working on his account in any capacity. If Abigail quit on that note, so much the better. Firing her would only raise her profile as a wronged woman. Some maverick Yalie straight out of law school could take her on as a poster girl for mother's rights.

There was an even better way to send her out the door to legal oblivion. They could tell her that they had decided, in light of the firm's current financial troubles, not to make her a partner. She would have to accept that; there had never been any guarantee. They would then kindly suggest that she look at smaller firms, or perhaps take a position as in-house counsel to a minor corporation. Such jobs provided better hours for working mothers and might be ideal for her in the long run. "Up or out" was firm policy. They really had no provisions for disappointed associates— especially those who felt sorry for all the legless widows of the world.

Something just like this had happened to Richard Trubridge, Fudim remembered. He'd had a great career until he'd switched sides in the middle of a custody suit. Trubridge had claimed he "could not ignore" evidence brought to his attention: that the Fletcher, Caplan client—the father in question—was a bigamist, with another family upstate. (The other wife had called him collect from Troy; the records were plain.) Trubridge himself had disclosed this ruinous information to the judge. But it went beyond that. Not only had Richard Trubridge not been penitent; he'd gone and reported some of the partners to the bar association for "suppression of evidence," as though he himself were ethical judge and jury.

Fudim knew the bottom line: it was good to see the back of the "goody-goodies." Such people really had no business becoming lawyers.

Once Fudim had settled on his strategy, it was time to call Dave Biddle-Kammerman in. He lifted a cigar from his humidor and decapitated it.

"Say, do you want one of these big boys?" he said, offering Dave his first official partner's smoke.

"Thought you'd never ask," said Dave, so moved that his hands shook as he took the prized Cohiba.

"I'll tell her she won't make it here. This is no place for panty-waists," Fudim said to his protégé. Leave them to traipsing around kiddie parks, he thought. Rumors reaching Fudim had suggested as much about the late, great Richard Trubridge. He was said to be haunting city playgrounds like a perv. Sad.

"Will you actually say 'panty-waists'?" Dave laughed. "Isn't that an archaic turn of phrase? And somewhat sexist?"

"I know! But just between you and me and the doorpost, that Trubridge kook and this girl we're discussing, they're both panty-waists of the first order. Am I right?"

"Yes, you are!"

"I mean, all terms come from somewhere, OK? Someone must be wearing big granny panties! And I'm thinking, for starters, old MacAdam—"

"Of course—" Dave reached for Fudim's big lighter and flicked it.

"And Mr. Dickhead Sell-Your-Firm-Out—"

"Natch," puffed Dave, trying not to cough. "No question Richard Trubridge is also a prominent wearer."

"And their ranks are now joined by our darling young Ms. Thomas."

"To whom we will now say goodbye."

"In the kindest possible way."

Having resolved not to directly fire Abigail Thomas, but merely to pass her over for partnership (which would amount to

271

the same), Fudim could wait until she decided to come back to the office. There was no point calling her in and sending her into hysterics, only to send her back out to some kind of permanent leave.

Privately, Fudim felt sorry for the kid; she'd had some spunk, some drive, some good ideas. And she could work her tail off! But lawyers like him couldn't keep her in the clubhouse. Smart young things with a compulsive work ethic came off the ramp every day lately. But a client like Cranebill? A goldmine? Once a decade, maybe.

33 But matters with that annoying associate just wouldn't stay put. As soon as Bertram Fudim had set his mind at ease about his recommendation in re Abigail Thomas, his secretary patched through a call from Grenada.

"Oh, god, I thought we'd settled this," he groaned. Wasn't it enough that the old coot was about to win the case?

"Not in the slightest," rasped the voice of Mrs. MacAdam. "New information keeps pouring my way. I've got pictures printed and nicely blown up here that make your client look like the idea-stealer of the century. He's probably growing cucumber-peppers right now!"

"No, he isn't" said Fudim. "He happens to be in New York City, getting wined and dined by one of my finest associates." And hopefully learning to forgive and forget—as long as they got rid of that viper in their midst.

"Which associate do you mean? That wonderful girl you sent?"

"No, no," he laughed. "Abigail Thomas? No chance Fertile Myrtle will ever see Cranebill again."

"What happened to her? Did she have the baby?"

"What do you think? Of course she did."

"Girl or boy?"

"I don't know! Girl, I think. Call her up and ask her."

"What's her number?"

"Oh, hell, I don't know!"

"What do you mean? Isn't she still working for you?"

"Leave of absence, maternity." Fudim thought it was strange and unorthodox, chatting like this to a former adversary, but something about the Thomas situation annoyed him so much he didn't care. How had an emotional young mother and a daffy old dame gotten him into this fix? Thank goodness he could get out of it.

"She was a very interesting girl," Mrs. MacAdam was saying. "And she's a good girl, too. With a heart and a soul and a conscience. Don't know why she'd waste her life working for a bunch of thieves and liars."

"Is that what you told her when she was down there—that we were a bunch of thieves and liars? Or is that what she told you?

"She isn't stupid. Hey! You admit it, do you?"

"No, I don't admit anything! It isn't in evidence, is it?" Fudim gave a little chortle.

"Is that some kind of lawyer joke? I don't get those."

"Sure you do. If it isn't in evidence, it isn't real. Even if he knows it, she knows it, you know it, and I know it."

"I'll tell you what's real. My beautiful settlement."

"I'll say," said Fudim, sighing. He reached for one of his white antacids.

"You know what else was real?" he added, sucking. "That kid was soft on you. You took a potentially great lawyer and ruined her."

"Oh, I know I ruined her!" said Mrs. MacAdam proudly. "Someone had to do something."

"She was driven, laser-sharp. But she lost her focus big-time."

"Abigail's my kindred spirit, you know. She's prone to great flights of passion, like me. But she comes down to earth when she needs to. When important things come up. New information, new priorities. That's what makes both of us gals so challenging to the likes of you."

"I'm not clear on what you're talking about. But you're both about as challenging as—as—" Slightly rattled, Fudim couldn't think of any conclusion to his simile.

"At a loss for words? I know we threaten you."

"'We,' huh?"

"We're alike, I said. She and I."

"So maybe you had a kind of mother-daughter thing going on? No kids of your own, I can understand the need to connect."

"You can? Good. Because I think we did. Maybe I needed to leave some kind of lasting legacy."

"What about my legacy? OK? What about all the training the firm put into her? Here she was, working for me, but feeling something for you, taking notes and e-mailing me, but somehow looking for depositions, listening to what she shouldn't have listened to, and looking at things she should never have seen."

"I applaud her ambivalence. Best sign of moral balance."

"Applaud all you want," said Fudim, as his voice descended to a quiet, settled sneer. "Your darling girl's history anyway," he added vindictively.

"What do you mean? You said that Abigail's on leave."

"You said it yourself, she doesn't belong here."

"You're not firing her?"

"Of course not! What kind of people do you take us for?"

"She's up for partner, isn't she?"

"She tell you that? What a mouth on her!"

"We're all big mouths, aren't we, Mr. Fudim. That's why we like each other so much. Anyway, Abigail told me a lot of things. We had a nice conversation. I shared my hopes and dreams, and she shared hers. She even peed on my floor. I tell you, that girl put me right at my ease."

"She had no business letting down her guard."

"You mean she can't be a lawyer if she's loosey-goosey?"

"Not with the opposing side. No." He paused. "I mean it's different, me and you, right now. We're settled, we're not in the thick of litigation."

"She did keep her mind on the case—your side, that is. I remember there were moments where she seemed frighteningly litigious. Isn't that what you wanted?"

"In many ways, yes. I'm glad to hear that. Thomas, she's a good thinker, she works hard, and sure, there were moments of competency. She had the hunger in her eye, I'll admit. I mean, we did hire her, but—"

"But?"

"But now she thinks with her, I don't know what to call it." Fudim's melting antacid coated his tongue, making his words more slurry.

"Her vulva?" she blurted. "Is that what you think of us females?"

"Her heart—please, the language, all right? Now, if you don't mind, I need to go. I happen to have a date with my son."

"You have a son?"

"Sure, I got a great kid," said Fudim, brightening. "He's ten now. Every three months we have dinner at 21 and I check his stock listings. If they go up, he gets dessert."

"How good of you," said Mrs. MacAdam.

"Really? My wife thinks it's crass, says he's still a child, blah, blah. Like there's a string attached to my affection, moan, moan. But I tell her, everything has its price, and it's good for the boy to learn it."

"What do you get out of it?"

Fudim took a moment to reflect.

"I like having him look up to me. Teaching him what he needs to know." Despite himself, Fudim was enjoying the conversation.

"I could get something out of teaching you, too."

"Oh, you've taught me, lady. That settlement hurt."

"I'd like to teach you something else, if you'd let me."

"Let's not get ahead of ourselves," said Fudim. Why did everyone, from young damsel to old coot, eventually come on to him? "Anyway, I really have to be going."

"Just a minute," said Mrs. MacAdam. "Everything has its price on my end, too. You'd better offer that Thomas girl a partnership if you know what's good for you. I'm taping this conversation and I'd be happy to excerpt the part about 'he knew, she knew, I knew.'"

"You're not really taping this conversation."

"Yes, I am. Cora-Lee! Am I taping this conversation?"

"Yes, you taping it."

"You bitch!" said Fudim. "You panty-waisted Trubridge!"

"What did you call me?"

"A bitch, which you are."

"The other part."

"Oh, I named you after the guy who tried to bust us for suppressing evidence before. He got a lot of us in trouble, and the firm pretty well almost folded. We had to pay fines, baby. Don't ask."

"You'll pay more fines with me if you don't make her partner. On the other hand, if you do make her partner, I could send some business your way, baby. That will teach you to be good to people who have dedicated their lives to you."

"Like who? My first wife?"

"Abigail Thomas, of course. She's worked for you like Jacob for Rachel. Seven long years."

"What business will you send my way?" said Fudim, still wondering about the Jacob reference. Biblical, maybe? It had been a few years since Sunday school.

"The business of my agricultural patents. They're worth millions."

Fudim stifled a laugh.

"Thanks. I'll consider it very carefully."

"She'd make an excellent partner."

"You've known her for a very short time."

"Long enough to know that her head's attached to her heart, like mine. And see where it got me?"

He sighed, as though to say, Lonely and legless in Grenada.

"Give up?" she said, laughing. "It got me to the point where I'm rich and powerful enough to do a good turn for someone else. Especially one who's been kind to me. And that's just what I'm going to do."

34 ❀ When Chloe was three months old, Abigail decided to call the firm again and see how everything was going. If they let her, she had decided, she would like two more months, unpaid of course, with the baby. (There was a precedent; Rona DeWitt Miller was on unpaid leave.) And when she returned, she had decided, she could work only part-time, which in her world meant fifty hours a week instead of seventy. They could prorate her salary accordingly.

Mr. Fudim, sounding pleased to hear how well she was enjoying motherhood, had told Abigail she could take the extra few months.

"Take your time," he had said. "There's one thing money can never get back for you, and that's time. One day the baby's here, the next it's a kid or a teen or a daughter you walk down the aisle. And one day your mom, who you've known all your life, she's a bag of bones and you're next. Follow?"

"I—I think so." He still had a mom?

"Yeah, you're no dummy. Take care of your nearest and dearest, and the rest kind of falls into place."

Abigail had hung up amazed. But then, amazing things were happening all the time now. She and Arlie were getting on better than she ever could have imagined. That early tension between them was gone. Abigail no longer felt like a stranger in her own home, deferential to an alien "expert." Arlie, for her part, seemed happy to play the part of helper, lending a hand to Abigail whenever she needed it, taking over when Abigail was busy, and sharing impressions when the three of them went out together. Chloe had started to make a sound like "Ma" just for Abigail. Abigail had lit up when she had said it the first time, and Chloe had noticed.

"*Ma*," she had repeated. "Ma." "Ma."

"What she say?" Arlie had come running.

Chloe had not repeated it then. She'd simply smiled and produced a few bubbles. Arlie had walked away, and Abigail had picked up the baby again. Only then had she repeated it, to her mother's joyful laughter:

"*Ma!*"

Arlie and Abigail shared a park bench now. They sat neither in the mothers' area nor the nannies' area, but in a third area that seemed to accommodate fathers, grandmothers, and the two of them, talking as though nothing was stronger than their common interest, Chloe.

Already, the little girl had forged a bond between them. Who else would Abigail have talked to when walking her daughter in her stroller, admiring how she kicked her feet to the beat of the tune her mother sang? Who else would have glowed with pride when Chloe rolled over from stomach to back one day on the Great Lawn, looked at the sky, and laughed?

"She's a gift, this child," Arlie had said, as they walked to the park together. "A real gift from up there."

"You'll have one of your own one day," Abigail had responded, touched by the comment. She leaned over to fix Chloe's hat, to feel her soft chin, so warm even as the weather chilled.

"I think so, too." Arlie had seemed so lost in thought that she had stopped pushing the stroller. Abigail had taken over, like a relay, so that Arlie could walk along unburdened.

What a luxury to have this woman share her life for so many hours, each day! Arlie was no longer imperious or cold. Something had come over her in the last few months, a feeling of confidence, of right being restored to the world. It was because of Tim, Abigail knew.

"Don't you think he's adorable, Arlie?" Abigail had ventured, one evening after he'd had dinner with the two of them. "And not only that, but he cooks, teaches computers to children—I mean, he's got numerous soft spots."

"He's not bad-looking," Arlie conceded. She was clearing the dishes but moved slowly, as though she wanted to pursue the conversation further. That was another clue that Tim had made an impression. Tim was so handsome that every woman in his orbit had to at least consider what he would be like as a boyfriend.

"And you're good looking, too, Arlie. Plus you're smart, you're decisive, you're stronger than you think. Don't you think it's time you tried to be with someone again?"

Arlie was rinsing a big pan in the sink. She took a scouring pad and scrubbed at it, then rinsed again.

"Tim and I are not in a 'relationship,' you know," Abigail offered. "Maybe at the beginning there was something in the air, but now we're just friends. I'm not sure why we never really clicked, but—" She hadn't known how to finish the sentence.

Arlie remained silent.

"You know what I think?" said Abigail. "I think you and Tim should go on an actual date or something. You might find you have a lot in common. Do you want me to mention it to him?"

Finally, Arlie spoke. She wiped her hands on her apron and said, "What does that mean, 'date'? We go out to a movie, we eat popcorn or something like that?"

Abigail sensed a passion rising in Arlie, something like anger, but not exactly that. A grievance. A misunderstanding that needed to be cleared up.

"You'd have fun."

"Oh, fun, is that it for me?"

"It could be that. Or it could be more."

Then Arlie said, "You may not believe it, Ms. Thomas, but it is more than that already."

"You mean—"

"We are already very well acquainted with one another."

"Well acquainted?" Abigail repeated, feeling foolish. Arlie seemed the expert again, as she had with Chloe. "You don't mean?"

"What?"

"Like, physical relations acquainted?"

"Yes, very good physical communications. But more than that. Some honest conversations. And some mutual respect, beginning to be there as well. You know?"

Abigail was surprised to feel a little hurt. Arlie had gone to places with Tim, it appeared, that she had not known were there. And without either of them telling her about any of it.

"Don't feel green and jealous, because you don't love the man and you never did," said Arlie kindly. "He's not so real to you, you know?"

"I think you're right."

"He kinda interests me, Abigail. Can I call you that, since we are talking so privately this girly-girly way?"

Abigail nodded. "Of course you can call me that."

"Tim is also interested. He is beginning to let himself know who Arlie is. I know him, too. I understand what makes him weak and what makes him strong."

"I didn't even know he had those options," said Abigail. Had she missed some wonderful opportunity?

"Tim needs your approval. He is too much in awe of certain women, maybe all of us. He needs our strength, not to fear us or be jealous of us. I think you were like a goddess for him, big belly with a child, which men can't do. . . ."

"Me?"

"They're all looking for that big, big woman, you know? The mother, the caregiver. Whoever gave them that tiny bit of love, so long ago. They shrink up without it. But the need makes them angry, and they fight back against it with all their man pride. They pretend to look down on us, to have that snobby sneer, you know. I fight this every day. If I let him get away with putting me below and him above—"

"He has contempt for you? How dare he—"

"Not really me, Abigail, but you know, for the, the soft one, the servant. The one he needs so much. You know, the mother that takes care of all of it."

"You're not a—a servant!" said Abigail, feeling embarrassed. No one ever called their help "servants" or "maids" anymore. "And of course mothers are not servants, either! They're the furthest things from—"

Abigail stopped herself. And what if they were? What shame was there in service for others? It was good work, tending to the young and the old, nursing the sick and dying. Pushing the elderly in their wheelchairs and the young ones in their strollers, wiping the chins. So many women doing it, for so many years, and for so little obvious reward. She remembered her good sister Annie, and her own faithful mother. She wondered if she herself had ever been that kindhearted. Only for moments, so far, she thought with some shame. But it was a good shame, because she felt herself growing from it.

"We're the bottom of the heap," said Arlie. "A great place to be. They think they stand so tall? They stand tall because of us. If we move, they fall all the way down. Should we feel insulted that they don't admit it?"

"No, and it's not our flaw if they're too proud."

"So let them learn at their own slow pace, eh?"

"If they ever do," said Abigail, pensively. "And even if they don't, it's true, and the truth is all that should really matter."

"Anyway," continued Arlie, "things are going to change for me now. I'm thinking to go into computers. Maybe in a year, don't worry," she hastened to add, seeing Abigail's face cloud over. "I won't suddenly disappear. And then you will call the agency again. They'll find you someone just as good as me. Better maybe. Older, like a real mother type for you. You need that, too, right?"

"I think I could go for a caring husband, actually."

"All right, so then call that man who was looking for you like crazy lately anyway."

"What do you mean?"

"Tim never told you about his call. But I heard him talk to someone, and he admitted that he gave him the runaround. Not because he wants you for himself. Right now, for the time, he wants me. But the one who has been calling here—Richard—he might be waiting for you, you know, even though Tim does think he's a married man."

"What would Tim know about it?"

"Not one thing."

"But on the other hand, sadly, Richard is married, Arlie."

"You saw the wife with your own eyes?"

"No, but I heard him on the phone, talking to his wife about the kids."

"So you ask him and he admit it?"

"Well—it seemed pretty obvious. But no, I didn't cross-examine him or anything."

"Well, I say he has no wife of his own, and no kids, except for Chloe, of course."

"How do you know that?" Abigail's heart billowed for a second.

"That is my educated hunch. And anyway, 'innocent until guilty,' right? Isn't that what you smart lawyers always say, eh?"

"Right, that's the law," said Abigail, distracted. "Or, you know, maybe it was just an ex-wife or something. People can stay in a close, cooperative parenthood, even after divorce, right?" It killed her not to know.

"Stop studying it in your mind. Call up and hear him. Listen to his proofs. A man with a rotten heart doesn't call, call, call like that. It was more than once, I seem to remember. Maybe two times, he try, and Tim was no help to him. Maybe this man even worried about the baby, you know? Maybe he want to help you out."

"He doesn't even know about the baby," Abigail protested, though she knew how absurd this objection was. He ought to know, and she ought to tell him, come what may. No more hoarding facts from those who were entitled to possess them.

"You're holding this child in your hands and you don't say nothing to him about her? It isn't right for you, or Richard. How long can you go on like that?"

"It's OK," she said, no longer certain that it was.

"No, it's not! You're keeping the truth boxed up," said Arlie. "You're like Chloe with gas trapped up in her guts. Get it straight and let it go free. Come on out with it."

"Tell Richard everything?"

"All the pressure will be gone. And he will tell you all about himself as well. So do that right away."

Abigail could see why Arlie had been so good for her and her daughter. She could see what Tim could see in her, and how much she might be teaching him.

35 Richard had been regularly visiting his sister-in-law, Lauren, at the Willows, the mental-wellness facility at which she was convalescing from what used to be called a "nervous breakdown." This was a vast, luxurious retreat for the anxious and depressed who could no longer function optimally outside, and for those whose moods had led to addiction to alcohol or other substances.

Richard was surprised to learn that Lauren had fit into most of those categories. She had been incapacitated by anxiety and depression, periodically self-medicating with alcohol, and also given to taking tranquilizers on a regular basis. Her husband's heart attack had sent her careening down to full addiction and collapse.

How well people hid their essential selves, Richard thought, and how often the truth (as in pregnancy, or breakdown) had a way of finding its way to the light. Lauren, much like his own older brother, had once seemed to him impervious. It was a shock to see her crumble, even temporarily. Still, Richard had been happy to take care of her three children. It had given him real joy to be helpful to her and to Allen, and to get to know his nephews and niece.

Lauren Trubridge was beautiful and elegant—almost six feet tall, and blessed with a mane of gleaming auburn hair that she wore in a sporty ponytail or elegant chignon. Her hazel green eyes now belied the sportiness and elegance. They were fathoms deep with sadness, noticed Richard, annoyed at himself for not detecting even a hint of this mood in Lauren before her bout with debilitating clinical malaise. Could he have done something to prevent it? And couldn't the chronically overworked, self-driving Allen have seen this coming?

Still, there were moments when Lauren's spirits lifted, and she seemed almost ready to meet the world again. On this day, her hair was down and freshly washed. Richard sat with her in the greenery-filled solarium, where palm fronds waved and the scent of lilies filled the air. It was a bit depressing in this facility, which Richard thought counterproductive (not to mention its name, the Willows, with its suggestion of weeping). How could anyone get better in a place where all were so urgently struggling, as though willfully going through emotional boot camp? That very effort was the opposite of relaxing, but simple stress (and marital lone-liness) seemed at the core of Lauren's sorrow.

The solarium's brightness made him want to shut his eyes, and its cloying floral scent made him think of the funeral of his parents—both killed in a boating accident when Richard and his brother were scarcely out of their twenties. Perhaps that was why Allen drove himself so—busy hours and enormous bushels of dollars might provide some sense of safety, insulate him from the inevitable barbs of life. But this insulation hadn't protected his broken core; he'd nonetheless been struck from within.

Something in the sadness of the sunlit room and its forced,

false spirit of spring made Richard himself suddenly burst into tears. These were hard tears, accompanied by shaking shoulders and a convulsing chest. These were sobs. Richard was crying not only for his lost parents, about whom he rarely thought, but about his own fragility, and his brother's, and his sister-in-law's. So tiny a margin separated people from the edges of disaster.

"Oh, my goodness," said Lauren, with a trace of a smile. Yes, her expression seemed to say. Life can be sad. Take a minute, why don't you, and cry about it. It will do you good, and I will be there.

And suddenly, Lauren began talking openly, telling Richard how she'd so often wanted to cry when at PTA meetings led by belligerent, autocratic hausfraus, or when she'd see one of her children hurt by another's cruelty. About the many times she'd suppressed tears, and how many more times she had spilled them, when first one child, and then another, and another, had spoken its first word, and then spoken back, or taken its first step, and then stepped away. More than anything else in the world, she told Richard, parenting children called upon indescribable reserves of courage, shown on the field, on the spot—or sometimes not until much later. But knowing these feelings helped. And crying helped.

Lauren poured her soul out. She spoke about how often she'd cried at her many mistakes, her tendency to scream too much at the children when they wrote on the walls or yelled, clamoring for attention, during their father's weekend naps. Her tendency to buckle under pressure, to let them quit lessons they didn't like. Her tendency to pity her children, and herself as their shield, for the harshness of the world they all had to confront. A world in which they would be forced to prevail.

All this talking—and he'd listened. But when she stopped, Lauren looked shocked to see Richard weep again.

"I've never said this much about myself," she offered. "But to see you, Richard, strong, logical, legal-eagle Richard, crying!"

Richard didn't answer, but Lauren gave him a moment. That was the mother in her, he saw.

Then he sniffed, cleared his throat, and said, "Wow. I really didn't know I was going to do that."

"What is it, Richard? What's happened? Is everything all right?"

"It's this woman," he said, shuddering with some purging finality, reaching into his pocket for a tissue. He wiped his nose and continued.

"I seem to be falling deeply in love with a woman who won't give me the time of day. And I just don't know why."

Lauren sighed with relief.

"You don't know why she won't give you the time of day, or you don't know why you love her?"

"Oh, I know why I love her, Lauren. She's magical and good. I just can't figure out why she's been consistently avoiding me."

"She might have met someone else, Richard. Have you considered that possibility?"

"Yes, I know, of course, but I think it's more to do with me, somehow. She seemed a little curt or angry the last time we were—together. As though she were annoyed, or hurt, by something I'd done. And for the life of me, I can't imagine what. And I feel if I could just find out—"

"She'd forgive and forget?"

"There's nothing to forgive or forget! I meant to say I'd know how to strategize. What to say, what on earth to apologize for."

Lauren played with a lock of her coppery hair.

"There's no need to shout," she said, but she was smiling again.

"I actually admire you, Richard. It's nice to see a virile and competent man lose his boundaries a little. Or a lot. If only Allen had let go once in a while, fallen all over the place, cried and shouted. Maybe then his poor heart would not have had to explode," said Lauren, now with a trace of anger. "If only he'd been sensitive, like you."

"I'm not usually like this," Richard said, slightly abashed.

"Oh, but you are. The way you speak. The work you do. The fact that you'd take our kids in as if they were your own. And especially Martin, and all his demands and his needs. I can't imagine Allen doing any of that."

"Well, he'll have to think about making some changes," said Richard. "The kids need him back. And more than anything, Lauren, they need you."

36 ⚖️ Abigail now found herself trying to reach Richard Trubridge, as Arlie had advised, if only to tell him about the baby he'd sired. But when she called the number she'd tracked down online there was no answer. No machine, nothing.

Of course, there was another way to reach him. Rona DeWitt Miller had told Abigail about sighting Richard in her park on the East River. She'd seen him several times, and each time with the same kid. Rona had told her, frankly, that he seemed devoted to this little boy.

"How old is he?" Abigail had asked.

"About three, I'd say. And a handful."

"Really, a handful?"

"A nightmare. Really spoiled, screams a lot, calls his dad by his first name."

Rona had had to concede, though, that Richard did seem to be acting pretty nice to his little boy. And he came there every day, without fail. The kid was challenging, but no matter what, Richard never yelled at him. Sometimes, she told Abigail, Richard knelt in front of the boy, holding him by the shoulders, looking into his eyes, until they both were in agreement. Nodding together.

"Well, maybe he is a good father," she had admitted. "That's possible, even if he is a philanderer and a crook lawyer. I mean, people have different sides to them—most have something they're gaga about. And men do cherish their heirs."

Rona's talk of Richard's tenderness brought back bittersweet memories of how tender he'd been with her. Coupled with the fact that he'd called her home (along with Arlie's hunch), it was all too much for Abigail to resist. Determined to head straight to the East River playground where Richard would be found, she dialed Rona's number and began talking immediately.

"Take me to him, Rona; I can't stand it anymore."

"All right," said her friend, "I can see you've got it bad. I used to have it bad for my husband, but then it passed, thank goodness. It was like the influenza. Actually, sometimes I miss it, being lovesick. This is Abigail, right?"

"Of course it is! Who else says 'take me to him, I'm lovesick'?"

"You actually said, 'I can't stand it anymore.'"

"Same difference. What's that obnoxious sound I hear in the background?"

"Processor. I was just making some more mashed yams for Dylan," said Rona. "You want to help me? I've got to get organic, my cooking teacher says. Otherwise, what's the point?"

"What is the point?" said Abigail distractedly, trying to keep up her end of the conversation.

Rona turned off the processor. "OK. I'll shop for the organic and then we'll do the park thing. I'll meet you at East End and Eighty-Fourth, OK? Then if it goes like a disaster for you, we'll spend the afternoon baking. Sound good?"

"Maybe he's not married, Rona. Maybe this whole time, there was only me."

There was a long pause.

"Who says he's not married?" said Rona.

"My babysitter, OK? I mean, she can't be sure, of course. But she thinks he's a nice guy, and so there must be some explanation besides that he's the son of Satan. She's really cool. You met her briefly when you came over. Arlie, remember?"

"I didn't pay attention, sorry. I was focused on your dot boards."

"I happen to trust her judgment."

"Whose—your sitter's?"

"Yes. Arlie Rajani. She's the one who made those boards you seemed to appreciate," said Abigail loyally. "And she's been really astute about Tim, too."

"In what sense, 'astute'?"

"Let's save that for now. It's pretty rich material. Right now, I just desperately want to see Richard."

"Well," said Rona thoughtfully. "As a matrimonial lawyer, I am paid to be professionally cynical, but hey—whatever makes you happy. Wait—Abigail, are you crying?"

"No, I think I'm just nervous!" said Abigail, shaking with hope. But she was crying, a little, single drops falling down her face.

What would Richard say when he saw her?

She bundled Chloe into her new winter overalls and jacket, tucked her feet, wrapped in thick socks, into her pink moon boots, and lifted her to her chest like a warm, fragrant pillow. Some things were uncertain, romantic love foremost amongst them, but that she and this child belonged together was a truth never to be shaken.

Perhaps Richard Trubridge would feel the same way about her.

◆ ◆ ◆

Richard was not in the park when Abigail and Chloe got there, but after a while, Rona came in, wheeling Dylan.

"Got the yams!" she said, flourishing the bag.

"Good, that's good," said Abigail mindlessly.

"Have you seen him?"

"Not yet, I'm looking around, though. You didn't see him anywhere, did you? Can you look around? Maybe he's here and I just can't see him."

"You really have it bad, Abigail," said Rona, kindly. "You're all red in the face."

"Well, Rona, I haven't set eyes on him since that time in Palm Springs. We did have a romance there, like everyone said, but I've had to hold it in until now. I thought he was married, because he was talking in this low voice to someone he called Honey. I thought I was just a one-night fling."

"Yeah, I know. The dreaded 'honey' phenomenon," said Rona, speaking as a divorce lawyer. "Poor you. I can just imagine how you felt when you heard that."

"But I got pregnant anyway. Honey or no honey. And the rest is—well, Little Miss Blue Eyes, here."

"You know, Abigail," said Rona, "even though everyone suspected this little romance, we also believed that with your little suits and scarves, and your nose to the grindstone ways—"

"Me? Nose to the grindstone?"

"Are you serious? More than anyone else in the firm, ever. So no, we thought you could easily have had the Immaculate Conception or something. That somehow you managed to just order up a baby, no muss, no fuss. You always seemed to be so in control, so perfect—"

"Oh, I'm not too perfect anymore. Having a baby makes you stumble around a lot. You fall a lot, in all kinds of ways." She'd tumbled down on Broadway, on the day she'd first met

Tim. She'd fallen on the turbulent flight back from Grenada. But most of all, she had to admit, she'd fallen, all the way, for Richard.

"That's good," said Rona, fervently. "It means we're human beings. We're mothers." She squeezed Abigail's hand. Abigail squeezed back.

"And all the time it hurts, I mean it hurt, but I hid it," Abigail admitted. "I tried to hide it well. But anyway, now I'm telling you everything, and I'm looking for Richard Trubridge to tell him also. Because Arlie—here's the crux—she says he wouldn't be chasing me like this if he were married."

"Arlie?"

"I keep telling you, Arlie, my babysitter. Don't you get it? She's like us—without all the diplomas—and she's learning as she goes. I trust her instincts. She found out Richard had called me, and that Tim picked up the phone—and by the way, that's why I never found out about it. Tim hid it from me!"

"Schmuck," said Rona.

"Jealous, threatened," said Abigail, more compassionately.

"Anyway," she continued, "Arlie says Richard's not necessarily the type to be messing me around. She can tell by what Tim told her. I guess Tim could hear his tone of voice, I don't know. . . ." Abigail broke off, disheartened. Hunches were all she had to go on, hunches and missed calls and a missing father to this beautiful child. Her courage momentarily flagged.

"Tim and she are buddies now?"

"OK, you should know that he's kind of over me, and he's Arlie's boyfriend now," said Abigail, rallying a little. It was good to have Tim move on; it made her feel less guilty. Abigail could never be what he wanted, and she kept thinking of Richard.

"It's a little weird, I know."

"Just a little unusual."

"But it's fine. It makes sense for them. It's what they want and I'm all for it."

"Uh-huh." Rona took this in and absorbed it with professional aplomb. "So who in the world was 'honey'? I mean, assuming the argument that Trubridge is not married?"

"An old girlfriend, maybe an ex? I don't know exactly. It was a really quick conversation."

"It's plausible that it wasn't a wife. Just. If it was, he might have been more nervous that you'd pop out of the bathroom and say, 'Great sex, babe!'"

"Well, I don't generally do that."

"But theoretically—"

"No, it was really—it was actually that and more."

"Not my point, sorry. I mean, but what kind of intelligent man would have taken the call with you in the room, not knowing what you'd say—what noise you'd make? He could so easily have been busted—"

"So it is plausible that he's unattached, right?"

"Sure. I guess. But about Richard Trubridge 'chasing' you," persisted Rona, "that one's harder to agree with. I mean, if he doesn't even know you were pregnant, and you're kind of following him here into the kiddie park, how does that constitute his chasing you?"

"Richard called me several times. Not just at home, Rona. At the office, too. Which was hard to do—you know how they felt about him. But of course Tina never let him through—she's like my guard dog."

"Good old indiscriminate Tina."

"Good old idiotic yet somehow indispensable Tina. But my point is that he called repeatedly. And even Tim let on that Richard sounded forlorn when he called, like he—"

"Like he what?"

"Like sad, you know—like, alone, longing—"

"Like as though Richard Trubridge were actually—what—madly in love with you?"

"Well, it's possible! Don't you think I'm the least bit lovable?"

"That you are, 'the least bit lovable,'" Rona teased.

"Oh—there he is!"

Richard had strolled in, holding Martin's hand. He stopped and leaned over the child to talk to him. Then Martin bounded over to the curly slides. Richard followed, his long legs loping.

"That's him and the crazy kid," Rona whispered. "You sure you're up for this?"

The two friends watched them for a while. Abigail nodded.

Rona said, "I think I'll just wander off and take Dylan for a little stroll along the river."

"You sure? Won't you two be cold?"

"It's not that bad. The experts say babies need to get used to all kinds of weather, anyway. You don't want them crumpling at the first frost. Why don't you stay here for a while, see what happens? I'll be home in about an hour, doing the damned mashed yams."

"Sounds great," said Abigail distractedly. "I'll probably see you soon, then. I mean what could happen that would stop me?" said Abigail. Her entire body was beginning to feel odd. Her knees were going wobbly. But she couldn't fall, not now, with a baby on her chest.

Chloe was bundled up in a baby carrier that placed her against her mother's heart. Abigail touched the fuzzy pom-pom on top of the baby's head as though it were a talisman. Then she trained her eye on Richard, stiffened her resolve and announced, "Here we go."

"Hey—Abigail, wait," said Rona suddenly. "I feel I have to tell you this. I've been talking to people at Fletcher this week. My leave is ending, so I called them to touch base. And there's talk that this guy you say is the father has got a screw loose. Maybe you and Chloe here are better off without him."

"I know, I know, they've been saying that for a while. But Richard's not even at the firm anymore!"

"Of course he isn't—he left in disgrace—but I brought him up. They asked me how my life was going, and I was trying to sound like I wasn't the only lawyer in the park on leave, you know, so I name-dropped him, kind of. Said I saw him here from time to time. I made up that we talk about the principles of family law while we watch the kids in the sandbox. He is kind of a big guy compared to us, and he's very well regarded at his new firm.

"And everyone I spoke to said to keep away from him, that he's a nutcase. Now, I realize that they're angry about him leaving over that custody case. I mean, they lost the case, and they got penalized, too. But they implied that it's more a mental thing than anything to do with the law as such. That Richard Trubridge is soft in the head. I mean, that boy he's with? That's not even his own kid, they told me. He hasn't even got a kid. So what's he doing?"

"Hasn't got a kid?"

"Right—it might not even be his."

This was good news to Abigail.

"Soft in the head?" she mumbled. Somehow, Abigail was not turned off by that description. She had had enough of hardheads. She was getting soft in the head herself.

"I will do some research, Rona. Some diligent fact-checking. I will determine, for the record, how soft in the head Richard Trubridge is. I will find out who this feisty three-year-old who intimidates you so is."

"I'm not particularly intimidated. I just think he's a handful."

"He's a boy. A three-year-old boy."

"Well, get the scoop."

"I will. And I will tell the world, concealing no evidence."

Rona stared at her. "I hope you don't mind my telling you all this. I felt I had to make a disclosure."

"You had to. The truth, the whole truth, and nothing but the truth, according to the best of your knowledge. Appreciated. And I hope you're wrong."

"Good luck then, sweetie," said Rona after a moment, wheeling her baby away.

37 Abigail took a deep breath and walked over to the climbing frame. Two curly slides emerged from either side of a wooden suspended bridge. Richard was crossing the bridge, running first to one slide landing, then the other. He and Martin laughed as the bridge shuddered beneath them. They had done this before and knew the structure, though flexible, was sure. It would carry them, together, and no matter how it shook, they would not fall.

Richard chased Martin over to one slide, put him in his lap, and rode him down with his legs in the air, shouting, "Whee!"

They did this over and over. Richard, whatever his faults, was a very patient man.

Then Abigail climbed up. She crossed the shaky bridge with her child, and went down the other slide. Legs in the air, she shouted:

"Whee! We're flying!"

Chloe let out a beautiful, bell-like laugh. It rang out clearly on this still, cold day. There were few other people in the playground.

Richard turned his head and looked over at Abigail and the little girl.

Abigail turned her head and looked over at Richard and the little boy.

"Abigail?" he called out uncertainly.

"Yes?"

"Have you had—is this your—your own baby?"

Nodding, Abigail turned Chloe around to face Richard.

"Voila," she said, idiotically.

"She's very—very pretty," said Richard, coming closer, his expression still unsettled, confused. His eyes remained focused on Abigail.

"Yes, she's a looker," Abigail replied. "Especially that dimple in her chin," she added, a bit sharply. Richard had one, too, and Abigail stared fixedly at it as Richard grew near. How like Chloe's it really was.

"A dimple in her chin?" he stuttered. His hand flew up to play with the cleft on his face—a little notch he could feel in the skin, and in the bone below.

"And I've always really loved her combination of black hair and blue-green eyes," said Abigail. "Really loved it ever since— ever since I met you, as a matter of fact. Never saw it before then, or since. But now, I get to see it every single day. And I'm seeing it again, as I look at you right now."

Richard couldn't take his eyes off Abigail's round, dark eyes.

"What—what exactly are you telling me?" his voice was a bit harsh. "Are you saying that my eyes are the same color as—"

"Please take your hand off your chin dimple and just take a good look at this baby," she said, just as sternly.

"But when—when on earth did you get married?"

"Married?" How stupid could this senior partner be? He was staring at the baby openmouthed, as though he were, in fact, an idiot.

"Richard," she all but shouted, "How could I get married and whom would I marry?"

"What do you mean? Who is this child? Are you—are you actually saying she's mine?"

"Isn't she yours?" Abigail answered, meeting Richard's gaze steadily.

"Are you saying that? I don't think I fully grasp what's going on here."

Abigail was almost angry at him. Would he be one of those men who made you take a test, even though they were the only man in your life, and even when the baby was practically their clone?

Richard looked fixedly at the child. He began trembling.

"Yes, you two," said Abigail, her voice trembling, too. "Both of you. Look hard at each other."

"You want me to look at her hard?"

"Yes, I do. Chloe's good at this. That's her name, this baby here. Chloe. She's a starer. Try it. It's about time she looked her father in the face. And it's about time you looked at her, too."

Abigail held Chloe up so she could see Richard more closely. He looked into the baby's honest, innocent eyes. They were indeed the same turquoise blue as his own—and they shone as her lips parted slowly in a smile.

Still trembling, Richard reached for her. Abigail lifted Chloe out of her carrier and Richard took her up into his arms, where she immediately nestled.

"She—she looks like—"

"Like you, like her father, like Mr. Richard Trubridge, Esquire."

Instinctively, Richard put his hand out to touch the baby's cheek. He had never seen or felt such soft skin. Chloe grabbed his finger and put in into her gummy mouth. She gripped it there, gnawing.

"Is she—what's the matter—is she hungry? Ow!"

"No, no—teething," said Abigail, trying to stay angry but wanting to laugh. Chloe could really hurt you—her jaws were vise-like.

"I just fed her," she continued. "Me, I'm the hungry one, Richard. Always."

"I know. I remember."

"Yes, that's who I always was, but I never understood what I was hungry for. I thought it was being a law partner, but that didn't really cover it at all. Love, and goodness, and honesty. That's what I was hungry for. Someone to rely on. All the things I thought I saw in you. There I was, being such a clever girl on the partnership track, when I found myself falling—well, literally falling down onto the grass of some golf course. I tried to get up, but I couldn't. Not only did I have to deal with the fact that I loved you unrequitedly, Richard, but as it turns out, I became pregnant."

"You got pregnant in Palm Springs?"

"Seems so. I mean, obviously. Wasn't that when we saw each other? Richard, your brain seems to have just died!"

"I'm just in shock. But of course, Palm Springs. Of course. When else?"

"That was a pretty significant watershed for me, as you can see." There was a tiny edge in Abigail's voice. She was angry at Richard for all this time—an entire precious year now—spent without him. For possibly being married, too. Because maybe he really was. Why else was he balking?

"So you're saying that this baby is really yours and mine?"

"It's either that or the Immaculate Conception, Richard."

"What a wonderful thing," he replied.

There was a long pause as Abigail regrouped.

"Really? Wonderful?"

Then darkening, he added, "but then it was truly wrong of

you, in my opinion, not to take my calls. It was my right to know. As a father. I don't want to get legalistic with you, Abigail, but—"

"Yes, it probably was wrong. I didn't think of it that way at the time. And it so happened that I didn't even know about all the calls. I mean, they weren't all delivered to me, certainly not when you tried to reach me at home. . . ."

"Yes, and who was that very unhelpful man, if I may ask?"

"A friend, Richard. Something more for a time, maybe, but not any longer."

"A friend, even one who is 'something more,' would have told you that I called, especially knowing the circumstances. Which I take it he did."

"Yes. I guess he was jealous."

"Fine. But what about the calls at work, Abigail? Those you heard about, I presume?"

"Yes, but I didn't—I really couldn't face you."

"Why on earth not? Why didn't you tell me anything, even while I kept trying to reach you—to see you again?"

"I wanted to but I held on to my dignity, such as it was. I didn't want to face any more humiliating scenes. Remember how I left your room so fast that last morning?"

"Of course I remember feeling terribly puzzled about it. Hurt, in fact."

"You were hurt? I was positive you were married! That I was no more than a stupid fling. I heard you talk to your wife on the phone, jabber on about kids of your own—so why would you need one more? One little mistake with a girl you didn't—didn't actually care about?"

"You thought what? Whom am I supposed to be married to?"

"I don't know her name, do I? But come on. Let's be honest with each other for once. You were talking on the phone to some woman, your wife probably, about your kids. Don't you remember?"

"But Abigail, for heaven's sake, that was only—"

"Uncle Richard, my goodie! Slidey! Again! SLIDEY AGAIN!"

"Excuse me, Abigail, I'm taking care of my brother's kids. This one is Martin; he's the youngest."

"Your brother's kids? What about your own kids?"

"Martin is my nephew. My brother is recuperating from a serious heart attack, and his wife isn't doing well either. In some ways I'm more worried about her—say hello, Martin," said Richard, as the little boy dashed under the bridge.

"No!" said young Martin from below. "You find me now. I am hiding!"

"Was that who you were talking to that morning?"

"Well, it certainly wasn't my wife!"

"Why—don't you talk to your wife sometimes, or do you forget her when you're on vacation or something?"

"I don't—I don't actually have a wife, Abigail! For heaven's sake, what kind of person do you take me for?"

"A bad one? A cad, actually."

"Well, that does explain your silence, I'll admit. It explains everything."

"It does. Don't sound so hurt. I'm hurt. I was very hurt."

"Are you still hurt?" he said, concerned. "I'm shocked about all this—you must be, too."

"Of course you are. I've had time to adjust—you know, nine months, et cetera. And now she's three months old. But now you can get used to these facts: you're a father, I'm a mother, and furthermore—"

"Yes? Furthermore?"

"And furthermore . . . I—I think I'm losing my heart to you, Richard."

She hadn't meant to say that. All this time, unable to say it to Tim, and there it was. She could really love him.

"Well, it so happens that—I've been falling in love with you, too, Abigail. You've been special to me since the first time I laid eyes on you. I've thought of you so many times since then. And I have missed you since Palm Springs. About a year now, right?"

"Oh," she said softly, for a moment at a rare loss for words.

"But back to that phone call. You need to know this: my brother, Allen, had fallen seriously ill around that time," said Richard. "He had a heart attack and almost didn't make it. I needed to keep in touch with Lauren, his poor wife. She was falling apart emotionally. Never strong, three kids, and a sick husband was too much for her. I didn't—I never imagined you were listening in on my phone call. If I'd known, I could have explained it right away—"

"Of course I was listening! Wouldn't you? I cared about you!"

"I suppose I would have, and anyway, one can't shut one's ears."

"No. So I was listening very hard. As though my life depended on it, which it did. And after that, I felt so miserable, so disappointed and ashamed, that I ran away. I had never felt worthy of you. All those years, I'd had this tiny little dream that you'd somehow notice me. Think about me. Want me. Even come to love me, the way deep down I knew I could love you. And all of a sudden, it all came true—for three little days. The man that I'd yearned for, deep down and for five years, was mine. And then it was all abruptly taken away from me."

"I did notice you. Boy, did I ever. And I cared, too, all along, and I—how do you think I felt when you ran out on me like that? And don't you realize I liked you all the time, even back when I was working at Fletcher?"

"You liked me, too? Come on," she said, a deep joy beginning to rise, "you practically never showed it."

"'Practically.' So you did see something. How could anyone resist you? And then there was that chemistry between us—a strange connection I'd never felt before. I did want you, if you must know. Painfully, both body and soul. Is that a cliché thing to say?"

"It's a delicious thing to hear."

"Yes, it is delicious, especially now," said Richard, savoring the electricity as she now stood before him. "But you know I couldn't make obvious overtures then, Abigail. I was a partner and you were an associate trying to please the partners; it would have seemed like—and perhaps been—an abuse of power. Seasoned man and younger woman, that old cliché. It wouldn't have made a good beginning. Of course I noticed you. I couldn't help it. You seemed very responsible, very hardworking. But that's not all of it. It's not even that you were—are—patently attractive. There are quite a lot of diligent, beautiful women in the world."

"I know, there are," she said humbly. Abigail felt herself flushing with delight at the word "beautiful."

"Well, actually not so many. Not ones with sterling hearts. And a valiant, brave spirit. But however many there might be in the world, the one I kept track of was you. I got to know your passionate spirit, on many levels. For one thing, I knew how hard you worked, like your life depended on it."

"It was that obvious?"

"Yes, and it was admirable; we naturally like that in associates. But that's certainly not all of it. It was just the framework. Because I also knew that your mother got sick, and how, in that context, your work fell off. I saw that: you took care of your sick mother when she needed you. The contrast, how you changed your priorities—that's what I really noticed. Your good and noble soul. You touched me with that beauty. And that made it even harder to withstand your external charm, I can tell you. Didn't you see it in my eyes, sometimes, when I looked at you?"

"I think I did sometimes, yes." There was a long and pleasant pause as Abigail took in the fact that Richard had essentially called her irresistible.

"You knew about my hours?" she said finally.

"You were notorious for it," he replied, smiling. "First, you had the highest number of billable hours, and then you had the lowest. One of the partners on the budget committee was ranting about it at the racquet club. I remember he complained that you were leaving early every night. And he said he'd called you in to explain, and you'd told him your mother was ill, and you had to be with her. It must have been hard for you to overcome that kind of stupidity. Here you were, doing what love requires, and then you get challenged for it—"

"And then, what's worse, I saw you again after she died and I got soft again and I got pregnant, and a lot more uncontrollable feelings followed, that's for sure, and big mistakes."

"And some wisdom, too?"

"I never thought you'd be there for me. I admit I was stupid about that."

"My poor Abigail. I'm sorry I scared you so badly."

"No, it's been a great lesson. It's been a privilege to know what it feels like to be so—so alone, and to bear so much, and such deep, responsibility. I never really understood all that before. It was all about me before that, and now it was about everything but me. What an awesome thing.

"It's been an honor to bring this child into the world. And when I look back, it was an honor to be with my mother as she left this world. Everything was quiet; her life was ending," said Abigail, stroking her daughter's head.

"Sweet, good Abigail."

"No, stop, it was a privilege, I said."

"Yes, an honor."

"Yes, it was."

"I understand. It's wonderful. It's how I sometimes feel about being with Martin."

Martin was still under the bridge, but he seemed very still. Sometimes, he got fascinated by looking at ants, at bits of moss or lichen, or even a flake of glinting mica. Richard smiled, just thinking about this little boy.

"I used to look forward to coming in to feed my mother supper," Abigail continued, as Richard listened intently. "The nurses sometimes did it, but some of them did it too fast. It wasn't their fault; they were busy. They didn't know her. I knew my mother liked to eat slowly. I knew she liked peas but not potatoes. I knew she needed sips of water between bites. Loving someone means knowing these kinds of details. Noticing, caring, and doing these very small things. You don't just grow overnight. You can't cram for this test, you know? It takes time, and your progress is slow, and sometimes no one even sees it."

"Yes, you're right. Maybe the greatest things do need time, Abigail. And patience, I suppose. It took years after I first met you to finally come over that day on the golf course—I yearned for you, but to really be able to touch you—"

"And here I thought you didn't know who I was."

"At Palm Springs, that day, you were looking over to me, sort of lost. You made me feel like you knew me, you trusted me. Remember, I offered you some help?"

"Of course I remember," she said shyly. "But at the time, I hadn't fully recognized you. I was trying to place you. Was this actually the man I'd had the mad crush on? But it seemed more than that, suddenly. You seemed so deeply familiar, like someone I'd always known. Your kind eyes, the wonderful timbre of your voice. I knew I'd liked you, but maybe it was more. Have you ever heard the expression 'coup de foudre'?"

"Yes, I have, and although I couldn't act on it, I'd felt similar lightning bolts and thunder claps when it comes to you. Yes, there was always something there. But I couldn't and wouldn't act on it when the power dynamic between us was what it was. But that ended when I left the firm. Fletcher's old history to me now, Abigail. Except for you—and fondly, because somehow it brought us together—I hardly think about that place anymore. Murdock & Hill let me be more of a maverick than Fletcher ever did. Before this leave, I'd been working pro bono on children's rights, actually."

"Really? What rights don't children have, by the way?"

"The right to have time off from all their homework, school, and lessons. The right to play without practical purpose. The right to see their parents in the evenings."

"That's—that's revolutionary."

"There's more. Weekends, too, should be off limits to any stress."

"Like the Sabbath day, you mean? Unplugged peace and rest?"

"That's exactly right, Abigail. I love that idea. And when they're really little, say under the age of five or six, I think they should have the inalienable right to be read to before bed, and snuggled for as long as they need. I read to Martin every single night."

"Are you planning some kind of class action about this, Richard?"

"It's hard to think about the bigger picture now. Right now, the 'class' is simply my brother's children. There's Martin, and also Ellen, who's ten now, and Hal, who's twelve and a bit. I'm planning to take care of them until Allen and his wife get better. They're all great kids, really, especially given the circumstances."

"So their mom's sick, too?"

"Just her nerves, and she's improving, but yes."

"I totally understand."

"Do you really?"

"Yes. To be solely responsible for a child can make you very unstable." Abigail sighed a deep, convulsive sigh.

"I know," said Richard, looking over at Martin, who sometimes tried to go to the ice cream man all by himself. But he was safe, no longer under the bridge but playing close by with a piece of chalk some other child had left behind. He was writing his initial: "M."

"I'm not all that stable either. Life's not that stable. But I'm learning to balance every day," he humbly concluded.

"And you're wonderful. Would it help our balance if we—if we held onto each other and kissed?" she ventured.

"Won't I squeeze the baby?" All this time, Chloe was lying quietly on her father's chest.

"You're always gentle, I seem to recall," Abigail said, and Richard leaned his long torso over Chloe. His face met Abigail's and they kissed, with their child between them.

As they parted, Abigail said: "Can you believe she's here? All the time we were apart, she was growing. All that time. And look at her now."

"Yes, she's wonderful," he said, flushing with joy. "She's a miracle. My first child."

"Mine, too."

"Oh, honestly, why didn't you call me, even if you did think I was married? For heaven's sake, everything doesn't have to be perfect, Abigail! Life does always have loose ends."

"Yes," she replied. "But I didn't tolerate them well before. I didn't like feeling foolish. I've grown to realize that folly can bring lots of good surprises."

"Uncle Richard you are a baddie! Why don't you play with me?"

Abigail laughed. "I guess that's what's in store for me with this little one, huh?"

"Well, they are related, right?"

"They are. They're—what are they?—first cousins. And from now on, I'd be happy to take them both to the park and give you a break, you know?"

"No, let's go together."

"That's the best word."

"Uncle Richard who is that lady and who is that baby?"

"Martin, darling, could you wait a moment? Uncle Richard's talking to his good friend Abigail."

"No you are not! You are talking to a baby!"

"If you wait nicely, Martin, I'll introduce you to this lady and the baby."

"I *cannot* wait, I can run away and I can go *far!*"

"Oh, all right. I'll put you on a swing."

"Uncle Richard you are my goodie!"

They all walked over to the swing area, and Martin got to meet Chloe and Abigail.

"I want *her* to push me," he said. "You keep holding that little baby."

"Would you like to do that for Martin, Abigail?"

"I would like nothing more."

All this time, Richard held his daughter to his heart. Chloe's little pom-pom sank slowly as she fell into a deep, contented sleep.

"Higher! Higher!" said Martin impatiently, even though Abigail was pushing for all she was worth.

"I'm trying!" she shouted, as he flew toward her, and away.

"OK, THANK YOU, YOU ARE VERY NICE LADY!"

With Martin safely flying, Richard said, "How's it going with work, or have you not been back?"

"I have been back, but they sent me away again. I'm not sure why. They're supposed to be deciding now about my partnership. Can I ask you something about you and Fletcher?"

"Sure."

"Why did you leave?"

"Hmm. Tough question. You still work there."

"Who knows, Richard?"

"All right. I'll tell you in confidence. It might be valuable information to you. In those days, the firm had a nasty habit of suppressing evidence. It was actually an unwritten policy of the partnership, of which I was a member. But I didn't come across this policy until I worked on a particular custody case, in which my client, the father, was about to win. I realized, based on some information that the firm and I had, that this man should not get the child. And it finally made it hard for me to get up in the morning and work for them. I prefer to make up my mind based on the truth. On what's right, and all that. Not on who's paying the bills. I probably sound like an old hippie to you."

"You sound great," she said, pushing Martin, sailing up to the sky and back. The little boy squealed with happiness. "How'd you get that way?"

"How'd I get this way? Oh," Richard laughed easily. "You know the saying. Hard cases make bad law. Well, I guess after all this time, I'm just a bad lawyer."

"But a pretty good person?"

"You'll have to decide that for yourself. After much deliberation, of course."

"I don't think the firm has changed yet, Richard. They tried to play 'hide the evidence' with a case I'm working on, too." Abigail hesitated. "So I think I'm becoming a bad lawyer, too."

"We're a pair, then," said Richard.

"You're so sweet, Richard," said Abigail. "But—just to be pedantic—we're technically a trio."

The long kiss they then shared was anything but pedantic.

38 ❀ Richard may have handled things well in those moments with Abigail, but his composure utterly abandoned him after she and Chloe left the park. And though he was loathe to cause his brother any stress after his suffering a heart attack, he felt he had no other choice. He had to tell him everything, and soon. Allen was his closest friend in the world, the only person he ever confided in. But he had never told Allen about his brief romance with Abigail. And now there was the baby to talk about as well.

He was due for a visit to his brother. And though he generally came over with the children, on weekends, Richard waited for the week to begin so that all three of them could be back at school. There were things he wanted to tell his brother that weren't completely comprehensible to, or appropriate for, a young child like Martin.

Even for grown men, there would be much to explain, to ponder, to discuss. How he'd fallen deeply and irrevocably for a woman—one who'd broken his heart by seeming to leave him, one whose heart he'd broken by seeming to betray her. How he'd unknowingly fathered a child. And how he felt about it all, now that he knew—now that he'd seen Abigail and their little girl.

Allen was only forty-five years old—a mere slip of a boy in these days of perpetual youth, but he had always seemed much older. Richard had his slow and quiet ways, but Allen was born quick and efficient and hard-driving, a banker type who loved calculations and checklists. His type A personality may have contributed to the cardiac infarction, if not also to Lauren's sinking into depressive darkness in the chaotic weeks that followed.

And it was hard to be happy, Richard thought, in a house as dark and full of "gravitas" as Allen's—the floors polished mahogany and Persian-rug smothered, the walls adorned with valuable oils and lit by brass fixtures that would have been at home in a good insurance firm. Lauren had been almost too ready to be the wife and helpmate to a man who had looked so good in a three-piece suit and silk tie, shoes polished and laces twice-knotted.

The heart attack had grayed and stooped Allen in a way that almost made Richard cry—to see him in his pajamas, in a robe (albeit an expensive, velvet one), in slippers (albeit monogrammed ones), sitting at home, shuffling miserably as though he were afraid to be betrayed again by his own fragility. Still, every time Richard visited his brother, Allen seemed that much better. He was told to do no manual labor, but he'd begun to work again at his accounting, and his partners had been kind enough to send some fairly standard things his way.

Now Allen sat in a brocade-covered wing chair, feet up on a hassock, and listened to his brother's surprising tale.

"I hope I haven't shocked you," Richard was saying.

"No, go on," the older brother responded, almost expressionlessly.

"These things happen, and they did—to us. But the point I

want to make, Allen, is that I want to marry her as soon as possible."

"To make an honest woman of her, as it were."

"Well, there's never been a woman more capable of honesty—though I wish she had kept fewer secrets from me at the relevant times. But I think we've both grown from the experience, and will only continue to grow. But anyway, Allen—she's making an honest man of me. I'm the one who needs to learn to really father this child."

"You're doing so well with my kids, and I'm so grateful, Richard. It can't be easy."

"It's not easy. But it's worth it. And I suggest you really start to think about becoming more involved in their lives."

"They've got a great mother," said Allen.

"Who's way overloaded. Overwhelmed, and not only by them but by you. The one who's most overloaded happens to be you. How much money do you need? How much power? What title? Don't you want to see them grow up? Why is it so hard for you to take the time for them—which is to say, for your own precious, irreplaceable, personal life?"

"I really don't know."

"Well, think it over. There are four people in this world who love you very much, and they all need you to be healthy."

"How is she doing?"

"Lauren? She seems much better to me. I know they don't want you to drive out to see her yet—"

"No, it's not that. She's mad at me, says I'm part of the problem, and that I'd have been a lot healthier and happier if I'd spent more time at home."

"Well, you're getting that chance now."

"Not really. It's awful being here alone, and frankly I can't wait for those three scamps to come back."

"What did the doctor say about that?"

"A few more weeks, and then we'll all be good to go."

"Well, I can't wait either. Not that I don't love them or enjoy their company. But I'm committing to a life with this woman and child, Allen, and I want to move on with that life, and soon."

"I will step up. I promise. Although one thing—no carrying Martin for me anymore. That boy did love to be piggybacked," said Allen, smiling. He'd done so on special occasions. "Do you ever carry him?"

"Oh, yes—I give him rides all the time."

"Well, apparently, I won't be able to from here on—not that these events were all that frequent—but I'm sad about that."

"Just explain it to him," said Richard kindly. "That your body was sick but the doctors made it better. That he has to be gentle with you. Martin's very smart and will more than meet you halfway. He'll understand."

"Lauren says he's the brightest of the three."

"Well, I don't know about that," said Richard, "but he's got a good head on his shoulders and a very good heart to boot."

39 When they finally met, Owen Thomas heartily approved of Richard, formerly the "cad." He was equally proud of Abigail's final agreement with Fletcher, Caplan. Surprisingly, they were letting her start up a division of children's rights within the firm. Although they had offered her a partnership (to Abigail's astonishment), she had refused, preferring to be "of counsel." This meant that although she would work on the premises, and with a partner's prestige, unlike the partners she would be a free agent. Richard would help her, behind the scenes.

"It all sounds great, but you'll be paid less, too, girl," Owen had protested.

"Maybe so," Abigail had explained, "but so what, Dad? You were always so proud to be your own boss. Why would I work for a bunch of lying thieves who think they're doing me such a big favor? What kind of power is that?"

Abigail also took Evelyn on as a client, representing her agricultural patents. While Mrs. MacAdam's potential in the field of agricultural crossbreeding had initially caused Mr. Fudim no small amount of bemusement, she and Abigail had the last laugh. The plants turned out to be quite lucrative for both women. There wasn't a table in America—particularly one laden with pasta or pizza—that didn't seem naked without some "basmary" on it.

But Mrs. MacAdam seemed sad somehow, to Abigail. She seemed forlorn.

She denied it, of course.

"Me? Sad? Horse patties! Cow duggers! I'm laughing all the way to the bank and carrying back big bags with dollar signs on them, like Scrooge McDuck."

"Who?"

"Donald Duck? Disney? Heard of them? Yes? Good! Scrooge was the rich one, counting his gold coins. Laughing to the bank, like me. Quacking and laughing. Half-and-half, you know? A mélange, as they say in France."

"Sure," said Abigail. These attempts at merriment seemed flat and forced.

"Not," added Mrs. MacAdam, "that I'm literally laughing."

"No, you actually seem a little—"

"I'm not laughing," Mrs. MacAdam interrupted forcefully, "because I'm not a total lunatic, despite what everyone and his half-brother and illegitimate cousin says about me. Got it?"

"Of course I've got it. Whatever you say."

"That's right. Whatever I say, you say, and you'll actually like it. And I'm not going to the bank. I'm disabled, and it's hard to perambulate. So if you must know—and I'm guessing you must know, as I'm a rich McDucky client in whom you take a great interest—I prefer to do my banking online so I don't have to wheel myself around and make a big to-do."

"Mmm hmm," was all Abigail said at this point.

Soon after, she managed to get Cora-Lee on the line. On her motorized wheels, Mrs. MacAdam was an ace at swiping up the phone by the second ring. But Abigail called late, after she knew the dowager had surely gone to bed.

"Cora-Lee, I'm worried about the missus."

"What is troubling you about her?" said Cora-Lee, sounding a bit defensive.

"She just seems—off, somehow. Sad, remote, grouchier than usual, sort of deflated."

"Everything here is the same, mostly. She go on with her routines. No more trial business, and that's a good thing, she rest better at night, I think. But—no, she not herself, that is so," said Cora-Lee, after a pause. "She hardly speak. Never yell at me these days—and you know what? I tell you, I miss that. And she hardly eat. Nothing to rush and get her. She hardly drink, either, not even her evening cocktail, and she did like her evening cocktail, you know?"

"I'm sure she did. Oh, Cora-Lee. I'm worried! They settled handsomely—you must know, right? Mrs. MacAdam has been vindicated, scientifically, market-wise, legally. She's getting paid and her patents are safe. And she's going to make a fortune with those plants!"

"Sound so good, Abigail. Good for all of you." It was good for Cora-Lee as well. Mrs. MacAdam was generous, and would probably give her a substantial raise.

"And through it all, I know you've taken the best care of her. So what's the matter, do you think?"

"She rich and successful, I know. More than ever. And she like having the victory and all that. She used to having money, from before, she tell me how much she and her husband Jock had luxury, luxury. So nothing new. But—but maybe winnin' take the fire out of her."

"You mean, like she likes—maybe she needs—some kind of challenge?"

"Sure, she need to be vexed, to scrapple and scrape with people. She mischievous. 'Now what,' you know? She win, so OK, that's that. Now where's the fun gonna be?"

"Let me delve into that. It sounds right. Thanks, Cora-Lee."

◆ ◆ ◆

The best way to delve was to call Jackson Moss, so Abigail did.

"New case?" he said, excited to hear her voice.

"Not exactly. But wow, we killed the last one, that's for sure."

"I know—congratulations, Ms. Attorney. And I hear the firm's finally treating you great. Like we all know you deserve."

"Who told you?"

"Mrs. M; who else?" Jay laughed gently.

"Yeah, in their way, they have been acting decent to me. And she's a great client. But I might leave one day and start my own thing."

"You always gotta think independent, I say."

"On that topic, thanks again for sending me the camera."

"No need to say more."

"But really—it was so nice—"

"*No need to say more*," Jay said firmly, in a way that Abigail finally understood. Initiative, a nascent sense of independence? Yes. But discretion? She didn't have too much of that.

"I get it. I won't say more about confidential evidentiary matters," Abigail said, belatedly aware that she was, actually, saying more with those words. "Oops, sorry."

"Now I know why Mrs. M. likes you so much. Both of you don't really know the first thing about keeping a poker face, do you?"

"No, we don't. We have that in common. And I'm actually calling for a different reason than to thank you or even to catch up on work. It's personal, and it is about Mrs. M."

"Sure. What's on your mind?"

"I'm beginning to get worried about her. With your help, I'd like to dig a little into her moods. Have you seen her lately? Have you heard anything about her state of mind?

"State of mind? Hmm. That's a complicated question anytime, isn't it?"

"It is."

"But no, anyway I haven't seen her, not much, Abigail. I mean, I've been over once or twice to give her my best for her success in the case."

"But nothing else?"

"Well, Cora-Lee and I have gone out for a Ting or a cold beer or two now and again, but—"

"Jay, I think Mrs. MacAdam is depressed, and Cora-Lee says she can see it, too," Abigail finally blurted. "You know she gets that way. That's what they say, like when Jock left her, and other sad times. She gets very low, very down. She's—she's a very emotional woman, Evelyn is."

Abigail noticed that her own voice was shaking. She really cared about Mrs. Evelyn MacAdam, just as Mr. Fudim had always said. Personally. On the most human level.

"She's a human being, is all," Jay said, as though reading Abigail's mind. "We can't all be happy-happy all the time. Right? But if you want, I'll go over and see her and tell you what I see, OK?"

"I'd really appreciate that."

"It's no problem, I'm going presently."

"You mean now?"

"Why not? I just got my bike tuned up. It's a fine evening. I'll bring her some flowers and just say I was in the neighborhood."

"She knows you helped her win the case. I know she'll be nice to you," said Abigail, thinking aloud. "I mean, she'll try to be." Mrs. MacAdam could be mean, and if she was feeling as low as

Abigail suspected she was, her nerves might show with a curt or crass comment.

As though reading her thoughts, Jackson replied, "Hey, if she treats me rough and rude, we'll know she's just her old self, after all. So it's all good."

"I hope it is."

◆ ◆ ◆

But Jackson's report was not all good. In fact, it didn't sound good at all.

"OK, Abigail. I have to admit I was kind of worried when I saw her."

"What happened?"

"She was in a daybed downstairs, in the broad daylight. I was surprised. In pajamas, you know, like a nightdress, and not ailing, you know what I mean?"

"Oh—"

"And with half her teeth out. Like an old, old lady suddenly."

"Why would she—oh, Jay, did she say anything? I mean, what did she talk about? And wasn't she self-conscious? I mean, she's a proud woman."

"She just kinda sigh-sigh-sigh like the whole world was over."

"But—as you know better than anyone—things couldn't be better on the legal and financial fronts! And Mr. Fudim—my boss, you know—is totally under her thumb. There is literally nothing in this case that did not go optimally—she ought to be the toast of the town!"

"Yeah, of course I know everything about her and whatever else on this island, for that matter. And what I saw was a little disturbing. I'm just reporting what I saw and heard in this particular instance. Mrs. M. also talked about you a lot, and the past, and she talked about Jock. You know, her late husband?"

"I remember, the one who got her mad by cheating on her, right?"

"I think they loved each other a lot."

"Oh."

"The way she talked about him. She always does, you know. Every time I've ever spoken to her, she brings him up. And now, she sounded as though her life was over."

"But her plants are wonderful! They taste great! And they're profitable! I could show her how great she's doing financially! And what a vindication to all the skeptics, naysayers, and greedy pigs!" Even Abigail could sense the hollowness in her own enthusiasm. Maybe Mrs. MacAdam was about more than her plants. Maybe she was lonely in the wake of all that past excitement. Yes, of course she was.

"Yeah, true, but now what?" Jay was saying.

"What do you mean?"

"I think she likes a little battle, this lady, Mrs. M.," he said, echoing Cora-Lee's view. "The way she teases everyone. The anger in her eyes, the spit and the bile you see. What do you American lawyers call it? Piss and vinegar? It's almost funny, right? But I think it—the piss-vinegar—it helps keeps her alive. It moves her blood."

"Now that I think of it, she hardly ever calls me anymore."

"She's hiding—in a kind of retreat, you know?"

"What could I do for her now? Can you think of anything, Jay? Some way to give her a reason to live?"

"Good point you make, and I'll give it some thought. Maybe another agricultural invention?"

"She was working hard on expanding the basmary. More stores, more countries. She was getting somewhere in Italy— and you know they eat a lot of pizza in Italy. Basmary's great with pasta, too. And then there was that cucumber hybrid—but no," Abigail continued, "It's got to be along more personal lines. She's conquered almost everything but the question of being part of a family. Do you think she's up to that challenge?"

Jackson laughed.

"You mean, your family? Be part of that? Are *you* up to that?"

"Yes, and I won't be alone. Richard and I are getting married—"

"Finally!"

"Hey—I wanted to finish the case first, and Richard has been taking care of his brother's kids—"

"No, I'm just teasing. Take your time, there's no rush."

"Well, my father—and most of the conventional world—might disagree. But anyway, Richard's brother and sister-in-law are finally getting much better, and I'd like to plan a wedding. A small one, but it's still all new to me, and—well, I don't have a mother to advise me. . . ."

"So you want Evelyn MacAdam to come to New York City?"

"I really do. Do you think she'd be up to it?"

"She's up to any challenge, that one. But are you ready to push some old woman around for the rest of her life?"

"Yes. But I won't have to. Because first of all, as you know, given your powers of keen observation, her chair is motorized. But secondly—secondly, Jay, I think I found another actual challenge. A good one that might change her life."

Abigail paused dramatically. But because she was not a poker player, she continued immediately after that momentary breath and blurted:

"Evelyn MacAdam will learn to walk again. It's ridiculous to keep a dynamo like that sitting down."

"Bravo! Love it! Love to be there to see it," said Jackson. "That's a photograph I'd like to have, for sure."

"I'll take it and I'll send it to you," Abigail promised. "You'll see. And of course, you'll come to the wedding and you'll see her walk in person."

40 ⚖ But first, of course, Evelyn MacAdam would have to fly from Grenada to New York.

"I've always hated planes," she grumbled on the phone to Abigail. "And since one actually fell on me, you can't really call me a 'fraidy cat.'"

"I never liked them much either," Abigail admitted. "I nearly lost Chloe in one, remember?"

"No, I don't," said Mrs. MacAdam crossly. "I've never met Chloe, simply saw her in your enormous tummy."

"Well, you will now. And Richard. And Martin, his little nephew. I was just saying that I had a bad flight, too, so I know how you feel." Sensitively, Abigail avoided mentioning that a large part of her legal business, up to now, had been aviation disasters.

"You're giving me no comfort with your selfish reminiscing. Now, how am I going to travel up north if I can't get on the damn things?"

"We could rent a yacht for you. Put all your stuff on it."

"What stuff? Stop wasting my time and my money. I'm going to face my fears."

"I'm going to applaud that," said Abigail, hoping that Evelyn would also rise to the occasion of walking again.

"And I'm not taking 'stuff.' Bunch of creaky chairs and a couple of cushions. It's junk, it's old, it's yesterday. I'm looking at tomorrow, so long as I can get there."

Abigail hesitated. "Would you like me to come with you?"

Mrs. MacAdam seemed to stop breathing for a moment.

"You mean, fly all the way down to get me, and then fly all the way back to New York with me?"

"Yes," said Abigail. "That's what I do mean."

"You would do that for me?"

"Love does entail some sacrifice, Evelyn," said Abigail warmly.

"You're not supposed to love the clients, stupid!" Mrs. Mac-Adam suddenly bleated, sounding wonderfully like her old self again.

"Well, yes, I know, but I do. I love you like family."

"I'm not like family, you ninny. I *am* family."

"Yes, you are."

◆ ◆ ◆

It had been a good idea to bring Mrs. MacAdam up to New York. After a short time, her troubling listlessness was gone, and she was back to being cranky and argumentative.

"Look, I appreciate this a lot, but I can't stay here," she'd say. "I'm useless and I'm in your way."

"Nonsense," Abigail reassured her. "Besides," she began adding, "I need you to help me plan my nuptials."

"I thought you'd never ask. By the way, in my day, these things tended to happen before the baby came," Mrs. Mac-

Adam grumbled. "But if you want my advice, wear shocking pink—that way everyone knows you've been the Great Whore of Babylon."

Plans for the wedding rarely progressed with banter like this. Abigail knew her first big challenge was not the ceremony but getting her friend on her feet, in every sense of the word.

Sometimes she wanted reassurance, and other times, Mrs. MacAdam just wanted her own space—the bustling household drove her mad. For now, she lived in Abigail's small apartment. Abigail took the sleeper couch in the living room, moved the table out of the dinette and put the baby there, and gave the older woman her own bed. Arlie helped them adapt to these new arrangements. But it was all a bit cramped, especially with a wheelchair to negotiate.

Until their parents came home, Martin and the older children, Ellen and Hal, continued to live in uncle Richard's place. But they often came over to Abigail's, and they got to know Mrs. MacAdam. While Hal and Ellen were at first a little intimidated by the imperious woman on wheels, Chloe and Martin gradually began to love her just as she was. Martin had begun by calling her "Chairy"; Mrs. MacAdam had soon fixed that, and was now allowing him to call her "Grandam."

Eventually, Abigail, Chloe, and Mrs. MacAdam would also move into Richard's Village townhouse, where there was plenty of room. The stairs were not yet navigable for Evelyn, but in time, they would be. Perhaps, Abigail thought, they could also hold the wedding there. The parlor level was gracious, if drab, but they could festoon it with flowers, as well as a traditional wedding canopy. Abigail began to imagine Mrs. MacAdam standing by her side as she took her vows with Richard. The unwieldy wheelchair would be gone, and with it, a world of pain.

◆ ◆ ◆

Happily, Mrs. MacAdam had finally agreed to see about getting a new leg. Abigail had ordered a catalog, and Evelyn had leafed through it, marveling at the options—even running legs that looked like they had steel rockers on the bottom, poised for a sprint. But the lifelike ones were the ones that drew her wistful eye.

"The new leg will be prettier than the other," she noted, fretting slightly. "They forgot to add the age spots and the varicosities."

"I bet they can customize it for you in any way you like," said Abigail.

And she was right.

Mrs. MacAdam had insisted on talking to "the man" herself, at an enormous prosthetics emporium in New Jersey that boasted "Advanced Design, Ergonomics, and Expert Fittings." Their phone call had reassured her.

Abigail drove her there, and she and Mrs. MacAdam found themselves in the most peculiar waiting room, surrounded by a glassed-in panoply of hands, legs, and feet. Male, female, white, black, brown. There was also a glass cabinet full of eyes—every variation of color and striation—and another case of prosthetic ears along the wall, leading Abigail to experience a literal sense of the phrase "the walls have ears."

"Why don't I wait for you out here?" she said, her voice and face revealing far more apprehension than Mrs. MacAdam herself felt. Aspects of her mother's cancer crept into her mind. "Or should I just leave and come back in about an hour or so?"

"So you're a bigger 'fraidy cat' than I'll ever be!"

"No, of course, no problem, I'll come in with you."

The anatomical displays, while perhaps troubling to Abigail, seemed deeply reassuring to Evelyn MacAdam. Trying to relax, Abigail watched her pick up the pamphlets about how you could actually improve your speed and strength with some of the latest designs. She read them, too, and tried to shed her sense of pity. Unlike her own mother, Mrs. MacAdam wasn't dying— she was getting better, in fact. Maybe she could someday win a marathon (or even an Olympic event), bursting through the ribbon, her gray updo flying out of its pins. Maybe this world of replacement parts wasn't sad at all. Maybe it was, as was so much else that one usually overlooked, a portal to redemption and restoration.

Inside the consultation room, the older woman spoke openly to the expert. Her agenda was touchingly modest: "I want to be walking by the time this one goes down the aisle," she said, pointing to Abigail.

"But I was thinking of having the ceremony in Richard's townhouse, and there's really no aisle—"

"Oh, shush," said Mrs. MacAdam. "These details bore me."

"Is this your daughter?" said the prosthetics man.

"As close as one can get, yes. I love her dearly, but don't tell her that, or she'll be spoiled rotten."

"And you say she's getting married soon?"

"But not before this one's on her feet," said Abigail. "And right by my side."

"And I want to look good, no clumpy brogues with Velcro," said Mrs. MacAdam. "I shall attend the festivities like a real lady, in high heels. Can you make me a leg that can wear elegant silken pumps?"

"That we certainly can. In fact, I'd be happy to make you a couple of options—and you can try some of the samples today. This one here"—the man took a half leg (from the shin down) out of a large closet drawer—"is for flat shoes, like sneakers or walking shoes. You'll find it gives you the best balance. And then we'll make another that's perfect for those heels.

"Let me look at your leg now, please."

Evelyn obediently raised up her ankle-length skirt and showed him what was left of her right limb.

"So much is still there," the man said kindly. "Amazing and wonderful. Because you happen to have an incredible amount of muscle and joint to work with. Not only the knee but that nice bit of leg below it."

Kneeling before her, the man examined the stub of Mrs. Mac-Adam's fibula. About a quarter of it remained, along with the miracle of an intact, functional knee.

"The cut end healed up a bit ragged—"

"That's Grenada for you—"

"No matter, we'll make a nice mold and put a comfortable and snug cushion right there. You'll love it. Nice thick piece of foam."

Abigail thought she saw tears in Evelyn's eyes.

"Is this hurting you?" she asked.

"It's repairing me, and for you and this dear man I shall always be grateful."

Evelyn MacAdam then ordered two legs to be made for her— one for high heels and one for flats, and both with the "veins and varicosities." The man took notes and snapped pictures, for which she posed with alacrity and joy.

41

"I'm restless now, and I want to go home," Mrs. MacAdam suddenly announced in November. She stood before a full-length bedroom mirror, admiring her new leg from every angle. It looked splendid in a new white sneaker, fresh from the box.

"This could be your home," Abigail replied, kneeling to do up the laces. "Right here with me and Richard and the baby." Several months had passed, and Mrs. MacAdam was walking. She and Chloe had taken their first tentative steps at the same time, and Abigail delighted in watching them both on their feet. They had all moved into Richard's town house now, where Mrs. MacAdam had her own room and bath.

"Fine, I'll have two homes. But it's getting cold up here, so maybe I'll just winter where I won't freeze my nethers. And I do need to tend to my business—our business, my clever attorney, or did you forget?"

"That might be a wise compromise," said Abigail. The crops did need supervision, and besides, every day Mrs. MacAdam seemed to have another good idea for a culinary herbal hybrid. She had come back to life with her new mobility, and if she now felt strongly that being in her own home, on her own land, would do her a world of good, who was Abigail to challenge her? Abigail felt that this growing sense of self, of individual purpose, was the very thing her own mother had never fully enjoyed.

But there remained the matter of the flight, which Mrs. Mac-Adam still dreaded. Of course, Abigail was again willing to accompany her. But this time, she decided, Richard, Chloe, and Martin would come down to Grenada, too. Even after Martin's mother, Lauren, had returned home, he'd stayed close to his beloved uncle Richard and to Chloe, who was like a sister to him.

Abigail wanted them all to see where "Grandam" MacAdam had lived, alone for all those years, her own dreams seemingly broken off. And how successful she'd become.

Little Chloe would be too young to remember any of this, but Martin, who was now four, probably would. His parents had assured Richard and Abigail that the boy could miss a few days of coloring, counting, and describing the weather in pre-K. Arlie could help Lauren with the older children until the family returned.

Arlie had decided not to study information technology with Tim. She'd wrestled with computer jargon for several miserable months until she admitted that she hated it. It was boring, impersonal. She had no gift for it, and it meant nothing to her. Arlie realized that her calling was caretaking.

Most of all, they were lucky to have Evelyn MacAdam in their lives, Abigail thought. She was lucky to have found them, too. Under a heap of wreckage and a squabble over claims they had all found lasting treasure.

A few weeks later, they flew through the air, en route to Grenada. Richard paced up and down the aisle, pausing here and there among his loved ones. There was slight turbulence at times, but Chloe, perched high in her car seat, seemed entranced between worlds.

"P'lows," she pronounced, as she gazed at the clouds.

"No, they're not pillows, silly, they're water vapors," Martin corrected. "Right?"

"Right," Abigail replied, smiling at the way he always understood whatever Chloe said, or tried to say.

"You're a clever little man," Mrs. MacAdam declaimed. "I want you to be the ring bearer."

"Yes! I'll do that! What is it? When?"

"Uncle Richard and I are planning to get married soon, Martin. We'll give each other wedding rings. We're not sure exactly when, but soon."

"I happen to know when, Martin," said Mrs. MacAdam. Abigail turned to look at her with surprise. "Just before New Year's, as a matter of fact. You'll be off from school, then, and so will your brother and sister."

"Is that right, Evelyn?" said Abigail, with an indulgent smile. "That wouldn't give us much time though, would it?"

"It's certainly a nice time of year," agreed Richard. "But didn't you just say you want to avoid the New York cold?"

"I will avoid the New York cold, and more to the point, so will you."

"I'm not sure I follow," said Richard.

"That's why you're coming down, actually," said Mrs. MacAdam. "Cora-Lee has to measure the bride for a pretty frock— there can be touches of white, if you insist, Abigail—but it will be so warm outside that you can float in gossamer and silk. And after I check my basmaries, we'll see if they're good for the centerpieces. And Richard's boutonniere. Not to mention the wedding canopy."

"Oh, I'm sure I'll find pretty flowers in New York," said Abigail, pleased that Mrs. MacAdam understood that she'd want the traditional Jewish chuppah. "I really don't want to put you to any—"

"Don't you see? I thought lawyers were supposed to be rather intelligent. The wedding will be in Grenada, my dears. On my estate and on my dime—I'll fly down everyone you wish. Family, friends. You do have friends, don't you?"

"Well, not so many," said Abigail, "but I was planning to invite Rona and her husband and maybe baby Dylan. And Tina, for sure. But you mean, you'd fly my sisters, and their husbands, Annie's kids? My father—and even Darlene?"

"I couldn't ask you to pay for my brother and sister-in-law," added Richard.

"You don't have to ask. And I'll put them up all up in style, too. The sky's the limit. I'm a rich woman, as you both know. Richer than ever, thanks to this blushing bride here."

"That's very generous, and we're very grateful," said Richard, "but there are so many details to settle. First of all, I'll need to get a license."

"That shouldn't be a problem," Abigail considered. "We are lawyers, after all, aren't we?"

"And it is just simple paperwork," he agreed. "We'd need to take care of that in any case. But who would perform the ceremony?"

Abigail reflected for a moment. Whoever they chose, wherever they married, she wanted to add a few touches from the Jewish tradition—a mazel tov blessing for luck, the traditional breaking of the glass. She wanted Evelyn MacAdam and her father to walk her to the wedding canopy, and to stand by her side underneath it.

"What about that handsome man you know down here?" said

Mrs. MacAdam. "The one who's always calling me to see how I am?"

"You mean Jay—Jackson Moss?"

"Yes. Mr. Moss seems able enough for the task. He could get certified to marry you in no time. He and I can make things move around there."

"Jay would be wonderful," said Abigail. "Would that be OK with you, Richard?"

"Of course it would. We'll touch base with him right away and ask him. Once he's qualified to marry us, the State of New York will naturally give full faith and credit—"

"OK—I've had enough soul-crushing legalities for now," Mrs. MacAdam interrupted. "Let's talk about the celebration. Festive music and piquant food, I'd say."

"Jerk chicken is always good," Richard offered.

"So we will have a big beach barbecue?" Martin burst in, pealing with joy.

"He knows you live by the ocean," Abigail explained.

"With fireworks so loud you'll need cotton in your ear," Mrs. MacAdam replied, nodding forcefully.

"No, thank you," said Martin, upon consideration. "It would scare Chloe too much."

"Mabby! Mabby!" he shouted a few minutes later, using his pet name for her as he reached out for Abigail's arm.

"What?" said Abigail, looking up from her papers. The wedding venue settled, she was going over some transfer documents for Evelyn. Everything looked good, but she was being meticulous, as ever.

"I want to come down *right now!*"

"Don't be afraid, we're flying, not falling," she said, calmly meeting the child's worried eyes. "And we're almost there. We'll be there soon. Everything will be all right."

Abigail had no fear anymore of being aloft. Her family had grounded her, and gathering Evelyn MacAdam into the heart of it had given her focus.

"Yes, loves, we'll come down very soon," said Richard, walking over to Martin and little Chloe and smoothing their shoulders.

"Uncle Richard, *please* explain again what's Mabby doing," said Martin, turning his gaze upward.

"A favor for an old, good friend," said Richard.

"Grandam is our good friend?"

"Yes, that's right, darling." He ruffled his nephew's hair. "You can be a friend and a grandparent and a generous, great person—all at the same time."

Martin ran over to Abigail, scrambled onto her lap, buried his head in her chest, and inhaled. They looked out the window together for a long time, and then the little boy began to close his eyes. Chloe, too, dozed calmly.

It was windy in Grenada, Abigail could see. Several hours had gone by, and now the azure sea was capped by small white waves. Then the land came into view, yellow and brown and green. Palm leaves swayed from treetops, all growing closer. A faint ridge of dormant volcanoes rose in the distance. The plane turned, swooping gently.

"Look up, everyone—see how beautiful!" Abigail said. She took Richard's hand in hers and squeezed it. Soon, down there, they would be married. She would wear a summery dress and stand, beloved, under the basmary boughs.

Abigail looked at the family around her and the sky around them and felt nothing but gratitude. Then she descended, from heights, past swirling waters, to the sturdy earth below.

ACKNOWLEDGMENTS

I would like to thank Ellie McGrath, Jan Olofsen, Anne Greenberg Bookin, Debra Berman, Bonni-Dara Michaels, Susan Weinstein, Jean Rosen Cohen, Lynn Auld Schwartz, John Patrick Shanley, Tammy Williams and Yona Zeldis MacDonough for their friendship and support, both literary and personal.

I would also like to thank Lawyers for Children; Donovan, Leisure, Newton & Irvine; Cravath, Swaine & Moore; and Coudert Frères for allowing me to practice my legal skills, such as they were. A special nod to the late Charles Black for showing me that attorneys could also be artists, mensches, and more.

To my mother and father, Gita and Simon Taitz, whose wisdom and courage continue to animate everything I do.

To my brother, Emanuel, and nieces, Jenny and Michelle—great parents all.

And to my family—husband, Paul, and children, Emma, Gabriel, and Phoebe—endless gratitude for embracing me with the gift of love.

1. Abigail's mother, Clara, is the child of Holocaust survivors, and her father, Owen, is a lower-class immigrant from Wales. To what extent does this background motivate Abigail to focus on the "American Dream" of professional achievement as a lawyer?

2. Does having a baby conflict with those dreams?

3. Abigail's decision to keep her baby is a very personal one. What would you have done in her situation and why?

4. Abigail is self-conscious about the lush curliness of her hair as well as the curviness of her body (which becomes only more pronounced in pregnancy). She thinks they conflict with a professional, corporate image. Have you experienced shame about your appearance and its supposed contrast with how you are "supposed" to look?

5. To what extent is it possible to say, as Abigail says to Mr. Fudim, that having a child will not change her work life? Should employers expect women (or men) to say this?

6. Tim rescues Abigail from a fall on the street, then takes care of her in other, more interesting ways. What thoughts come to mind when a character enters a story as a "knight in shining armor"?

7. Abigail is determined not to be "just" a housewife like her mother. Does she lose anything in the act of running away from the traditional feminine role?

8. As the novel progresses, a legal mystery unfolds that suggests corruption in Abigail's firm. Do you think she is right to challenge the status quo?

9. Which male archetype do you find more appealingthe boyish Tim or the experienced Richard? Does your perspective shift throughout the novel?

10. Abigail feels many conflicts with regard to her child's nanny, Arlie. Arlie, too, walks a challenging path as her employee. In the course of their power struggle, what separates these two women, and what unites them?

11. Evelyn MacAdam, the dowager of Grenada, enters the novel as something of a comic character. At the same time, she is a formidable legal opponent. What role does she play in Abigail's professional, emotional, and ethical development?

12. What does the title *Great With Child* mean to you?

A NOTE ABOUT THE AUTHOR

SONIA TAITZ is a playwright, essayist, and author of three novels and two works of nonfiction. An award-winning writer and Yale-trained lawyer, her work has been praised in *The New York Times Book Review*, the *Chicago Tribune*, *People*, *Vanity Fair*, and many other publications. She is also the mother of three children, who are now all taller than she is.

CPSIA information can be obtained
at www.ICGtesting.com
Printed in the USA
LVOW08s0739210417
531624LV00003B/4/P